*The Scandalous Confessions of*

# LYDIA
# BENNET,
Witch

## Also by Melinda Taub

*Still Star-Crossed*

*The Scandalous Confessions of*

# LYDIA
# BENNET,
Witch

MELINDA TAUB

GRAND
CENTRAL

*New York Boston*

Copyright © 2023 by East Pole, Inc.

Jacket design and illustration by Caitlin Sacks. Jacket image by Shutterstock. Jacket copyright © 2023 by Hachette Book Group, Inc.

Grand Central Publishing
Hachette Book Group
1290 Avenue of the Americas, New York, NY 10104
grandcentralpublishing.com
twitter.com/grandcentralpub

First Edition: October 2023

Grand Central Publishing is a division of Hachette Book Group, Inc. The Grand Central Publishing name and logo is a trademark of Hachette Book Group, Inc.

The publisher is not responsible for websites (or their content) that are not owned by the publisher.

Grand Central Publishing books may be purchased in bulk for business, educational, or promotional use. For information, please contact your local bookseller or the Hachette Book Group Special Markets Department at special.markets@hbgusa.com.

Library of Congress Cataloging-in-Publication Data

Names: Taub, Melinda, author.
Title: The scandalous confessions of Lydia Bennet, Witch / Melinda Taub.
Description: First edition. | New York : Grand Central Publishing, 2023.
Identifiers: LCCN 2022057832 | ISBN 9781538739204 (hardcover) | ISBN 9781538739228 (ebook)
Subjects: LCGFT: Paranormal fiction. | Novels.
Classification: LCC PS3620.A8944 S28 2023 | DDC 813/.6--dc23/eng/20221213
LC record available at https://lccn.loc.gov/2022057832

ISBNs: 9781538739204 (hardcover), 9781538739228 (ebook)

Printed in the United States of America

LSC-C

Printing 1, 2023

*To Daria*

# PART ONE

# CHAPTER ONE

I suppose if this were a proper book I'd begin it something like, "Miss Lydia Bennet, youngest of five daughters to a father hopelessly entailed, had few advantages in life, but not too few to squander." That sounds fine, and important, and promises that no matter how exciting the story may become it will all resolve with a tidy boring moral at the end. That is why Kitty and I prefer to skip the last chapter of novels.

However, that bit about squandering isn't true. Oh, I daresay many in Meryton would whisper that I had indeed squandered all my advantages of birth and position; and that much is true, and Lord knows I have shed many a tear over it. However, I was born with greater gifts than one silly girl can use up in a lifetime. Kitty is proof enough of that. For another thing, I am not the youngest of five daughters. I am the youngest of seven.

Those who knew me in Meryton would frown over this, and perhaps discreetly count on their fingers. As far as the public remembers, we Bennet sisters number but five. There is beautiful Jane, the eldest; Lizzy, second in beauty and first in her own mind; dull, moralizing Mary, so mortified by her own lack of beauty that she was doomed to become clever; my darling Kitty; and me, Lydia, the baby.

This count is wrong in two respects. Firstly, three of my elder sisters died shortly after birth. No doubt the world scarcely remembers them, for unless Mamma wanted something from my father and wished to remind him of all she had gone through on his behalf, Charlotte, Anne, and Sophia were rarely spoken of in our household. Quite right, too. Deceased progeny are hardly a jolly topic of conversation, I think.

Nevertheless, this makes me, Lydia, the seventh daughter of a seventh daughter. Strange, is it not, that being born so late and a girl should be a source of both my misfortune and my strength?

Those readers diligently counting Miss Bennets will have noted that the count is still off by one. Five living girls and three dead ones bring the total to eight, not seven. Is all this arithmetic making your head ache? It is mine. Perhaps I'd better begin again.

It is a truth universally acknowledged that the seventh daughter of a seventh daughter must be a witch.

My earliest memories are of my sisters' backs. I remember toddling along after them, calling for them to wait. Jane was always kind, and Lizzy only slapped me if I tangled her embroidery; but Mary loathed me. She would begin to cry and whine to our mother the moment I came near. "Mamma, Lydia pulled my hair! She stained my dress! Take her away! Mamma!"

Quite often I did pull her hair and stain her dress, but I was only trying to get close to her. I adored her, and yanking on one of her long, neat plaits was one of the most reliable ways to get her attention. I thought of nothing but attracting attention in those days; in our large family circle I was often forgotten. They do not remember it so, of course—in a large family, every child is sure that they alone were uniquely neglected. Lizzy says I was Mamma's favorite from birth, which is quite possible, but Mamma was often abed with her nerves or another failed attempt to produce an heir, and quite often no one was looking after me at all. Once my mother, after bringing me on a morning visit to show me off to Lady Lucas, forgot me in the carriage, and no one found me until tea-time. Another time I fell in the stream that ran through the garden, and despite my cries no one came. It was one of my father's tenants who fished me out, and that, I believe, because he heard my cries and thought me one of his lambs. Jackson brought me into the house, dripping and sobbing, and *then* the house was set in as much of an uproar as I could wish. I spent the evening on my mother's lap, being squeezed and kissed and lamented over, while my sisters petted and caressed me and brought me sweets and bits of ribbon.

The next day, I threw myself in the creek again. Well, what did they expect? A good thing witches float.

I wanted hugs and sweets and smiles from them all. Failing that, I would accept scolds and slaps. Mary was my primary object. I adored her, worshiped her, thought she was beautiful. (She should have enjoyed it while it lasted—I was the only one who ever thought so.) In my foolish baby mind, if I glued myself to her side firmly enough, she would eventually return my regard, and we would form a pair like Jane and Lizzy. Alas, even then Mary loved nothing but solitude and study, and her legs were long enough to escape me.

And so I found myself, in a house crowded with sisters, servants, and visitors, usually alone. It did not suit me. Mary is born for solitude, but I am born for company, as much and as merry as possible.

I took to spending my time with Mamma's cat. My father gave the little gray kitten to Mamma after one of her indispositions, and for a time she enjoyed cuddling the sweet little ball of fluff. But it soon grew into a stringy, mottled gray cat with a piercing yowl, and Mamma took no further notice of it.

I began to follow the cat about as I had my sisters. At first I had no better luck winning its heart. Indeed, when it saw me reaching my jammy hands toward its fur, it would make a sound of dread low in its throat and leap for the nearest open window. But cats are simpler creatures than sisters. Neither scratches nor howls deterred my lavish embraces and sticky kisses. My love needed an object, and the family cat could not escape. Generous gifts of cream and kippers soon had the creature following me from room to room, much to Mary and Papa's disgust. Indeed, Papa would leave the room when he saw us coming, claiming that my pet made him sneeze.

I did not care. I only hugged my cat close, glorying when she purred instead of fleeing, and whispered my secrets into her fur.

So far, ordinary enough. Many a lonely young girl makes a companion of a pet. What happened next, though, was far from ordinary. I made believe that my cat was my sister, and my family indulged me, as one does with an imaginative and spoilt child. "And how is Kitty today?" they would ask me.

"Kitty is hungry," I would say, or "Kitty wants to go to the market," and my elders would nod solemnly. Do you know the difference between pretending to believe a witch, and truly believing her? There isn't one. Kitty this, Kitty that, was the refrain in our house, until one day, they were not humoring me—they saw her, too.

From that day forward, my parents had not four daughters, but five. The world saw Kitty as a tall, thinnish girl, not terribly bright, but with a great gift for learning things she wasn't supposed to know. She had a rather carrying voice, and spoke almost exclusively to me.

This was my first spell. I thought nothing of it at the time. All small children think they can control the world around them. Years later, my aunt explained to me what a tremendous working my first one was—I would not match it till the events of my sixteenth year. Later still, we talked of the price of it. All magic carries a price, of course, and if you do not pay up front and in full, it will extract the cost in its own way.

My aunt's theory on the price for that first, unconscious spell was an heir. Perhaps my mother would have had one more child, maybe even a boy to save us all; but my unknowing childish gluttony for love snatched its soul from her womb to fashion Kitty. I tend to disbelieve this theory. On the day my father first referred to Kitty as his daughter with no hint of mockery, his favorite horse dropped dead at four years old and he could never afford such a fine one again. No further explanation, I believe, is necessary.

# CHAPTER TWO

If you were to tell Lizzy's story, or Jane's, I suppose you would begin with when they met their husbands. I don't say that to slight them! I've often wished that my own life had turned out like theirs. They seem very happy with their rich husbands, and though neither man is to my taste, who am I to judge? I am a foolish wretch and usually racked with misery of my own making. Ask anyone. Ah well! At least I've known such fun as they will never come within a hundred yards of. La! Imagine what Lizzy would do if she knew I made that spot on her chin pop back out whenever she vexed me.

The story of Lydia Bennet must linger in her childhood for a while (but take heart, dear reader, there are handsome rakes and ardent suitors to come). Luckily for me and my family, I was not the only witch in our connection. My aunt Philips, my mother's sister, lived in Meryton and she had the gift. When all the town began referring to a ragged mouser as Miss Kitty Bennet, she realized that one of us must have it, too. Shortly after that, she cornered me after a family supper.

"That is a very pretty bit of magic you worked, my girl," she said. "They all see Kitty as your sister now, even your father, who still sneezes when she comes near."

"I know," I said complacently. I was too young to be astonished at the mention of magic. "Papa thinks he avoids her because she is so stupid. He dislikes me for the same reason, so it's easy for him to believe. Pooh, I hate sherry." I withdrew from the scent of sherry on her breath. I had not yet learned to be polite. (Some would say I never did.)

My aunt merely chuckled, sending more clouds of sherry breath my way. "Careful, my girl. If you're to be a witch, you needn't hold your tongue generally—it's the good Christian folk who must take care not to offend *you*. But I'm a witch myself and you'd better mind me, or I'll disenchant that cat of yours and the Bennets will find themselves with only four daughters again. There, don't cry." She chucked me under the chin, which had begun to tremble, and glanced nervously over her shoulder at my mother sitting by the fire. I had a piercing voice when I cried.

"Don't take Kitty away," I whispered. My mother still hadn't noticed anything amiss, but Kitty, curled up next to her, narrowed her eyes at us and came stalking over.

"Take me where?" she said.

"Nowhere," said my aunt hastily. "I'm proud of the glamour she cast over you, Kitty dear. And as long as you both behave I'll do nothing to alter it."

Kitty slipped her hand into mine and squeezed it. I was glad I'd made her my older sister instead of younger. Lifting her chin, she was nearly as tall as my aunt.

"As if you could," she said scornfully. "I'm in this shape because I choose to be." But I saw a flash of doubt pass over her face. We had never met another witch before.

My aunt laughed. "Isn't that just like a cat. Everything has to be your own idea. I believe I've frightened you two, and that's the last thing I would wish, my dears. Come, let me make it up to you. Let's have some fun, eh?" And from the depths of her dress she produced two lengths of lace and handed one to each of us. We gasped.

"This is the new lace from London! Mrs. Pierce said she wouldn't have any till next week. How did you get it?" I demanded.

She looked sly. "When you're a witch, there's much folks will do to oblige you, if you know how to ask."

That was enough for me. The promise of new lace made me clamor to learn all she had to teach, and she readily agreed.

"I'd better train you up, yes, for Lord knows who you'll kill, else. I'll teach you. You too, Miss Kitty. You won't be able to work human magic, of course, but Lydia's power is bound up with you."

Naturally I agreed. From then on Kitty and I spent all the time we could in the village with my good aunt. She made me promise not to tell anyone of our lessons; however, I think she must have laid a powerful silence spell on me as well, for I was such a chatterbox in those days and never could have kept mum on my own. I suppose she had to do it, but I'm sorry for whatever alley cat or street mongrel sacrificed its life's blood so that a middling witch like my aunt could perform such a spell. I have always been powerfully fond of animals.

# CHAPTER THREE

Aunt Philips was no seventh daughter of a seventh daughter. She was a simple hedge witch, with a little talent for the craft supplemented by a great deal of guile. Her first Great Working did not come until she reached the age of seventeen, and was mortified to discover that her younger sister—my mother—was considered far more beautiful than she.

Up until then, as the eldest, my aunt had been first in everything. And so she had assumed it would always be, for my mother admired her as much as she could wish. When my mother came out, and suitors flocked to young Anne Gardiner while ignoring Margery, the elder Miss Gardiner's rage was so wild that it forced her gift into full flower.

For many of us, you see, the first working is one of the greatest. The power of dammed-up youthful passion is considerable. So it was with Miss Gardiner, although even at the height of her powers, she was not strong enough to cast a glamour on herself that would make her appear a beauty to the whole town, or even just the young men. But what her gift lacked in power, she made up for in deviousness.

"My father was an attorney in town, and very prosperous for his station," she told me. "Our brother had no wish to succeed him, so Papa established him in manufacturing in town and prepared to pass the business to his clerk, a handsome young man named Philips."

I can remember sitting at my aunt's knee, the ruddy light of the fire playing over her face as she told me the story. Even years later, it filled her face with glee. "My sister adored Philips," she said with a chuckle. "From the time she was a tiny girl, she followed him about, declaring that she would marry him. A childish passion, but it did not fade.

"The young man did not object to the affections of his master's daughter. They would have been married, I suppose. But when Anne came out, the attentions of other young men turned her head, and she became a great flirt." She shook her head. "For what came next, she has only herself to blame."

She stirred up the embers with a poker. "My girl, here is the truth about witchcraft: We have been given immense power, and we *must* use it. To squander it would be wicked—especially if we do not use it to right wrongs, such as the wrong the world had dealt me. Well, use it I did. I cast a glamour, and young Philips found himself ten times as devoted to me as he ever was to my sister." She chuckled. "You should have seen Anne's face when we announced our engagement! It was as though I had slapped her. I'm sure she thought that when she had had her fill of flirting, he would still be waiting for her. Let that be a lesson to you, Lydia. The power of beauty is considerable, but it is no match for the craft. Now cast these bones and tell me if it will rain tomorrow."

Luckily for family harmony, my mother's respect for her older sister was stronger than her passion for her father's clerk. After a brief outcry when she learned of their engagement, she found comfort in half a dozen new flirtations, until finally marrying my father. She never seemed to bear my aunt any ill will, perhaps because in the eyes of the world, my father was the much better match. Still, sometimes when we were all together, I would catch her looking at my uncle, a little knot of worry between her brows, as though she was trying to remember a pleasant dream long forgotten.

Anyway, that's my aunt in a nutshell. And that, pray, is the woman who shaped me! I do think that excuses some of what followed, don't you? I could not help but turn out terribly wicked and selfish when guided by such a woman. Lord, even she thought me wicked! Most of her stronger spells required an animal sacrifice of some sort, and I refused outright to take part. Indeed, she once bought a snow-white kid goat to sacrifice at the full moon, and I snuck out while she was asleep and stole the kid away. I brought her to one of our tenants and said she was a gift from my father. When Aunt Philips found out what I'd done, she boxed my ears and said I was the most selfish creature she'd ever encountered, and it was my fault if the harvest was blighted that year. I've no idea if it was blighted, but Papa still receives regular gifts of goat cheese.

La, how my hand hurts! I have been writing for two hours together and I have never felt such an ache in my life. My hand is smeared in ink, too, for I'm left-handed. And fancy, I have just counted and only ten pages are done! This writing is the dreariest business I have ever undertaken. But I did promise to do it, and every witch knows the importance of keeping one's promises. (Promises to people who matter, I mean. I promised to pay Jane back for lunch and I never shall.) I know what: Our bargain was that I must write an "account of my experiences," so I shall fill these quires of paper till the last page and then stop—even if that leaves off in the middle of the Battle of Brighton. That would serve you right.

Where was I? Oh yes, my aunt. After her great triumph of landing my uncle, they took a house in Meryton. She still practiced the craft, and often bragged to me that she had brought the rain for the farmers; but only after the rain was already falling.

Her house was like a second home to me and Kitty. At her knee I learned all she knew about the craft and, I thought, all there was to know. I learned herb lore and glamours, knot-magic and mirror-magic. Before I was ten years old I knew how to spy on any household in town that had a mirror. I couldn't do it very often, for our mirror was in our front hall, and I could rarely be alone there, but once I saw the vicar picking his nose, and another time I caught Lady Lucas saying that Mamma was an "empty-headed, vain peahen," and I was overawed to learn that adults were as rude as children when in private. Magic was immense fun to me then. When Mary fell in a patch of nettles and got a rash across her neck and cheek, I told her, quite seriously, that I would fix it. I pestered my aunt to tell me what herbs would cure it, and snuck out at midnight and sprinkled them into a pool of water reflecting the full moon, and the next morning Mary's rash was gone. She didn't believe that I had fixed it and refused to thank me, so I pushed her into the nettles again. I would also tell fortunes for my sisters and girls of our acquaintance.

Our parents thought this was harmless make-believe and allowed it. If only they knew! I told my sisters that Jane would marry a beautiful fool, and Lizzy the most disagreeable man she had ever met; and wasn't I right?

My magical education was rather patchy, but my aunt did teach me the most important thing a witch must know: the law of sacrifice.

"Some spells are more difficult than others," she explained, "and some witches are born with more power than others. Being the seventh of a seventh, and having a familiar, my dear, you've a tidy little sum of magic to your name. If magic were coin, I should say you had about ten thousand pounds. But there are other things that will affect your success—your skill, and the quality of your herbs, and the position of the moon, and so on. But most of all, every magic you do, Lydia, you must pay for. The more difficult the magic, the more you must sacrifice." And she leaned over and plucked a hair from my head.

"Ouch!" I said.

She ignored me. "Try that spark spell again now."

I did so, and found that I could raise a spark from my fingertip. It fell on my apron and left a little black spot. I had never managed real fire before, only illusions. "Gracious!"

I plucked three more hairs from my head, expecting to be able to produce a whole shower of sparks, but again there was only one.

"Three hairs do not hurt more than one, do they?" she said. "The magic knows that."

"How does it know?"

"Little witches should not be so inquisitive." (It took me a few years to realize this is what she said when she had no idea.)

"But then how am I to do great magic without plucking my head bald?"

"Ah." She looked sly. "There are all kinds of sacrifices, are there not? What matters is not what the sacrifice *is*, but what it *costs*. And it need not be you who pays it."

I pondered her words. This, of course, accounted for my aunt's habit of slaying small animals. "If magic keeps such minute reckoning of the cost, why does it allow you to make others pay?"

She shook her head. "It is the way of the world, child. Farming your father's lands requires a great deal of sweat, but how much of it is his own?"

None, of course. "Oh, I see." I said the spark spell again, then, just before sealing it, reached over and ripped a handful of hairs out of her head. She cried out in pain. A whole shower of sparks burst from my fingertips. My aunt's hair had begun thinning, causing her great distress, so I suppose it was a greater sacrifice.

"Now you're thinking like a witch," she said, "but I am not your black cockerel." And she boxed my ears.

My aunt didn't teach me much protective magic. Her own talent was paltry enough that she never attracted much notice from anyone who might endanger her, and I suppose she did not know that my case was different.

She did, however, offer one piece of wisdom that I should perhaps have taken more note of, although at the time, she never made much of it.

"Never offer an open boon to another witch, niece. Your word is your bond where magic is concerned," she told me. I nodded solemnly, but I was not even sure what a boon was. I vaguely pictured a sort of exotic animal. As if I would give one of those away if I had it!

I soon had reason to wish she had spent less time teaching me parlor tricks and a bit more time preparing me for the actual dangers of being a witch. I had never so much as heard of the Great Powers up until the day I met one.

It happened on the way to Meryton when I was seven and Kit eight. Kitty did not like magic lessons above half. She didn't enjoy the walk to Meryton, which was often muddy and soiled the hem of her gown or—if she was in cat-form, as she often was if we were alone—caked the fur of her paws.

"Drat this walk," she said one particularly cold March day as we picked our way across the Lucases' south field. One of her hands clutched at her bonnet strings and the other held back her skirts. I saw her then as others did—a girl of eight in a fine dress and a handed-down bonnet. She preferred to take human form when we passed near Lucas Lodge, so the dogs would not chase her. If I let my eyes relax with a certain laziness, I could see through the disguise to what she really was: a mottled gray cat hopping between puddles with weary distaste, shaking one paw and then the other. "Why must we go so often to your aunt? The hearth is quite as warm at home, and though nobody strokes me anymore, Cook will give me all the cream I want now that I am a Miss Bennet. Come, let's go home!" Her voice rose to a plaintive yowl.

I focused my eyes and Miss Kitty Bennet snapped back into place. "You may go home," I said, "but I shan't. Aunt is teaching me tea-reading today. Fancy being able to tell the future whenever someone comes to tea! You're just jealous, Kitty, that she won't teach you."

Kitty put her hands on her hips. "We cats know things of magic that your aunt can never teach you," she said loftily. "And if I go home, Mamma will scold me for leaving you to walk alone, and send me to bed without tea. How cold it is. And there's Sir William's dratted dog. Come, Lydia, let's go home." She continued in this vein for some time. If you ever have the chance to give your cat the power of speech, I strongly advise against it.

I was trying to raise little whirlwinds as we walked, by knotting the ribbons on my purse. It was my latest trick, and not an easy one—it's far easier to change the way things seem using magic than the way they are. Kitty's whining upset my concentration. Besides, if she did go home, my spells would not work nearly so well. My magic was always strongest when she was by my side, as well she knew. "If you know so much magic," I snapped, "why don't you tell me my fortune now?"

"I could," she said. "Cats can tell the future, you know. Haven't you ever heard of how we can predict earthquakes? Or how we crouch at the bedside of those about to die?"

I snorted. "There's never been an earthquake here, so I suppose you've never been wrong. But when the old groom died of fever last winter, you slept soundly in your bed all night." She pushed me into a mud puddle at that, and I launched myself back at her and grabbed a handful of her curls and yanked. We often had such scraps in those days. We never felt easy when we were apart—my magic weakened, and she had a harder time remembering not to have a tail. All that enforced sisterly closeness found an outlet in fighting, especially on the way to my aunt's to spend the night. We knew that she would wash our gowns for us, and would not betray us to our mother.

Eventually I got the upper hand, for though she was taller I was more ruthless. I sat astride her. "Do it then," I said. "Tell my fortune with your cat-magic."

She scowled. "Shan't."

"You mean can't."

A flash of claws across my arm left me with three bright scores of pain. I fell back and Kitty got up, trying in vain to brush the mud from her dress. "Very well," she said. "But remember, you asked for it. Cats care nothing for anyone's feelings. Cats are honest, and so is our magic."

I would have scoffed at this, but just then she grabbed my hands in hers.

We often held hands when I was doing magic, or when one of us was frightened, or so we could squeeze each other's hands in warning when it would not be polite to giggle aloud. I knew the feeling of her palms well. But this felt different. Though she still wore a girl-shape, she no longer looked human to me. Her face went blank, her eyes far away. Then she spoke—but the voice was not her own.

*Well, well,* said the deep voice that came from her mouth. *What tender young lambs have wandered onto my lands?*

Her lips shaped the words, but the sound seemed to come from all around us—if it was a sound at all. It was as though the earth itself was speaking, the words vibrating up from deep underground to rattle my bones.

"Stop it, Kitty," I said nervously. "I don't like it."

"It's not me," she said in her own voice. I could see the fear in her eyes. I tried to pull my hands away.

*Ah, ah.* Her hands gripped mine even tighter. *Hold still, witchling and witch-beast. Let me have a look at what's been creeping across my territory.*

It was as though red-hot claws raked through my brain—a bit like the three scratches Kitty had left on my arm, but deeper and more precise. Bits of memory flicked lightning-fast across my brain—the thing in Kitty was examining my life.

*So that's how it is now,* said the voice in disgust. *Courtesy and lace caps. Visiting cards and dancing slippers. You foolish folk have forgotten the deep, wild power in this land.*

"Who are you?" I said. My voice was shaking now. My aunt had never told me of anything like this. "I warn you, I am under the protection of the witch Philips."

The voice laughed so loud it made my teeth ache with the hum of it. *You mean that hedge witch who lives up yonder? Yes, I can feel her. Her power wasn't even enough to stir me. As to who I am—bah, what an impertinent question. I am your liege, of course. You may call me Lord Wormenheart.*

My father has a book in his study that has illustrations of exotic animals. I used to sneak in and look at it sometimes—a great risk, for if any small fingerprints were found on his precious colored plates I'd have my ears boxed, but the illustrations were irresistible to me anyway. There was one that fascinated me—a man being slowly strangled by a boa constrictor. The way I felt now reminded me of that picture. Wormenheart's tendrils of power seemed to be wrapping themselves around the heart of me, slowly, even lazily, but I could not escape.

*Do you know what poaching is, little one?* he asked conversationally. *It's stealing game from the lord of the land. Your own people frown on it most harshly. Well, I am the rightful lord of this land, and you have been poaching its magic from me.*

"You're not the lord of this land," I gasped. "This is Sir William Lucas's land, and he does not hunt game here anymore, because of his gout."

Wormenheart chuckled. *Such spirit you have. You certainly speak your mind, child. Is it bravery or idiocy? Ah well, in many folks they are the same.* I felt the mental coils constrict. *Enough chatter. Nourish me.*

"Wait," I gasped. "I—I—if you have waited this long, surely you can wait till I make more of a meal."

The squeezing slackened, just a little. *More of a meal?*

"My—my aunt says witches don't come into their full power till they're women. I'm j-just a little girl."

*Hmm.* There was a long pause, and I held my breath, hardly daring to hope. If he ate me, what would happen? Would my body drop lifeless to the path? Or would I disappear, erased from the world as wholly as Kitty had been imprinted on it?

*Very well*, it said. *A few years are as nothing to me. I will let you go—if you apologize for your discourtesy.*

"Discourtesy?"

*You did not make yourself known to me when you came upon the county, witchling. As lord of this land, all magical creatures within are my subjects.* The coils flexed. *Make it right.*

Jane says that the rules of etiquette exist to make everyone comfortable. The most important part of politeness, she says, is putting everyone at their ease, whether or not they deserve it. Sweet Jane! She would think that. She would rather burn her tongue off than say the porridge is too hot. But etiquette is also a weapon. A velvet-wrapped cudgel that the powerful use to prettily brutalize the weak. I hate it, I hate it, I hate it.

I willed my shaking muscles to still. I dropped the deepest curtsy I could and inclined my head. Jane herself could not have done it prettier. "I am sorry, my lord," I said. "Please accept my most humble apologies and allow me to live and work magic on...your land."

*Very well.* The voice was practically purring now. *You are free to go. I'll content myself with this one.*

Before I could gasp, the tendrils had left me and tied themselves around Kitty.

"Stop!" I shrieked. "Leave her alone!" All the wild panic I'd kept at bay when my life was at risk was now clawing at my throat.

*But she's so interesting*, he said. *A cat and a girl at once! I've never seen such a thing. Quite a unique delicacy.*

Kitty hissed and bared her teeth. She'd let go of my hands and now her shape was flicking rapidly, cat-girl, girl-cat, as she struggled to escape. Not even a creature this powerful can easily hold a cat who doesn't want to be held. But slowly, he was closing in.

A wave of possessive rage swept over me. Kitty was *my* sister. *My* companion. How dare he!

"I'll give you a boon!" I blurted.

Again, Lord Wormenheart paused. *A boon?*

"Yes."

And just like that, he released her. Kitty gasped and stumbled into my arms.

*You owe me a boon of my choosing, witchling*, Wormenheart's voice said. He sounded farther off and a bit sleepy, but very smug. *I will let you know when it comes due.*

And then he was gone.

Kitty began to cry and sat down. I did, too. "Who *was* that?" I said again. He certainly was not a lord. *They* did not eat people, I was sure— not even the Prince of Wales. But then, Wormenheart claimed we were his subjects, and he evidently had the power to enforce it—perhaps that was all a lord was.

"I don't know," said Kit, her arms around my waist. For long moments we clung together, sniffling, until the cold and damp made us get up and continue on our way. We were still teary and frightened, but there seemed to be no words to discuss what had just happened. Indeed, as we walked on, the details of the encounter began to shred away and disappear, like a dream does when you wake in the morning. Long before we got to Meryton we had forgotten about Lord Wormenheart, and resumed our previous squabble. We arrived at my aunt's house in Meryton muddy and still bickering, but together, as we almost always were. Kitty was frostily aloof the rest of the day, and made a point of speaking mainly to my uncle at dinner; but the night was a cold one, and when we went to bed she crept small and furry into my arms, and slept purring against my side.

# CHAPTER FOUR

Bother. Do you know what I've just realized? *You* will be a character in my story before long. How tiresome. For I did promise you to tell the story thoroughly and honestly, and I could hardly do that if I left you out.

But my goal in writing this wretched, hateful book is to get you to grant my request, and how likely are you to do so if I'm honest about you? Not that I will say anything so very bad, for I have the greatest ~~respect admiration friendship fear~~

There, you see? As soon as I tried to address you I sputtered to a halt. I know. I'll write you in the third person, as though the *you* reading the story and the *you* in it are quite different people. Perhaps that will make it easier. I suppose you will still be offended—but remember, the Lydia who met you and the Lydia who now writes this volume are quite different people, too.

For some time after the Wormenheart incident, my interest in magic waned. I didn't remember it clearly, as I said, but I kept a vague impression that magic was not the fun romp I'd enjoyed thus far, but something much more dangerous.

It was not just that. My sisters and I were growing up, and even with such neglectful parents as ours, we could not but notice that certain aspects of our education were lacking. Jane and Lizzy were moving more in society and had grown alarmed at how we Miss Bennets compared with the girls they now mixed with.

"You ought to have a governess for us, madam," Lizzy said. (She'd begun to call our mother "madam.") "I thought myself very widely read, but all the ladies in town talked of poets I'd never heard of. And we have no accomplishments at all."

"Except for Mary," Jane said.

"Yes, but that's *Mary*."

Our mother, after waving off the mention of Mary, on whom she and Lizzy quite agreed, said, "No accomplishments? Nonsense. Jane can draw very well and you can play and sing ever so much better than the Miss Lucases. And what is better, you are both very pretty. Believe me, my dear, men do not care a straw whether a girl can net a purse."

But Lizzy pressed her point, and Jane, in her quiet way, backed her. In the end it was agreed that Kitty and I should be kept much more at home and learn to be accomplished.

Masters were engaged. I studied drawing and Italian, Kitty singing and piano. I think sometimes of those girls we were becoming. Where would they be now? Still respectably unmarried, I suppose, visiting their rich older sisters and mixing with wealthy young men in pursuit of an eligible alliance. Wherever that Lydia would be, she'd probably be living more comfortably than in these cramped, cold quarters of ours. I could have done it. I am not so lazy as my sisters like to believe. I can net a very elegant purse, you know.

But it was not to be. My aunt missed my worship and was determined to have me back as her student, and she wooed me with all her ability. She magicked Lizzy to make her forget a red hair ribbon she'd lent me, allowing me to keep it. She made Papa send Kitty's singing master away—though, whether that was really magic, I doubt, for we were all heartily sick of her noise. And, greatest wonder of all, she convinced Mamma to let me and Kitty come out. It was ridiculously early for me to be attending balls and parties, as I was just fourteen, but in our small provincial town few people were more than vaguely aware of that. I was wildly excited to go to balls with my sisters. If magic could attain such wonders, did I really need accomplishments?

For a time, I tried to do both—learn to be a proper young lady, and a proper witch. It proved impossible. Not even magic can make more hours in the day. I was always rushing from my aunt's house, where she would shake her head over the half-crushed herbs I'd hastily picked, to my home, where my sisters would scold me for being late to my drawing lesson.

The problem wasn't just time—my two fields of study were fundamentally incompatible. Becoming a young lady is a bit like being a topiary bush. You start out wild and unformed, and highly paid experts snip away at you until you're beautiful and thoroughly tamed. Only then are you considered proper company. A witch is more like a young willow tree. You may start as a scrawny weed, but every root you send questing through the ground, every shoot you send toward the sun, strengthens you. If you're not checked, your roots can crack walls.

So, gradually, I stopped drawing and sewing. At first, my family tried to force me to apply myself, but none of them had much energy to spare for the task. Once I stopped, I felt I'd been a fool ever to start. Nobody seemed to give a fig whether I was accomplished or not! I was still pretty, merry, and a Miss Bennet, and that was all it took to be welcomed heartily into every salon and ballroom in the country. Why, Mary had accomplishments coming out her ears, and where did that get her? Ignored, mostly.

You see why I turned out so bad? It's really not my fault. When someone has warned you that there will be dire consequences if you do a thing—and you do it—and the consequences do not appear, it leaves you inclined to take a dim view of consequences more generally. Everything, I decided, would generally work itself out, so I could do as I pleased. Young ladies are met with prognostications of doom for the slightest transgression, and I feel that this is unwise. For we will transgress, of course. Unless one is as perfect as Jane, one can't help it. What they ought to do is tell us what the really big mistakes are—the ones that will end life as we know it.

Lord, maybe they did tell me. I probably wasn't paying attention.

So much for my happy childhood. I must now pass to the period that you most want to hear about—and that, I own, I least wish to speak of. Must I really go over the whole tiresome business again? You already know the particulars as far as the public is concerned. Rich Mr. Bingley came to Meryton; mooned after Jane; Jane mooned after him; Bingley brought the even richer Darcy; Darcy looked down his nose at us all, and set up a year's worth of trouble by refusing to dance with Elizabeth; Jane and Bingley continued to be moon-calves; the regiment came to town, full of delectable officers, the handsomest one being Wickham; Lizzy set her cap for Wickham in the most shockingly forward fashion, whatever she may now say; Caroline Bingley made her brother leave town without offering for Jane, which just goes to show how dangerous it is to pay too much heed to one's elder sisters; Lizzy met Darcy again near Rosings, where he offered for her; having now heard from Wickham what a shocking rascal he was, she refused him; then later, after seeing the extent of his estates, she accepted him; I went to Brighton, married Wickham, and left with him for London, though not in quite so correct an order; Jane married Bingley and became rich; Lizzy married Darcy and became richer; and at some point Mr. Collins was there.

I daresay nearly all those involved would cry foul about the above account. I know, I know, I am doing them wrong, but that is how the world sees it, and the world thinks well of most of them and terribly of me, so they ought to be content.

Of course, nearly everything the world thinks it knows about my part in the affair is wrong. As far as society is concerned, an empty-headed young girl (me) went to Brighton, where she was seduced by a rake (Wickham), ran off with him to live in disgrace, and was only saved from utter ruin by Mr. Darcy's willingness to pay him off to marry her.

They know nothing of me! Not even my own family knows what I sacrificed and went through in Brighton—what I'm still sacrificing! It's not fair!

Bother! I'm crying. I will have to leave off writing for a while. I'm almost out of ink, and if this page splotches I can't afford to rewrite it.

I took a turn about our quarters until I was calm again. It took quite a number of turns, for our quarters are the size of a mouse-hole, and about as well maintained. All right, I'm ready.

"My dear Mr. Bennet, have you heard that Netherfield Park is let at last?"

# CHAPTER FIVE

We were all assembled in the parlor when my mother walked in and uttered those words. It was a fair September day just before Michaelmas, and the windows were open to let in the breeze.

It is remarkable how much time we all spent in that room, living entirely different lives. I was not paying much attention to the others, for Kitty and I had our heads together trying to work a spell that would allow us to become the best dancers in Meryton at the next assembly, at the low cost of Mary's ability to dance at all. That wasn't so bad, you know—Mary never did dance, for she said she detested it (I think she was actually just afraid that no one would ask her). She never missed the dancing ability we took from her.

Though I was paying little attention at the time, I find I can call the scene to mind if I remember what everyone was wearing. Jane wore the simple light-blue morning dress that so brought out the hue of her eyes. Most morning dresses are white, you know, so this was a rare sprig of vanity in her. She sat near our mother, sewing a shirt for Papa. Mamma worked on another. Lizzy, in a white morning gown that used to be Jane's, sat at the desk by the window writing a letter—she always had someone to write to, seeking any mental escape from our company. Mary despised white, and had dyed her hand-me-down morning dress a deep brown.

I found this unutterably selfish as she would someday hand the dress down to me or Kitty—and in fact, I'm wearing the horrid thing now, and it does not become me at all. She was at the piano. Papa sat in the best chair, reading the paper.

"My jewel, I had not heard such a thing," he responded to our mother's fluttering announcement. "Therefore you must be mistaken, for as you know I am the town gossip, and always up on the latest news."

There followed a scene that was common in our household, and which Kitty and I had learned to tune out until actual information arose from it. My mother fluttered around my father's chair, worrying at him, trying to make him join in her urgency; this only made my father retreat farther into his paper. Kitty always said the scene reminded her of a young kitten trying to induce its mother to play when she would rather sleep. For my part, I am reminded of a sparrow pecking at a tortoise.

My sisters and I began, one by one, to take notice, though, as we realized that Mamma had genuinely important information to impart. Lizzy dropped the pen, Jane laid her sewing to the side; Kitty and I allowed Mary's dancing ability to flow back to her unmolested.

"Why, my dear, you must know, Mrs. Long says that Netherfield is taken by a young man of large fortune from the north of England; that he came down on Monday in a chaise and four to see the place, and was so much delighted with it, that he agreed with Mr. Morris immediately; that he is to take possession before Michaelmas, and some of his servants are to be in the house by the end of next week."

"What is his name?"

"Bingley."

"Is he married or single?"

"Oh! Single, my dear, to be sure! A single man of large fortune; four or five thousand a year. What a fine thing for our girls!"

"How so? How can it affect them?"

"My dear Mr. Bennet," said Mamma, "how can you be so tiresome! You must know that I am thinking of his marrying one of them."

"Is that his design in settling here?"

"Design! Nonsense, how can you talk so! But it is very likely that he may fall in love with one of them, and therefore you must visit him as soon as he comes."

"I see no occasion for that. You and the girls may go, or you may send them by themselves, which perhaps will be still better, for as you are as handsome as any of them, Mr. Bingley may like you the best of the party."

My father, as you can see, is a monster. You know how it was with our family, yes? Our lovely house, Longbourn, was our father's, along with enough land to keep us in gowns and lace and a serviceable carriage; but it was entailed to the male line, and we had no brother, and altogether our situation was a bit like eternally picnicking at the edge of a crumbling cliff. My father's favorite pastime was mocking my mother's fear of falling.

While they continued to argue, Kitty suddenly growled low in her throat, the way she did when I stroked her fur the wrong way.

"What is it?" I whispered. "Is there a dog in the yard again?"

She threw me a look of reproof. When she was a girl, she did not like to be reminded of her catlike tendencies.

"I have had," she said, "a Premonition."

"How diverting! There is going to be an earthquake then? Or am I going to die?"

"Of course you're not going to die," she said impatiently. "Not for years and years, I'm sure. And no earthquakes, either. This is about us. Something about that Mr. Bingley she mentioned—things are going to change for us—all of us." Her face took on a faraway look. "Except for Mary."

I was beginning to believe her. Kitty loved to give herself airs, but she never lied to me, and the look on her face was one I'd never seen before.

"Perhaps this Mr. Bingley is the Chevalier," I whispered.

The Chevalier was a code word Kitty and I had for a certain kind of man. We had never encountered him, except in novels, and only imperfectly there. The Chevalier was the man I was going to marry; sometimes there were two Chevaliers, one each for Kitty and me, but he was primarily my fantasy. He began dimly to appear when I was around eleven, and by now his image had so sharpened that I could almost see him. The Chevalier was tall (very important, for I was already the tallest of my sisters, and still growing) and handsome. He always looked straight past my sisters and fell in love with me. Sometimes he was blond, sometimes dark; but always his face was comely, his manners beautiful, and his history tragic.

That was my primary objection to the young men in the neighborhood. Nothing very tragic had ever happened to them. Oh, some of them had lost parents or siblings, but always to something prosaic like the fever or childbirth. Never anything truly heartbreaking like a centuries-long feud with another family or an illegitimate uncle bent on revenge.

What I wanted was someone with a story. A story I didn't know. I tried not to think of marriage much, because when I did, I found my prospects so bleak that I was tempted to try out one of Mamma's fits of hysterics. I knew my father would never take any of us, let alone the youngest, for a London Season (like I said: monster), and my aunt and uncle in London were not terribly fond of me, so my best chance to find a husband was someone who lived near Meryton, and they were all utter bores. I would probably end up married to Tim Lucas—never mind that when Tim stayed with us once while his siblings had measles, he cried every night for his nurse, and my mother had to rock him to sleep—and he a big boy of eight! Who could marry *that*?

Sometimes the Chevalier was rich, but not usually. A lack of fortune was a barrier, you see, and barriers were romantic above all. Besides, he would be pure of heart and swift of sword, so in the course of our romance a fortune would sort of naturally accrue to him, to allow us to live passionately ever after.

But Kitty shook her head at the idea that Bingley could be the Chevalier. "I don't think so," she said. "When I think of him, I taste money, and fun—but no romance. Not for us. No, he is a—a harbinger."

This was a rare word and I was not at all sure Kitty was pronouncing it correctly. "A harbinger of what?"

"I don't know. Change." She frowned. "Lydia, we must go to the Lucases' ball in a fortnight."

"Of course we must! The last public assembly was canceled because of the fire at the inn, so we've not danced since Mr. Herriott's ball in August. We don't need a premonition to tell us to do that."

"No indeed," Kitty said, and giggled. So did I. Mary told us to hush, and Mamma told her to hush, and Papa told us all to hush.

Lord, how cold it is in here! I can hardly write for shivering. Thinking of that day, with the sun streaming in the south windows, makes this horrid place feel even colder. Stupid, isn't it? With my gifts I could make the Archbishop of Canterbury dance naked in front of Buckingham Palace if I chose, yet I cannot make a fire to warm my chilblained hands—at least, not during the waning moon, and not in such an unmagical place as Newcastle. Oh, I expect I could make sparks, but what good is that when we've no coal and no money to buy more?

I do envy Jane and Elizabeth their money. If I were the mistress of Pemberley, I should light a roaring fire in every fireplace in that ancient pile, cost be damned—then I would drag a tiger-skin rug (I have never been to Pemberley, but surely there is a tiger-skin rug. If not I would buy one) in front of the biggest fireplace of all—and toast myself on it until the tiger and I were both warmed through. Don't you think Darcy ought really to have married me instead?

I am never invited to Pemberley, so I do not know what it is like there, but I can guess, for at the Bingleys' house it is never above half warm. Those who have never been cold do not understand how beautiful it is to be warm.

Just now I sent Wickham out to get us some money. He was not eager to leave his bed, for all that it is nearly eleven. I suppose he drank enough last night that the deep chill of our shabby little rooms could not touch him.

"You must go and find something to burn, dear husband," I said to him. "Or I will take my death of cold."

"If only you would," he growled.

"Go," I said, "or I will tell your father."

"My father the steward of Pemberley is dead, rest his soul."

"That would be no obstacle. I'm a dab hand at necromancy."

He turned away from me and splashed his face with the icy water in the basin, growling something about foul witches burning in hell.

"In any case," I said, "I meant your real father."

He whirled on me, his eyes gone hard, all traces of his hung-over daze gone, and growled, "If you do, I'll tear your heart out."

"You already did," I reminded him. "But I was younger then. You know well what a ruthless monster I can be these days. I know you've got those pretty silver cuff links hidden away where you think I won't find them. Go and sell them, or I'll make you sorry for it."

For a long moment, he did not move, staring a challenge into my eyes. He was right in front of me now and I could feel his chest rise and fall when it brushed mine—the first warm thing I'd felt all day. In public he was always perfect in appearance—hair oiled, coat brushed, shirt points starched. A waste of time, I now knew. Having seen him first thing in the morning, tousled, shirt hanging carelessly open, and still handsome enough to take one's breath away, it was quite clear that all his elegant attire was just gilding the lily.

Stupid Papa. Stupid Darcy. Stupid busybodies of Meryton and Brighton. How could they blame me for following such a creature anywhere, whatever his so-called morals?

Of course the truth is far more complicated. But even if it was just a question of a silly girl's seduction by a rake, they should not have blamed me.

"Go," I said lightly, and shoved on his chest. "Or next time you're in a stupor I'll empty a chamber pot over you."

He stepped forward, the insolent press of his body pushing me up the wall an inch. I fought the urge to squeak and merely met his gaze steadily. His ogreish expression failed to frighten me anymore. Realizing his bluff had been called, he stepped back, made me an ironical bow, and departed.

I breathed a sigh, long and shaky. I declare, there are times I wish that nasty creature and I really were married.

# CHAPTER LORD, I DON'T KNOW—SEVEN?

I could go back and look, but I'm feeling mulish. I feel I've written a hundred chapters by now. Time goes ten times as long when writing as anything else. It drains one awfully.

I shall bear down and get some of it done today, but it is most awfully hard, you know. My mind will not settle. From our grimy window I can see the entrance to one of Newcastle's most fashionable dressmakers. I suppose there must be an important ball coming up, for all day long I see richly dressed young ladies going in and out, their hair styled in the latest fashion.

Most of them are the daughters of manufacturers, I suppose. If they had tried to join in Meryton society they would have been severely snubbed. Now not one of them would be at home to me if I called—a poor soldier's wife with a dubious reputation. I am as far from my old life as if I'd been flung to the moon. A pity. Those ringlets tumbling over one shoulder would, I suspect, look charming on me.

I left off writing for an hour or so, to try the style out. Difficult to do on my own, with no lady's maid, but a witch manages. As I suspected, it looks elegant. Are you sure you would not rather I write you an account of the latest fashions? No, I know you would not, you bore. It would at least be fun, though.

But I suppose I must get on with it. Back to that fall. My father, after having his fun, did indeed make Bingley's acquaintance. Shortly after, so did we all, and immediately he singled Jane out. I was not terribly impressed with him—he reminded me too much of the Lucas boys—but the way he looked at her left nothing to be desired. It was exactly the look I wanted from the Chevalier.

The next time we all met him was at Maria Lucas's coming-out ball, a few weeks later. Poor Maria! She was nowhere near as plain as her eldest sister Charlotte, but she was such a shy, meek little thing, and her looks so unassuming, that hardly anyone remembers it as her night. Bingley and Jane talk of that night fondly as the beginning of their love; Lizzy remembers it as the night she met her husband; and I—well, I remember it as the occasion of several important events, not all of them connected to the ball. For that night was the very first time I attended a gathering of a coven.

That was later, of course, however. The ball came first and I was far more excited about it. I wore a dress of pale rose, covered with a slip of white tulle, with pale-rose silk flowers braided in my hair. (You see I will make this an account of the latest fashions whether you wish it or not.) My sisters and I attended Maria's ball all together, but Kitty and I were engaged to leave with Aunt Philips and stay the night with her. I thought she merely wished me to spend the early-morning hours gathering herbs under the light of the moon, as we had several times before, so I thought little of it, except to hope it meant we might be able to stay later at the Lucases' than the elder three. It was a warm night, and I leaned my head out the carriage window as we drew near. How different everything looks the night of a ball! Lucas Lodge, so shabby and familiar during the day, glittered with lights at every window. Nestled at the top of a hill, it could almost be a fairy castle.

When we arrived, Lizzy fixed us younger ones with a stern eye and said, "Behave." After she turned her back, Kitty stuck out her tongue. We were heartily sick of Lizzy acting as though she was in charge of us instead of Mamma. Mamma herself said nothing but that we should have a good time, and for the next few hours we made certain to do so.

Inside, the ball was everything one could expect from a Lucas affair:

crowded, hot, poorly organized, and great fun. There were not nearly enough gentlemen and many a lady had to sit down, but Kitty and me had partners for every dance. (*Kitty and I*, I can practically hear you saying. Shush. Few pleasures are left to me in this life, so allow me at least to make free with my pronouns.) How I love to dance! One forgets how it feels until one is doing it—and then one feels that this is what bodies are *for*—moving in rhythm, twirling, dipping, and just when you think you've become muddled and forgotten the steps, you turn round and your hand slips into your partner's, and you realize your body knew the way all along. Tap! A dozen dancing slippers hit the floor at the same instant. Whoosh! You dash down the line of the dance, so lightly it feels you're flying. Boom! Your heart keeps time with the music and the clapping hands of everyone not lucky enough to be on the floor. Many say that I am the best dancer of my sisters, for though I am not so pretty as Jane, nor so precise in my steps as Lizzy, I enjoy dancing the most, so even the clumsiest partner may feel at ease with me.

Besides, I am the tallest. It's very easy for me to meet a gentleman's eye across the crowd, and once he has done that, what can he do but ask me for the next dance?

When I wasn't dancing, I passed a very enjoyable evening gossiping with Kitty over glasses of punch about what a goose Maria was to wear that violent shade of green that did not suit her at all, and how proud Bingley's friend Darcy was, walking up and down the assembly looking down his nose at us all, and eavesdropping on what someone's Oxford chum said to Mrs. Long's niece going down the dance.

"La!" I said to Kitty. "I am sure some of the things he said were quite improper. Is a gentleman allowed to say 'milky knees' to a lady?"

"I'm sure not," Kitty said. "A cat could, though. The barn tom used to sing praises to every part of me, tail-to-whiskers." She gave a little shudder of pleased remembrance.

"The barn tom is no gentleman," I said.

She smirked into her punch. "By cat standards, he was."

I did not know how to continue that conversation so I changed the subject. Leaning closer, I said, "How goes your premonition? If it was not about Bingley, perhaps it was about his friend, Master Stinkface."

I nodded across the room to Darcy, who was just then standing coldly near Elizabeth, declaring with every rigid line of his body that he would not ask her to dance. I wonder sometimes that anyone minds my behavior when men like that exist. At least I like people.

Kitty frowned. "Mr. Darcy? No, I do not think so. That is—oh, I don't know. The feeling's long gone. Perhaps it was only a fancy after all—oh look, here comes Lady Lucas."

Indeed, our hostess was bearing down on us, beaming. In her wake trailed a skinny girl of perhaps sixteen. "Just the girls I wanted to see!" Lady Lucas said. "My dears, allow me to introduce Miss Mary King. Mary, Miss Kitty Bennet and Miss Lydia Bennet."

As we made our curtsies and said how d'ye do, I eyed the newcomer. She had a very elegant fascinator trimmed with feathers in her hair, but it did not quite match her gown. The gown itself looked expensive, but it sagged in the bodice—it had not been made for her, and she had not enough bosom to fill it. Two strikes against her in the marriage market, if that was what she was here for. Perhaps husbands were not yet on her mind, though. She was tall enough, but her figure was rather thin and childish, and her face young. She had ginger hair and—worst of all, if landing a husband was her aim—her face, her arms, and even her bosom were covered in freckles.

Lady Lucas's gaze flitted between us as we sized each other up. "Miss King and her mother are new to the county," she said. "Her grandfather is ill and needs rest, so she is come here to visit, aren't you, poor lamb?" Miss King looked vaguely insulted at being addressed as a poor lamb, but Lady Lucas gave her no time to reply. "Well, I told her, I know two of the liveliest young ladies in the county, and just your age, too, and if you will allow me to present you, I am sure you will all soon be the most intimate of friends." By the end of this speech she was already looking over our shoulders, and when she was done she departed without another word, intent on seeing to some other crisis of hostessry, leaving us to stare at one another.

Why is it that grown-up people always assume that young people of the same age and sex must necessarily be intimate friends? They do not abide by such maxims themselves. If they did, Lady Lucas would be bosom friends with Mrs. Cantby, instead of cutting her dead whenever they meet. (Mrs. Cantby's niece declined Fred Lucas's invitation to dance, and then danced with another man for the very next set! It was all we talked of for weeks.)

Kitty and I tried not to stare, of course, but the newcomer regarded us with an amused smile, as if she expected us not to be able to tear our eyes from a creature as magnificent as her. She was indeed eye-catching. Her dress was a vivid shade of coral that clashed horribly with her ginger hair. Most of the young ladies in the hall wore shades of pastel or white. She stood out among us like a flamingo among doves. And yet, the effect was not displeasing, exactly. Her clashing hues were so riotous they seemed almost a deliberate statement, an arch, witty remark I could not quite follow.

Kitty broke the silence. "I am very sorry to hear your grandfather is not well. Has he been indisposed long?"

"Oh, ages," our obligatory new friend said in a drawling accent. "I declare I am dead tired of it. He persists in not dying, and Mother and me are left in low water." We must have looked confused, for she favored us with a smile. "In low water? Skirting the river Tick? Low on funds, you know."

Kitty and I exchanged a glance. We had never heard a girl of our own age use such slang. She gave us an airy little laugh that sounded like she'd learned it by rote. "I suppose country girls like you are not allowed to use such terms," she said. "Lord save me from provincial manners."

"You're from London then?" I asked.

"London! Oh no. What a bore. I am from *Brighton*." She said it like *I am from Buckingham Palace*.

Have you ever met someone who you could not decide if you loved or hated? So it was with Miss Mary King. I was a child still really, and had seen nothing of the world—but even I could see that our new acquaintance was not quite the thing. And yet she behaved with such utter careless rudeness that she gave the impression that it was all of us in Meryton who were beneath her notice! Her manners seemed to say that every guest in attendance ought to be paying their respects to her august personage. She was so self-assured that she made me doubt my own sense of the social order. Maybe it was we country bumpkins who were ignorant of the social supremacy of a lawyer's daughter from Brighton.

And oh, how she spoke of Brighton! The balls, the tents, the amusements, the sun, the sea, the officers on parade. It did make me feel small and countrified in comparison. Even apart from the slang, her speech was peppered with words and phrases that she made no further attempt to explain. They were alluring in their incomprehensibility.

"In general we go walking on the Steyne in the early afternoon," she was saying. "Of course the heat is oppressive, but it is a much more exclusive time to walk. If one goes later there is always the tiresome crush of people about HRH, and Mamma cannot abide it."

"HRH?" I ventured to ask.

"Why, His Royal Highness, of course. The Prince Regent. Fancy you not knowing that! We see him all the time in Brighton, naturally." She paused to take a swallow of punch.

It was a bit like saying you lived next door to the man in the moon. The Prince Regent was so removed from our sphere that I never even thought of him. He belonged to Papa's tiresome discussions of politics with his friends. Miss King, however, spoke of him casually, as if he were a nodding acquaintance. I did not quite believe it, but in the fairyland of Brighton, who knew what might be possible?

Our conversation was interrupted periodically by the dancing, when partners came up to claim Kitty's or my hand for a round. No suitors came for Miss King, which was not so very surprising—she was a stranger, and men hereabouts were generally shy. When I danced with Tim Lucas I tried to get him to ask her next, but in vain—when Tim returned me to her, despite my elbow in his side, he made his bows and swiftly retreated. Miss King did not look at me, her gaze drifting languidly over the dance floor.

"How glad I am that none of these tiresome country boys have asked me to dance," she said. "Their skill is sadly lacking. It is all right for you, I suppose, having grown up among them."

This I would not stand for from an outsider, even about clods like Tim. "I think there are many gentlemen here who are fine dancers."

She widened her eyes and flung her hands up. "My dear Miss Lydia, I meant no offense. They are the finest dancers in the land, if you wish it. I meant merely that, having been raised in the ballrooms of Brighton, I expect a different standard, and should hardly enjoy myself with any of the men here." Her keen, small eyes scanned the room. "That gentleman, perhaps, knows how to acquit himself. When he asks me to dance, I may acquiesce, if I am not too *fatiguée*."

I followed her eyes and laughed. "You mean Mr. Bingley?"

"Is that his name?" She watched him, talking animatedly to Jane on the other side of the ballroom. "He patronizes a decent tailor at least. I fancy I may even have seen him in Brighton."

"Perhaps, but he is—" I hesitated. "He is certainly a fine gentleman, and they say he has four thousand a year. But he is hardly acquainted with anyone here. He is new to the county."

"Then we will have much to talk of. Besides, we are acquainted. Sir William made us known to each other."

Kitty's eyes met mine, and we shared a moment of silent commiseration over a situation that had become distinctly uncomfortable. Bingley was still hanging on Jane's every word, and anyone could see that he was gathering his nerve to ask her to dance again. Acquainted or no, he clearly had no intention of asking Mary King. But then a group of punch-seekers swirled by, obscuring our view, and when they had moved, Bingley, with a startled look on his face, was moving toward us.

"Miss King," he said, with a bow. "May I have the honor?"

"Oh, I suppose." She lay a gloved hand in his and they were off, without so much as a backward glance. Her back was straight and proud; Bingley had the look of a man who did not quite follow what was going on. But then, that was not so different from his normal look.

Kitty and I were soon claimed by our own partners, so we had no time to gape. Bingley, recovering from his apparent surprise, chatted amiably with his partner, and her bright laugh trailed with him down the line, her eyes never straying toward the incredulous and, in many cases, envious looks the young ladies of Meryton cast his way. I was not jealous—to me, despite his lovely fortune, Mr. Bingley seemed like an overgrown Tim—but it was certainly perplexing. Perhaps his disagreeable friend had dropped a word in his ear about dancing two sets in a row with a young lady he had only just met. Yes, that was probably it.

I ought to have guessed the truth then, of course, but I was busy trying to remember the steps to the new gavotte.

# CHAPTER EIGHT

When the evening ended, Kitty and I departed in my aunt's hired chaise, yawning. It was still many hours till sunrise—Lucas balls were too hot and stuffy to dance through the night—but I could hardly keep my eyes open.

"Please, Aunt, must we really gather herbs tonight?" I said. "My feet ache awfully—and look at Kitty."

Kitty was so tired that she had given up on girl-shape altogether and lay curled up on the seat on the coach, her tail over her nose, grumbling whenever we went over a bump.

Our aunt clucked. "Kitty, stop that at once. You'll get fur on the seat cover. And who said anything about gathering herbs?" She drew herself up. "Wake up, girls, and gather your wits, for tonight we go to a gathering of the coven."

Kitty and I looked at each other. Despite my exhaustion, my heart began to pound. When we got to my aunt's house, we found the maid who should have waited up for us snoring by the door; there was a tiny sprig of lavender beneath her chair, tied with a blue ribbon—a simple charm for sleep. My aunt winked at us, and told us to make ready.

If there is any better feeling than putting on your finest gown, and slipping into your new pair of dancing slippers, and having your mother's maid dress your hair in the latest style—it can only be the feeling of taking the tight, itchy gown off again at the end of the night, kicking off the cursed slippers that have rubbed your feet raw, and letting your hair down again. What a pleasure it is to scratch what needs to be scratched, and otherwise attend to all the parts of one's body that a young lady is supposed to pretend do not exist. Every one of us experiences that delicious sensation, but only we witches know what it is to then run into the night wearing nothing but your sleeping shift. Imagine if my sisters could have seen me then!

My aunt ushered us through the back door—none of her other servants appeared, either—and through the garden and out the back gate to the fields. She, too, was in her shift, her hair loose in a frizzy wave, and thinner without the hairpiece she normally wore in front.

Kitty and I chased each other in circles around her, laughing. We ought to have been careful—it would not do at all for anyone to see us—but that thought could not touch me. I laughed and whooped until I could hear my voice echoing off the hills, but somehow I knew we were safe from the everyday world.

All my tiredness was gone. I felt immortal. It was October, and there was a hint of crispness in the air. The trees above us were touched with orange and yellow, just visible in the moonlight. The dew-slick grass cooled my dancing blisters and I ran even faster. Kitty, sprinting out ahead of me, looked like a pixie or a will-o'-the-wisp. Her dark hair streamed behind her, over the billow of white shift and the flash of long, pale limbs. Any passing farmer could have seen us, but I knew they wouldn't. The night belonged to us witches.

My aunt allowed us to run wild for a time, focused as she was on puffing along in the darkened field without tripping on the uneven ground. Presently, though, she brought us to heel. "Now, girls, not too much of that," she commanded. "Of course, some carrying on is appropriate for such dread creatures of the night as we, but let us not go too far. Kitty, come back here! You'll catch your death if you splash in the creek so. We've serious witching to attend to tonight, and I'll box your ears if you shame me in front of the coven."

"Shame you how?" I asked. I was engaged in conjuring cold little winds to puff against the back of Kitty's bare neck and make her shriek.

"None of that, for one thing," my aunt said firmly, and she grasped my spell-hand (my right, since I am left-handed) and pulled it down to my side. "Proper young witches do not perform magic before their elders without being asked to do so. And if anyone asks your name, you will say you are Lydia, apprentice to Mistress Philips. Oh—and I nearly forgot. Kitty, stop being a girl at once."

Kitty stopped dancing and looked at her. "I beg your pardon? Not an hour ago you were scolding me for getting fur on the seats."

"That was in society. It's nothing to do with what's right on a night like this." She shook her head. "I have been sadly remiss, I think. I ought to have taught you two how to behave in the company of sisters of the craft long ago. Go on with you now, Kitty."

Kitty looked about apprehensively. We had come to the edge of the field and stepped over the stile into a small woods—small by daylight, but the shadows now were dark and thick and made it seem immense. "Out here? Now? What if a fox gets me?"

"We'll keep the foxes at bay, but you'll change now and no mistake. A glamour is a kind of lie and witches are honest before their betters. Lydia will be the youngest witch there tonight and it would be the greatest insult to imply that older and more experienced witches could not see through the glamour she's placed on her familiar."

I blinked. "My what?" It was the first time I had ever heard Kitty called that.

"Your familiar, dear. Surely you didn't think the bond between you was mere sisterly affection? Come, Kitty, we haven't got all night."

"Very well," said Kitty, "but I'm not getting my paws wet." She jumped toward me and transformed in the air, landing in my arms in cat-form. She scrabbled a moment for balance, digging her claws into my arms, then climbed up onto my shoulder, where she rode, grumbling and swishing her tail the rest of the way.

Our destination was a hill out by Struble's Mill, with a circle of standing stones at the top. There were perhaps thirty people there, milling about in the moonlight. After squinting for a few moments I noticed several things: One, they were all women; and two, they were all naked.

Before I could exclaim, a woman appeared at my elbow, holding a bucket. "Dram of Hecate, dearie?" she asked. My aunt drank some, then passed me the ladle, and I also drank it down.

It was a bit like Lady Lucas's punch—oversweet and overstrong. But this drink had subtler notes as well. Herbs and something spicy. I smacked my lips dubiously.

"Good, isn't it?" the woman said with satisfaction. "Mistress Stickle's is not half so delicious, though they say hers can show you more than any mere mortal can see. The secret is, I adds mint."

As the woman wove off into the crowd, a glowing, floaty feeling began in my stomach. I was not drunk—in fact, my senses were sharper—but I felt perfectly calm, and when my aunt, who was naked now, gestured for me to disrobe, I did so without hesitation. It would have been rude, I felt, to do otherwise. Does that sound very dreadful? Everyone thinks we country folk are so conservative, but we end up seeing an awful lot, you know. In a house of five sisters and little money, the womanly form was hardly embarrassing to me.

For some time, I stayed on the outskirts, stealing glances at the assembled witches. I had never seen so many naked women before, and certainly never had leisure to study them. Such variety astounded me. Old, young, thick, thin, firm, wrinkled—all so different, and all so unashamed. If only the young rake who'd whispered to his dancing partner about milky knees could see us now—more milky flesh than he'd know how to handle.

No one seemed to object to my staring. The witches mostly paid me no mind. Occasionally one would nod to me. One woman of about forty, with faded ginger hair, asked me to do credit to my teacher by showing what I had learned. She handed me a cup of milk, and I soured it. She and her friends applauded and said I was a good girl. She clicked her tongue, causing a shower of sparks, and something dropped into her cupped hands. She slipped it to me—it was a boiled sweet, one of the ones they sold in the Meryton shop, and I realized she was the shopkeeper's wife. I said thank you, but she and her friends had already turned away to resume their conversation.

After a little while, I began to discern patterns in the swirling chitchat. Some women, it was clear, were more important than others. They stood in the best spots—near the bonfire, but not so near that their naked flesh was at risk from sparks—and others gravitated toward them. Some they acknowledged, gracing them with conversation, while others, less fortunate or less respected in this society perhaps, milled on the outskirts, putting in an occasional word that was usually ignored. Sometimes the shifts of the women's bodies would shuffle these unfortunates out of the orbit altogether, and they would move away toward another clique, as if they'd always intended to seek another acquaintance just then.

It was all so much like Meryton society at a ball that I almost laughed. I'd have thought witches better than all that. The difference was that in Meryton I knew the rules. Here I did not. Was my aunt respected here? Would I be? Who should I try to talk to, and who should I scorn? As I watched, some of the faces came into focus in the flickering firelight— women I knew. One of the important women was Sadie, the vicar's cook's daughter, who was pointedly snubbing the Honorable Miss Charing, spinster daughter of the old baron.

Occasionally one of the women would do a bit of magic—casually, as the shopkeeper's wife had, but showily. I saw a woman complain loudly of the cold, then make a fire in her hands. She cupped it close to her chest, trying to look as though she wasn't concentrating hard, and allowed the flame to drift in lazy circles around her body. When it reached her head her hair caught fire, and she swiftly beat it out, looking embarrassed. The women she'd been talking to pretended not to notice.

I felt an unaccustomed shyness creep over me. Back home I needed to know only three things to discern a woman's place in relation to mine: who her father was, who her husband was if she had one, and how much money she had from them. In our magical society, which was entirely free of men, how was I to judge? I'd always hugged the secret of my witchcraft to myself with glee, reminding myself that I was not just another young lady—I was a witch. I was special.

But among witches, who was I?

*Indecent, is who you are,* Kitty yowled from my feet.

"Oh, hush," I said. "This is normal among witches. Don't show your ignorance, Kitty. Besides, you're naked, too."

*It's all right for me. I'm a cat. We're not meant to be clothed. When you grow a decent coat of fur to cover your unmentionables, I'll cease to mention them.*

"You're only cross because Aunt wouldn't let you come as a naked girl."

Kitty delicately washed a paw. *I'm not the only one at least.*

She was right, I saw. Some of those gathered also had animal shadows following them about. More cats, a dog, a raven, even a goat in one case. I wondered if any of them were people I knew. Most of the women I had identified as important had such companions. Perhaps I was special after all.

Before I could muse any further, a woman clapped her hands. "Friends," she called, "the time has come. Let us begin."

At her words, one old witch, so wrinkled and bent that I thought she must be a hundred, took a place by the fire and began to beat a drum. A large woman stood next to her and played a pipe—a wild, thumping, skittering tune that could not have been more different from the tame Scottish airs that had graced the Lucases' ballroom an hour before. And yet it gave me the same feeling that diving down the line of the dance did.

Everyone seemed to know more or less where to go, although it was evident that there was no set place for each woman—there was a fair amount of shuffling and giggling and changing of positions. Witches called their friends over to them—"'Ere, Dorcas, stand with me and me big bum'll block the wind!" "Oh, Sophie, how very kind, I should be delighted," and so on. But their movements were not aimless, either. Quite often a woman would find a spot, look about, and then, muttering in dissatisfaction, go somewhere else. Feeling more awkward than ever, I sought my aunt, hoping that she would tell me what to do, or at least let me stay at her side. However, she was deep in a fawning conversation with the tall woman with the goat, and merely hissed, "Not here, dear, not here, get in the virgins' circle."

I was at a loss, but luckily Kitty nipped at my ankle and said, *There. Those must be the virgins.*

It was a line of young women of about my own age, and a few plain-ish older ones as well. The Honorable Miss Charing, who was sixty if she was a day, was one of them, and none too pleased did she look. I hastened to join them. Of the ones I knew, I realized, all were unmarried.

Gradually, the shape of the thing became clear. We were arranged in three circles. One, the one I was in, was made up of, it seemed, virgins. Another contained most of the other women, and the third held the women I'd identified as leaders. The circles interlocked, our linked arms passing over and under each other, like the rings left from Papa's teacup on his desk because he refused to use a coaster.

We began to move. Slowly at first, passing in and among the other circles without ever breaking the chain. Then the beat of the drum sped up, and we moved faster and faster. The chains should have broken—it should have been impossible—yet somehow, we kept our hands clasped tight.

What is magic, anyway? Perhaps you know. You have always been wiser than I, irritating as that often is. It's been explained to me many times, but no explanation has ever seemed enough. A scientific-minded young witch once told me it was the reverse of entropy—witchcraft is the only force in the world that can unbreak a teacup. My aunt told me it was a gift from the spirits—when I asked what spirits, she merely tried to look wise and said nothing.

That feeling that rushed through me as we danced—was that magic? Were we binding our powers together, we ladies and chambermaids, heiresses and beggars, naked and hand-clasped? Or were we just a lot of

country women making an unnecessary fuss to convince ourselves that
we were wild, wicked, magical creatures?

What happened next, of course, I have no doubts about at all.

We spun faster and faster. Finally, with a great shriek and a final
drumbeat, the circles flew apart. We stood, panting as one, and the
woman with the goat stepped forward and raised her hands.

"Sisters!" she called. "We are called forth tonight to do a Great Working together."

A few women gave wild, eerie cries in response. A few more tried to
give wild, eerie cries.

The woman waited for silence. The goat stood perfectly still at her
feet. "One of our own has asked a boon of us."

A murmur of anticipation went through the crowd. It seemed they
were not called together often. Now they would learn why.

"She is in need," the woman went on. "What is rightfully hers is with-
held. In the flower of youth, the rich earth she needs to grow is kept from
her. I ask you—is that any fate for a witch?"

"No!" came the cries.

"Will we witness her right this wrong tonight?"

"Yes!"

"Will we grant her aid?"

"Yes!"

"Then let her come forth!"

With that, a figure stepped up to join her. A slender girl, her pale skin
ruddy in the firelight. She wore streaks of bright-blue paint across her
face and body. I started. It was Mary King.

If she saw me, she gave no sign. She was leading a small white animal.
At first I thought it was a familiar, like the other beasts there, but then
I realized that she led it by a rope, while all the familiars walked free.
Goose bumps rose on my bare skin.

"Bear witness to my Great Working," Mary called to us. Even under
the ritual formality, she still sounded slightly bored. "You are the vessel,

and I the blood. You are the channel, and I the ship. With my power and yours, I act!"

With that, she threw a handful of herbs into the fire.

Smoke billowed forth, and I began to cough. I heard others try to smother their coughs, but I couldn't. My eyes watered.

I could not see precisely what she was doing. None of us could, I suspect. When Mamma is working on an especially intricate bit of needlework, I can tell she's doing *something*—a line of black stitches here, a blotch of red there, and a riot of rainbow-colored threads hanging below her hoop—but it can take days or weeks to see the final shape. This was much the same. It felt to me like Mary was trying to blow up a dam. On one side, there was a stagnant pool—on the other, a dry creek bed. What she wanted was to let the water flow, that was all. The creek cried out for wet, and surely the pond took no joy from its sluggish stillness.

It was all of our power, as she'd said, but Mary was in control. I could feel her laughing as she drove us along. Perhaps she was right to scorn most of Meryton society. The fools certainly had no idea of the pillar of flame who walked among them. We rocked against the dam—once—again—again—and then, with a creaking sigh, it dissolved.

I came back to myself with a blink. The lamb lay in the embers of the fire, a knife in its heart. Whatever had held us together, it was gone now. A sliver of sun peeked over the horizon.

As daylight began to touch us, a hint of embarrassment permeated the crowd. We found our shifts and dispersed, avoiding one another's eyes, and hurried home before the milkmaids could see us.

Kitty and I slept that day at our aunt's house till nearly one o'clock. When we woke, with that half-cross, half-luxurious feel of having slept the entire morning, my aunt's maid brushed the leaves and dirt from our hair without a word.

Two weeks later we were at our aunt's house again when our uncle wandered in. "You've missed your chance to say goodbye to your new playfellow," he told us. "Those King females left town first thing today. Seems as old Mr. King has taken a turn. Won't last out the month."

I drew in a sharp breath. Kitty dug her nails into my arm to silence me.

My aunt continued to untangle a skein of wool. "Very tragic, I'm sure," she said placidly. "At least he'll leave the girl well provided for."

"Yes, five thousand pounds, I believe," my uncle said. "Wonder what it was that brought him low at last? Been a very long illness, so they say. Ah well, it's for the best I daresay."

I felt a little sick, and stammered out our excuses. Kitty and I walked home in queasy silence.

"We did something very wicked," I said finally.

"We didn't do it," Kitty argued. "It was Miss King. No one told us what the spell was for."

"But we helped."

My legs trembled beneath my skirts. I could not meet the eye of anyone who passed. I was sure my wickedness showed all over me. When I got home, I rushed past Mamma's welcoming embraces and dived straight into my bed. But the strange thing was, as I discovered over the next few weeks, that nearly everyone in Meryton seemed to share my uncle's opinion. The death of an unknown, sick old man was a blessing if it allowed a widow and her single daughter to find more prospects. One might almost suppose that the old gentleman had been rude to refrain for so long from dying, and infer that, after all, it was a good deed to remedy his faux pas.

If the good folk of Meryton had known what I had done, they would have condemned me as a murderess. However, I distinctly got the impression that if any of *them* had the power to hurry along their inheritances, they'd have done so almost to a man.

# CHAPTER NINE

My dress is tight about my arms and chest. The hem is too short, too. I've grown since my wedding. Can you believe that? Fancy a married woman not yet grown to her full height! It's a shame that I've fallen into this position. Not my shame only. I was a *child*.

Do you know what Lizzy was like when she was fifteen? She may have forgotten, but I haven't. She drove the entire household mad for a year. She got hold of the wrong sort of books, declared herself a Wollstonecraftian, and told our mother that she was repressing her rights as an individual. She would not let the maids style her hair and said that learning women's accomplishments was "an attempt to stifle her intellect." (You see I was not the only one who found such things tedious! You ought to see how strident Lizzy used to become about the liberation of the female when it was time to practice her piano.) Such rows she and Mamma used to have! Up and down the stairs, in and out of the parlor, Lizzy quoting *Vindication of the Rights of Woman* and Mamma begging her to please just wear a *few* curls in her hair.

Jane was nothing like that of course, but in her own way she was equally trying. She always acted completely correctly, but such an effort it cost her! Before her first few balls she got completely ready to go and then melted down into hysterical tears, frantic with the certainty that she would make some error of etiquette and be utterly disgraced. Several times we were all in quite a fright, for Jane said she could feel her heart beating out of her chest and she was sure she would die of it. It would take her up to an hour to calm down. Kitty and I used to sing duets to her, changing the words to make her laugh. Jane never knowingly caused trouble, but for three months after her presentation, her fits of nerves turned the entire household upside down.

My point is that every girl of fifteen is trying. I was not some remarkable example of wickedness. Jane and Lizzy grew up, and grew calmer. Lizzy discovered that the algebra and geometry she'd insisted on learning were even duller than piano, and Jane found that the world did not end if she missed a dance step. My mistakes just happened to be of the sort that time cannot remedy.

Forgive my digressions. I'm sure you don't want to hear about anything but what we agreed I would relate. But really, you are lucky not to have sisters. Whether you adore them or loathe them, they never quite leave you alone.

Kitty turned eighteen today. I'd have liked to send her a gift, but I haven't the money to post the smallest parcel, let alone to buy something to put in it. Perhaps that is why my mind is even more scattered than usual. At home, they are just having a quiet birthday celebration like any other, I suppose. Papa might give her a book she doesn't want, and Mamma will ask the cook to make her favorite supper. Perhaps Papa will even take her for a stroll, just her and him. He always said that eighteen was the age when females became somewhat able to hold a conversation.

I would have done something. We like birthdays. Kitty is fascinated with how old humans get. If she were still a cat she'd be a great-grandmother, too old to do anything but lie by the fire. Instead, she's only just passed the verge of womanhood.

I wish Kitty would write to me.

Enough. I am going out. I haven't seen that so-called husband of mine for three days, there isn't a thing to eat in the house, and I am going to buy myself something pretty with money he doesn't have.

*Later*

Well, that was quite an unusual day. Newcastle has some decent merchants after all.

I made my way to Northumberland Street, where I bought myself a pie and ate it while walking. Not something I would have done in days past, but before I left home I had covered myself in charms to keep myself and my too-short gown unnoticed. I was a little anxious—charms to stay unnoticed were not much a part of my repertoire when I was a Miss Bennet. But fallen, shabby Mrs. Wickham is another matter.

Newcastle is an astonishingly ugly place. Full of smoke and muck and people. So many people! It seems more crowded even than London, with great masses of humanity flooding to and from the factories at the appointed times, chattering in accents I find as incomprehensible as Greek. The hints of magic I can usually smell on the air in the country or at the seaside or even in London are almost entirely absent here.

And yet—I like it. Just a little. It's such a vigorous place. People come here to make money, and they make gobs of it or go bust or both in succession. Newcastle has a brutal honesty about it that I find appealing. Perhaps if I had been born a boy in the north, all those "high spirits" of mine that everyone deplored would have borne me to a great career as a man of business.

I drifted through the shops one after the other. My stomach was growling again, but I did not want to spend my few coins on more food. I tried to feed my soul with pretty things instead, stroking my fingers over racks of ribbons, leaning down to examine snips of lace: It was a balm to my sore, bauble-loving heart.

I was in the haberdasher's, trying on a frilled cap—I could make such a one myself without much trouble, but the thought of setting out to make something so dowdy made me feel a thousand pounds heavier—when I saw them. To my own eye, the cap made me look like I was a little girl dressed up in her mother's clothes, but I knew that from behind I looked every inch the dowdy matron. That is why women submit to wearing those hideous caps, I suppose. They are the most depressing items imaginable, but they do declare to the world that one is safely married, and that buys one a bit more freedom than those dangerous creatures, unwed

ladies, are allowed. As I glumly contemplated my reflection in the mirror
held by a bored clerk, a flash of color caught my eye.

There was a group of young ladies behind me. I eyed them curiously
through the mirror. At first, they all looked the same: half a dozen girls,
all clad in the same deep-blue cloaks. They were accompanied by several
maids, a footman carrying various packages, and an older lady whose
smile was so pinched you could use it as a clothespin.

"Hurry up, girls," she said. "Marianne, be quiet, or I'll send you back.
Margaret, mind you don't outspend what your father sent. Frederica,
cease that tittering." She continued on in this vein, apparently neither
noticing nor caring that her charges did not heed her.

A school, then. I'd heard that there was a school for fine young ladies
near the city—very expensive indeed, it was said. Most of such estab-
lishments, I have heard, are awful places. Jane went to one for half a
year when she was thirteen and begged not to return. She was cold and
hungry always, she said, and the mistresses were cruel, and punished her
daily for not knowing all that a girl of her age ought, and if she was made
to return she would throw herself in the river and drown. The only time
I have ever seen her put her foot down, I believe. Sometimes I think the
real reason she was so sweet all the time was her terror that Papa would
force her to go back.

Most families would only send their girls to such an establishment
if they could not afford a governess. The exceptions are certain highly
exclusive schools where the elite send their daughters to mix with the
right people. But there could hardly be such a school here, so far from
town, surely. Who would pay exorbitant school fees to introduce their
daughters to the society of *Newcastle*? More likely something the first
families would pay to avoid.

And yet, these ladies looked neither cold nor hungry. Their round,
healthy faces and rosy cheeks spoke of such hearty meals and roaring fires
that my own stomach growled jealously. And the fond contempt with
which they ignored their teacher's anxious monologue said they were

hardly being terrorized by tyrannical teachers, either. No, these girls, I was sure, were rich. They had the easy assurance of the very wealthy. They laughed and called to one another and seemed so full of life that the rest of us looked even shabbier than we were.

All except one of them, that is. While the rest of the girls twittered about the shop, I saw one hanging back. She moved slowly, carefully, like a donkey finding a path through a stony brook, afraid that any false step could mean a broken leg and a trip to the knacker's.

As I craned to see her, the clerk holding the mirror cleared his throat. "If madam is finished—" He glanced pointedly over my shoulder at the girls behind me. Clearly, he knew I wasn't going to buy the cap, and wanted to attend to his real customers.

I was tempted to magic him into thinking I'd paid for it—serve him right!—but the truth is I wouldn't have bought it even had I had the money. I took it off and handed it back.

"On second thought, I think I'd better order the one I saw in London after all," I said. "Much better quality, of course."

"Very well, Mrs. Wickham," he said, already turning away.

As I replaced my own bonnet, I turned around and looked at the girl again. She was as well fed and well dressed as the rest of them—but half asleep. She looked as though her cloak were made of lead instead of wool. She was around my age, perhaps a little older, which made her one of the oldest of the girls here, but her hair was done in a childish style, half down. If I looked like a child dressing up as a matron, she looked like a woman dressing up as a girl.

What was wrong with her? Was she ill? Without thinking about it, I slipped a hand into my pocket and brushed it against the herbs I had picked in the churchyard that morning. As the spiny little balls of burdock seed pricked my skin, I could suddenly see a network of spells flung over the girl.

No wonder she walked like her cloak was made of lead: Effectively, it was. Protection spell after protection spell had been thrown over her, tied hastily to her cloak or arms or hair or eyelashes or lips, tangling with one another until they became hopelessly snarled. Someone was trying very hard to protect this girl—someone, I realized, who did not remotely know what they were about.

Oh, their basic spellcasting was all right. I could see many of the simple protection rhymes I'd learned at my aunt's knee. But either the caster was ignorant of anything beyond those basics, or they were astonishingly stupid, or both. They seemed to believe that casting the same simple spells over and over would multiply their power, but in fact they just made the whole thing more cumbersome. One minor spell against injury was cast at least ten times, but I could tell that despite the repetition it would still be ineffective against anything worse than a scraped knee.

Some of the spells did not even make sense. A spell to prevent her being deceived in love, fine; but why was it knotted to one that would keep her from being eaten by sharks? I was fairly certain that someone had simply sat down with a book of spells and cast every one of them with *protection* in the name. The clumsiness of it was downright offensive.

Who had done this to her? The girl could not have done it herself. She was no witch—beneath the heavy, sodden blankets of her spell-cloak, I could see a boringly prosaic little soul—but even if she had been, warding herself with all that would be as difficult as smothering herself to death with a pillow. At some point, self-preservation takes over.

"Come along, dear," a warm, sweet voice said. "Let's not fall behind the others." It was the teacher. Her dry voice suddenly oozed with cordiality as she tenderly took the sleepwalker's arm. "There's all sorts in this town you've no need to mix with." She threw me a sharp glance as she spoke.

Ah. I had my own delicate web of pay-no-attention-to-me spells covering me again. If this lady could see me, she was probably the witch who had cast this teetering pile of spells. I did not think much of her. Less than a hedge witch, probably. I made a sign with my fingers that should have provoked a countersign from her—*hello, I'm a witch; hello yourself, so am I*—but she made no response. Yes, she could see me, but she had no idea what she was seeing; when she looked at me, she perceived nothing but a shabby young wife, insolently staring at her grandest and most precious charge.

The charge in question blinked slowly and turned to her teacher. "I am to buy a hat," she said uncertainly, more a question than a statement.

"That's right," her teacher replied, squeezing her arm. "But we'll find you a better one than they have here. Come along, my dear Miss Darcy."

Well. You can imagine what that name did to me.

I am not angry at Mr. Fitzwilliam Darcy. Not precisely. It was my own wickedness, of course, that led me to my current situation, and in fact he helped me avoid falling into even worse circumstances. I ought—so everyone from Lizzy to my father to my aunt's lady's maid told me—to be eternally grateful to him. I shall certainly endeavor to do so. Eternal gratitude, however, does not seem to be in my nature. The more I attempt it, the more I imagine punching him right in his proud, disdainful face.

Miss Darcy. This, then, must be his sister. Now that I knew that, everything fell into place. No doubt that proud man had wanted time alone with his new bride, and had sent his young sister off to school—but after the events of last year he knew something of what dangers awaited vulnerable young ladies. Of course he would not let one who belonged to him venture out unprotected from magical perfidy.

I have never been sure how much Darcy knew. Of course he was aware that what was going on was not quite natural, but none of us sat him down and gave him an explanation. (Unless you did? I had the impression that you did not consider him worth talking to at all.) Clearly, he gleaned enough to decide that his sister needed magical protection—but he would not have had the slightest idea how to go about acquiring it. Obviously, Miss Carr's School for Young Ladies provides such a service. An excellent idea, when one thinks about it! Perhaps I ought to open such a business on my own, what do you say? Except no, of course not, no decent parent would entrust their daughters to the scandalous Mrs. Wickham. Ah well. I hate children anyway.

Miss Darcy glanced back at me for a moment, as though she had felt my stare; but a sharp word from her teacher made her turn her head obediently. Perhaps, I realized, the pile of spells was not quite so purposeless as I had thought. The heaviness might not actually protect her from harm, but it made her very biddable. Some people think that obedience in a young female is the same as safety.

They were heading for a warm, dry carriage, waiting right outside. It had begun to rain. I was going to get soaked when I walked home. Without thinking about it, I brushed past the girl and plucked a little loose thread off her cloak. "Excuse me, miss," I said in my most humble voice, then walked home, becoming drenched within moments as her carriage no doubt drove off to a nice warm fire.

I have that bit of thread in front of me now. Wickham is still not back. I magicked the butcher to let me have a bit of cold meat—don't scold me, I did not steal it, merely stretched our credit, I will pay him back—and now here I am, shivering, wearing Wickham's spare trousers and jacket because they are dry, and staring at that little thread on our kitchen table.

There is all sorts of mischief a wicked creature like me could do with this. I could, for example, steal Miss Darcy out from under their noses. That cloak of hers is so thick with magic that it would probably move around on its own for several days. Only a slight illusion spell would be needed to keep them from realizing it wasn't her underneath it.

Or I could leave the girl where she is, but take her under my control. She's already half asleep—would they even notice if I stole her will away and made her my servant? I could slip a scrap of paper and a sachet of herbs into her pocket and make her assassinate the Duke of York if I so chose. And not just I—anyone with more than a smattering of magic could.

I'd wager a thousand pounds that there is some old woman among

Darcy's tenants who could have given him a deft, lightweight protection that would have kept the girl safe and never so much as caused an itch on her nose. Maybe she'd have done it for free, too—I'm sure she'd have been thrilled to be noticed by the lord of the manor. All he'd have needed to do was to ask his housekeeper or his gardener—that is, if he did not already know himself, from growing up on the grounds. He'd probably heard things as a child, before he became too proud to hear and too hidebound to believe. But he'd prefer not to know that, wouldn't he? Even now, he wants to think of magic as something that happens rarely, and in the wicked city, not in his own backyard. And if he must have spells, well, obviously the best ones must be done expensively by a woman of impeccable reputation and birth. His snobbery is only putting his dear sister in more danger.

All right. I think I know what to do to those tiresome Darcys. I'll get started in the morning. It's dark already, and I can't afford more candles.

# CHAPTER TEN

I've just finished my little Darcy project. Heavens, it is awfully nice to do magic again. It turns out there is magic in this town after all, though it feels very different to what I'm used to. It smells of smokestacks and sweat instead of greenery and fog. If I live here long enough, maybe I'll learn to do spells with a bit of factory ash instead of wild herbs. (*If* I live here long enough? There is no earthly reason to think I shall ever live anywhere else, except the precariousness of our circumstances.)

I know this isn't what I'm meant to be writing about at all, but I do think I was clever in how I went about it, so perhaps you will indulge me a little longer.

After doing my wards, I put the little blue thread in the center of the table and told it, quite firmly, that it stood in for Miss Darcy. Thread is good for that; it's obedient to a witch of authority, but it feels some loyalty for the skin it used to lie against. Then I took some scraps of white linen—my mother sent me yards of it, assuming I would be sewing shirts for Wickham, but he won't let me, because he believes I would sew hexes into the seams, which I certainly would—and laid them over the blue thread. Each one represented a layer of that pile of spells, as best I could remember—the top layer being sort of a catchall for anything that was left.

Then I propped my hand mirror (a present from Jane—the most useful thing her wealth has ever got me!) against a teacup so I could see into it, and cast a smoke-scry, calling forth Miss Darcy. I was betting she'd have a large mirror in her room, and I was right—when I'd cleared the soot, there she was, sitting next to a dressing table and staring blankly at the wall.

The only thing left was the cost, and that was easy. I am now so poor that practically everything I do have is precious enough to serve as spell-tithe. I took the last of the meat I'd got yesterday and tossed it out the window to a passing cur, which snapped it from the air. I was already ravenous and knew I'd be completely out of magic after finishing all this, so I wouldn't be able to get more food today—giving up one's only chance at a decent meal was surely payment enough for a middling magic like this one. (I'm very careful about the price these days, you see. I have learned my lesson about *some* things.)

I tried to use knitting needles to poke the spells off, but they proved too unwieldy—the bits of cloth had gleefully taken on their role as inept spells, and some slipped against one another, while others clung wetly, making the whole mass quite difficult to manage. In the end I had to use my hands—eugh, I hate touching someone else's used spells!—and flung the whole clump off Miss Darcy in one quick swoop like a stack of pancakes. There was a very satisfying *ripping* feeling, like pulling off an old scab, as the spells pulled free. Then I took the very top layer, which was a decent enough general ward, and flipped it back over Miss Darcy. That should keep her looking roughly the same from the outside, and whoever cast it won't notice that I've excavated beneath, if she is as much of an idiot as I believe.

I took the remaining spell-clump and flung it out the window as well. The yip I heard from below leads me to believe there is now a street dog somewhere in Newcastle who is very well protected from fortune-hunters and shark attacks.

Miss Darcy, as tiny as a locket portrait in my mirror, suddenly jumped to her feet and looked around at the little room as if she'd never seen it before. There was certainly no doubt that my magic had worked—she looked like a different girl. Her cheeks flamed, her eyes lit with an intelligent gleam, and she drew herself up to her full height. She looked down at herself in utter perplexity—

And then she looked straight at me.

Or so I thought, for a moment. Of course she was only looking at herself in her mirror. Goodness, I am out of practice! She has a very sharp, intelligent gaze, you see, so for an instant I could have sworn that she could see into my tiny room with the cracking paint just as easily as I could see into her comfortable sitting room.

In my shock I leapt back, which smudged the salt I'd put down as a ward, and that was enough to break the spell. Miss Darcy disappeared from the mirror, replaced with an unflattering look at the underside of my own startled face. I've a spot coming on my chin.

Despite that silliness at the end, I'm quite pleased with the whole process. I don't even mind being a bit light-headed from hunger. Even you cannot fault me for rescuing an innocent young heiress from an oppressive clump of magic that never would have protected her anyway. I was doing a good deed, really. And if in performing it I had the pleasure of undoing something that Darcy paid a great deal of money for—well, as we know, I am very wicked underneath it all. There is probably nothing to be done about that.

*Later*

I've just had a note from Miss Darcy. She wishes me to call upon her. Bother.

# CHAPTER ELEVEN

I have looked back on what I've written so far and I find that I begin almost every day by making excuses for the actions I am about to relate. I shall endeavor to break myself of this habit, but not today, because really, I must explain that what happened with Miss Darcy is not my fault.

I have never heard of such a thing, and I daresay neither have you. Perhaps an inverted protection spell can act as a counter-scry. Or maybe after she trudged around carrying so much magic, she wound up absorbing some of it. No witch could have predicted such a result.

In any case, I am afraid I was right the first time. Miss Darcy did see me in the mirror when I was unmagicking her.

It's been a few days since Miss Darcy's teacher's footman arrived bearing an invitation for me. He looked around doubtfully as I read it, which I did as quickly as possible—he was the first person other than our landlady or her daughter who has come to Wickham's and my flat, and my cheeks burned as I saw it anew through his eyes. The dingy, cracked paint, the smell of food, the clothes hung across the room to dry—every fiber of me burned to get him away and leave me to my solitary shame.

*My dear Mrs. Wickham,* it read, *I hope you will not think this letter too forward, as I have never had the pleasure of making your acquaintance, but there are such connections between your family and mine that I really think we need not stand on ceremony. I am sorry that you were unable to attend the nuptials between your sister and my brother, but if you will do me the honor of calling upon me, I will be very glad to tell you all about the happy event at which you were most sorely missed.*

Ha. Sorely missed. If my husband and I had attempted to attend Lizzy's wedding, we would have been barred from Pemberley's gates. I read on.

*I also wish*, she wrote, *to thank you for the most kind gift that you have so recently made me. It has imbued me with such lightness of spirit that you would think me an entirely different woman. You must allow me the pleasure of thanking you in person, and inquiring as to its provenance. I hope it did not cost you too dear.*

So there it was. She'd realized I'd stolen her spells. No doubt she wished to see me to demand that I repay the Darcy coffers for the money they'd wasted. Well, she'd wait a long time for that. I have no money and when I do get hold of a few shillings, they are from the Darcy coffers as like as not.

*My dear Mrs. Wickham, do not delay. Come to my school, Miss Carr's School in St. James's Square, any morning and I will be honored to receive you. Cordially, Miss Georgiana Darcy.*

Did you ever read such insincere lines in your life? Miss Darcy of Pemberley, honored to receive me! The idea that I would fall for such flattery was utterly insulting. I dashed off a few lines politely regretting that I was too busy to pay social calls (true enough—busy not having anything suitable to wear, or a carriage to wear it in) and sent it back with her man. I breathed a sigh of relief when he was gone. Poverty is ten times as painful when seen through respectable eyes.

I expected that to be the end of it. For several days I endeavored to put it out of my mind—very difficult, for I have very little else to occupy my mind at present—until yesterday, when I heard from her again.

*My dear Mrs. Wickham—*

*I am sorry to hear that you are too much occupied to wait upon me. I shall instead wait upon you. I hope to find you at home tomorrow morning. Cordially, Miss G. D.*

The rich always get their way in the end. I would rather die than let Miss Darcy of Pemberley see how I live. I told her servant that Miss Darcy could expect my call that very day.

Luckily, the school was not as far as I'd thought. I was well able to walk it. If I arrived a bit dusty and sooty—well, such is the way of life in Newcastle, whether one walks or takes a carriage. We all live in the belly of the great dragon of industry, and she has indigestion.

The school was in a fashionable part of town. It was rather an elegant building and had a large walled garden off to the side, but still, it could not hold a candle to Netherfield or even Longbourn. A quick charm before I rang the bell shook off the worst of the dust, and a light glamour hopefully hid the too-high hem and the faded sleeves of my gown. Luckily I had received a letter from Mamma the day before. The promise to burn it unread caused such a pang of pain in my chest that it more than paid the spell-tithe. Mamma would approve, I am sure, of my sacrificing a mere letter from her so as to look pretty for a call upon someone from a rich family who hated me.

The servant who came to the door looked haughty but not shocked, so I suppose the glamour worked. I was led upstairs to Miss Darcy's private sitting room, which was larger than my entire home. She was not there and the maid bade me wait, with a look that told me not to lay my poor, grubby hands on anything. There was a roaring fire in the grate, before which sat two comfortable-looking green velvet chairs with footstools, and a pianoforte in the corner. I was just peeking at the music on the stand to see how skilled she was (frightfully so, it seems) when Miss Darcy herself appeared.

The girl in front of me could not have been more different from the somnambulist I had seen in town days before. Gone was the look of drowsy, biddable stupidity. This young lady's eye was lit with a sharp intelligence. She was still dressed simply, though her hair was no longer in that childish style, but rather pulled back into a bun. It was too severe for her strong features, but at least she looked her age.

"Oh," she said. "Mrs. Wickham. There you are. I mean, how do you do."

"Miss Darcy." I curtsied.

"Please." She nodded to a seat by the fire. "Won't you sit? Clayton will bring us tea presently."

I joined her by the fire. Her hands fluttered a bit before she folded them firmly in her lap. There was something of a shy and awkward air about her that reminded me a bit of my sister Mary. I did not detect any of Mary's pompous air, though. Miss Darcy's gaze was forthright and honest. No beauty was she, but she had a great deal of countenance. If she were a witch I should not like to try one of my hexes against hers.

"I know what you did," she said abruptly. "I know what you are."

"I beg your pardon?" I murmured.

She blushed—not a romantic blush, but a blotchy one of embarrassment. "I do not suppose you meant me to realize it," she said, "but of course I felt it the second you took it all off, and I saw you in the mirror."

I could not help a sharp intake of breath. "That's not possible," I blurted before I could think.

"Possible or not, it happened. Just what is it that you did? Please—"

I had risen to take my leave. "I thank you for your hospitality, Miss Darcy, but there seems to be some misunderstanding. Good day to you."

She held up a hand. "Pray don't go. I'm not angry, you see. I really am grateful for—whatever it was."

"And just what do you think I did, miss?"

"Oh, don't make me say it. I'll sound so foolish." She sighed, and blushed even harder. "Very well. You're a—a—a witch. You witched me the other day."

I might have left, but just then tea came in, and I couldn't resist. A steaming, fragrant pot of tea! Three kinds of cakes! Fresh fruit and bread and butter! I hadn't had a meal like that in months. My stomach practically turned itself inside out with longing at the sight.

I waited till the maid had laid the spread out for us by the fire and left before I replied. "I didn't witch you. If anything, I unwitched you." I sat in one of the chairs and pulled it a little closer to the fire. At least I could get warmed through before I left.

She nodded eagerly. "Yes, I know that. Ever since Miss Carr came to see my brother about me, I've felt like I was watching life from ten feet underwater. I could hardly think. I slept fourteen hours a night. Every girl here thinks I'm an utter half-wit, and so do the teachers." She waved a lesson at me. "Look at this! They've been teaching me to conjugate *être* like a seven-year-old." She shook her head in amazement. "And I got it *wrong.*"

"What is it you want from me?" I asked.

She leaned forward. "I want to know where I stand," she said. "I heard Fitz and Miss Carr talking, so I know all those spells were supposed to be for my protection. Am I in danger now that they're gone?"

"You're as protected as you were," I said. "More so, really. At least now if someone attacks you, you might notice and run away."

She nodded. "So I thought. Miss Carr thinks very highly of herself but she's really not a very clever woman—it's the other teachers who run the place. It doesn't surprise me that she's not much of a witch, either."

I bit into a cake and had to stop from moaning when raspberry preserves and cream exploded in my mouth. It tasted better than anything I'd had in months, and for once didn't smell of soot. After a sip of tea, I added, "I didn't leave you totally vulnerable. There's still a touch of protection. But all right, yes, I took most of that muck off."

"Why did you do it?" she asked. "Are you planning to attack me?" She did not sound particularly frightened of the prospect.

"No! Why should I?"

She shrugged. "You are married to George Wickham. Perhaps you—" She frowned and looked down. "If you are jealous, you needn't be."

"Jealous?" I said. "I don't know what you mean." But I found that I did. I passed a hand wearily over my forehead. "He made love to you, didn't he. The devil."

"Not recently." She made another quick, abortive movement. "He grew up on our estate, you know. A few years ago, he and I—but that was nothing. I am sure he is a perfectly loyal husband to you."

"If you are sure of that, you don't know him at all," I said drily.

She stared at me hard, with those sharp brown eyes of hers. Her brother's gaze can seem so haughty and cold, but those same dark eyes in her face burn right through you.

Abruptly she stood. "I wish to engage your services," she said, and began to pace.

"What services?"

"Your magical services. The only reason my brother allowed me to come away to school was because he ensured that I would be thoroughly protected. He made a muddle of it, but I cannot walk about unguarded." She seized my hand. "My dear Mrs. Wickham, do not be offended—I know you are no tradeswoman. But I do not know where else to turn. I enrolled in this school to study mathematics, because we could find no governess who had more to teach me. But I haven't been able to learn a thing since coming here! Please, I need you. Tell me you can reset those odious wards without making me feel as though I'm slogging through pudding all day."

"Certainly it's possible," I said. "But would your brother really want you associating with George Wickham's wife?"

There it was. Out in the open now. She dropped my hand and was silent for a long moment. "No, he wouldn't," she said. "But I don't care."

"Don't you?"

"All right, of course I care. But I've been nothing but trouble for Fitz since Mamma died. He deserves time to enjoy his new marriage without worrying about me." She looked suddenly fierce. "And I deserve to live away from Pemberley for a few months and prove Goldbach's conjecture."

"Do what to whom?"

I won't bore you with the details. Miss Darcy grabbed a slate and chalk and tried, at some length, to explain to me a thorny mathematical problem that she was determined to solve. Suffice it to say, I did not follow at all. I learned mathematics from Mamma, and though she is better than you might suppose—she may not be the cleverest woman, but she keeps strict household accounts, down to the last farthing—we never advanced beyond multiplication and division. Miss Darcy, however, has gone quite a bit past that. Indeed, her version of mathematics contains almost no numbers at all, just a series of letters of different sizes that she calls variables. Some of them are Greek, which seems excessive.

"Enough," I said at last. "Since I cannot understand this in my right mind, I am sure you cannot do so while drugged with protection spells. But what do you mean for me to do about it?"

She brushed the chalk dust absently from her hands on her gown. I nearly shuddered to see the finely made dress treated with such carelessness. How unfair it is that wealth seems to stick to those who have no appreciation for it.

"My clear head will not last," she said. "Miss Carr puts more spells on me every Sunday, I am sure."

"How can you tell?"

"There's a funny taste in my tea, and then I fall asleep all the afternoon."

I nodded. "Sounds like a casting. It's a good thing I got to you when I did. If she'd kept on as she has been, you might have smothered to death under all that magic."

She shuddered. "Heaven forbid. I'd rather be drawn and quartered."

"She had a spell on you to prevent that."

"I don't like magic," she said abruptly. "It oughtn't to exist. The reason I like mathematics is that if one plus one equals two, it will always equal two. No one ought to be able to wave a magic wand and make it be three."

I considered this. "I don't believe I could make one and one be three. I could make you believe it was three, perhaps."

"Regardless," she said. "I do not like it. But a woman of science must never let what she *wishes* to be true keep her from seeing what *is*. Magic is real and it's a problem. Can you be the solution? I can pay. Not much, for I'm not given much pocket money of my own, but I will do what I can."

I considered this. "You need two things," I said. "Competent protection spells, and regular scrapings-off of the incompetent ones. I would have to see you weekly." I was sure she would say no to that.

She nodded without hesitation.

"It will not be easy," I pointed out. "The only reason you could possibly have been allowed to see me today is if Miss Carr did not properly know who I was." A bitter taste filled my mouth, but I made myself continue. "When she does, you will find that I am not someone whose friendship she will allow you to cultivate."

"Can't you do a spell to make her?"

"Yes I could, but I will not. Are you sure you don't care for magic? You're very quick to demand its worst applications."

She looked abashed at this. "I'm sorry. I'm sure there are all sorts of rules governing you of which I am ignorant."

I tried to look wise and virtuous. I was glad she did not know I had just yesterday done a very similar spell to charm the butcher out of a bit of meat. It was only a small spell, though, and I was hungry, and I *did* promise that I would try to avoid using magic that way if I could. I had already made up my mind not to do as she asked—I was sure it was only Darcy's pride that made him believe that his sister was the target of some magical conspiracy, and I had no wish to attract his attention—but there were still a few sandwiches left so I resolved to let her continue.

She moved over to her pianoforte and began moodily to play a few minor chords. I am always resentful of those who are so proficient with an instrument that they can play it for fun. "I suppose you're right. I can't just strike up a friendship with you. Your reputation in this town is quite bad. I oughtn't to be seen with you. Perhaps you could disguise yourself as a charwoman?"

That was enough. I rose to go, trying to maintain my dignity while also slipping a slice of fruitcake into my pocket. "Good day, Miss Darcy."

"Wait, don't go. That was awful, wasn't it?" She shook her head and banged out a few more stormy notes. "Fitz is always telling me that I am too shy in company, but this is why. When I do speak, I am sure of saying the wrong thing. Please, Mrs. Wickham. Don't leave me here to slip under the waves again. I am quite sincere when I say that I would rather die."

I was sorely tempted. In truth, I would have done it for the cakes and the warm hearth alone. But I could see no way of managing the scheme. If word reached Darcy that I was interfering with his sister, I did not care to find out the consequences. "Why not return home?" I suggested. "The old great houses are stiff with ancient wards. You'd be quite safe there, I daresay."

She shook her head. "I can't. I must be here. My work is too important."

"Your work?"

"Goldbach. I'm close to something, I know I am. Would you deprive the world of a proof it has sought for over fifty years?" Her eyes burned, and she looked more like her brother than I had ever seen her. His pride is for his house, his lands, his ancient line—but this peculiar girl's pride was all for her mind.

I opened my mouth to refuse once more, but just then the door opened. The maid entered and bobbed a curtsy to Miss Darcy. "Letter for you, miss. It just come."

"Thank you, Clayton." She took it and the girl retreated. Miss Darcy frowned at the thick, creamy envelope addressed to her in green ink. "Another invitation to a tiresome Newcastle card party, I suppose. Fitz says I must go and learn to be sociable."

I swallowed my envy at the thought of attending literally any party. "How terrible for you."

"Yes, it's most—what on earth!" As she unfolded the envelope, revealing a piece of paper closely written with lines of green ink, the letters slipped and slid off the paper over her hands. In moments, her hands were covered in the ink, dripping onto the floor and her gown. A sour-sweet smell, like green apples, filled the air. She dropped the paper on the ground, where the remaining ink, as though running down a steep hill, flowed up her boots.

An ugly spell if I ever saw one, and directed unerringly toward her. The green spread in blotches over her hands, feet, and, after she put a frightened hand to her mouth, her face—but that was a good thing, I realized. A curse this strong ought to have absorbed immediately into her skin. Instead it beaded and dripped, like rain off oilcloth—for now. How long until it made its way past her defenses? She had to shake it off immediately. How? "Miss Darcy—sneeze."

"What?"

I grabbed her slate, covered in chalk dust, and blew it straight into her face. "Sneeze!"

She opened her mouth to tell me off, but instead gave a mighty sneeze. Green droplets flew everywhere. I shielded my face.

When I lowered my arm, she was sniffing, her eyes streaming and swollen as though with hay fever. "What was that?" she said stuffily. "That was awful."

The room was now dotted with green splotches from floor to ceiling—as was, I noted ruefully, my second-best gown. It looked like a bottle of ink had exploded. Miss Darcy, however, was perfectly free of its stain.

I bent to examine one of the droplets that stained the carpet. The green apple smell was fading. "A hex," I said. "A nasty one, I think."

"Do you know what it was meant to do to me?"

"No, but I can guess, partly. You've only got one protection spell on you right now, you see, and it's one that I accidentally inverted."

"Inverted? Is it still protecting me?"

"Strictly speaking, it's protecting the rest of the world from you." I gestured at the green constellations all around us. "That's why this curse didn't work. It must have been intended to make you do harm to some-one else."

"Eugh. I hate magic." She looked grim. "Now will you agree to help me?"

I considered her. Nothing had changed, really. I still did not want to attract Darcy's notice. I certainly couldn't think of any respectable way we could meet. But now I knew for certain that someone really did mean this girl harm—and through her, someone else.

"Let's discuss terms," I said. "First of all, I want those raspberry cream cakes every time we meet."

# CHAPTER TWELVE

You do not disapprove of my meeting with Miss Darcy, I assume? I know that we agreed I was to limit my magic to that which was strictly necessary—but necessary for whom, pray? She certainly needs help from someone, and if I am meant to be a reformed character, surely it may as well be me. I will learn to love the role of selfless protector. Well, not entirely selfless. A married woman must have some pin money, you know, and right now I haven't so much as a pin.

I'll tell you more of that Darcy girl later. For now, I really must return to the narrative I promised you. I've filled nearly two quires of paper, crossed front and back, and I've only covered the very beginning! Too many digressions, I suppose, and my handwriting has always been rather large and swooping. I think it looks more elegant that way, and I never had to pay for my own paper and ink before. I shall try to be more succinct henceforth.

The regiment arrived a few days after that wild night on the hill. We had had officers in town before, but none since Kitty and I were old enough to take notice of them. I do not exaggerate when I say that their arrival was the greatest thing that ever happened to us.

In our entire lives, Kitty and I had never left the environs of Meryton, except for a couple of short trips to town when we were small. We had never been acquainted with anyone but the Meryton families and those who drifted through to visit them. Is it even possible to fall in love under such circumstances? It always seemed to me that the most romantic part of romance was about choosing and being chosen. I wanted someone to look at me among a throng of other young ladies and think, *You, only you.* But how could they truly choose me when there was hardly any alternative? And how could I make a choice myself when the only options available were Tim or old maidhood?

And then the ——shire arrived. It was the autumn before last, in mid-October, when the air had turned golden and the leaves were bursting with color. Their red coats looked very fine against such a backdrop, I assure you. I wished passionately that I had kept up with my drawing lessons, so I could paint them marching into town. I tried, but I never got the hang of paints. The final result looked rather like a lot of apes in red jackets.

My aunt soon proved that she was of more use to me than just as a witch-tutor. The very first day they marched into town, she not only let Kitty and me leave off practicing our fortune-telling, but actually leaned out the window with us to watch. "How thrilling," she sighed. "Your mother and I spent many an afternoon in our youth flirting with the officers quartered here. Such happy days were those! Officers are so attentive, and have such beautiful manners, and they have beautiful figures, too, for they're not stuck at a desk all day. What flirtations we shall have, girls."

Kitty stifled a giggle at that. *We?* she mouthed at me. I made a face back at her.

My aunt's taste for officers was to our benefit. She dispatched her husband to wait on Colonel Forster the very next day, and before the week was out we had made the acquaintance of any number of officers.

Here is a scrap of paper I found that Kitty and I made out sometime that fall.

*Denny*

*Captain Carteret—youngest son of an earl! Just fancy! Even if he does have seven older brothers*

*Colonel Forster—old, but so commanding, and K. says it would be disrespectful to leave him off the list*

*Pratt—nicest eyes*

*Smith—looks best in his coat*

This is a list, as you can perhaps perceive, of which of the officers we found the handsomest. We made several lists of the kind, and every one was different. Sometimes we "accidentally" let them fall into the hands of the men in question. It was most awfully fun.

I did not, as I had expected, fall in love with one of them—to do so would have felt rather unsporting, when we were all having such fun as a group. I assumed I would eventually, however. There were more than twenty officers in the regiment, and they came and went often. Denny was my favorite—too short and weak of chin for real handsomeness, but he had lovely blue eyes and the most charming smile, and soon we were such friends it was as though I had known him all my life. Denny was like me, I think—he needed society, was not especially bright, and was willing to make himself agreeable to anyone in return for a bit of fun. I first met him at a garden reception that Colonel Forster gave to meet the neighbors. It was a poor choice of events—there was no dancing, and many of the officers looked ill at ease. They were active men who showed to best advantage doing something vigorous and athletic, like dancing, or fistfights.

Denny was introduced to us by Colonel Forster, but we scarcely noted him at first. Everyone was stiff and formal and Kitty and I were bored to tears. We decided to wait by the refreshments. We were just whispering to each other trying to figure out a way to excuse ourselves and go home when Denny sidled up to us.

"Hello again, Miss Kitty, Miss Lydia," he said. "Care to see a bit of magic?"

We both whipped our heads around to look at him. "You! Do magic?" said Kitty. "Don't be foolish."

He looked taken aback by our intensity, but rallied with a flirtatious grin. "It's you who's foolish, miss," he said. "Strongboxes are the place to keep your coin, you know. Not here." With that, he reached out and appeared to pluck a coin out of her ear. His gloved fingers brushed her hair, setting one of her curls swinging. She clapped a hand to her ear.

"*What was that,*" she hissed. "That wasn't magic. *What did you do.*"

"Kitty," I said. "Don't worry. We're well warded. He cannot hex us."

She thrust an arm in front of me. "Get behind me, Lydia, I'll scratch his eyes out if I need to."

Denny swallowed. "I—it's just a trick. I'm sorry, I've not spent much time around ladies. I didn't mean to offend." He gave us a little sheepish half bow.

Kitty narrowed her eyes. "A trick? Explain."

He showed us how the coin was concealed in his palm. When she saw how it was done, Kitty laughed in delight. "How capital!" she said. "How diverting! Do it again."

He did, as many times as we wished. Then I did it to him, but not as well—I had trouble stopping the coins from pouring from his ear. There was quite a little pile of them at his feet before I managed to cancel the charm. "By Jove, you *are* a quick study," he said. "I could never palm that many. You'll have to show me how you do it."

Kitty scooped the coins into her purse before they could turn back into pebbles.

By that time, our little group had been enlarged by several of Denny's brother officers. They shouted encouragement to us, and applauded vigorously when I managed the "trick" at last.

"The misses Bennet are not merely the prettiest young ladies in the county, but the most amiable," Ensign Fulton shouted. I lowered my eyelashes and tried to blush.

"And the most gifted at magic," added Denny, and they all laughed. The shadows were lengthening and the light growing golden. A number of the older members of the party had left to seek their supper, and it was mostly we young people who were left.

"This fine assembly can be improved by only one thing—dancing," said Denny. "Do you dance, Miss Kitty?"

"We certainly do," said Kitty. "But not at garden parties. How should we? There's no music."

"That's quickly remedied, isn't it, lads?" cried Denny.

The best thing about the regiment was the sheer energy they put toward any problem when motivated. Normally, even the smallest dance in Meryton took weeks of cautious planning and discussion before it was deemed wise to proceed. This pack of impatient puppies had no such scruples. No sooner was the idea proposed than they sprang into action. Captain Carteret, with his winning manners, took himself over to the older ladies and sweet-talked them into permitting the entertainment. Two men produced out of nowhere a fiddle and a pipe. Another three moved the refreshment tables off to the side, clearing the wide lawn for use. And Denny sidled up to our host, his commanding officer. I was sure he would not secure Colonel Forster's permission—but he knew his commander better than I.

"Sir," he said diffidently, "I wonder if you would object to a bit of music and dancing, for the entertainment of the ladies."

Colonel Forster shook his head at him. "Now, now, none of that, my boy," he said. "I told you lads this was to be a quiet, well-mannered party. We've got to show the neighborhood we're not one of those harum-scarum regiments kicking up larks and bothering respectable people."

"Certainly not," Denny said promptly. "But surely, a good part of nice manners is making sure that our guests don't grow bored? I fear the young ladies are awfully restless. Miss Smith, for example, wondered several times what kind of dancer you are, sir, and expressed a wish to see you."

Forster harrumphed. "She did, did she? Saucy female…Well, the young ladies may wish to cut a caper, but we cannot make those matrons over there comfortable on a floor made of grass."

"They will be as comfortable as they are now, and better entertained," said Denny. "They will not wish to dance themselves, but the Reverend Apthorpe and the other elderly gentlemen can keep them company, while we young men"—his gesture included himself and his brother officers, as well as the colonel—"do our duty by the young ladies."

Colonel Forster was a man of about forty. His hair was silver at the temples, but his luxuriant mustache was raven black. He stroked it now, and stared over at Miss Smith, giggling with her friends. "Hmm," he said. "Must be a good host, I suppose. A bit of respectable dancing can't hurt. But no waltzes, mind you."

"Of course not, sir," said Denny, and turned and winked at us.

And so in the dying sun and under the rising moon, we danced. Benton's fiddle wailed, and Caspar's pipe did its best to keep up, with what it lacked in accuracy being made up in spirit. Our aunts and mothers, charmed by Carteret's noble-bred manners, clapped and kept time, and the dullest party I had been to in a month became the greatest fun of the season. In the dim light, the music seemed wilder and faster than it did in a ballroom. It put me in mind a bit of the dancing at the witches' gathering, only this was better, because there were boys. None of us were as careful about our steps as we would normally be, and there was a great deal of shrieking and laughing as we slid in the grass. At one point Kitty tripped and would have fallen, but Denny, who was partnering her, swung her up in his arms and carried her to the end of the line, while she laughed so hard that tears poured down her cheeks. No matter what anyone says, I shall never regret my friendships and flirtations with those gentlemen as long as I live. I don't wish to write any more today.

# CHAPTER THIRTEEN

La, I am already on the thirteenth chapter! I thought I would get this whole tiresome task done with in just a few dozen pages. I am quite the authoress.

Now that I have the responsibility of keeping Miss Darcy out of a permanent stupor, I find myself looking forward to my writing interludes. She is dreadfully hard work, I must say. I have been to see her three Sundays now, and I will tell you I earn my five shillings and cakes. I was relieved at first to find that her Miss Carr let me in without a word of objection, until I discovered how Miss Darcy managed it. Do you know what that girl did? She told Miss Carr that I was a poor sinful woman, and that she was studying the Bible with me as a charity project! When she told me that I gave her a piece of my mind, and a great shiny spot at the end of her nose to boot. Not that she cares. Now that she has possession of her faculties and can study her precious conjecture, she is happy as a pig in mud, and cares nothing for her appearance. How she will ever get a husband, I don't know.

The thirteenth chapter is an appropriately cursed, witchy number, for the time has come to introduce my own dear sweet love.

The dear sweet love in question has at last reappeared, and is trying his utmost to get on my good side. He brought me a new bonnet, and is full of smiles and soft words and promises to squire me about town.

"Awfully sorry to be away so long," he said this morning, when he came in, dashing and neat in his uniform. "They've had my company out on maneuvers for days. I hope it wasn't too dull for you."

"Oh no," I said politely, just to vex him. "I amused myself quite tolerably." Maneuvers! Ha. His company up here is nothing like as respectable as the ——shire. Its men are those whom no better regiment would take—sullen men trailing vague clouds of scandal and ill repute. Like Wickham. I've scarcely been invited to a single social event since he joined them, but I do not think it is a deliberate snub aimed at me— they're simply not having any parties they could invite a lady to. Even a lady such as I, who is possessed of her own (though comparatively small and fluffy) cloud of scandal. Wickham is practically the only married man among them—though I am sure there are any number of women who keep company with them.

My dowry bought his colors in this regiment, but it is barely worthy of the name. As far as I can tell, the only regimental activities that bring the men together are drinking, cockfighting, and the occasional slovenly roll call. The rest of the time, they draw their meager paychecks and tend to their own—mostly petty and suspect—pursuits. Heaven help us if a foreign army ever invades Newcastle. These men will not be able to do much but drink them for it.

Wickham looked put out not to find me more on edge after all these days alone, but he quickly recovered. "I should know better by now than to treat you like any other lady," he said. "Of course an enchantress of your powers would be well able to pass the time."

I snorted. "I'm not doing much *enchanting* these days, as you well know. And why do you call it that, anyway? I'm not an *enchantress*. You make me sound like the fairy godmother in a tale. I am a plain witch."

He held up his hands in surrender. "Peace, Lydia. I don't want a quarrel. Here, I brought this for you." With a flourish, he opened the basket he had brought and produced a feast: a large smoked ham, fresh bread, a roll of cheese, even some hothouse strawberries. There might be more still in the basket, but I refused to dig through it.

He looked at me in triumph. Clearly he expected me to be ravenous and to fall upon the food. Luckily, I'd been careful with my five shillings a week from Miss Darcy and wasn't the starving waif he'd expected. "Is that all?" I said. "You should have gone to Croft. He's a much better grocer than the Naughton Brothers."

"You never stop, do you, witch?" he said. "I mean this food as a peace offering, I swear to you. No, more than a peace offering—a white flag. You win, Lydia. You always win."

I crossed my arms and stared at him through narrowed eyes. "I win what?"

"Whatever fight we're currently having." He sliced off a few hunks of bread and cheese. "I've been thinking," he went on. "I've been a beast to you, I know. An utter beast."

"The whole world knows that."

"I'm not talking of what the world thinks it knows. I'm talking about us. Two people stuck together against their will. We can't escape each other, Lydia. So why not make the best of it?"

I frowned in confusion. "I thought we were making the best of it."

"Oh, I'm certain we can do better than *this*." He looked around at our shabby quarters with distaste. "If we work together, that is."

He set the plate down in front of me. My mouth watered in spite of myself. A bit of cold meat, cheese, and bread—it would never be seen on the fine tables of Pemberley, or among the elegant cakes and fresh fruits of Miss Darcy's sitting room. But it was just what I wanted.

"What is it that you want?" I said.

"A truce. That's all. I swear." He took a mouthful of his own hunk of bread and grinned at me cheekily. "You know what I am. A selfish, lazy wastrel with no redeeming qualities and not a friend in the world he hasn't betrayed or disappointed. I won't pretend to be otherwise. But Lydia—in the world's eyes, you are married to that sorry reprobate. We will never escape each other. Don't you think we ought to find a way to live with that?"

There was undeniable truth to this. We may not be married, but he and I are bound in a way that is deeper than marriage, and certainly more insoluble.

"What would this truce entail?" I asked.

"Well, since we both like dancing, and I am sure you are as starved for a bit of company as I am, I thought that on Friday it could entail a trip to a public ball." He produced two tickets with a flourish. "But for now, it entails a meal."

Dash it. I took a bite. It was good.

"There's a girl." He gave me a friendly kick under the table and grinned with his mouth full. "It wouldn't really be so bad to lay down our arms, would it? You and I used to be chums, after all."

Do you know, I have been thinking and thinking, and I can't remember if that was ever true.

I did not fall in love with George Wickham at first sight. I know that much. It was Lizzy who did. He came when autumn was shading into winter, when the daylight looked pale and sickly and it seemed to hurt the sun to rise for a few hours. (Gracious, that sounds fine! Perhaps I should be a poetess.) When I think of that day, it seems to be accompanied by the mournful strains of a French horn, because it was. Our cousin Mr. Collins had arrived for a visit the previous day, and was following us everywhere, and he was the most odious, pompous windbag you ever heard of. The night before, he actually read us sermons for an hour! Well, it felt like an hour anyway. Everyone but Mary was yawning before long. I *tried* to help everyone by delicately changing the subject to something of more general interest—every book on etiquette says one ought to stick to topics of general interest, you know, and Fordyce's is not interesting to anyone, except Mr. Collins—but when I ventured a remark about how my uncle meant to turn his manservant off, I was quite severely quashed by Lizzy and Jane.

I am sure, however, that they were secretly grateful, for the odious fellow got offended and stopped sermonizing. People are forever getting cross with me for doing things they wish they could do themselves. After that, Kitty and I put our heads together and came up with a plan. That night we took vervain, willow, a rook's feather, and an old piano string and tied them into a little bundle and threw them in a fire. Then we both went to bed without curling papers—rather a steep spell-tithe, for there is nothing more devastating than knowing your hair will be lank and flat the next day, but we wanted to be very sure it would work—and from the moment we woke the next morning, when Mr. Collins spoke the only sound that reached our ears was the oomphing of a French horn. It was such a relief, I cannot tell you.

We had not specified what music we wished to hear, and I'd have preferred a pretty piano concerto or a lively fiddle, but I suppose the spell could not *completely* do away with Mr. Collins's spirit. And the oom-pa-pa of his horn was funny at least. We were quite in transports at breakfast when Mamma politely asked him questions about his parish and nodded while he blatted away in a minor key. Luckily he seemed to take our fits of giggles as a compliment. I am sure he thought we were in awe of his wit.

Anyway, it was a gray-brown autumn day. Lizzy, Kitty, Jane, and I were walking into town, accompanied by Mr. Collins. Kitty and I had grown bolder, and were now actually inviting our cousin to speak.

"It is a prosperous parish you have taken, Mr. Collins?"

He smiled smugly and replied, "Oomph-a. Ooomph-a-a."

"I see. And how many families do you dine with there?"

"Oomph-a-a." He gave us a slight bow.

"How marvelous. Do you not find this hilltop offers a beautiful view of Netherfield?"

He swept his hands out, indicating aesthetic transports, and assented, "Blaaat."

Lizzy glared at us behind his back, but she could not actually identify anything wrong that we were doing, so she said nothing. Indeed, we had rarely been so polite in our lives.

We had tired of the game by the time we reached town, but there was a new diversion in the form of our friend Denny, whom we saw walking with ever such a handsome fellow. We managed to contrive a meeting—not that we needed to contrive so very hard, for the high street is only about five buildings on each side—and were greeted by Denny.

Whatever Lizzy and Jane may think, I did not insist upon the meeting just because of Wickham. I had not seen Denny in days, and Kitty and I had matters of great importance to discuss with him, such as the dance Kitty owed him after leaving the Longs' ball early with a headache, and whether our bonnets still looked up-to-date compared with the ladies of London.

"I don't know," he said. "A fellow don't pay much attention to bonnets and fripperies, you know. Yours are awfully pretty so I'm sure they're all right."

"Thanks, but that's no help," I said. "What did the London bonnets look like, specifically?"

"Like yours, but with not such pretty faces inside."

"Stop flattering," Kitty said severely. "We don't look pretty at all today. Our hair's quite flat."

He grinned at her. "Is it? Looks full of bits and bobs to me." And he pulled a coin out of her ear again.

I was just going to scold him for this—his coin trick might have been charming once, but really, it was too pathetic to keep repeating—when Kitty did something odd. Denny's fingers were still curled by her ear, and as he pulled them away, she bent her head toward them, just for a fraction of a second, as though she was going to butt his hand with her cheek. You've seen this gesture, if you've ever known a cat who's affectionate or hungry or trying to manipulate you.

"Er—uh," said Denny, and dropped the coin.

I'd have said something, but there was an impatient honk from behind us and I realized that it was Mr. Collins clearing his throat. My curiosity about my sister's behavior would have to wait.

"Ensign Denny, may I present our cousin, Mr. Collins," Jane said. "Mr. Collins, Mr. Denny."

"Brrt brrt thbbbbrrrt," Mr. Collins tooted, and bowed in his typical obsequious style, then looked inquiringly at the handsome stranger at Denny's side. "A-bbrrrt brrt oomphrrtt?"

"Ah." Denny turned to his friend. "Wickham, may I present the Bennet sisters: Miss Bennet, Miss Elizabeth, Miss Kitty, and Miss Lydia, as well as Mr. Collins. Ladies, Mr. Collins, my dear friend George Wickham. I was lucky enough to run into him in town, and told him what a cracking good outfit the ——shire is, and it emerged that he was looking to join up, and, well, here he is."

I turned my attention fully to this new playfellow he had brought us. Wickham bowed politely and struck up a conversation with Lizzy and Jane, giving me ample chance to regard him. He was tall and slim, at least a head taller than Denny, and he had the easy grace of an athlete. A handsome fellow, too. More than handsome. There was something about him. He outshone Denny as the sun outshines the morning stars. I looked forward to his addition to my merry band of flirts. I had found that my playfellows responded best to a sort of half-scolding, half-flirting tone, and I opened my mouth to upbraid him for not joining up sooner when he turned and looked at me.

You walk on the earth every day, taking it for granted. You never think that one day it may shake beneath your feet. When Wickham locked eyes with me, I felt that everything I thought I knew was in question. I could feel the earth quaking beneath me, heat pouring up through my soles, as though a volcano was going to erupt, as though all of Meryton rested on the thinnest skin over a lake of fire. I was frozen, unable to speak, caught in the beams of his burning brown eyes. He had little crinkles around his eyes, I noticed, as of someone who smiled a lot. I couldn't breathe. My palms were sweaty. A scalding hand seemed to clench my stomach.

*Something is beginning.* The thought came to me unbidden.

Lizzy said something, and his gaze shifted back to her. I could breathe again.

Just before we parted, he bowed goodbye to me, and then to Kitty. I meant to say something arch and witty to send him away with, but just then, Kitty began to cough. She'd had a touch of a cold all month, and it was evidently back. I tried to glare her down from making such a racket in front of such a man, but she could not stop.

Indeed, she coughed all day. She coughed while we told our aunt about Wickham, and that evening at home when we told our mother. She coughed while I braided her hair for bed and while she braided mine, till I took over the job. It wasn't until we lay down that she finally stopped.

"Gracious, you sound awful," I said. "You'd better get over it, or Mamma will send for the apothecary. You know what horrid medicines Jones makes one take."

"I'm all right," she said. "What was wrong with *you*, when we met Wickham earlier? You looked as though you'd swallowed a toad."

"I am not sure," I said. "I think it may be that I am in love."

She rolled over to look at me. "In love! With Mr. Wickham? What's it like?"

"I rather think I must be." I described the symptoms I had experienced earlier.

"It does sound like love in novels," she admitted. "Are you sure?"

"No. For one thing, I thought love would feel nicer. This was awful."

"Sometimes it sounds that way in novels, too. For example, I could never see why Pamela married Mr. Whatsis in the end of *Pamela*."

"I know, she ought to have pushed him out a high window." I considered this. "So perhaps I am in love."

"Perhaps." Kitty stared at the ceiling. "And he is much nicer than Mr. Whatsis. He is rather like the Chevalier."

"Yes. He's handsome, and poor, and good-mannered."

"And he's a soldier, so he must be brave."

"Not necessarily. Have you seen Pratt around spiders?"

"Yes, but that's *Pratt*." She took a deep breath. "So. Love."

I tucked my hands under my cheek and looked at her. Kitty had grown two inches in the last six months, and her face suddenly looked very grown-up in the flickering light of the candle. The planes of her nose and cheeks were more like Mamma's than mine. I tried to trace the lines of her cat-self in her human face, but it was harder than it used to be. "Maybe."

"We should ask Denny what he knows of him," she said. "We'd better make sure Wickham is respectable before we cast a love spell on him or anything."

This reminded me. "Speaking of Denny, what was that earlier?"

"What was what?"

"You did that thing you do when you want your ears stroked." I butted her shoulder with my head.

"I did no such thing!"

"You did!"

"Didn't!"

I tickled her. I could always win fights that way, for though Kitty was stronger, she was absurdly ticklish. But this time, instead of subsiding into gasping giggles, she began to cough again.

Her cough had sounded thin and fretful by day, but amid night's shadows it was worse. It seemed to come from somewhere deep inside her. She coughed so hard her whole body contracted with it. I had never heard someone our age cough like that.

But presently she caught her breath and said, "Dash this dratted cold," and all was right again. By the time I remembered to ask her about Denny, she was asleep.

## CHAPTER FOURTEEN

No one cared that Kitty was ill. When Jane had been sick a few weeks earlier, it had turned our lives upside down. She was stuck at Netherfield, Lizzy went to stay with her, and Mamma and the rest of us flew back and forth with anxious visits and messages. Now no one seemed to notice there was something amiss with Kitty at all.

Of course, her illness was not as picturesque as Jane's. Isn't it unfair that Jane looks pretty even when sick? Leaning against the fine pillows at Netherfield, her blond locks damp with sweat, she looked like a Renaissance saint being martyred. No wonder Bingley's *tendresse* for her was deepened.

Now, however, Kitty's illness was seen as little more than an annoyance. Mamma snapped at her for irritating her nerves whenever she coughed. To be fair, she was not as ill as Jane had been. Kitty never got fevers—she called them a "human affectation," which I do not think can possibly be right, but I don't know enough about cats to contradict her—and she wasn't weak enough to be stuck in bed, so it did seem for some time that she was just prolonging her cold to vex us. She just coughed and coughed and sniffled and coughed, and, when no one was looking, ate little bits of grass.

We had little time to worry about Kitty, for a few days after we met Wickham, I made the worst magical mistake that I had ever committed. It started with Mary's piano.

People think the country is quiet, but our house was always filled with racket. Mamma never stopped talking except to draw breath, whether anyone was listening or not. There were the servants, clattering about in the kitchen and the bedrooms, and some members of the household were known to complain about the noise Kit and I made, too. But the most constant sound, from morning till night, was Mary's piano. She would wake early in the morning and the first thing we would hear was Mary thundering up and down her scales, DUM-dum-dum-dum-dum-dum-dum-dum-DUM-dum-dum-dum-dum-dum-dum-dum-DUM, again and again. Kitty and I were sure she played as loudly as she could on purpose to wake us and scold us for our sloth. Then there were concertos and arias, hours of them, precise and dull as the ticking of a clock, and if you interrupted her, even with a compliment, she'd bite your head off. Finally after luncheon she'd go up to her room for a few hours and read sermons, and we'd have a bit of quiet (unless Lizzy seized the chance to practice, but even then it was a relief to at least hear the poor piano being tortured by a different pair of hands). Why couldn't she have read her sermons in the morning and let us sleep? you wonder. So too did we. I assume it is because she hated us and wanted us to suffer. We all need such small rebellions.

Such was the background noise to nearly every day of my life. Then Mr. Collins arrived. His first night there, Mary was quiet—well, Mary was always quiet—but, during a lull in the conversation, she asked him about his taste in music. He named a certain composer of hymns, a Mr. Charles Wesley.

"An excellent composer," Mary said warmly. "Mr. Wesley." Then she nodded as though committing his name to memory and bent over her meal again.

The next morning, instead of concertos, we had hymns.

None of us took any notice—except our father, who told her to "stop that churchy racket"—least of all Mr. Collins, who was busy fawning over Lizzy. Mary did draw his attention to her recital eventually, when his trailing of Lizzy brought him near the piano.

"You are right, Mr. Collins," she said. "Mr. Wesley truly embodies the Christian spirit that dwells within our breasts."

"Yes," he said. "You play marvelously, Cousin Mary. A pleasure to hear you. I daresay even Lady Catherine, who is used to a very superior kind of music, could find nearly no fault with it." Mary launched into the same hymn over again, a tiny smile on her face.

We rarely paid much attention to Mary, so it took a few more days before it dawned on us what was going on. It was raining and we were all stuck in the house, and had not bothered much about our appearances. Mary never did, so I was astonished to find her in my room going through my hair things. As I watched, she took out a silk rose and held it up behind her ear, testing its effect in the window reflection.

"What are you doing?" I demanded. "That's mine!"

She whirled around, whipping the rose behind her back. "You have so much frippery, it's astonishing," she said.

I tilted my head, looking at her curiously. Mary never wore anything in her hair. "A woman's virtue is her greatest ornament," she intoned when anyone asked her about it, so mostly we didn't ask.

"Why are you playing with my hair things?" I asked. "You never dress your hair even when there's a reason to. And now we're all stuck inside and there's no one to see us but that windbag Collins."

"Don't speak of him that way!" Mary flashed. "Mr. Collins is an educated, clever, moral man, and he's worth a thousand of a silly girl like you."

"He's worth two thousand of you, then, Mary!"

"It would be well for you," she hissed, "if you could see his worth! Stupid, can't you see he's here to marry one of us?"

After thinking about it for a moment, I could see. Mr. Collins had first followed Jane about, showering her with compliments and telling her what a good housekeeper she was. Then, after a day or so, he switched his allegiance to Lizzy. Probably Mamma had told him about Bingley.

The thought of seeing that fleshy, greasy face across the table every day for life made me shudder. "I believe you're right," I said. "Poor Lizzy!"

"Lizzy!" Mary said angrily. "He's not going to marry *Lizzy*. Once he gets to know her, he'll see how shallow and unaccomplished she is, how totally unsuited to be the wife of a serious man, and then—he *will* see. A man like him is more concerned with character than frivolous things."

Oh. Oh dear.

"Do you want to wear that hair-rose to the Netherfield ball on Tuesday?" I asked. "You may if you like, for I am going to wear the blue ones."

"Of course not," she muttered. She threw the rose on the vanity and left the room.


"I think Mary has formed an attachment to Mr. Collins," I whispered to Kitty that evening as we shared the sofa. The rest of the family was in the sitting room, too, but Mary's enthusiastic playing of hymns provided a noisy cover for our conversation.

"How is that possible?" Kitty said. "Even for Mary, that's astonishingly poor judgment."

Mary just then reached the end of a hymn, playing and singing the final chords with a flourish and an attempt at vibrato that sounded more like she was riding over rough cobblestones. She looked at Mr. Collins with a smile that begged for compliments like a dog begs for scraps.

When he ignored her, continuing to ask Elizabeth about the book she was reading, Mary said loudly, "I find that hymns are the perfect accompaniment to a quiet family party in the evening. Dancing music livens up the blood far too much, while quiet hymns put young ladies in the frame of mind to contemplate the divine, a pursuit to which their weak and frail natures ought always to be directed as much as possible. Do you not agree, Mr. Collins?"

"Oh—er—yes, quite, Cousin Mary," he said. (The horn spell had unfortunately worn off by then.) "Fair cousin Elizabeth, will you not favor us with an example of your playing, which I am sure is as exquisite and superior as all your other myriad accomplishments?"

"I'm nowhere near as good as Mary," said Elizabeth firmly. "Let her continue."

"I am sure no lady in the county can play half so well as you, dear Miss Elizabeth," he said gallantly, and Mary quietly closed the piano and left the room. There was an unusual glitter in her eyes. Mary never cries, but she gets a sort of hard look, and if you speak to her in that state she's likely to call you a jezebel and quote reams of scripture.

Mr. Collins did not even seem to see her go. He had already turned back to bothering Elizabeth.

Poor Mary!

"I say we cast a spell on Mary to make her forget him," I said, after Kitty and I had gone up to our room to discuss the matter freely. "Watching Mary try to flirt is the most painful thing I have ever seen in my life."

But Kitty shook her head. "I think we should help her. He does mean to marry one of us, after all, and she's the only one who actually likes him. Wouldn't they be perfectly suited?"

I wrinkled my nose. "How could anyone be suited to that obsequious toad?"

"They like all the same things: church and sermons and looking down their noses at the rest of us. I think they'd make a fine match, actually."

I thought about it. Mr. Collins's main subject of conversation, besides long, absurd compliments he thought were polite, was the brilliance of his patroness, Lady Catherine de Bourgh. Lady Catherine sounded like a tiresome old bore to me, but she was certainly very grand and wanted Mr. Collins to marry so that his wife could be a sort of unpaid companion for her. I could not see Mary excelling at that role. She had told us many times what a waste of time social outings were when one could be reading. On the other hand, if Lady Catherine liked Collins, why wouldn't she like Mary?

And indeed, where would Collins find a better wife? They liked all the same things. They could live out their days quite happily, quoting sermons to each other and abstaining from reading novels. "He's all but said he means to choose a wife from among us, and here Mary is, practically throwing herself at him—and he looks right through her."

If Mary did not marry Mr. Collins, we might lose our home. And if Mr. Collins did not wed Mary, probably no one ever would.

"Human men," said Kitty wisely, "only care about looks. And Mary does not look at all well."

It was true. Mary had always been the plain one in our family, but that wasn't saying much, for the rest of us are awfully pretty. However, she was unlucky enough this week to have a rash of spots across her face, including a big, red, shiny one on the end of her nose. Unfortunately, I hadn't caused them, and non-magical spots are harder to cure with spells than consumption. Her hair, too, disagreed with the wet weather, puffing out in a frizzy cloud around her face.

"Still," I said indignantly. "She's a good deal too pretty for *him*. Why, he should be on his knees thanking the Lord that a girl as fine-looking as Mary regards him with favor."

"Men don't have to think that way," she said. "When Papa dies, Mr. Collins will have all our money. He'll have our house. No wonder he thinks he can select from among us like sweets in a shop window."

"All right," I said. "We'll just have to make sure he picks the right sweet then."

The next morning Kitty and I rose even earlier than Mary did and went down to the living room to consult our aunt. (The trick is to drink a large glass of water before bed. You'll wake up ever so early.) I had never done a love spell before, so we decided to seek her advice. Luckily Aunt Philips had a mirror in her bedchamber, and my uncle sleeps at the other end of the corridor. She was still asleep when we cast the mirror-spell, snoring dimly, half in and half out of the frame. We rapped on the glass until she woke and came to her dressing table, her long grizzled braid poking out of her cap and her eyes dim with sleep.

"What is it, girls?" she asked. "Is someone ill?"

"Sorry to wake you," I said. "But it's raining still, so we can't come into Meryton to visit you, and we want to make Mr. Collins fall in love with Mary."

She blinked awake at that. "You what?"

We explained the situation—Mr. Collins bride-hunting among us, his apparent attachment to Lizzy, Mary's embarrassing attempts to get his attention. "So you see," I concluded, "it would be very sensible for us to make him love Mary instead."

I had expected my aunt to be in raptures at the scheme—she loved any demonstration of my power—but she frowned uneasily. "I can see the merit of it," she said. "But love spells are a tricky business, girls. It's very hard to make one that sticks, especially for a witch as inexperienced as Lydia."

"You cast one on Philips when you were only a little older than I," I pointed out. "That's stuck, hasn't it?"

She looked uncomfortable. "Yes, of course, but—well, aside from duration, there are all sorts of other ways they can go wrong."

"We'll be careful," I said firmly. "Just tell us what to do."

"And hurry," Kitty added. "I can hear the chambermaid starting to stir."

"Very well." She straightened up. Whatever her misgivings, I could see that she was gratified to have us clamoring for a lesson. "There are a number of kinds of love spells. Some work merely on the physical passions. Others work on the mind to create a deep admiration. Still others plant false memories to make the victim think he's been in love with the target all along—you'd be surprised how well those work," my aunt said. "People's passions are very persuadable."

"That sounds perfect," I said. "I am sure Mr. Collins is persuadable."

"We can give him a memory of Lady Catherine de Bourgh telling him to love Mary," Kitty said with a giggle.

But Aunt Philips shook her head. "It requires months of preparation—you would essentially have to craft every detail of the false memories, like you were writing a novel for his brain."

"We haven't got time for *that*," I said, "And I wouldn't want to write a romance starring Mr. Collins and Mary anyhow." Kitty gagged her agreement.

We didn't want to think too much about their physical passions, either, and we didn't have the supplies to create a deep and lasting admiration, so in the end we settled on a rather small spell that would create only a brief infatuation.

"This will last only a day—two at the most," our aunt cautioned us. "So you must choose your moment to deploy it wisely. And, girls—"

Just then, the chambermaid started down the stairs, and we quickly broke the spell and pretended that we were practicing hairstyles in the mirror for the Netherfield ball.

The temporary infatuation spell luckily required nothing we did not already have, or at least could easily access. Ginger to whet the appetite, a pinch of hemp to stimulate the senses, black tea to focus the mind. Add a little bit of young mint, plucked and dried while the leaves were still curled, and brew it all in rainwater fallen under a full moon. Serve with biscuits. However, there was a problem.

"He's got to be looking *right at her* when he drinks it," my aunt had cautioned us. "Whoever his eye falls on when it passes his lips will be the object of his desire."

"How are we to manage that?"

"I don't know, my dears," she had said tartly. "I told you such spells were tricky. It's up to you to figure it out."

Kitty and I talked it over, and in the end, we could see but one way.

"You're a *what?*"

"I'm a witch," I said patiently. "Do calm down, Mary, that's only the beginning of what we have to tell you."

We were sitting with Mary in the small back parlor that overlooked the garden. The ceiling leaked a bit, so it was a good place to have a private conversation when it rained. It had taken hours to pry Mary away from her pursuits and get her to come with us. In the end we had to tell her that we needed her advice on a matter of womanly duty. She loved giving advice about womanly duty.

"You are being absurd," she said. "Lydia, Catherine, you are much too old to be playing such silly games. Your time would be better spent in study or useful labor."

"She'll go on like this all day," Kitty said. "Show her."

So I magicked one of the ducks out by the pond to look ten feet tall. Mary fainted. We chafed her hands and fanned her face until she came to. We guided her to the sofa and Kitty ran down and brought her a glass of lemonade.

"You are making a fool of yourself," she said. "I don't know how you did it, but I am not silly enough to believe your practical jokes."

So I magicked the duck again. Mary fainted again.

This time, when she woke, she gave me a cautious look and said nothing but "Don't do the duck again."

"I shan't," I agreed. "That's not what we're here for, anyway. We want to help you."

"Help me how?" She pushed Kitty's fanning hand out of her face and struggled to sit up.

"Help you to marry Mr. Collins."

Mary went still.

"That is what you want, isn't it?"

She didn't look at us. "Any woman would be lucky to espouse a man as respectable and intelligent as Mr. Collins," she said stiffly.

"If you say so. Well, we're going to make a love potion to get him for you."

I explained briefly about the brew. "All you have to do is wait till no one else is about and tell him you've made him a cup of tea," I explained. "It's simple."

Mary looked wildly tempted for a moment, but then shook her head. "Let's say you two really are witches," she said.

"I'm not a witch," Kitty said. "I'm a cat."

Mary closed her eyes briefly, then said, "Let's say Lydia is really a witch. I would never use such unholy methods to attach anyone. When

I marry, it shall be because my husband sees in me a true and virtuous partner and helpmeet."

"Very well," I said. "We were only trying to help."

For the next two days it continued to rain and Mr. Collins continued to pursue Lizzy. Mary's hymns grew louder and more desperate, but to no avail. The morning after the Netherfield ball, Mr. Collins proposed to Lizzy. She would not have him. The process of not having him took several hours, for Mr. Collins refused to believe it and Mamma refused to accept it. In the end, however, Lizzy was freed from the burden of his love. This did not open his eyes to Mary's virtues, however.

"Oh, Mr. Collins," Mary said, rushing up to him. "Pray believe that not all members of this household share my sister Elizabeth's shortsightedness. Would you care to join me in my study of what Mr. Fordyce has to say about the inconstancy of woman?"

However, Mr. Collins was so stung by Lizzy's rejection that he stormed right past Mary without seeing her, nearly knocking her down.

Mary came to my room an hour later. Her eyes were red but her chin was determined. "Very well," she said. "How do we do that spell?"

It was a simple matter to get the kitchen to ourselves. I told Mrs. Pond, the cook, that Mr. Collins was going to propose to Lizzy again in the garden, and she hurried out to see. Quickly, we brewed up the spell. Mary watched with wide eyes as Kitty and I joined hands across the fragrant steam and chanted a few lines of verse.

"Power of water, herb, and moon,
Grant us now a humble boon.
Let he who drinketh what here steeps
Dream of she whose heart he keeps."

I don't know why spells use words like *drinketh* and *boon*. I suppose there's no one to modernize them like the dictionary.

"It smells—rather good," Mary said hesitantly, sniffing the steaming cup in her hand.

"Of course it does," said Kitty with scorn. "How would we get him to drink it, otherwise?"

"I don't know if he keeps my *heart*, though."

"Poetic license. Spells are very dramatic. Go on now, it's ready," I said. "Bring it to him in the parlor. He's alone in there."

Mary hesitated for a moment, looking doubtfully at the brew in her hand. "Do you think," she said, "do you think, without this, I'll ever get anyone to marry me?"

Kitty and I looked at each other in alarm. I opened my mouth and closed it again.

As I've said, it wasn't that Mary was ugly. If anything, it was that she was never *herself.* Mary seemed always to be putting on a show of some kind. Trying to convince everyone that she was the most accomplished girl in the room, or the cleverest, or the most moral. Anything but the plainest. It was exhausting to be around. For her more than anyone, I think—you could always see the lines of tension in her face during even the gentlest venture into society. Still, this was practically the only moment of vulnerability I had ever seen her display. Say what you will about my sister Mary, but I have never seen her accept pity.

It was Kitty who answered. "If you want to get a husband the natural way, Mary, you will," she said. "A girl as determined as you always gets what she wants. But if what you want is *this* husband, now, then you need the spell."

Mary nodded. Then she squared her shoulders, raised her chin, and marched toward the door.

This next bit is a bit hard to explain. Let me lay out the particulars as clearly as I can.

At the moment that Mary took the love potion, which to all appearances was merely a cup of tea, out of the kitchen, Mr. Collins was in the parlor writing letters. Kitty and I left out the back door and circled around to the side of the house to peep in at the parlor window. We wanted to be sure that he was looking at Mary, you see, not at either of us, but we had no intention of missing the fun.

Mary marched into the parlor. She looked white with tension. "I brought you some tea, Mr. Collins," she said in a high, affected voice that I suppose she thought was flirtatious.

"Eh?" he said absently without looking up. "Very well. Put it down there, girl."

He thought she was the maid. Collins's ability to ignore Mary was truly unparalleled. Mary shot us a look of despair over Mr. Collins's shoulder. *Get his attention*, I mouthed. Luckily his back was to the window.

"I do hope you will enjoy it, cousin," she said loudly. "I myself am passionately fond of a good cup of tea. Are you...fond of...tea?"

Finally, at this, he looked up in bewilderment. "I suppose so, Cousin Mary," he said. "If you are so passionately fond of the beverage, would you care to drink this cup yourself?"

"No," she said firmly.

He looked even more startled at this. Mary had not done anything but simper and assent since he had arrived.

"What I mean is," she hastened on, "I brewed it myself, specially for you, and it would give me great pleasure to see you enjoy it."

A normal man might have found this peculiar, but luckily Mr. Collins's ego had no trouble believing that a woman was panting to watch him drink tea. "Far be it from me to disoblige a lady," he said, with an oily smile, and reached for the cup.

Just then, the parlor door opened and Jane stuck her head in. Mr. Collins turned to her immediately. "Ah, cousin," he said. "I was just about to enjoy the cup of tea your charming sister has so kindly brewed me." And, staring straight at Jane, he raised the cup.

Mary can move very fast when she chooses to. Before a drop could pass his lips, she threw herself across the room and snatched the cup from his hands.

"Forgot the sugar," she said. "Do pardon me, dear cousin. You do take sugar, don't you?"

"Only three or four lumps," he said. "But really, it is not necessary—"

"I'll just be a moment," Mary said. "Jane, our mother wants you upstairs."

Jane blinked in surprise. "Are you sure? I just saw her a moment ago."

"Quite sure," Mary growled.

Jane, obliging as always, withdrew, and Mary withdrew to the kitchen. Kitty and I ran around back to meet her.

When we came in through the back door, Mary had her back pressed against the kitchen door, her eyes a bit wild.

"That was close!" I said. "Well done snatching the cup back, Mary. That could have been awfully tiresome for Jane."

"She should be used to it," Kitty said. "Men don't need spells to fancy her."

Mary glared at us. "What am I to do now?"

"Add sugar, of course, and get back out there," I said.

"Sugar won't disrupt the—well—you know?"

"The spell? Oh no. You can add sugar to just about any spell. A lot of them taste too vile to get down otherwise. Witches don't believe in enduring unpleasant sensations."

Mary pressed her lips into a firm line, bore the cup to the kitchen table, and with quick movements tonged in four lumps from the sugar bowl. *Ting, ting, ting, ting.* She was about to bear it back out to her paramour when several things happened at once.

First, Cook came back in from the garden. "You were wrong, Miss Lydia," she said reproachfully. "That Collins en't making a spectacle of himself in the garden. And Miss Elizabeth has gone off for a walk." She returned to the stove. "By the way, Miss Lucas is coming to see you all. I saw her coming up the lane just now."

We exchanged alarmed glances. If Charlotte came in, the first thing the maid would do was show her to the parlor. Kitty flew out into the hall without another word.

I do not know what Mr. Collins thought when the parlor door banged open, Kitty sprinted in from the kitchen, gasped, "Excuse me, Mr. Collins," and immediately sprinted out the door to the hall. Where we waited in the kitchen, we just heard her say "Charlotte, dear, you're back! No, don't take your coat off, let me admire it for a moment," before being distracted by my father's arrival in the kitchen.

"Heard the kettle was on the boil," he said. "Why didn't you send some tea to my study, Cook?"

"I didn't make no tea, Mr. Bennet," she said coldly, banging a saucepan. Like most of the servants, Cook's allegiance was firmly with Mamma, which she showed by being as disobliging to my father as she dared. "I'm sure if you wanted a pot you could have let me know."

"Never mind. There's a cup ready here." And to our horror, he took the cup Mary had just prepared from the table and drank deep.

Cook, who knew she hadn't made tea, turned in curiosity, to see my father grimacing at the taste. "My God, why's there so much sugar in it?" he said, his eyes closed in a wince.

"In what?" said my mother, who had just come in from the hall. Papa opened his eyes and met the soft, watery blue ones of his wife, currently red-rimmed from attempting to sway Lizzy with weeping and her hair peeking out rather untidily from beneath her cap.

Papa stared at her for a long moment. Then he put the cup down.

"It was for Mr. Collins," I said in a small voice.

"What?" Papa said.

"The tea," I said. "It was for Mr. Collins. That's why it was so full of sugar."

"Ah," Papa said. "Well, best make him another cup then. Far be it from me to deny that man anything."

"How can you say that, Mr. Bennet," cried Mamma, "when you have this very morning denied him the tenderest desire of his heart?"

"An extremely wise observation as always, my dear," Papa said drily, "but if Lizzy was the tenderest desire of his heart after knowing her only four days, I daresay he shall find tea even more fulfilling. He has been acquainted with it longer."

Mary and I exchanged glances. Papa sounded just like he always did—dry, sardonic, a little cruel. He certainly didn't sound like he loved Mamma any more than usual. Apparently the spell hadn't worked—on him at least.

Either that, or he had loved her all along, and was determined not to show it. But how likely is that?

In any case, Mary is not one to give up easily. She poured out another cup from what remained in the teapot and marched back into the parlor. I went back round to the window to watch.

Mr. Collins, apparently having finished his letter, had risen and half put on his cloak.

"Here, Mr. Collins," she announced. "I've poured you a fresh cup."

"Thank you again, fair cousin. There really was no need to put yourself to such trouble. In fact, I was about to go out for a stroll—"

"*Drink it,*" hissed Mary.

Startled, Mr. Collins did as he was told. He put the cup to his lips and drank down a deep gulp.

At that very moment, Charlotte Lucas entered the door.

"Good day, Mr. Collins," she said. "A pleasure to meet you again."

Collins's eyes locked on her as he swallowed the spell-tea. Straightaway his face changed. It went a sort of mottled purple. He nearly dropped the cup. "My dear Miss Lucas," he said. "The pleasure is all mine."

Mary tried to distract him, to bring his attention back to herself, but it was no use, of course. As soon as he could Collins slipped off with Charlotte to spend the day with her family. The very next day, they announced their engagement.

As I watched Collins's face as he told us of his wife-to-be, I could tell the spell had already worn off. Not love, not even infatuation, could get much of a grip on Mr. Collins's pedestrian little soul. But it didn't matter. Infatuation might be gone, but pride remained. He had made a good match, and that was all he had ever really cared about.

Mary took to her bed, claiming headache. As soon as we could, Kitty and I slipped up to see her. Jane and Lizzy shared a room, and Kitty and I another; but Mary slept alone. Her room was small, tucked under the eaves at the top of the back stairs; only the color of the paint in the hall distinguished it from the servants' rooms. But Mary liked it. She preferred solitude, and said she liked to look through her small window up at the stars.

She was not crying when we crept in—I hadn't seen her cry since we were children—but she wouldn't show us her face. She stayed buried in the sheets and wouldn't emerge.

"Mary?" I said cautiously. "Mary, are you all right?"

No answer. I patted the lump of bedding where I thought her shoulder was. She rolled away.

"We're most awfully sorry, Mary," I said. "We didn't know it would go so wrong."

Kitty nodded. "We'll make it up to you. Honest we will. Cook is making sweet buns. Shall I sneak you one?"

Still more silence. Kitty and I looked at each other.

"Mary," I said. "Say something."

At last she rolled over and pulled the covers down. Her eyes were red and her face damp. "Thou shalt not suffer a witch to live," she growled.

Mary did suffer us to live, of course. She could hardly burn us in the town square. But after that she wouldn't speak to us unless absolutely necessary, and never about affairs of the heart.

# CHAPTER FIFTEEN

It's been several days since I wrote. They've been busy days—almost, I would say, happy ones, at least as compared with the dreary weeks that led up to them.

That so-called husband of mine has been as attentive as I've ever seen him. He's purchased coal for the stove, paid our rent, and bought me fabric for a new dress besides. It's a lovely dusty blue, with sapphire silk for the trim. Nothing too fancy, but I must own he has good taste. I've been sewing day and night to finish my new gown, and I'm going to use the scraps to let out the hem and sleeves on my day dress. I ought to demand to know where all this sudden wealth has sprung from—it's certainly not from his salary, for that is small and I know he's already gambled it away and then some—but I've been too delighted with the feel of a gown that fits and doesn't cut me across the arms and bosom to care.

We went to the public ball as promised on Friday. Oh, it was lovely—lovely—lovely. Terribly crowded of course, and a little shabby, but I don't *care*. I got to dance.

I was surprised when we arrived to find many of the guests greeting Wickham warmly by name. Apparently his reputation has not yet caught up with his charm. Some of them certainly snubbed him or looked sharply at us, but quite a few were amiable. It wasn't just his brother officers and their ilk, either—quite respectable members of Newcastle society hailed him as a friend. When did he have time to worm into their good graces, I wonder?

He certainly acted the part of the respectable, doting husband. He squired me about, introducing me to this gentleman's daughter and that officer's wife, finding me suitable dancing partners but never straying far from my side. It felt almost like being back in Meryton again. For the waltz, he claimed my hand himself, and smiled into my eyes the entire time. I could feel the gaze of the assembly upon us. *Who is that handsome young couple?* I imagine they were saying. *They look so terribly in love.*

All right. I'm not stupid. I know he's up to something. But while he tries to get round me with dresses and waltzes, can't I enjoy his kindness? It may be the only sort of kindness I can enjoy for the rest of my life. I'll watch him like a hawk, I swear it. The way I should have done last year.

A sort of terrible hilarity took over Kit and me in the new year. We never walked if we could run; never smiled if we could laugh; never dallied if we could dance. It felt as though there was an immense energy building up restlessly in my breast, and if I paused to think, it shrieked at me to move. The glory of freedom, I supposed, when I bothered to consider the sensation. Jane went to London in January and Lizzy to Hunsford to visit Charlotte Collins in March, and there was no one to scold us for our high spirits. We could be as loud and flirtatious as we deemed necessary.

Often, it was great fun. Such pranks we had with the officers! We snuck a cockerel into the colonel's bed, and replaced old Mrs. Templeton's organ music with sheet music for a Scottish reel and she played it at church, thinking it was a new hymn, and lots of other larks like that.

Kit took part in all of this with as great enthusiasm as I. "I feel as though there are hot coals under my feet," she gasped to me and Denny once, after a fast reel, "and I've no choice but to dance and dance." She was laughing breathlessly when she said it, hanging on Denny's arm. Her cheeks were flushed and she was starry-eyed with pleasant exertion. Denny offered to take her to sit down, but the next dance was beginning, and she seized his hand and dragged him back onto the floor.

Oh, I hate remembering that time. When I think of it I hear my own stupid shrieks of laughter ringing in my ears. I'm a selfish willful brat, and normally I don't mind being one (that's how selfish I am!), but when I think of what could have happened to Kit...

But I'm getting ahead of myself.

Mary King came back to town, and seemed to take a fancy to Wickham. They often waltzed together, and passed whole evenings murmuring to each other in corners while the rest of us played cards. She was no longer clad in awkward secondhand plumage—she had a fortune of five thousand pounds now, and everything she wore was impeccably cut. Fortune can't buy taste, though, or a bosom, and her skinny form and brightly colored ensembles still made her look like a flamingo.

I burned when I saw them together. Now that Lizzy had left town I felt that Wickham ought to be my property to flirt with. How dare this scrawny social upstart try to steal him, five thousand pounds or no five thousand pounds! I plotted elaborate schemes to get back at them. Denny and Kitty listened patiently as I outlined pranks to play on her. But somehow, I never followed through on them. Mary King frightened me. She was the only witch I had ever met who I was sure was stronger than me.

And truthfully, I did not really want to attract Wickham's attention, either. Infuriated as I was at seeing him with another woman, I found it easier to love him from afar.

At the public ball in Meryton in May, I stood in a corner complaining to a few friends. They had heard it all before, but what are friends for, if not to listen to the same complaints over and over?

"They look absurd together," I said. "He's so refined and she's so—*bright.*"

"Yes," said Harriet Forster. "Like a thoroughbred and a donkey." She was the colonel's new wife, and had quite unexpectedly become a close friend of mine. She was only a few years older than I was and seemed to feel no need to behave with the gravitas of a senior officer's helpmeet. She was nineteen and full of fun, and if the colonel minded, it was buried deep under his pride at having landed such a young, pretty wife.

"Oh, I don't know," rumbled a voice behind us. "My breeding is not as pure as you might think."

I turned in shock. It was Wickham.

He bowed slightly to us. "Mrs. Forster," he murmured. "Miss Kitty. Miss Lydia." We all curtsied, but he never took his eyes from me.

I knew I ought to apologize for the rudeness he'd overheard, but as so often happened when I locked eyes with him, I found that I was unable to speak, or even look away.

"Are you enjoying yourself, Wickham?" Mrs. Forster asked. "You certainly seem to enjoy the company of one particular young lady. You've danced with Miss King three times tonight."

"Have I been showing her too much favor?" he asked. "I had better remedy that. Miss Lydia, may I have this dance?"

I found myself holding out a hand to him. I felt a flash of heat through my glove as he took it and led me onto the floor.

I was sure the next dance was to be a gavotte, but the musicians struck up a waltz. A murmur went through the room. Waltzes were uncommon in sleepy, conservative Meryton, and unheard of at public balls. Even my mother, who normally encouraged me to do exactly as I liked, might scold me for dancing one with Wickham. But it was too late now. I shivered as his hand closed on my waist and we began to move.

You can't get away from your partner during a waltz. You never turn away or step apart or take hands with other dancers. Always, his gaze is on yours. I still felt that my tongue was frozen in Wickham's presence, but when it became clear that he had no intention of conversing, I forced myself to speak.

"Sorry," I said. "That was awfully rude of us. I'm sure Miss King is a delightful companion."

He laughed. His voice was low and seemed to rumble through our points of contact—hip, hands, his legs brushing against my skirt. "Are you? Sure of that, I mean? It seems like you two despise each other."

I wasn't sure what to say to that, so I gave him my best arch look and changed the subject. "Are you enjoying your time with the regiment?"

"Yes. More than I expected. I thought I would find it too quiet, but the life of an officer is full of unexpected pleasures."

"Like drinking and cards?"

"Yes," he said. "You can win all sorts of interesting things at cards. And then there is the pleasure of befriending the young ladies of the town. All the young pups of the regiment seem constantly tangled in some scheme or other of yours. I wonder, why haven't you tried to ensnare me in your games?"

"I suppose a man of your years has better things to do."

"I'm not as advanced in years as you seem to think."

We whirled in silence for a bit. He was a good dancer, for certain. Under the music I heard snatches of sounds from around the ballroom— Lady Lucas hissing my name to my mother, Kitty coughing, an officer's loud laugh—but I could not tear my eyes from Wickham.

"I've been wanting a chance to speak to you," he said. "I believe you and I could come to a mutually beneficial arrangement."

*Mutually beneficial arrangement?* That was the kind of phrase whispered about women of ill repute. My eyes narrowed. "What are you talking about?"

"Come now, Miss Lydia. Surely we needn't be coy when it's just us. I know you've felt it."

My face went hot. We whirled past a window and I caught sight of my reflection. I was blushing, certainly, and it wasn't as becoming as I'd hoped. I felt like I would burst into flames.

Somehow, the tempo of the dance seemed to be getting faster. I saw the Forsters, dancing nearby, glancing at me with concern, but Wickham whirled me away. He leaned a little closer.

"The heat pours up through the soles of your feet," he said in my ear. "When you look at me you choke. When I touch you, you freeze, like a frightened rabbit."

I cleared my throat. I might not be as refined as some, but this was no way to talk to a lady. "You are mistaken, sir," I said. "None of that is true, and it is very presumptuous of you to think that you've won my affections."

He threw back his head and laughed. "Ha! Is that what you think is happening? The pain, the heat, the weakness—you think you're in love with me? I knew young ladies were stupid, but not to this extent. Look." He slowed us for a moment and I saw Kitty, sitting with Denny. Denny was holding her hand in one of his, the other offering her a glass of water. But she was coughing too hard to take it.

Horror bloomed in my chest as I looked at her. How long had she looked that thin? That feverish? Dear Lord, her hands were shaking! How had I stopped noticing that that dreadful cough of hers was actually getting worse? And Denny—Denny had been worried for weeks, I realized. His normally cheerful face had grown increasingly anxious when he looked at her, and he was always trying to get her to sit and bringing her glasses of water. He'd even mentioned taking her to a physician, but I'd been busy winning a hand at cards and didn't listen. Why didn't I listen?

"You're not in love with me," Wickham said quite conversationally in my ear. "*I'm eating you*—cat first."

His mocking gaze raked over me. I swallowed with difficulty. I felt as though his eyes could burn away my gown, petticoats, smalls, leaving me naked before his gaze and everyone I knew. I wanted to pull away but couldn't.

The music stopped then. He kept my arm tucked solicitously through his. Those around me no doubt saw him as they wished to—a fine young man with beautiful manners, delicately supporting his young partner who was unused to the vigor of the waltz. Only I could feel the iron grip his arm had on mine. I felt that without it my legs would scarcely support me. He leaned in and, through a smile as though we were merely exchanging the usual pleasantries, said, "You're lucky I like it here, or you and your cat-sister would be quite eaten up already. That's certainly what my father wanted."

Mary King was smirking at me. I had the sudden impression that she knew exactly what was going on—which was more than I did, certainly. When she saw me looking she raised her cup of punch to me, which looked even more poison green against the magenta hue of her dress, in a silent, mocking toast.

"Your father?" I said stupidly to Wickham. "Darcy's steward? He's dead."

"Yes, the father of this body's previous owner is dead," Wickham said pleasantly. "But he lost it to me in a card game, and Father ate his soul. A mean, mealy, misused little trifle. Yours tastes much better. It's what my father sent me for. Come, you must have figured out who he is."

And suddenly, I had. The heat, the smoke, the coils tightening unnoticed for months. The memory of that day on the path in Meryton came crushing back. How had I ever forgotten? "Wormenheart."

"Lord Wormenheart, to you. Come to the standing stones tomorrow at midnight." He escorted me back to Kitty, bowed, and walked away.

# CHAPTER SIXTEEN

Wickham wants to know what I am writing about. Shall I tell him? I must own it amuses me to write in front of him, knowing he can't make head or tail of it. In some ways, reading is what he's best at—what he was made for. Reading people. Manipulating them. He can look at a love letter and see not only every word on the page, but which of them are lies, which ones are unwritten but should be, probably even what the writer had for breakfast that morning.

But I'm not a person. I'm a witch. I don't leave my emotions imprinted on the things I touch the way normal folk do. And while Wickham can read people and the slightest traces they leave, the fact is that he cannot read the alphabet.

I'm probably lucky he hasn't thrown this manuscript in the fire. He's threatened to, but he's not quite willing to stretch the delicate détente between us that far, I think. I caught him looking at a page, once, when he thought I was sleeping. He was holding it upside down.

What would he say, I wonder, if I told him I was writing about last year, when I thought he was going to kill us? Trying to remember that however charming he may be acting at the moment, he once tried to eat me alive? No, definitely best to keep my mouth shut.

*Later*

I told him. Keeping my mouth shut has never been a gift of mine. Besides, Miss Darcy canceled our weekly spell appointment (for the second week in a row—what's that foolish girl about?) and I've got no one else to talk to.

To my surprise, he only laughed. That's the nicest thing about Wickham, I think (the nicest real thing, I mean, once his initial charm wears off). The things you think will most insult him are the ones he cares the least about. "Ah, yes, the good old days," he said. "How foolish I was. I should have just eaten your soul in one gulp and been done with it. Such a sweet little morsel it was."

"Was?" I said sharply. "What's wrong with it now, pray?"

He laughed again. "Vanity, thy name is woman. Don't worry, Mrs. Wickham, your soul would still be tasty, I'm sure."

"Don't call me that."

"Very well. I suppose you are still Miss Bennet, even if I am the only one who knows it." He turned and looked at me intently. I felt his gaze rake over me with more than human eyes. "Yes," he said. "Still tasty, I think. Not quite as fresh and tart as it was, but riper. And a little singed around the edges, which would no doubt bring a delightful complexity to the flavor. Like a baked apple."

I crossed my arms to cover a shiver. "Stop that."

He shrugged. "All right. You did ask." His impudent gaze was still on me. "Can't blame a hungry fellow for dreaming of a meal."

That was quite enough of that. I clenched my left hand—the one with my "wedding" ring—into a fist and yanked. He stumbled to his knees with an *oof*, as though he'd been jerked forward by a chain around his middle—which, of course, he had.

"If you're hungry," I said sharply, "go and buy us some meat pies for supper. And mind how you speak to me."

"Mind how you speak to me, Mrs. Wickham," he said. "The world doesn't look kindly on disobedient wives." And with a bow, he left.

I wonder how long we can keep doing this dance. "The rest of my life" is the current plan, but surely something will crack long before then.

I hope it's him that cracks and not me. It's like sharing a home with a tiger—a declawed, muzzled tiger, whose leash is in my hand. But still, tigers are tigers.

The sun was threatening to rise when Kitty and I left the ball. I tucked Kit into the carriage next to a dozing Mamma, but I could not stand being shut up in the dark with them. Instead, I cast a slight don't-notice-me glamour, and I walked home.

For me it was the end of a night, but for many in town the day was beginning. Though it was the sleepiest time of day, the strange, itchy energy I had been feeling seemed to have left its mark on Meryton, too. Two tired drunks were still stumbling through a fight, hours after they should have passed out. A hen was pecking its chick to death—I rescued the bloody lump of fluff and put it on a fence post, but I knew it would probably fall to its mother's beak in the end.

I stopped to rest in the town square at the lip of a well. As I shook a pebble out of my slipper, I heard a hiss and saw steam rising into the cool morning air. The well was boiling.

Lord. Who *was* Wormenheart?

"Very kind of you, I'm sure," I said to the empty air, as steadily as I could. "Much more convenient for breakfast tea." And, ignoring the pain in my feet, I marched across the fields toward home.

Kit was asleep when I got there, still in girl-shape but curled up as much as a girl can. If she'd had a tail, it would have been across her nose. Little tendrils of hair escaped her curling papers and her sleeping cap to frizz around her face. Even in sleep, her cheeks were flushed, as though she'd just danced a vigorous quadrille. I laid a hand on her forehead. She was burning up.

Oh, Kit!

She stirred with a groan when I slipped into bed beside her. "You're all cold," she whined, trying to pull away from me toward the wall.

"Sorry," I whispered.

An apology from me was rare enough to wake her up a little. She rolled over to look at me. "Where have you been?"

I told her about Wickham. "Did you know something was wrong?" I asked. "With you, I mean?"

She nodded. "I hoped I was imagining things."

"You should have said something, stupid."

"Well, why didn't you? You all heard me cough. No one seemed to think it was important. Not you. Not Mamma."

"That's part of the magic, I think. It kept us from noticing. Or maybe not. We're not a very attentive family."

"Denny noticed," she said quietly. She'd rolled over to look at the ceiling. One hand rested at the base of her throat, her fingers stroking her pulse point. "He's been begging me to see a doctor for weeks now. He hardly dances anymore, so that he can keep a chair for me."

I curled my cold fingers under my cheek and asked her the question she had asked me weeks ago. "What's it like to be in love?"

Her chest rose and fell in a slow sigh. "Not smoke and fire and choking. Not for me, anyway."

I nodded.

"It's more like the floor in the breakfast parlor at Lucas Lodge," she said. The Lucases had added a wing to their house this summer. As usual, Sir William had chosen his workmen poorly, and the new parlor was a slapdash affair. They were very proud of it, however. Kitty continued, "The floor looks straight enough, but if you set a ball down on it, wherever the ball starts in the room, it rolls to the southeast corner. That's what it's like for me. I don't mean to, but I always come to rest next to Denny."

"That sounds nice," I whispered.

"It is."

*I'm eating you—cat first.*

He clearly thought of Kitty as simply an extension of me. Well, he was hardly the only one. Aunt Philips looked on her the same way. Our

own family mostly spoke of us as though our names were one word—
KittyandLydia. Gracious, even I tended to make decisions for both of us.
For all our scrapping, I knew she'd follow where I led in the end. But if
it had ever been true that Kit was merely a part of me, it wasn't anymore,
was it? What she felt for Denny was completely alien to me. Oh, I liked
him well enough, but there was no shred of romance about him. He had
a nice smile of course, and fine broad shoulders. And his singing voice
was lovely. Kitty always appreciated a man who could sing to her. But
Denny, barely half an inch taller than I, with a slightly soft chin and a
crooked nose, was hardly my idea of a lover.

For all that, though, in some sense Kitty and I *were* still one. I could
feel the connection that bound us, vibrating between us like a heartbeat.

"Kit," I whispered. "Do you have the cough as a cat, too? Colds and
sore throats don't usually follow you across transformations."

She didn't answer. I thought of something and grew cold. "Kit, when
did you last transform?"

She curled away from me. I realized she was crying. "Kit," I said, and
put a hand to her shoulder.

"I can't," she said. "I can't transform anymore. Lydia, I'm scared."

I slid an arm around her waist. "Rest, Kit," I said. "You rest."

Presently she fell asleep, but I lay awake, watching the sky turn from
gray to blue.

# CHAPTER SEVENTEEN

I did eventually get to sleep, though I had strange, anxious dreams. I was running down a long corridor, looking for Kitty, and I knew she was behind the door at the end, but no matter how fast I ran the knob was always out of reach. Cat-Kitty ran at my feet, urging me on, her yowls increasing in pitch.

I finally woke to a monstrous headache and an empty bed. I found Kitty downstairs eating toast and marmalade. In theory, anyway. She was really only nibbling at the edges, though she ought to have been ravenous after dancing all night. Again I felt that surge of irritation. Why hadn't I noticed how thin she'd become? Why hadn't she said something? We'd lost so much time!

After breakfast—I ate about half a loaf of toast and marmalade myself, and bullied Kitty into at least finishing a slice—we went to my aunt's. I wanted to take the carriage so Kitty wouldn't have to walk, but Papa refused.

"The longer it takes you to walk to Meryton and back, the longer this house will be blessedly quiet," he said.

"But Papa, Kitty's not feeling well."

"What does she want to go to Meryton for then?"

I'd have pressed the case, but Kitty whispered, "It's all right. I'd rather walk."

So we set out on foot, as we usually did. Kit said the exercise made her feel better, but we still stopped to rest far more often. If anything happened to Kitty, I resolved, I'd make my father suffer. No witchcraft.

I'd burn his library to the ground with my own hands. The thought cheered me immensely.

My aunt's maid Hester tried to turn us away when we got to her door. "The mistress ain't woke up yet," she said. "If you young misses would come back later—"

"We'll wait," I said.

Hester pressed her lips together—perhaps remembering how loudly we waited—but let us into the parlor. Sure enough, Kitty and I had hardly had time to play one round of lottery tickets before my aunt appeared in her bedclothes, yawning. "What are you doing here, my dears?" she asked. "It's not even two o'clock."

"Morning, Aunt," I said. "We're in terrible danger."

I told her everything. At first, she didn't believe us. "Eating your soul! Young Wickham? Nonsense. He has such a lovely blue coat," she said.

"It's not just him. His father is Lord Wormenheart," I explained.

Her face went rather white. "You—you girls have been approached by Wormenheart?" Then she shook herself and said, "Nonsense. What an imagination you have. No one has fallen prey to him for a hundred years. If one of the Great Powers had woken, why wouldn't he have tried to devour *me*? *I* am the most senior witch of the village."

"I don't know," I said impatiently. "But he contacted us when we were children, and made us forget it till now, and I promised him a boon, and—"

"You what?" She went very still.

"Promised him a boon," I said weakly.

She sank into a chair. "You stupid, *stupid* girl," she breathed. "You know better than to give an open-ended promise to anyone, especially a magical creature."

"I know," I said, "but I had to. He was going to take Kit."

"Better for you if he had."

"I beg your pardon!" said Kitty.

"Sorry, Kitty, dear. But this is very serious, you know."

"We know," I said. "But you can fix it, can't you? You can't just let him take us. Things like that don't *happen*."

"They do, sometimes," she said. "The Great Powers and other powerful spirits, that is. The outside world never notices. Your body keeps walking around, but with a . . . different inhabitant. It's my opinion that's what that rascal Napoleon is." She tilted her head, considering. "Of course, Kitty was never supposed to have a human body in the first place. She might disappear altogether."

Kitty drew in a sharp little breath and began to cry. "I shan't! I shan't disappear!"

Aunt Philips looked distressed. "There, there, dear. Of course you shan't. Auntie's here. Lydia, go and get some brandy, would you? And bring a nip for Kitty, too. I'm sure it will do her good."

I hurried to the sideboard and handed round the brandy glasses. "But, Aunt—who is Wormenheart?"

"He is one of the Great Powers," she said. "That is all I know."

"And who are they?"

"Do not be a fool, Lydia. Surely I taught you of the Great Powers. No? Ah well, I suppose you have forgotten. Your mind is like a sieve." She stared into space, swirling her brandy absently. "The Great Powers are the aristocracy of the magical world," she said. "Once they were well known by all men, but most have passed into legend, or been forgotten altogether. No two are alike, and many have been greatly weakened by the passing of the years. But one thing is for certain: Any witch who draws the attention of a Great Power had best be extremely careful." She blinked, gulped the rest of her brandy, and glared at us. "Not that I believe you *really* woke a Great Power. Far more likely some brownie or sprite is making sport of you."

"You're the best witch we know, Aunt," I said. "Please, can't you stop this?"

"Of course." She gave us a smile that I tried to draw confidence from. "You just leave it to me."

While she made her preparations for the night ahead, Aunt sent Kitty and me out to gather herbs. On the way back we were caught in a rain shower. We were just about to duck into the church to wait it out when we heard a sudden, "Coo-ee!"

We looked across the road. There, in her smart little phaeton with the cover pulled up snug, was Mrs. Colonel Forster, waving madly. We made a dash for it and tumbled inside with a sigh of relief. How nice it was to have a friend who had her own carriage.

"Thanks awfully, Harriet," I said.

"Of course. But what on earth were you doing out there? And why were you grubbing about in the dirt?" She nodded to our handfuls of herbs.

"Oh, um—"

"Still life," Kit said. "Lydia wants to practice her watercolors. She's going to paint them."

"How nice," said Harriet, casting a dubious look at the herbs, half crushed and trailing long, dirty clumps of roots. "But I *am* glad I ran into you, Lydia. Such exciting news we've had about the regiment!"

"Oh?" I said politely. The day before I would have hung on every word about the regiment, but now I could barely attend.

"Yes! We're moving to Brighton! Isn't that marvelous? It's the most delightful place in England, I think."

"Leaving!" Kitty said. "All of them?"

"Well, yes, Miss Bennet. The regiment moves together." I had always got the sense that Harriet found Kitty rather trying. She sighed. "Ah, Brighton! I hope you won't take this the wrong way, for I know it's your home, but Meryton is truly one of the dullest places I've ever lived—and my father was stationed in Durham for four months. But I will miss you awfully, Lydia. You ought to get your parents to bring you there for the summer. I'm sure you would all have such fun."

I was sure of that, too, if summer ever came for us. I looked at Kitty, who was leaning her head against the side of the carriage. "Denny told me he could swim like a fish," she said wistfully.

Before I could think of a tactful way to turn the conversation away from Brighton, Harriet said, "Why, it's Wickham!" She stopped the carriage and waved to him. "I wish I could offer you a ride, Wicks," she said, "but as you can see my little phaeton is already full to bursting. What are you doing out in this nasty weather?"

"How do you do, Mrs. Forster, Miss Bennet, Miss Lydia." He made us an elegant bow and a friendly smile. The rain had disarranged his neat coiffure and, truthfully, it only made him more handsome. But his beauty repelled me now. I imagined that I could hear hissing when the raindrops struck him, like droplets of water on a hot stove. "I'm after some more blacking. My man used the last of mine, and I've an important engagement later." On the word "engagement" he looked past her and straight at me.

"An engagement with Williams and his cockfights, no doubt," Harriet laughed. "Well, mind you don't drink too much, for I require you to dance with these ladies when next we all meet."

"Oh, I'll lead them a merry dance, I assure you," he said softly. Then he tipped his hat to us and was gone.

Harriet gave me a playful blow on the arm. "Lydia! Why didn't you flirt with him? He couldn't take his eyes off you! I declare, he must like you, you lucky thing. Don't play shy, for I know you are not, and he's not at all the kind of man on whom false modesty works."

"I don't believe he does like me," I said. "And anyway, I don't like him."

She looked at me oddly. "Don't you?"

"No," I said. "I'll be glad when he's gone."

"Well," she said dubiously. "You'll soon have your wish. *I* think it would be much more fun to have you both about me, though. Here we are." And she dropped us at our aunt's doorstep.

We slept a few hours in my aunt's spare bedroom in the afternoon, then arose to find the house nearly empty. She'd given the servants the night off and encouraged her husband to go round to his brother's.

It was a wise decision on her part, for she'd transformed her parlor into a sort of magical war room. Every surface was covered in potions, herbs mid-chop, and dark dripping candles. In the middle of the floor she'd put down a large gray sheet, then poured out a protection circle in salt on top of it—"For ease of cleanup," she explained.

I squeezed Kitty's hand when I saw it all, and she gave me a hopeful smile. We'd never seen our aunt go to such great lengths before. It was clear she was bringing out every weapon in her magical arsenal to protect us.

We spent the next couple of hours chanting, anointing one another, and drinking foul brews to protect us and drive away evil spirits. "There!" she said finally. "If that won't protect us I don't know what will. Off we go, now." And we stripped to our shifts and set off into the night.

The giddy excitement we'd felt the night of the coven felt a million miles away. It was May, but it had been a cold and damp day, and the muddy grass and sharp wind turned our trip to the stones into a dreary slog. My aunt was a better witch than Miss Darcy's idiot teacher is, but the protection spells still weighed us down, like wearing a sodden gown. Kitty's cough grew worse the longer we walked, and her teeth chattered. I longed to return to my aunt's warm hearth—but the knowledge of the ordeal that lay before us made the safety of her fireside seem farther away than ever.

The top of the hill, bare to the wind as it was, was even colder, though a bonfire had been started. A few women were already waiting for us. I recognized the woman with the goat from last time. She brought us yet another spicy brew to drink while we disrobed. This one, at least, warmed me on the way down and took away some of the chill. I think it was mostly whiskey.

"Well met, Goody Philips," she said formally to my aunt, then more casually, "Couldn't you have given us a bit more warning? Most of the coven can't get away on such short notice. They've got children to mind, and Miss Charing has her niece visiting."

"Well met, Mistress Pell," my aunt said. She made a deep curtsy (a peculiar sight, for she was naked), and nodded to us to do the same. "You remember my niece Lydia and her familiar."

"Of course." Mistress Pell sized us up. Next to her, her goat did the same, his yellow eyes glowing in the moonlight. He butted his mistress's thigh. She addressed herself to me. "Dante would like to know why your familiar here is rudely cloaked in human form."

"I can't *help it*," Kitty said querulously.

Mistress Pell sniffed. "Stuck, is it?" she said, still speaking to me. "You should have come to us long before this. The glamour was always in poor taste. Who ever heard of a human girl familiar?"

"She's just jealous because that *Dante* can't do it," Kitty muttered. Luckily, a gust of wind kept anyone but me from hearing.

"You'll help us, won't you?" I said. There was a quaver in my voice. "Please?"

Mistress Pell looked at us with narrowed eyes. I found myself wishing that there were gentlemen witches. Older gentlemen tended to be highly susceptible to that quaver, and I hadn't even had to feign it this time. Mistress Pell did not melt, however, and merely gave a curt nod.

"You're a member of my coven," she said. "We don't appreciate outsiders like this young city rake Wickham causing trouble. We're a decent country coven, we are, and we want merely to practice our dark arts in peace. I'll expect some spell-prices for my pains, of course, but we'll help settle this. Mind you, I don't think there's much trouble here to settle. Wormenheart risen? Pah. Young witches have such imagination."

I'd have argued with her, but it was too late. Wickham was there.

He hadn't come alone. To his left stood Mary King. Both of them held torches. She was naked, as we were, her pale skin practically glowing in the firelight, and Wickham wore only a pair of trousers. He looked rather nice like that, and I felt faintly sick that someone who was about to kill me should be still so beautiful. Evil ought to be ugly. All the trappings of his respectable life as a soldier were gone. He seemed to have put off his gentle flirtatiousness, too. I stared at Wickham and tensed, but to my surprise it was Miss King who stepped forward and spoke.

"Well met, all," she said, sounding as bored as ever. "On behalf of my benefactor, the Great Lord Wormenheart, I greet you. May I present his son, known on this plane as Wickham." Wickham stepped forward and gave a slight bow.

An uneasy murmur went through the crowd. Mistress Pell, her chin set, stepped forward. "I don't know what your game is, Miss King, but I'll remind you of the help we offered you last fall, and ask you to speak to your elder witches with more respect, and not waste our time with these fairy tales. Wormenheart indeed."

Miss King looked rageful for a moment, then laughed a tinkling little laugh. "Gracious, how diverting! Have you grubby little hedge witches really never encountered one of the Great Lords before? I knew that things were dire out here in the country, but *really*." She turned to Wickham and put a hand on his back. "Do you mind, darling?"

Wickham stepped forward, away from her touch. He paused for a moment, looking hard at me, as though to convey something. Before I could puzzle it out, he turned away and threw an acrid gray powder into the fire. And then Wormenheart was there.

I could not see him, but he was, nonetheless, undeniably *there*. The hot, suffocating coils felt just as I remembered them from childhood. They seemed to lazily press in on us from all directions—not physically, but mentally, spiritually, magically. Wickham stiffened and stepped into the fire. He turned to us, apparently heedless of the flames and sparks licking all around him.

"*Ooh, lovely, witches,*" said Wormenheart with Wickham's tongue.

A gasping, shuddering moan went up from the assembled women. Next to me, my aunt clutched her chest. Kitty fell to her knees, coughing.

I give Mistress Pell credit: She did not give up her territory easily. She muttered a few words, and I felt the frail magical framework of the coven strengthen into something sturdier, pushing back firmly against

Wormenheart's coils. "Begone, demon or puck or spirit," she said. "In the name of dawn and dusk and midnight, this coven abjures thee. Leave this place. Leave the witch Lydia and her familiar. Leave all this coven in peace."

It was a mistake. I could *feel* Wormenheart swell and grow hotter. It was like trying to breathe inside an oven. "*Demon?*" he demanded. "*Spirit? PUCK? Have my subjects so far forgotten the true nature of their liege? Well then, I must needs remind them.*"

When I had tried to picture Wormenheart, I'd vaguely imagined the ghost of a country baron, or perhaps a long-dead petty king. That, I thought, was what my aunt meant by magical aristocracy: the spirit of a real aristocrat, from an age when such people wielded magical power as well as the mortal kind.

As Wormenheart gripped our minds, I saw how wrong I was.

Images came to me in a flash. Men and women in long robes, chanting in a circle of stones. Wolves prowling the cliffs. All of them savage, proud, fearless—except when the shadow passed overhead. Then they all cowered, hoping it would not see them.

*Dragon.*

A thousand years flicked by, the dragon ruling the land, picking off sheep and deer and children at its leisure. Then, more men came. Men determined not just to survive on the land, but to master it. They drove the dragon back with crosses and swords and spells of their own. For years, they were locked in a pitched battle. Finally they tracked the dread beast to its lair, a cave beneath the hills, and slew it.

"*There is one of your churches there now,*" Wormenheart drawled in annoyance. "*Built right over my head. The organ rattles my bones o' Sundays. And I can hear them sometimes, in my dreams, telling their young the story of how once beneath this spot dwelt the dread dragon Wormenheart.*"

"You're dead then," I said, as stoutly as I could. "You can't hurt us."

"*Death is not the end for one of my rank. Such power only sleeps. And a spark as bright as you, witchling, could be just what I need to be set alight again.*"

Mistress Pell, bless her, did not give up. I could see her trembling from across the circle, and rivulets of sweat ran down her cheeks, but whether out of bravery or lack of imagination, she continued with her plan. "No dragon has hunted in these lands for centuries," she said. "Whatever manner of creature you may call yourself, I'll thank you not to bother this young witch anymore."

"*I don't think so, mistress,*" said Wormenheart. "*Said witch made me a promise, and I intend to take my fill.*"

With those words, we were somewhere else.

The dark flame-lit hilltop became the blinding sun of midday. I was floating in the sky, looking down at a pasture. Far, far below, I could see two little girls clinging to each other. As far away as I was, I could hear my own little-girl voice ring out distinctly: "*I'll give you a boon!*"

We were back on the hillside. Mistress Pell looked at me accusingly.

"I had to," I croaked. "He was going to kill Kit. We were only little."

"*A promise is a promise,*" said Wormenheart silkily. Sparks framed Wickham's face, gleaming reflected in his eyes. I wondered if the flames didn't affect his human body, or if his father just wasn't allowing him to react. I hoped he'd be covered in burns. "*You know that, mistress. And in any case, do you really think you can stop me?*"

"Listen to my lord, witches," Mary King said. "He's your rightful lord, too, you know. Shockingly gauche of you not to pay your respects long before now."

The heat of Wormenheart changed, then. It was less like brute force and more like a sense of overwhelming authority. All of us cringed away from it. I felt small and silly, and had an urge to bow. It was like when I met an earl at a ball last year, and felt sure he could see that the ribbons on my gown were bought on sale.

"*There,*" he said coaxingly. "*Give me what is owed, my vassals. Your fealty will be rewarded.*" And he showed them how.

*Mistress Pell had never married. What if her father suddenly began to take fits and her pretty sister moved away to care for him, leaving the affections of the handsome widowed tanner down the road as Anne Pell's for the winning?*

*What if, after a better-than-expected year for the farms, the Honorable Miss Charing's brother decided to send his daughter to town for her debut after all? What if Miss Charing could chaperone, and finally, for the first time in her long, dry life, witness a London Season?*

*The growth in Carrie Powell's husband's belly that made him groan and swear and cry out for her in the night, that would, no matter how many tears she shed, and no matter how many pathetic healing charms she cast, kill him before the year was out—what if it simply went away?*

All they had to do, the dragon's voice whispered to us, was admit what they already knew to be true: They could not defeat him. They could not stop him from claiming what was his.

One by one, the witches of the coven fell. Tempted or overcome with fear, they bowed and gave way, and our protection circle weakened as they did. My aunt's spells blew away like dry leaves. All those hours of chanting and anointing, worth nothing. Kitty and I were the only ones who didn't give up—Kit and I, who must be special, I thought desperately, for we had attracted his attention in the first place—but it wasn't enough. It wouldn't be enough.

Despair and rage made me want to cry. I saw these witches, now, for what they were: a bunch of upstart country women, hardly a drop of magic among them, mumbling spells garbled by generations, scrabbling for crumbs of power they didn't understand and could barely perceive, let alone use. This was what I had been trained up to be. All the years of lessons at my aunt's knee, all my pride in my glamours and spells—this was all I was.

Kit and I gripped each other's hands so hard, I thought that if we made it through this we'd have broken fingers.

Wickham stepped out of the fire toward me and the flames went with him, leaving smoldering footprints in the damp grass. He reached a hand toward me.

"*Well fought, little witch,*" he said, a hint of amusement in his voice. "*I appreciate that even now you are standing strong. I tell you what. I will offer you the same bargain I did when you were small.*"

And he showed me.

*I was the most beautiful of my sisters. I always had been. I was cleverer than Elizabeth, more charming than Jane, more accomplished than Mary. The apple of my father's eye, he sent me to London for a Season, and I was the toast of society. Great men, lords, titans of industry—all of them fell at my feet. I would make a brilliant match, and I—I, Lydia, the youngest—would save my family from ruin.*

*All I had to do was give him Kitty.*

I had tears on my face as I saw what he could do. What could I say? If I didn't give him Kit he would take us both.

"*Just give her to me,*" he said. "*What good is she to you, anyhow? She's broken and weak. She can't aid you in your craft if she can't even take her true form.*"

My aunt gripped my other elbow. "Do it, girl," she muttered. "I'm sorry you must lose your pet, but you can get on very well without a familiar. I always have."

Kitty dug her fingernails into my hand, sharp as claws. "I may not look like a cat," she croaked between coughs, "but I still am one. And we cats can see through glamours, you know."

"*Can you, now.*"

"Yes." She turned to me. "Listen to me, Lydia. He's not as strong as he seems. That's why he's bargaining instead of commanding. He's dead, remember? All these promises—he can't keep them. If he could, why is he still slumbering beneath the church, and not flying about eating sheep and whatnot?"

She was wrong. I could see that she was wrong. His power shimmered in the air, glowed unbearably bright in Wickham's eyes.

But what if she wasn't?

So many rules I had been taught had turned out to be little more than social glamours. *You must be accomplished, Lydia, or no man will ever seek your company.* Nonsense. Plenty of lovely men sought my company. *Behave yourself always with propriety, or society will turn its back on you.* Piffle. Society did nothing worse than sputter about my scrapes and pranks. What if the ironclad law Wormenheart laid before me was just another paper tiger?

It didn't look that way. I could feel his power around me, tightening like a vise. But if the last thing I ever did was to trust Kit and make a fool of myself—well, at least I'd go on as I always had.

"Wormenheart," I said, summoning slang I wasn't supposed to know to my tongue like a protection spell, "Wickham—whoever you are—get rogered."

My aunt, cowering in terror with the other so-called witches of the coven, wasn't too far gone to gasp at my vulgarity. Still gripping Kitty's hand tightly with my left, I grabbed my handkerchief from the grass with my right and cast the first spell I could think of: the whirlwind spell I had been practicing that day Wormenheart first found us.

My power had grown since then, just as I had. What emerged was no little dust devil, but a howling whirlwind. The bonfire became a twenty-foot pillar of flame. Our clothes whipped up and around it, spiraling with leaves and sparks in a mad dance. The screams of the witches were carried away by the cyclone.

I didn't care. My own scream was joyous as my hair lashed my face and bare shoulders. The cyclone carried some of the terrible heat up and away, and fresh air poured into my lungs. Even Mary King huddled behind a tree, her arms over her head. Kit and I held hands and as one, screamed our defiance.

I was sure for a moment that we had him. Then a lash of wind blew a handful of sparks straight into my face. I threw up my hand to shield my eyes. When I lowered it, Wickham was there.

His hair moved in the wild wind as though it were a gentle spring breeze. He stood his ground as though nothing were happening at all.

"*Not all power is an illusion, little country witch*," he said. Then he put one hand on Kitty's wrist, the other on mine, and began to pull us apart.

It hurt. It boiled. It would leave scars, hideous burns, handprints showing the world how foolish we'd been. Still, we held on. Still, I shrieked and ordered the wind higher. Still, we didn't give up.

It wasn't enough.

Kitty had been right—Wormenheart's power was mostly illusion. But even a tiny sliver of his original strength was, in the end, sufficient to overcome us. He'd already overcome our allies. There was no one else to help us. Our grip began to slip.

"*Don't cry, girls,*" Wormenheart said through his son's mouth. "*It's an honor for a peasant to serve her lord.*"

Then from behind us a calm voice said, "That's quite enough of that."

Wickham turned with a snarl. There, coming up the hill, was Harriet Forster. At her back were half a dozen men of the regiment, among them her husband and Denny.

"Shall we do it now, Mrs. Forster?" Denny asked eagerly. He was smiling, his eyes bright, as if this were just another of our jokes. The other men looked the same.

"Yes, I think so," said Harriet. Each of the men took out his dagger and sliced his left palm. They gathered around Harriet and held their closed fists over her handkerchief, and she gathered the blood on it before tying it in a firm knot.

Everything on our wild hilltop was suddenly still. My cyclone was a six-inch whirl of leaves again. The heat of Wormenheart's coils slithered away to little more than the natural heat of the bonfire. Harriet Forster stood before us, glowing with power.

"Gracious, Lydia! You have made a mess of things," she said cheerfully. "You really ought to have come to me from the beginning, you know. How foolish to try to fight him off with nothing but your little country coven! Don't you know that magic requires sacrifice? And there are so many nice men willing to make a little sacrifice for us."

"Did we do it right, my dear?" her husband asked anxiously. "It hurts, rather." A faint, sweet smell clung to him that I was to learn to recognize as the scent of his wife's magic.

"You did it perfectly," she assured him with a fond pat to his cheek. "It wouldn't work if it didn't hurt, you know. I explained about needing a sacrifice, remember, and the pain from your little cuts is perfect."

He brightened. "Oh. That's all right then."

I stared at her, gaping. Before I could speak, she looked past me and said, "Why, it's Mary King. Hello, dear. You look well. You ought to kill more of your grandparents, it suits you."

Mary struggled to her feet. Even covered in streaks of mud and soot, she looked terrifying and wild—a fire elemental. "Begone," she snarled. "Unless you'd like to join her as prey to a Great Lord."

Harriet laughed. "Oh, Mary, you're always so amusing. Go put some clothes on, why don't you. You're scandalizing my friends."

It was only then that I realized that, though the rest of us were naked, Harriet and the boys of the regiment were fully clothed. Mary shrieked in outrage at Wickham. "What are you waiting for!" she screamed. "Get them!"

And Wickham rose, Wormenheart's fire gleaming in his eyes—

And then he shook himself, and his eyes were Wickham's brown ones again. "No," he said. "You know, Mary, I don't think I will." He turned to Harriet. "Where have you been? Things were getting very tiresome here. I'm sure all this smoke can't be good for my complexion."

She shrugged. "Getting enough of these fellows was a bit like herding cats. No offense, Miss Bennet." She nodded to Kitty.

*What is this, vassals? This is not what we discussed.* Wormenheart's voice rumbled dangerously through the air, no longer through Wickham's mouth but all around us.

"Apologies, Father," he said, with a vague bow to the air. "When you dispatched me to this plane to capture your promised prey, you should have sent me to steal the body of a less handsome young man. Being George Wickham is *fun*. I'm not ready to give it up yet."

*Oh, aren't you, boy?* Wormenheart snarled. *I'll make you sorry.*

"What are you?" I said in a shaking voice. "Where is the real George Wickham?"

"Gone, extremely permanently," he-who-was-not-Wickham said. "Don't grieve, Miss Lydia. You never knew him. He was no great loss, anyway. The last thing he did before losing his soul to me was to try to seduce a fifteen-year-old heiress. I'm not at all sure the world is worse off with a demon walking around in his body instead." And that wretched creature actually winked at me.

"It's like this, Father," he said. "With my strength added to that of these fine witches here"—he nodded to me and Harriet—"you can't overcome us. That means you can neither eat this young lady and her cat, nor force me to return to my elemental form and rejoin you in that wretched pit beneath the church."

*Nonsense, boy*, the voice snarled. *You are my creation. I own you. You are* me. *You* must *do what I say.*

"I understand that it is quite a rite of passage for human fathers to discover that none of that is true of their sons," he said. "Now. Let us parlay."

*Parlay?* Wormenheart said with outrage.

Harriet stepped forward then. "My lord," she said politely, "I believe that if you let Miss Lydia Bennet go, she can obtain for you a much more valuable prize than her own paltry soul and her familiar's. My men and I"—she waved her hand to her husband and the men of the regiment—"are on our way to Brighton, down on the coast. Do you know what's there?"

Wormenheart stretched, curious, straining his vision toward the coast. I caught fragments of what he was seeing—a flash of light, a flare of power, a blinding glitter of purple—

*A Jewel of Propriety*, he snarled.

Harriet dipped her head. "It could be yours, my lord," she said. "I believe the child Lydia has the raw power to seek it out. Let me take her to Brighton with me and she will find the jewel for you."

*And what do you get out of the bargain?* he asked.

Harriet shrugged. "Lydia is my friend. Besides, it's high time I had an apprentice."

*A Jewel of Propriety,* Wormenheart mused. *With such a thing I could take my proper place in this land.*

"Certainly," she said warmly. "Just stay incorporeal or they'll start sending knights after you again. I don't think you'd enjoy our recent advances in weaponry."

*Very well,* he said. *The girl and her familiar may live. Take the young witch to the pleasure-city by the sea and seek me out this treasure. On one condition.*

"Yes?"

*The cat stays here. I need a hostage.*

Kitty looked at me in alarm. Since the time she first became mine, we had never been more than a mile apart. Even that had been uncomfortable. I was fairly certain that in her weakened state, she wouldn't survive a longer separation.

Harriet's sharp eyes caught the exchange. "That won't work, will it?" she asked.

I shook my head. "We can't be that far apart."

*You refuse the bargain, then?* Wormenheart said. A hint of hunger crept back into his voice. I looked at Harriet and Wickham. He shrugged. "We can't hold him off forever. Take it or leave it, girl."

"There must be another way," I said.

Harriet dusted her hands off briskly. "With magic there's always another way. Let's see—what we need is a sort of—slackening, is that right? You two are far too old to be tied this tightly together anyway. Yes, I see how it can be done."

The other witches had all fled by then, I realized, looking around—including Aunt Philips. So much for family. Harriet dug into her pocket and pulled out a few small sachets of herbs, neatly labeled and much more finely chopped than those my aunt and I used. There was more, too—a little violet crystal she called amethyst, some light-brown grains that she said were sand. She arranged it all into a neat, complicated shape with too many angles for me to quite make sense of, explaining to me out loud as she did so what each element was for. "Amethyst for the anchor, lavender to relax the bond, and sand because, well, we're going to the seaside, aren't we! And now for the sacrifice." She turned to our friends and said sweetly, "A bit more blood, gentlemen, if it's not too much trouble?"

They cried gallantly as one that indeed it was not and, reopening their wounds, they dripped blood at the place she indicated, in the center of the shape. Kitty bit her lip when Denny's turn came, but he grinned at her reassuringly, and she held her tongue. Harriet took my hand and Kitty's in hers, and cried out a few words in a language I didn't know.

Nothing happened.

"Ah," she said. "I was afraid of that." She squeezed my hand apologetically. "It appears the sacrifice has to be yours. This is a very personal spell, after all."

"I have to cut my hand?" I said.

"No. That won't be enough in this case. You have to make a real sacrifice. Something that won't heal up in a few days' time. Gentlemen, you can head on home, you won't be needed."

Agreeably, the men of the regiment waved a cheery, bloody goodbye. Harriet gave them each a swallow of something in a flask—"So they won't remember this tomorrow. Much less bother," she explained—and they marched down the hill. "Mind you wash those cuts in hot water!" she called after them. "And bind them up in clean linen! We don't want any of those small sacrifices turning into permanent ones."

Staring down at Harriet's spell-shape, I felt like I was seeing through it, to the shape of Kit and me. She was right. We were so tightly tied to each other that it would take a sizable amount of power to disentangle us. We were like two neglected rosebushes that had grown around each other. No gardener would risk the thorns to separate them for his normal wages.

What was needed, as Harriet had said, was a real sacrifice. Something that hurt. A loss that would ache for a long time, maybe always.

As I examined my life, I found, to my horror, that I didn't have anything like that.

What could I offer, after all, that was mine to give? A favorite ribbon? A blobby painting of the regiment? An imaginary love affair? My life, I saw, was little more than a collection of trinkets. The only thing of value I had was Kitty herself, and I wasn't prepared to give her up.

But Kitty had something.

Kit hissed, sounding almost like her old cat-self, as she realized what I was thinking. "No," she spat. "Don't you dare."

I looked to Harriet. "Can we sacrifice something of Kit's?"

"*No*," said Kit.

Harriet looked at me. "In the eyes of the craft," she said, "Kitty is yours, which means anything of hers is yours to give."

All right, then.

I held it in my mind, carefully, like a soap bubble, gathering all the things I'd ignored, overlooked, barely considered until today. The way Denny whispered jokes in Kitty's ear during dull recitals. The flower he'd cut her when we'd all gone berry-picking, now pressed carefully between two novels. The way she craned her neck looking for him anytime we entered a party. Their foolish grins. The way they leaned toward each other, like two cats about to rub necks in pleasurable adoration.

Kit was screaming at me now. "If you do this, Lydia, I'll scratch your eyes out! I'll tear you to pieces! I'll never, ever forgive you!"

I did my best to ignore her and continued on. This was the only way to save her life. She'd understand in time. If Kit was a normal human girl, what would happen from here? Denny would approach our father. He hadn't much money, but Kit was young, and they could have a long engagement while Denny sought his fortune. If he found it, he'd come back and they'd marry. Perhaps he'd advance enough in the ranks of the army to support her. She'd be an officer's wife, like Harriet. A commonplace little life, following their commonplace little love story.

All this I held cupped in my hands. I lowered it toward the center of the spell-shape. Kitty's red-rimmed eyes locked on mine. "Please," she sobbed. "Please don't."

"I'm sorry," I whispered.

Her eyes hardened. "At least let me say goodbye," she said.

I bit my lip and nodded.

She didn't wait. She yanked her shift over her head and took off down the hill, her long legs pumping, heedless of how her breath wheezed as she scrambled after Denny.

He was straggling behind the little procession of officers and he half laughed as she slammed into him from behind. "Easy, there, Miss Kitty."

She threw her arms around him and buried her face in his shoulder. He patted her awkwardly and turned. "There, there, love. What is it?"

She pulled back and looked into his eyes fiercely. "Don't forget me, Denny," she said. She didn't look like my sister anymore, or my pet, or my familiar. She was a woman rendered ageless and unrecognizable by agony.

Maybe whatever Harriet had given him to make him biddable was still in effect. Maybe he just trusted her. Either way, he asked no questions. He pressed his forehead to hers. "Never, Catherine," he said. "Never."

Slowly, she pulled back from him. "Go," she said. "Get that cut seen to." Then she turned back and looked at me with sullen rage. "Do it, if you're going to."

I lowered my cupped palms and offered Kit and Denny's love to the hungry spell. And it took hold.

There was a flare of something. Not light. It was a bit like when your hairgrips slide out in public. There's the relief, of course, of not being so tightly bound. But there's also a wrongness to it. That terrible slackness, the feeling of something carefully constructed sliding away. The shame of it. The knowledge of how hard it will be to put back.

I felt as though I had gone numb. It was Kitty's absence, I realized. I had always been able to feel where she was without thinking about it, the way my left hand can find my right elbow in the dark. After a moment of groping, I located the thread connecting us, but it was too loose now to tell me where she was. I found her only by opening my eyes and looking down the hill.

It was done, then. We were—not separated, but separable.

I looked at Harriet. She nodded.

"If you and your son give back what you took from Kit," I said to Wormenheart, "and you promise not to hurt her, we have a bargain."

*DONE,* that horrible voice roared. A great flood of power flowed through me to Kitty. The unhealthy flush left her cheeks. She stretched, took a deep, clear breath, and changed into a cat.

Wickham cleared his throat. "Well," he said. "I'll see you in Brighton." And with a bow, he set off down the other side of the hill toward the regimental quarters. Harriet followed him.

Kitty and I looked at each other. There was half a hill between us, but it felt like much more. I started toward her, expecting that she would wait and then jump on my shoulder, but she turned and trotted toward home without a backward glance.

For the first time in our lives, I lost her in the shadows. When I got home, I found her sleeping by the kitchen fire, still in cat-form. I tried to scoop her up but she scratched me. So, for the first time since I was a little girl, I slept in a cold, empty bed all alone.

# CHAPTER EIGHTEEN

Do you know I actually look forward to my writing time now? It's terrible sometimes, thinking back over it all, but it feels good, too, getting things sorted out in my mind. I always had a horror of thinking things out before. I suppose I didn't want to face what a foolish, selfish little minx I really was, but there's something bracing about facing it after all.

I haven't even got to the part you expressly wanted to know about—the Brighton bit. I will, I promise—that's a real promise, a witchy one, so I shan't wriggle out of it. But something has happened. I'm not sure what, yet. I walked to Miss Darcy's school yesterday and found it all closed up—no one there but an old caretaker, who said all the girls had been sent home. If he knew why, he wouldn't tell the likes of me.

When I got home, I had another surprise. A hansom cab was waiting outside our lodgings, and in it were all our trunks.

As I stared, openmouthed, Wickham turned and spotted me. "There you are," he said crossly. "Get in. We're leaving."

"Where are we going?" I managed.

He shoved a letter into my hand. Here is what it said:

*Wickham—*

*We're at the Bingleys' estate, Baily Hall. Come at once. I forget nothing that has passed between us, but much can be forgiven if you and your wife can put this right. And yes, I'll pay. For pity's sake, man, it's Georgiana.*

*In haste,*

*Fitzwilliam Darcy*

Before I'd had time to absorb this, he picked me up and set me in the carriage. "We've got to hurry or we'll miss the post," he said, and off we went, before I could even snatch one last look at the little lodgings where I sat and wrote most of this.

I'm in an inn, now, scrawling out this last page as Wickham snores beside me. I don't know what's happened to Georgiana, or what will happen when we get to Derbyshire. I may not have a chance to write for some time. So let's just call this the

## END OF PART ONE.

P.S. We caught the post in plenty of time. I think the real reason Wickham was in such a hurry was so he could skip out on the rent.

# PART TWO

# CHAPTER NINETEEN

We have been three days at Bingley's home and still no one will tell me what is going on. Everyone is acting exceedingly strange. Elizabeth remains at Pemberley—she is in "too delicate a state for this kind of shameful affair," her husband proclaims, which is a fine way to learn that one's sister is expecting a child—and Bingley has sent Jane to keep her company. I suspect what their husbands really wanted was to keep them away from me.

Baily Hall is usually a very pleasant house. It is like the Bingleys themselves: neither imposing nor elegant, but friendly and comfortable. I usually enjoy my visits here so much that I don't leave until I have positively worn out my welcome. Quite shameful behavior, I'm sure, but without my sojourns at the Bingleys' table I don't think I could keep body and soul together.

Now, though, everything has changed. Most of the staff have been sent away, whole wings closed off, and we are obliged to keep to the few open rooms and pieces of furniture not covered in Holland fabric. It is positively gothic and I'm losing patience with it.

Wickham, Darcy, and I are the only guests. Darcy walks about the place with a face like a thundercloud. Sometimes I think he's about to speak, but then he changes his mind and stalks off. With no other females about, it is impossible for me to talk to Darcy alone, and I refuse to ask Wickham to accompany me. Every time I see him, he gives me that ironical look as though daring me to beg his assistance. I shan't. Shan't, shan't, shan't. These three fellows brought *me* here, apparently to beg my help, and it's up to them to broach the subject.

I own I'm most awfully curious though. I hear the oddest noises, especially at night. Howls and shrieks like a wild animal. Has Bingley bought a tiger? It sounds like something he would do. Perhaps it ate Georgiana. She's certainly not here, as I expected her to be. There's no lady's maid here, either, and Mr. Darcy, Mr. Bingley, Wickham, and I are the only people sitting down to dine.

Oh, would it *really* be so bad for me to corner Darcy on his own? It is a little absurd that I, who have fought demons and transformed animals and called down cyclones, can't do something as simple as meet with a man alone. But that man is married to my most tiresome sister and I will *not* have him or Bingley carrying tales back to their wives of my impropriety. I am sure they all four glory in shaking their heads over my shameful ways and I shan't give them any excuse to do so.

Unfortunately, between my determination to spite Wickham and to behave correctly before my brothers-in-law, I am left with nothing to do but wander the grounds and continue with my manuscript. I wish Georgiana *were* here. Then at least I'd have someone to talk to, even if it was a someone who kept trying to teach me about isosceles triangles. What did Darcy mean, "It's Georgiana"? I hope she's all right.

I admit it—I'm more than curious. I'm worried. I have that tipping feeling in the base of my stomach I get when something is about to be my fault. Should I have laid more protections on her? Maintained them better? Did the person who sent that ink-spell strike again? For God's sake, why won't anyone tell me what is going on?

Georgiana was the first one in months to speak to me like I was a person and not a contagious disease. That may only be because she hasn't enough common sense to find me as disgusting as she should, but it was a pleasant change nonetheless. I hope she's merely eloped with some handsome young man and that's what's vexing Darcy.

Anyhow, there's nothing to be done about it for the moment, so I shall continue my tale for you.

The practicalities of how to get myself to Brighton were more difficult than expected. I thought that, having fought a dragon to a standstill, the non-magical aspects of the business would simply sort themselves, but I thought wrong. If there is anything fiercer than a dragon, it's Papa.

My original intention was to persuade my family to remove to Brighton for the summer. Kitty could stay behind, pleading illness or something. But I did not even get that far. The morning after we parlayed with Wormenheart, I went straight to Mamma and told her about the regiment going to Brighton. I did not even have to say anything else.

"To Brighton!" she said. "My dear Lydia! How dull, how empty your life should be without all your friends in the regiment! And of course Brighton is quite a healthy place, too—I am sure it is just what poor Kitty needs for that dreadful cough." (This was the first time I had heard her bring up Kitty's illness.) "As for me, my poor nerves have been an absolute plague lately—I am sure that sea-bathing would be the perfect balm." She stood up. "We must certainly ask your father at once to take us there. Brighton! They say the public balls there are some of the most amusing in the country."

The lovely thing about Mamma is that she understands things like this so completely. There are other things she doesn't understand. Witchy things, of course, and more than that—loyalty, sacrifice, anything that's difficult, really. But when it's a question of having fun, Mamma is as reliable as the rising sun.

Unfortunately, so is Papa. It would not have mattered if the Prince Regent himself was waiting in Brighton to make me an offer—nothing would stir my father from the comforts of his library and his fire and his chair that he had spent decades perfectly molding to the shape of his behind. Mamma and I wheedled him for days but he would not be moved. Kitty was no help. She had hardly left cat-form for days. The family still saw her as a girl of course, but she really put no effort into the façade. She even left a hairball on the sofa, which made the parlormaid look at her very oddly indeed.

It was a great strain on me. I could not tell them *why* I wanted to go to Brighton so badly—"I must go to save Kitty, who is a cat really, from a dragon who lives under the church" would hardly have helped my case—and in consequence my whole family thought I was demanding to go on a whim. It was a tiny bit mortifying to see that none of them found this at all surprising. I may be silly but I'm not *that* silly.

The wild energy that had filled us during Wickham's slow attack still shivered in the air, but it was weaker now, and easier to resist. Still, every time I ran into Wickham and he gave me that ironical smile, I felt sick. Wormenheart may have agreed to our terms, but we were still in his clutches. I *had* to get to Brighton.

I poured out my heart to Harriet one afternoon. "And the worst of it is," I told her, "now that Lizzy and Jane are back, Lizzy makes the most *scornful* faces whenever I bring up Brighton. I want to slap her! If she only knew. If we *did* go to Brighton, she would probably have a marvelous time and end up married to a viscount or something, while I'd have to spend all my time searching for that propriety thing."

Harriet made a sound of sympathy. "It's awfully hard dealing with the non-magical in one's family. My brother is forever telling me what to drink and when to sleep, because he says he takes much better care of his health than I do of mine. Little does he know I've twice cured him of consumption and once of the French disease!" She shuddered delicately. "They've no idea how hard our lot is. We do *so* much for them."

"Yes," I said fervently, although in truth it had rarely occurred to me to use magic to do anything for my family, and I wasn't sure what the French disease was. "Oh, Harriet, what am I to do?"

"Well, my dear, I see only one possibility. I'll have to invite you to come along with me."

I stared at her. "Truly?"

"Of course. It's better that way anyway. We don't want to be forever tripping over those hundreds of sisters of yours."

I acknowledged this. "Won't the colonel mind, though?"

"I'm sure he won't," she said. "He wants me to amuse myself. And he's always telling me not to bother him with my girlish prattle. I'm sure he would be delighted if I had a friend about to keep me company. I'll have him send the invitation tomorrow."

The colonel did as he was bid, and wonder of wonders, my father acquiesced. For the next few days I flew about the house in a frenzy of wild excitement and relief. Now that my travel plans were settled at last, I began to think of the trip as more than a dire necessity. Brighton! And on my own, too! No glowers from Mary, no scolds from Lizzy, no Papa of any kind. Of course the most important thing was to find the whatever-it-was to save Kit, but still: I was to see Brighton!

Kitty, the ungrateful wretch, did not share in my joy. The whole time I was packing my trunk, she wandered the house yowling at the top of her lungs. The rest of the family interpreted this as the sulky sobs of a girl feeling left out, but I could hear her plainly, and it was all I could do not to cover my ears.

In truth, I was a tiny bit glad to get away from Kitty, too. I was not accustomed to feeling guilty, but somehow she made me feel so. Every time I ran into Denny, he was as jolly and obliging as ever, full of cheerful stories about how he and three of his brother officers had all managed to cut their hands on the same broken gate. But something was off. He would open his mouth, as though about to inquire after Kitty, and then close it again, frowning.

Well, I'd acted for her own good! How could I have done otherwise? And besides, even if I had left their attachment alone, Denny could hardly have wedded a cat, could he?

Still, every time I turned round and found Kitty hissing at me, I felt a lurch of guilt.

I did my best to put it out of my mind. Mamma was glad to help with that—she was full of glad chatter of all the fun I would have, and all the dancing I'd do, and all the officers I'd meet. In their way, my father and sisters helped, too. Disapproval rolled off them in waves, so even if I had entertained some small private doubts about my upcoming journey, I could not give them the satisfaction of showing it.

On the day that Harriet Forster called to take me away, she brought several of the officers to luncheon with her, including Denny and Wickham. At the sight of her former love, Kitty deigned at last to transform back into girl-shape; but Denny gave her little more than a polite hello before turning away to speak with enthusiasm to his brother officers about a stallion one of them was thinking of purchasing.

I felt Kitty flinch; but when I turned to offer a word of comfort, she gave me such a fierce scowl that it died on my lips.

I wondered if she could still feel her love for him. Did she still have that need to be near him, that purring delight at his presence? Or had I left her with nothing but the memory of how it felt to love?

I turned resolutely away. Unfortunately, on my other side was Wickham. He gave me that charming smile that now made my skin crawl.

"Good day," I said coolly. "How is life as a demon?"

He laughed. "Profitable. One of my attributes is luck when my power is high, so I've won prodigious sums at cards of late."

"And why is your power so high?" I asked. "Have you been eating poor young girls' souls away?"

"Come, Miss Lydia," he said. "We ought to be friends, you know. We will be often together in Brighton."

"You tried to kill me."

"I *saved* you. And besides, you will never find what you seek without me."

"We'll see about that."

At last the luncheon was done. The servants packed my trunks in Harriet's carriage, and my family tumbled outside. I hugged everyone, even Papa, and Mamma cried and hugged me again; but when I came to Kitty she simply flickered back into cat-shape and trotted away.

While the servants and officers struggled in merry disorder to secure my trunk, I slipped after her. I found her by the hearth where she spent most of her time now. She hissed and put her ears back when I tried to stroke her.

"I do think you might be a little nicer," I said. "I'm doing this for you, you know."

She growled, low in her throat.

"I had no choice about using your attachment to Denny. You know that. There was nothing else."

At that she looked up at me, her yellow eyes enormous. *And whose fault is that?* she demanded. *If you hadn't led such a foolish, empty life, you would have had something of worth of your own to sacrifice.*

"You might have told me," I said. "You were there every step of the way."

*No one can live your life for you, witch. You must mend it yourself.* She curled up with her back to me. *And you'd better do it soon. I suspect this won't be the last sacrifice asked of you, and you've already used up the only thing in the world that mattered to me.*

I thought *that* was a touch dramatic. She and Denny had only known each other a few months, after all. But the insult implied in her words hit me as hard as she no doubt intended, and I couldn't speak for the lump in my throat.

It is about a hundred miles from Longbourn to Brighton—by far the longest journey I had ever undertaken. We spent a night in London and three more at inns along the road, then stopped to stay with the colonel's uncle in Eastbourne. Despite the jostling of the carriage and the indifferent food at the inns, my excitement never waned. Harriet smiled at me indulgently as I kept my face glued to the window of the carriage as we left the home of the colonel's relations. The men of the regiment rode around us as a kind of honor guard, and took turns riding next to the carriage to pass the time. I would have been swollen with pride to be the center of all this elegant masculinity if I weren't so overwhelmed. Luckily, Wickham had gone ahead, so at least he wasn't there to plague me.

"You look like your eyes are going to pop out of your head," said Harriet. "Come, have a sweet and sit back with me."

She unwrapped a twist of white handkerchief full of boiled sweets and held it out. I selected one and sat back, thinking. Her clean handkerchief had reminded me of the blood-soaked one from that terrible night. "Harriet," I said, "do you often get power from the men that way?"

"Only when it's necessary," she said. "Does it shock you?"

She said this very kindly, but I felt suddenly that it was quite important not to appear shocked. I was going to Brighton with a sophisticated witch of the world. I would not behave like a country mouse.

"No," I said as carelessly as I could. "I was just curious, that's all."

She nodded. "Not all of us are lucky enough to have a familiar like you do. I am quite careful, of course, never to take too much. I know you country witches prefer to sacrifice a cockerel or a snow-white lamb, but I always found that distasteful, don't you?"

"Ye-es," I said. "But... well, don't their hands get rather sore?"

"You funny little thing! I don't do it *that* often. And besides, there are plenty of officers to choose from."

The thought of the men's bloody hands still made me uneasy, but I did not want to appear ungrateful for all she'd done, so I changed the subject. "What do you know of this *Jewel of Propriety* thing?"

She frowned. "Very little, I'm afraid. I know it's an item of great power. There are supposed to be several of them in Britain, balancing the power of the craft. But truthfully I had barely heard of it until Wickham mentioned it. And I know a great deal about witchcraft."

This was true, it seemed. Like me, Harriet was raised to the craft by an older female in the family. In her case, it was her mother, and her education had been much more systematic than mine. I knew only one don't-notice-me charm, and she knew three that worked in different ways.

And when I mentioned that my aunt had told me to avoid love spells, because they so often did not work, she pursed her lips and looked away.

"Isn't that true?" I said.

"Well…perhaps for a woman such as your aunt. She probably never had proper training." Seeing my face, she leaned over impulsively and put her hand over mine. "But you're not to worry, Lydia. You may have picked up poor habits, but you've obviously a strong natural talent, or else you'd never have attracted Wormenheart's attention."

"What good is natural talent, if I'm ignorant of how to use it?"

"That," she said, "is why you have me, silly." She patted my hand. "I'll teach you all you need to know and more. Now take a deep breath. Do you know what that is?"

I breathed in. There was a wild, salty scent on the breeze. I had never smelled such a thing before. "The sea! It's the sea!"

"Yes, Lydia."

As we drew nearer to our destination, the smell grew stronger. At last we crested a hill and there it was: dazzling and vast, the biggest thing I had ever seen in my life. I felt rather small and humble—as humble as I ever do, anyway. The size of it, the *power* of it.

Once again, Harriet laughed to see me. "Those parents of yours are shameful," she said. "They ought to have shown you more of the world. It's not right for a young witch to be shut away in such a dull, shallow pool of magic as Meryton."

"They don't know I'm a witch," I reminded her absently. I stretched a hand out the window toward the sea. Its vastness called to me. It was like a high, wild fiddle wailing above a staid quadrille. It made my heart beat faster and whispered promises in my ear. If I could just—

Harriet gave me a sharp poke in the arm with her finger. "I wouldn't, if I were you," she said. "The sea takes more than it gives."

"But it's so—"

She shook her head. "I know. It *feels* like it could power all your spells for a lifetime and never feel the lack. And I daresay it *could*, but that kind of power isn't to be trifled with. Try to fuel so much as a simple charm with it and you may find you've swum a mile from shore with no way to return. The sea likes to keep what it attracts." She tilted her head. "I daresay the charm would work, though. And you'd be the prettiest drowned corpse in town."

I shuddered and pulled my hand back in. "No thank you."

One more change of horses, and we were nearly there. The grass had grown sparser, and here and there where it had been cut away I could see that the turf beneath was white. One of the hills we passed caught my eye. It was covered in the same long green grass as the rest, but in some spots the texture of the grass seemed to change. Certain lines and patches were a deeper green than the rest, as though furrows had been cut in the ground beneath and the grass had grown back even longer and lusher. If I squinted, they outlined the figure of a man, holding a staff in each hand. The figure must have been hundreds of feet long.

"Look!" I said, pointing it out to Harriet. "What's that?"

She frowned and said she had no idea. One of the officers, Ensign Fulton, pulled his horse alongside us. "That's the Long Man," he said. "Or the Green Man, some call him. He's been there for hundreds of years, they say."

Fulton was a very young man—a boy really—and usually too shy to talk. Now he was smiling. A hint of the southern accent crept into his vowels, making them longer and rolling. I remembered that he had grown up about these parts. "Hundreds of years!" I said. "Who made it?"

"No one knows," he said. "Some say it was the old papist monks, or the Romans before them. Me, I think it was the wild people who were here before the birth of Christ."

"But that would be nearly two thousand years!" I said. "How could simple turf cuts survive that long?"

"I don't know, miss. Where I grew up they used to say that the Green Man was a drawing of one of the wild people's old gods. Superstitious folk used to leave offerings for him sometimes. It was said he'd strengthen your hand against your enemies, or bring you knowledge you seek. Of course," he added hastily, "none of *my* connection would ever do such a thing. We're educated, God-fearing folk."

"Of course." I looked at the Long Man, and he seemed to look back.

At last we arrived in Brighton. Our lodgings were not glamorous, but still tucked within the boundary of the fashionable part of town. I would realize after we had been there some weeks that we'd been lucky to get them. It was late May, and Brighton would soon swell with visitors, as it did more and more every summer.

The morning after we arrived I woke bursting with excitement, wild to see the town. Imagine my disappointment when I found it was pouring rain. There was no question of our going out. After breakfast, Harriet joined me at the window where I sat disconsolately.

"Don't you fret," she said, with a mysterious smile. "The day is not quite spoilt." She pulled out a little bunch of ribbons and began to braid them together. I caught a scent of something sweet and flowery and lovely. I had a sense of her gathering power, just as her fingers deftly gathered the ribbons. And then the clouds parted and a brilliant sky appeared.

I stared at her, openmouthed. "Harriet! How did you do that?"

She laughed. "Don't expect me to fix the weather every day. It only works when the wind is just right. Still, rather a neat trick, don't you think?"

"Oh *yes*," I breathed, looking up at the clear blue sky.

When I think of Brighton, I think of color. Meryton was all respectable blue-grays and faded violets, but Brighton seemed to burst with an abundance of hues. The red stripes of the regiment's tents, the candy-colored pastels of the ladies' gowns at balls, the soft cottony white of the clouds. It all looked sweet enough to eat.

And, of course, in the corner of my eye, that glimmer of purple.

We settled quickly enough into a routine. Harriet had not been to Brighton in some years, but she already had various acquaintances there and brought with her numerous letters of introduction, and we were immediately welcomed into the social whirl.

In the morning (or the "morning," depending on how late we had been awake the night before), we would breakfast with the colonel. He was a kindly man, and always inquired as to whether we were amusing ourselves; when we replied that we were, he retreated into his newspaper. Once he had left to drill his men or whatever it is that colonels do all day, we would have a bit of magic tutoring.

Harriet was a stricter teacher than my aunt, but a kinder one, too. I could often see that she was shocked by my lack of knowledge, but she did her best not to show it, merely offering gentle correctives. Under her tutelage, I learned to weave much subtler, finer glamours than the brute-force don't-notice-mes and look-I'm-prettys that my aunt had taught me. She also showed me how to prepare and keep my herbs better so that even small spells were more reliable and powerful.

"Of course your aunt is correct that fresh herbs are best," she said. "But they are hardly the most efficient. If I were to spend an afternoon gathering herbs every time I wanted to do the slightest complexion-brightening charm, I would never have time for anything else—and my complexion would be quite ruined by all the time outside. If you dry and keep your herbs properly, you can do ten spells in the same time."

Harriet was wonderful. She was like an older sister to me—the kind of sister I had always longed for. She was as pretty as Jane, as clever as Lizzy, and had nothing at all in common with Mary. Perfection. Most of all, she approved of me, in a way that my sisters never had (except for Kitty, but she was different). I felt that she *saw* me.

"I'm so glad I found you, Lydia dear," she was wont to say. "A witch of the first water ought not to languish in obscurity."

I often felt guilty for how much time and energy she invested in me, but with the benefit of hindsight, I can understand her motives a bit better. My awe of Harriet made me treat her as a wise elder, but in truth she was only nineteen, with a husband over forty. I know now how lonely it can be to be the young wife of an officer. Colonel Forster was much kinder to her than Wickham is to me, of course, but he treated her with a kind of fond condescension that might have been galling had she not had a young friend to condescend to in turn.

All in all, though, they were a very happy couple. Harriet was not in the least romantic, and was exceedingly proud of her husband's position and the way he doted on her; and he, in turn, took every opportunity to show off his pretty young wife to the world. She told me that her mother had laid a web of spells to secure his proposal of marriage; something I was sure had been unnecessary given how he adored her.

She smiled when I told her so, but said, "You may be right, but she preferred to leave nothing to chance. From what I hear, my husband liked to dance and flirt with many a young girl before I came along, but none of them ever got him to the altar, did they?"

"I suppose not," I said. "But then, none of them was *you*."

"What an extremely agreeable houseguest you are," she said.

After magic lessons we would put away our herbs and thread and go visiting. If the weather was fine we would go and see some of our friends about town, and then go walking on the Steyne, to hear music from the band and see if we could spot the Prince Regent or his mistress. If the weather was bad we would stay at home and some or other of the officers would come to keep us company. Denny was usually among them, and Ensign Fulton, and Captain Carteret. Wickham was often there as well. Of course the roster of visitors varied, depending on their duties, and which of them were nursing an ale headache or occupied with avoiding debt collectors; but those four were so often in our company that they became known around town as "the honor guard." I found the attention extremely gratifying.

At first I felt awkward around Denny, remembering the devastation on Kitty's face that night on the hill. But it soon became clear that he really remembered none of it. He asked after Kit, but only as one who had been his particular friend; he did not seem pained by the memory of her. But nor did he seem inclined to pursue any other ladies, aside from a dance here or there, and he treated me with the same cheerful comradeship he always had, so I was mostly able to put his and Kitty's romance out of my mind. He was learning new "magic" tricks with cards, and it was going very badly.

Fulton was one of the youngest men of the regiment, and the shyest. He came along to Harriet's parlor with Denny or Carteret, who had taken a shine to him; but on days that they were occupied elsewhere he did not dare to come on his own. As for Wickham, Fulton worshiped him so thoroughly that he could hardly speak in his presence; friendship did not come into it. Fulton had grown up in Brighton, the son of a clergyman who had died when the boy was young. It had taken a whole family's worth of church uncles and lawyer brothers to scrape together the funds to buy his commission, and he lived in eternal terror of letting them down. The regiment's arrival in his hometown had given him a small measure of confidence, though. He knew the area as none of the rest of us did, and the surest way to draw him out was to ask him about the town and its environs. Brighton was the only subject on which he could state an opinion without looking anxiously at his brother officers after for validation. Except for his timidity, Fulton was considered an extremely promising young officer. He was diligent, clever, and one of the best riders in the regiment. Colonel Forster spoke of him often with approval, and it was widely expected that given a bit of luck he would climb high in the ranks. They were all careful not to tell him so, because the weight of those expectations probably would have paralyzed him with fear.

Carteret was a smoothly handsome man in his late twenties or so. He was always impeccably attired, and had the most exquisite manners you have ever seen. He was the youngest son of an earl, and had grown up among the first families; he could therefore put on a dazzling show of aristocratic charm that would admit him into any circle of his choosing. However, his exquisite manners were all the inheritance he had from his noble family. With seven older brothers, there was little money for him once his commission was bought—little from his perspective, anyhow. To a boy like Fulton, Carteret's small private income and employment of an excellent valet were the height of wealth, but they were certainly insufficient for Carteret, whose passion for fashionable clothes meant he was usually in debt. Many pretty young ladies set their caps at Carteret, but he paid them no mind. He swore he would only marry a woman of immense fortune. "For," he proclaimed, "I could betray my family for nothing less."

"Betray your family? By marrying?" I said. "What do you mean?"

"I am the youngest of eight sons, Miss Bennet," he said. "*Eight.* Did you know that every son of an earl has a different duty?" He took my hands and held them up, folding down my gloved fingers one by one as he counted. "The first son, of course, inherits the title. The second son inherits such property as his mamma brought to the marriage, and stands ready in case his older brother should die. The third goes to the church, the fourth dies in infancy, and so on, and so on down the line. By the time you get to number eight, the only thing he can possibly do for his family is to die honorably in battle and not leave any needy relations behind."

"That's horrible," I said.

"Yes," he agreed cheerfully. "But it's not so bad. Knowing one is to die in battle soon is a great weight off one's shoulders. And if you want to save my life, all you need do is find an immensely rich lady and get her to marry me."

"I wish I could adopt you instead," I said. "As my brother I mean. Your whole life is spoilt because of too many brothers, and my life is spoilt by the lack of even one."

"Now, Miss Bennet. We are neither of us spoilt yet," he said. "We've our wits and our pretty faces. Come, we are called to the card table. Let's rob young Fulton of his pocket money."

At first I was not best pleased that Wickham was always there, too, but it did not occur to me to try to make him go away. I was used to the restricted society of Meryton. One's social options were so severely limited that it was quite common to be friends with those one could not stand. And mostly, he left me alone. Sometimes I would catch him watching me; but he would quickly avert his gaze. It gave me great reassurance that I seemed to unsettle him nearly as much as he unsettled me.

In the evening there were balls, card parties, and dinners. Sometimes we would go out at night on the Steyne to watch fireworks over the palace. Every day in Brighton contained more excitement than a month back in Meryton. I adored it. I could not believe people chose to live any other way. Everyone in Brighton seemed to be exactly like me: determined to wring every drop of enjoyment out of life.

Yes, I know what you are thinking. What a frivolous manner in which to spend my days, when a dragon was waiting to eat me. I should have been searching for the jewel, not—quite literally—dancing my life away. I have no defense, except to remind you that I am inherently wicked, and was also at the time very young. Brighton at first so overwhelmed my senses that I could think of nothing but the next amusement.

Wormenheart seemed so very far off, and in the light of day I found it hard to believe that Kit and I were really in any danger. Surely such things did not *actually* happen, did they? Not to gentlemen's daughters.

Each night, as I fell asleep, I pledged firmly that I would make up for lost time in the morning. I would go straight to Harriet and insist that we begin our search in earnest. I would not waste another moment on frivolity until the jewel was in my hand.

But in the morning, I would feel lost at sea. I did not even know where to begin searching for the jewel. What if I couldn't find it? What if I let Kit down? Even more than I already had, that is?

Such thoughts were so painful that my mind shuddered away from them. One more day of distraction, I would promise myself. One more day of joy. That will fortify me for the difficult task ahead.

And so I went on, for nearly three weeks.

# CHAPTER TWENTY

Why did Darcy call us here in such haste, only to have us cool our heels? It's too vexing. I even asked him about it the other night on one of the rare evenings that he joined us for dinner—forget getting him alone, I want to *know*. I could not come right out and say *Is your sister under some dreadful enchantment?* of course—not in front of the others. But I dropped delicate hints.

"You know, Mr. Darcy," I said, "I became acquainted with your sister when we lived in Newcastle."

"I know," said Darcy.

"You did?" said Wickham.

"A dear girl," I said. "How is she, I wonder? I was sorry to see her school close so suddenly."

"Well," said Darcy. "That is...she has been ill. There has been some improvement of late, so we have hope that it will not be necessary to—" He cleared his throat. "I will give her your regards."

"Thank you." I took a delicate sip of soup. "A *dear* girl. I was quite—*enchanted* with her." Another sip. "*Bewitched* really."

"I pray you will excuse me, my man is calling me," Darcy said, and rushed from the room. Wickham looked at me quizzically, and Bingley went white with consternation and hastily changed the subject to the trout he had failed to catch that day. It is possible that delicate hints are not my forte.

So today I'm wandering the grounds again, folio in hand. I told them I was going sketching, and they nodded as though they believed me, though really the Bingleys' grounds are not much worth sketching. They are nicely laid out and will be lovely one day, I suppose, but right now they have that scrubby, depressing look a new place has when all the trees are too short.

There was one fly in the ointment of my Brighton delight. (Other than my imminent death by dragon, I mean.) It was a girl. Her name was Maria Lambe.

Long before I met Miss Maria Lambe, I began to hear of her. She was the orphaned granddaughter of a South Seas planter, and she was the heiress to an enormous fortune. The whispers were that her grandfather's lands comprised half the island of Sainte-Josephine, where she had grown up. The old gentleman's son had married a local freedwoman, who had borne Miss Lambe. She had sailed for England to find a husband and take her place in society.

One of Harriet's acquaintances, a respectable widow named Tomlinson, was to act as the girl's companion while she was in Brighton. "She's to rent the finest lodgings in town," she said proudly while calling on Harriet one day. "Finest still available at this late date, I mean."

"Was she presented in London this past Season?" asked Harriet. "I did not hear of it."

"Oh no, not her. Soon as she set foot on our shores, she fell ill, poor thing. The climate doesn't agree with her. That's why she's removed to the seaside, you see—to take the cure. She's spent these last few weeks in Sanditon, but didn't care for the company there. So to Brighton she comes. And as I told her in my letter, if it's gay and jolly society you want, Brighton is the only place to be." She winked at me. "I shall be sure of introducing you, Miss Bennet. A rich young beauty like her is sure to have lots of young men buzzing about, and those who don't succeed in winning her may look about for the nearest flower."

"How kind," I said sweetly. "I'm sure I shall be lucky to win the attentions of her cast-off suitors."

Mrs. Tomlinson roared with laughter. "You're a proud one, aren't you!

Especially for one whose fortune is no bigger than my little finger. I hope you learn a bit of humility, girl, before you lose your chance."

Lose my chance! I was fifteen.

It seemed to me that this Miss Lambe sounded exceedingly sickly and tiresome. However, this was an opinion I kept mostly to myself, for all of Brighton was awaiting her coming with bated breath. Everyone agreed that she would be a great beauty, and immensely charming, and wonderfully accomplished. Even her delicate state of health was spoken of as something that added to her charms—"For," as one would-be admirer said, "there is something very pleasing and feminine about a delicate constitution."

"Well," I muttered to Harriet, "that certainly makes *me* want to be sick."

I was predisposed to dislike Miss Lambe before even meeting her. Since my arrival in Brighton I'd been something of a novelty, and cries of "Here's little Miss Lydia Bennet and her honor guard!" often greeted our arrival at parties. I enjoyed this notoriety, but now it seemed to be supplanted with talk of Miss Lambe. However, this prejudice against her could have been easily overcome, you understand, if she had been at all agreeable. I like most people, you know. It is one of my few good traits.

In any case, I first met her in a ballroom. I was having a jolly evening, dancing with all my friends, and flirting with an excessively handsome captain from another regiment who was whispered to have a rich old uncle who was very sick and very fond of him, when Mrs. Tomlinson approached. "Come, my dear," she said, practically trembling with borrowed importance. "My charge has arrived, and you shall be one of the first to meet her! Look, there she is, isn't she lovely?" And she gestured to a tall girl near the door.

Is there anything more vexing than someone wearing the wrong clothes? As I've said, Brighton is all bright hues, like its name, and the gowns in the ballroom were a riotous rainbow of yellow and fuchsia and green. The girl I saw was clad all in gray, marring the pretty picture like a little rain cloud. Not only was her gown gray, but it did not have an ounce of fashion to it; no frills, no lace, just a severe simplicity that had not even the grace to be the Grecian style so admired these days. (Grecian gowns may be simple but they display one's bosom wonderfully.) Her hair, too, was barely dressed, merely scraped back into a tight bun. It was as though she had dressed specifically to downplay all her best attributes, or perhaps specifically to vex me. Many ladies in the ballroom could not carry off the bold hues they wore, but on this girl, brilliant scarlet or magenta would have looked charming with her golden complexion; and I could see from the tendrils that sprang free from the sullen mass of her hair that she was blessed naturally with the curls the rest of us tortured into our coiffures with curling papers and hot irons. But did she allow them to hang charmingly framing her face? No, she had clearly done her best to brush them straight back! It was too bad.

When Mrs. Tomlinson introduced us, Miss Lambe did not smile and curtsied rather coldly. "How do you do," she said, then sniffed and took out a handkerchief to dab at her nose.

"How do you do, Miss Lambe? I hope you are finding Brighton to your liking?"

"It's as well as it can be," she said indifferently, "given how dismal the climate is."

In fact the weather had been rather lovely that week—all balmy breezes and soft fluffy clouds.

"Miss Lambe grew up in the South Seas," Mrs. Tomlinson put in. "Our English climate is rather a shock to her delicate constitution."

"I am sorry to hear that. I hope you feel quite well now?"

She looked at Mrs. Tomlinson. "Is it quite polite to discuss ailments in a ballroom? I thought people found it tiresome."

"I suppose," I said, through gritted teeth, "it is impolite to go on and on, but I assure you, I am not impolite to *ask* after your health."

"No offense taken, I'm sure," she said, and dabbed at her nose again. "I do feel a bit better."

I waited in vain for her to ask me a polite question in turn, but she did not, merely stared at the ground. I was about to curtsy and take my leave when a male voice at my elbow coughed meaningfully.

"Good evening, Miss Lydia," said Captain Carteret. "How are you enjoying the ball?"

I opened my mouth to remind him that he had already asked me that while partnering me in a reel, and we had agreed that the punch was too sour but the musicians were superb, when he darted his eyes meaningfully toward Miss Lambe.

It's a very good thing I never harbored any *tendresse* for Carteret myself, or I would have been quite hurt at his use of me as a stepping-stone. As it was I was only annoyed. "Miss Lambe, may I present the Honorable Captain Willoughby Carteret," I said. "Captain Carteret, Miss Maria Lambe."

He bowed deeply and beautifully. "How do you do, Miss Lambe."

"How do you do."

Even under the full force of his charm, she softened but a little. After extracting a bit of small talk from her (no, she had not been to the Steyne yet, only to the bathing huts to be dipped; no, she had not seen the fireworks, for the night air did not agree with her), he said, "I would be honored if you would join me for a dance, Miss Lambe."

He said this quite humbly, but I could see that he expected her to say yes. Indeed, his left elbow was already rising to lead her onto the floor when she said, "No thank you."

The moment of shock on his face was comical—like Kitty on the rare occasion when she misjudges a jump from the top of the armoire to the shelf. Then, like Kitty, he instantly recovered his poise and affected an attitude of unconcern. "Perhaps your card is already full? If so, then the next time we meet—"

"You misunderstand, sir. I do not dance. I try to avoid unnecessary frivolity."

"But dancing is a very necessary frivolity, I assure you. Especially with so elegant a creature as you." He smiled that charming smile.

She turned to Mrs. Tomlinson. "Is this one of the beguiling, danger-ous fortune-hunters I have been warned to stay clear of?"

Mrs. Tomlinson looked as annoyed as I felt. "No, dear. Captain Car-teret is quite a respectable gentleman."

"Is he? How much is his fortune then?"

Mrs. Tomlinson turned quite red. "My dear Miss Lambe," she hissed. "I do not know how things are done in the Indies, but here we do not ask such questions."

"I do not know how things are done there, either, for I never attended balls back home. But I am quite certain that that *is* how things are done here. I have not been here above ten minutes and I have already over-heard multiple conversations about who has what fortune, simply by standing near the petits fours." Her stuffed-up, clipped voice continued as she nodded to me, "For example, Miss Bennet here has only a thou-sand pounds, and an entailed family estate, which, I am informed, is a fortune so paltry that even a much prettier face than hers could scarcely attract any suitors worth having."

My mouth fell open. Here was a rudeness so absolute, so sweeping, that one almost must admire it. Perhaps I would have admired it, had I not been its object. "At least if I do gain any suitors," I said before I could stop myself, "I shall know they were attracted by my moderately pretty face and not by my fortune."

At that point, Carteret intervened. "Your candor is charming, Miss Lambe," he said smoothly. "The truth is that I am, indeed, a man of little fortune. If my relative poverty makes me a fortune-hunter in your eyes, I shall not burden you with my presence any longer. Come, Miss Bennet, let me conduct you to your next partner." And he bowed.

He whistled lowly as he led me away. "What a sourpuss!" he said. "We'll have a hard time cracking that stony heart."

"Carteret! Do not tell me you're still planning to pursue her?"

"A man who owes as much to his tailor as I do cannot be overly nice about selecting a bride."

"Willoughby Carteret, if you marry that sour-faced thing I'll never speak to you again."

"I shall dry my tears with fifty-pound notes."

I saw Miss Lambe frequently after that. Brighton's ravings over her subsided for the most part. They had been prepared to be in raptures over an exotic hothouse flower, full of the passion and beauty of the South Seas; they got a reserved, sniffly woman who dressed like a Quaker and behaved like one, too. She seemed almost to revel in disappointing them. I suppose I can understand that; being expected to be a hothouse flower at all times sounds rather exhausting. However, I do think she took it further than necessary. A number of young men, drawn by her fortune, still endeavored to fall in love with her, but she rejected them all, and with little respect for their feelings. Indeed, she seemed to go out of her way to make courting her as painful an experience as possible. One young man wrote her a sonnet titled "To My Orchid of the Islands"; she corrected the spelling and gave it back to him, in public, loudly explaining the difference between *their* and *they're*.

Carteret's pursuit of her fell off. "I shall wait until all the less skilled adventurers have exhausted themselves," he explained. "Then I shall swoop in and dazzle the lady with the depth of my understanding of apostrophes." I wasn't sure if he meant it or was just covering his wounded pride.

I found Maria Lambe's behavior irritating. I tried to just ignore her, but somehow I could not. She was everywhere I went, Mrs. Tomlinson in tow—or perhaps it was the other way around. She seemed determined to have no friends. At concerts, she'd frown down anyone who dared to whisper during the performance and stayed glued to her program during intermission. At balls, she'd stand to the side, delicately hiding yawns behind her fan until she could wheedle Mrs. Tomlinson into taking her home early. When walking on the Steyne or by the seaside, she wore the deepest bonnet and carried the most enormous parasol you ever saw, the better to pretend not to see an acquaintance.

If I had behaved so, I would have been dropped by society at once. It drove me mad to see that this was not the case with Miss Lambe. Money covers a multitude of sins; and if she was not exactly the darling of the Brighton set, still she was invited to move in the best circles.

It drove me so mad, in fact, that I actually tried to fix it with magic. I had been practicing my glamours with Harriet and could use them much more precisely now. When I saw Miss Lambe waiting on the sidelines of another ball, wearing that hideous gray dress buttoned up to the neck again, I couldn't abide it any longer.

First I altered the color of the gown. I didn't want to do anything too radical—most people had entered this gathering not knowing magic was real, and it was probably prudent to make sure that they left in the same state. But I warmed the color of the gray gown with just a hint of soft lilac. I longed to do more, but first I congratulated myself on the effect of my small change. Some illusions require more time and preparation, but this one was easy—the gown *wanted* to be pretty.

Before I could do anything else, Miss Lambe glanced down at herself. With a cluck of irritation, she brushed her hands over the fabric and returned it to its dull gray. Then she turned and glared straight at me.

"Oh," I said. "I didn't realize you were a member of the sisterhood. Sorry."

She looked me up and down. "Ah, it's you. Of course."

"What do you mean, 'of course'?"

"It was a childish prank, and you, Miss Bennet, are a child."

My anger was all the greater because I was definitely in the wrong. "I'm not a child. I was trying to *help*."

"Help!" she said. "The only help you can give me is to stop wasting magic on my appearance."

"Very well, now I know that you're a witch, I'll stop using my glamours on you. Though to be frank, I was doing everyone a favor by giving them something to look at besides that gray gown."

"I do not care what the foolish people in this frivolous town think of my gown," she said coldly.

"Why?" I nearly exploded.

"What?"

"Why don't you care? What have these people done to earn your scorn?"

"I don't scorn anyone," she said stiffly.

"Oh yes you do! You hate Brighton. You loathe its amusements. You despise its people. So why are you here?"

She opened her mouth and closed it again. Finally she said, "It's not by choice."

"You have made that extremely clear," I said. "Good evening, Miss Lambe. I shall strive not to trouble you in the future. I am sorry I cannot promise the same on behalf of all the 'frivolous people' in this town who have tried to be kind to you." And I made my frostiest curtsy and walked away. Before I did I thought I saw a flash of something— surprise? hurt?—in her face, but I would not spoil my beautiful exit by looking back.

I was still fuming when Wickham claimed me for the next dance. Somehow he always managed to snag a waltz with me.

"I saw you talking to Miss Lambe," he said. "Does that mean you've begun your search for the Jewel of Propriety at last?"

A flash of guilt made my cheeks heat. I'd still made no meaningful efforts toward finding the thing. "I don't know what you mean," I said.

"Ah," he said. "I assumed that Miss Lambe had given you a lead of some kind."

"A lead? What kind of lead? She is a witch, right enough—did she say something to you?"

"No. But can't you see it?"

"See what?"

He shook his head in amazement. "I thought I'd seen the extent of your obtuseness when you thought you were in love with me, but clearly

I have just scratched the surface. Tell me, Miss Bennet, have you detected any sign of the jewel since arriving in Brighton?"

I frowned. "Just little glints here and there." Indeed, I'd often seen flashes of purple in the corner of my eye. There seemed to be no rhyme or reason to them—they appeared on the Steyne, out by the bathing huts, once in the lending library. Another time I'd chased one across the street and nearly got run over by the mail coach. It was maddening, and in the end I'd decided they were just a sort of meaningless miasma giving no specific information about the jewel's location, and did my best to ignore them for the time being.

"Indeed." He shook his head as he led me through a particularly vigorous twirl. It took me by surprise, but his steady hand at my back kept me from stumbling. He may be a soulless demon but the man can dance. "I never cease to be amazed by your capacity not to see what's in front of your face. Here, I'll show you."

The music had drawn to a close, and under the guise of giving my hand a gentlemanly kiss, he took it in his own and drew one finger up the inside of my wrist, rucking up the fabric of my glove.

I gasped. He'd given me something like a pair of magical eyeglasses. I could see every bit of magic in the ballroom, and it was immediately clear that Brighton was a much witchier town than I'd realized: There were far more illusions and glamours than just my own. One lady's diamond necklace flashed with a these-are-real glamour. A middle-aged dowager's midriff was belted in a don't-notice-my-arms charm. A beautiful young woman had a make-her-smell-bad jinx tied to her foot.

I swayed, clinging to Wickham's arm in disorientation. "There are so many of us!"

"Not that," he growled in my ear. "Look." And he nodded to the side, where Miss Lambe sat.

This time I almost cried out. The purple glint of magic surrounding her was so strong it hurt my eyes.

"Wherever the Jewel of Propriety is," said Wickham, "it is clear that Miss Lambe has spent significant time in its proximity."

My heart sank as I realized the full implications.

"Bother," I said. "I am going to have to be her *friend*."

I paused my writing for a few minutes because I heard voices coming through the grounds. I'm on a little stone bench at the bottom of the ha-ha, so Darcy and Bingley did not see me as they walked by above.

I ought to have announced myself, but before I could I heard my name.

"—Mrs. Wickham becoming rather impatient?" Bingley was saying.

"She'll wait," said Darcy. "I still have some hope that Georgiana may come out of it on her own. She knew me yesterday. Asked for bread and butter with cinnamon—her favorite when she was a child, you know."

"That's wonderful, Darcy," said Bingley in a hesitating voice. "But— the other part—is it no better?"

A long pause. "No," said Darcy.

"Then for God's sake, man, why not ask the girl for help? Isn't that why you brought her here?"

There was an even longer pause. I could hear Darcy whacking at the shrubbery with a stick. "Because," he said at last, "I cannot be certain that Mrs. Wickham is not the one casting this wicked curse."

Well, of all the cheek!

# CHAPTER TWENTY-ONE

O h Lord. At least now I know what's going on.

After the conversation I overheard, I was too angry to write. I went to my rooms and paced and fumed. (A good thing there's plenty of room for pacing here.)

I know Darcy and I did not exactly part on the best of terms. Nor am I precisely blameless for what happened last year. But nor is he! As well he knows!

And now to drag me from my (as far as he knows) happy home in Newcastle, all the way to Derbyshire, and then to have the gall to say that I'm to blame!

By the time the bell rang for dinner my fury had hardened into an icy rage. I dressed in my finest gown (all right, not precisely *my* finest. A tradesman delivered some new dresses for Jane yesterday and I've borrowed one. I'm sure she would want me to) and got one of the few maids remaining in the house to help me with my hair. I looked *very* pretty and much older—at least twenty, I daresay. It certainly produced an effect. When I entered the dining room Bingley and Darcy looked quite startled, and Wickham arched his eyebrows and raised his glass to me almost imperceptibly.

I waited for the conversation to die down, then said, "Do you think the weather will be fine tomorrow?"

Bingley smiled. "Yes. Yes, Miss Lyd—Mrs. Wickham, I daresay tomorrow shall be one of the finest days yet this year."

"Excellent." I dabbed my mouth with my napkin. "A good day for travel then. Be so kind as to send Palmer to the inn tomorrow morning?

My dear Wickham and I shall depart on the afternoon stage, if it has seats for us."

"Leaving! So soon?" Bingley cried.

"Yes," I said, still glacially calm. (I'm not really much good at glacial calm, but Lord, is it satisfying when one can pull it off!) "Mr. Darcy asked my husband to bring me here to help with some problem with his sister. Since we haven't heard anything about it, I assume he no longer needs our help. We must be getting back to our affairs in Newcastle."

Wickham glared at me. Whatever his "affairs" in Newcastle are, I don't think he anticipates getting back to them so soon.

Darcy reddened. "The situation is—delicate, Mrs. Wickham."

"By 'the situation,' I assume you mean the enchantment or hex that your sister is under."

A shocked silence fell.

"Well, really." I dropped my napkin on the table. "Is witchcraft one of the things etiquette bars us from discussing at table? I don't think it can be, for no book of etiquette I've ever read mentions the subject."

Wickham snorted a laugh at that. "She's right, you know," he said politely. "You did ask us here. Why bring a demon and a witch under your roof and then not even tell us why? I, for one, should be happy to remain drinking Bingley's excellent wine and shooting his plump birds indefinitely, but I don't see what you gain by it, Darcy."

"At least," I said, "tell me how I can satisfy you that I am not—what was it you said?—not the one casting this wicked curse."

Bingley drew in a sharp breath. "Were you listening to us using a—" He dropped his voice to a near whisper. "A *spell*?"

His money is lovely and he's very sweet but I truly don't know how Jane can endure living with Bingley every day. He is essentially a St. Bernard puppy. "No," I said. "I overheard you by accident, using a ha-ha."

Darcy laid his hands on the table. "Very well, Miss Bennet," he said. "You're quite right. I did call you here because my sister seems to be under the effects of a dangerous spell. You are the only—" His jaw twitched. "—the only *witch* of my acquaintance, excepting her incompetent schoolmistress. And your conduct this past summer, *while far from commendable*"—I rolled my eyes—"did show a great deal of ability. And Georgiana mentioned you in her letters home to me—went so far as to call you a friend. However, scarcely had I sent for you than I uncovered some correspondence between Georgiana and yourself in which I discovered that you had actually been taking off the spells I arranged for her protection!"

I raised my eyebrows. "You read her letters?"

He looked slightly uncomfortable, then remembered that I was the enemy. "Don't venture to tell me how to take care of my sister. I had to try to understand what had happened. For her own good."

"Oh yes, certainly." I turned to Wickham. "No matter what happens to me, don't you dare read my private correspondence."

"Too late," he said mildly.

"Darcy," I said, "I took those spells off because they were *smothering* her. Why on earth would I want to hurt her?"

"I saw in her ledger that she was paying you," he said stiffly.

"And you thought I was—what?—using her to get a bit of coin?" I lost my last shred of icy calm as my voice rose to an outraged squeak. I *do* wish I sounded less silly when I'm angry. "Why do you think so ill of me?"

"I beg your pardon, Mrs. Wickham." He looked a little abashed, but his mouth stayed set in a grim line. "But—she's my sister. My ward. A man must protect his family."

A lump rose in my throat. Who was this Mrs. Wickham whom he must guard against? Who was this scheming, venal, debased woman he seemed to see? I felt dirty. I wished I could disappear. It's one thing to know I'm wicked, and quite another to have respectable young men treat me like a monster. "From me? I am your family, too, you know," I pointed out as steadily as I could. "And yours, Bingley. Much as you would like to forget it." And to my horror, I burst into tears.

For a few moments, there was nothing but the sound of me smothering my sobs into a napkin. I was suddenly so *tired*. I wanted Mamma there to put her arms around me. I wanted Jane—the old Jane, who didn't look at me with that little crease of disappointment. Lizzy even, the old Lizzy, who might scold me up and down in private but would have delicately filleted anyone who insulted me.

Dash it, what I really wanted was Kitty. And she was lost to me. All I had was these three embarrassed men, staring at the tablecloth.

I took my time collecting myself. No need to make them comfortable. As I gulped down my last sobs, I started when I felt a warm hand on my shoulder—for a wild second I thought I'd actually conjured Kitty there with my longing. But it was only Wickham.

"Right, Darcy," he said coolly. "You've insulted my wife for the last time. We'll leave in the morning and I'll thank you not to trouble us in the future."

I looked up at him. He was the picture of outraged husbandness. Anyone would have believed he really meant it.

I drew a shaky breath and tried to match his tone when I said, "Agreed." I knew we would regret severing this bond—Darcy might not like us, but much of our income came from his household—but in the moment I was too angry to care. I rose to sweep out on Wickham's arm.

Darcy said, "No, wait."

I stopped.

"You're right, Mrs. Wickham," said Darcy. "Come along. I'd better show you."

Darcy took up a lantern and led us out of the dining hall and up the stairs. He stopped at the door to the wing of the house that had been shut up and gestured us through.

Beyond the threshold it was dark except for Darcy's lantern. I stumbled over a rug, and Wickham grabbed my arm to steady me. "Careful," he said.

"Were you really ready to leave back there?" I asked.

His arm was warm against mine. "No," he said, "but Darcy did promise to pay. You can always get more out of them if you seem willing to walk away."

"I'll bear that in mind."

Darcy stopped at the door of a bedroom on the third floor. "Mrs. Wickham, you come in and see her," he ordered, then jerked his chin at Wickham. "You—stay out here."

"If you're asking me to leave my wife's side—" Wickham drawled.

"Oh, do shut up, Wickham," I said. I nodded to Darcy. "Show me."

And he opened the door.

One hears stories about families who treat their unstable members in the most shocking ways—locked up in freezing garrets, chained in cellars, that sort of thing. I will say this for Darcy: There were no garrets or chains here. It was a comfortable room, with a roaring fire, a few chairs, and a bed. A kindly-looking woman of around fifty dozed by the fire. Other than that, the room was rather empty of furnishings, and it was immediately apparent why.

Georgiana Darcy stood scrawling on the wall with a bit of charcoal. Her hair was long and loose and wild around her face, and she wore a white shift. She muttered to herself as she wrote.

Every wall, every part of the floor, even the bedspread was covered with letters and numbers and strange symbols. As I watched she ran over to write something on a patch of floor, heedlessly smudging the scratchings she passed over.

"From this we can see," she muttered, "given steps eleven and seventeen, 2 to the $n$th over $-1$ plus 4a is not natural. Wholly, wholly, wholly unnatural. I dreamed I was a leopard and the number of my spots was divisible by pi. QED."

"Georgiana," Darcy said in a soft voice.

I looked at him in surprise. I've hardly ever seen the man express an emotion that wasn't somewhere between "disapproval" and "extreme disapproval." But now his eyes were actually glinting with tears.

Miss Darcy looked up at her brother's voice. She froze, then looked at her hands, as though unsure how they came to be so dirty. "Fitz?" she said.

The woman in the chair stirred. "Oh," she said with a yawn. "Hello, sir. She was about the same today, I'm afraid. Didn't seem to know where she was at all."

"Nonsense," Darcy said fiercely. "She knows me now." He crossed the room and took her hands in his. "Don't you, Snubs?"

"Fitz?" she said again, a little more certainly.

"Yes, well, she's always a bit better this time of the evening." The woman got up with a creak of joints. "Good night then, sir, Miss Georgiana. I'll see you in the morning."

Darcy nodded absently and didn't look up as she left. He was busy guiding Georgiana to sit, and smoothing the tangled hair out of her face. "All right there, Snubs?" he said softly.

Georgiana nodded slowly. "Careful," she said when he tried to take her hand again. "I'll get charcoal on you. Fitz, I'm having such a strange dream."

"I'm afraid it's not a dream," he said.

"It's not?" she said. "Are you sure?"

This uncertain girl was nothing like the bright, keen woman I'd been meeting with. I felt suddenly ashamed to witness the proud Darcys in this moment of such vulnerability. But when I backed toward the door, Darcy looked up and said, "No. Wait."

So I took the chair by the fire, and waited as Darcy softly asked her questions. Some she answered, but to most she responded with nonsense or simply stared into space. She didn't acknowledge me at all.

Then the moon rose.

It ought to have happened with a flourish. A rising wind, a flash of light, that sort of thing. But it was nothing like that. Say this for whatever witch is tormenting her: They aren't showy.

One moment Georgiana was there, staring at her folded white hands; and the next, a great gold-and-white owl stood on the chair in her place.

I drew in a sharp breath, and the beast swiveled to look at me with enormous black eyes. Then it flew to the windowsill and began tapping the glass with its beak. Darcy walked to the window and threw it open. The owl spread its wings and ghosted off into the night.

"She'll be back before dawn," Darcy said conversationally. "I have to let her out, you see, or she hurts herself. Breaks the glass or bites at her feet if they're bound to a perch."

I winced. I had the strangest urge to pat his shoulder. I never expected to feel a moment's pity for Darcy, but of course I know what it is to love a sister who's slipping away from you.

"Well, can you help her, Mrs. Wickham?" he demanded.

I truly had no idea. "Is she—" I began, then, "Does it always—"

"Yes." His hands tightened on the windowsill. "Every night, she's— like that." He jerked his head toward the window. "And the rest of the time, she's out of her mind. Scrawling symbols and ciphers I can't make any sense of."

Thank God I could help with this at least. "I believe," I said, "that she's trying to prove Goldbach's conjecture."

# CHAPTER TWENTY-TWO

Feeling rather shaky and delicate this morning.

I'm still in bed now. I've decided not to go down for breakfast and asked for a tray to be sent up to me. After last night's ordeal I think it's best for all concerned if I don't impose myself on the company. Besides, I'm exhausted, and what good is having rich brothers-in-law if one doesn't at least indulge in the occasional luxurious breakfast in bed at their expense?

After I set down my account of Miss Darcy's condition, I set to work trying to remove the hex. It should not have been too difficult; I have ample experience peeling spells off her. However, when I attempted removal using my usual white linen technique, the results were dire. The linen caught fire; my dress caught fire; and Miss Darcy transformed into something that was decidedly not an owl. What is it that has claws, scales, feathers, and spits acid? I do not know, but Miss Darcy transformed into one and nearly ate me.

So for once in my life I'm going to think before I act. (Before I act again, at least.) Before attempting to remove it, I must figure out what this hex *is*. I shall do some very careful divining spells first of all, using the best tools money can buy. I'm composing a list of things for Darcy to send for. Herbs, both common and exotic, and fine embroidery thread for stitch-spells. (And maybe for my new gown if there's enough left over.)

Until I have what I need, Miss Darcy will simply have to stay as she is. I don't think that will do any more harm—her mental state, while unfortunate, is not deteriorating, and the owl looks well plumed and healthy. No doubt Darcy will think I'm wasting time, but so be it. I'm not willing to endanger Miss Darcy's life further for the sake of her brother's good opinion.

Until then, I'll write as much as I can about the Brighton bit. I know you must be getting impatient, and I suspect that once things get under way here I won't have much time to write at all. Poor Miss Darcy. I hope I'm up to the task.

Befriending Miss Lambe was easier said than done. I'd made it quite clear I had no use for her, after all. I tried apologizing. I called on her and expressed my remorse at losing my temper, and suggested that, as fellow young witches, we ought to know more of each other. She accepted my apology quite politely but never returned my visit. I sent her gifts of lemon balm and burdock, thoughtfully dried and bound up into little sachets ready for casting. She sent them back with a note saying thank you, but she never used them. When we met in the street she did not cut me, but made no effort to stop and chat.

Luckily, Mrs. Tomlinson was on my side. She had been charged by Miss Lambe's relatives to introduce her into society, and she was grimly determined that society there would be. She let me know Miss Lambe's schedule, so that I could arrange to casually run into her.

It was hard work. Miss Lambe seemed determined to turn the gay town of Brighton into the dullest place imaginable to pass the time. She was the only person of my acquaintance who really appeared only to be in Brighton for her health. Everyone said they were there to take the waters, but most only took a dip or two before nipping off to the theater or a ball. Miss Lambe took it far more seriously. And tragically, that meant I must, too.

Taking the waters is stupid and I hate it. There are far less unpleasant health treatments to be had in Brighton these days—perfumed steams, massages, even an Indian gentleman who does something to your head called "shampoo." But no, nothing did for our Miss Lambe but the ocean itself. Every morning—and far earlier in the morning than I would have preferred to be out of bed—Miss Lambe went down to Russell House on the shore for her sea-bathing. One morning, smothering my yawns and suppressing a slight hangover, I contrived to bump into her there.

"Good morning, Miss Bennet," she said. "I did not know that you favored early bathing."

"Good morning," I said. "Yes, I've been feeling rather overtired lately, so dear Mrs. Forster consulted her doctor, and he said a bit of sea-bathing ought to put me right."

"I hope so," she said.

"Do you come here every morning, Miss Lambe?"

"Yes."

"And do you feel it helps with your ailments?"

"Yes."

"How so?"

"It is very invigorating."

"Do you find it too cold?"

"No."

Very well then. I let her lapse into silence and go back to her book.

When it was time for Miss Lambe's bathing, I had a stroke of luck: One of the dippers came puffing up the shore looking apologetic. "I know you reserved a private bathing-machine, miss," she said to Miss Lambe. "But old Charley's cracked a hoof so there's only enough horses for one machine at the moment. Would you mind very much sharing with your friend?"

Miss Lambe looked deeply offended that someone had called me her friend, but she could hardly say no. So, aided by two dippers with armfuls of bathing clothes, we went into the sea.

It was my first time in a bathing-machine and I was interested into the process. They call it a machine, but it's just a wagon, really. You get in on shore, and then some extremely patient horses walk you out to sea a ways while the dippers help you into your bathing-clothes. Then, once you are a sufficient distance from shore that no men will be titillated by your enormous bathing robe that covers you from chin to ankles, you get out and—with the assistance of the dippers if necessary, who are very strong—you bathe.

Once I'd changed into the loose robe and turban, I turned to find Miss Lambe regarding me. "Have you bathed in the sea before, Miss Bennet?" she asked me.

"No," I said.

"Keep a firm grip on your dipper's arm, then."

I thought that was rather strange, for the waters at Brighton are famously quite calm. But before I could ask more, her dipper Mrs. Gunn announced, "Here we are," and opened the door.

Miss Lambe immediately walked herself carefully down the steps and—again to my surprise—slipped an arm round Mrs. Gunn's neck, so the dipper could carry her like a baby. *How foolish*, I thought. Of course that's what the dippers are there for, but they're intended for small children or serious invalids—not great girls who could easily stand on their own. I thought Miss Lambe must be quite as much of an imaginary invalid as Mamma.

But when I got in the water myself, I understood.

There are several things I hate about sea-bathing. First, there's the cold. It hits you like a slap from an enormous hand. I gave a great gasp and wondered if my heart had stopped. That's the first thing I noticed, and it would have been quite bad enough. But while I was still gasping and stumbling to get my bearings, the sea itself took hold of me.

Ever since that first day that Harriet and I came into view of the sea, I had learned to ignore its magical presence. Like the crash of the waves, its wild song simply became part of the background noise of everyday life in Brighton. I had completely forgotten that early moment when I had reached out to it and it had seemed to reach back. But when my skin hit the water, the song suddenly rose to a joyful crescendo, drowning out every other sound and sensation. The slap of cold, the dazzling, headache-inducing glare of the sun on the water—it all seemed to be part of the sea's song. Even now, it feels almost indecent to talk of it. Young ladies are not supposed to endure such strong sensations. The words to describe it without shame have not yet been invented.

*A witch!* that joyous voice seemed to say without words. *A witch, a witch, a little witch! Well met, well met, well met.*

*Well met,* I answered shakily. *I think.*

*Come away?* it pleaded. *Will you come, won't you come, won't you come away?*

It showed me, then, what it offered. Bright colors and underwater gardens, quicksilver flashes of fish, a world where one could fly high above the floor or creep along the seabed, a world where nothing stayed still but everything swayed to the same great heartbeat of the sea.

*Freedom,* it said hopefully.

I shook my head. Bubbles and waving strands of hair tickled my cheeks. *I'm not free,* I said. *I'm sorry.* And I was sorry. The world she— the sea—showed me was so riotously beautiful, it made Brighton look like Meryton. But of course I couldn't. Not with Kitty waiting for me.

*Trade,* she offered. She showed me: Wormenheart's fire drenched by her waters (she had only the vaguest notion that there were parts of the land out of her reach), me and Kit wrenched from his clutches, and Kit freed to go her own way, or to swim by my side. She would wrap us up in fur coats like a mother would, and we would dart off on our furred fins, our hoarse barking cries joining her endless song.

I could feel the lonely ache of her, the longing, yearning heart. I caught glimpses of some of what she'd lost. Other beloveds of hers, who'd stepped out of their skins and departed for the land of men, promising to return but never coming back.

*I can't, ma'am,* I said again. *I'm sorry.*

She could have kept me there. But the sea was no Wormenheart. It didn't want to eat me, didn't need my power. It was just lonely, and it wanted someone to come to it willingly. It gave me one last sad caress—

*"Miss Bennet!"*

Strong arms hauled me out of the water. I coughed and coughed, seawater pouring out of my nose and mouth. I looked into the terrified face of my dipper.

"Are you all right, miss?" she demanded. "You just went under!"

"I'm all right," I croaked once I could talk.

Miss Lambe and Mrs. Gunn were looking at us. "Why, miss, your friend must have the same fainting affliction as you," said Mrs. Gunn.

Miss Lambe turned her head, out to the open sea. I followed her gaze. There, for a moment, a little ocean-spray cat danced: the image of Kit.

"It appears she does," Miss Lambe said, "and quite a powerful case of it."

They bundled me into the wagon and took me back to shore. I kept repeating that I was all right, thank you, but really, I scarcely heard their queries. The afterimage of the sea still seemed to fill my senses, like ringing in one's ears after standing too near a rifle report.

Miss Lambe sat next to me, her cool shoulder pressing against mine through our soggy robes, the sensation grounding me. "Who was the cat?" she asked presently.

"My sister," I said absently, still distracted by the thrumming on every inch of my skin.

It wasn't until we returned to the bathhouse and I scrubbed off the seawater and put on my own clothes that I started to feel like myself again. By then, Miss Lambe was gone.

I never felt quite the same about the seaside after that. It's very strange to see people parade along the shore in pastel walking-dresses, or wade in silly bathing costumes, for all the world as if they were safe.

# CHAPTER TWENTY-THREE

After my little adventure with sea-bathing, I asked Harriet about it. "Oh yes," she said. "Many witches feel a little discomfort in the sea. I always have someone hold my arm. It's terribly invigorating, though." However, she said nothing of hearing voices or seeing visions of a life underwater.

Miss Lambe was the only one who seemed to understand. After that day she seemed far more willing to at least tolerate my company. She would allow Mrs. Tomlinson to invite me over, and would occasionally respond to my invitations in the affirmative, provided the activity I proposed was something she deemed "not totally useless."

"Yes, it shows you things," she said when I broached the subject of my bathing mishap. "Poor sea. It tries ever so hard to be seductive."

"Then why do you go back every day?" I asked.

"I like what it shows me." But what that might be, she refused to divulge.

In her company, I spent a great deal of time doing dull things, like borrowing books of essays from the library, and embroidering. Luckily my lessons with Harriet had included a significant number of stitch-spells, which had the side effect of greatly improving my embroidery. Quite often I tried to entice Miss Lambe to do some spell-work with me, but she always refused. Half the time she also refused to go out at all—she would claim a headache or a cold, and though she allowed me to hang about her parlor, she spent all her time furiously writing letters in silence.

I feel I'm being unfair here. Spending time with Miss Lambe was not such a trial as I'm making it seem. After the incident with the sea, she unbent toward me a little, and I began to see glimpses of her true self. She had a wicked sense of humor, for one thing. She could imitate Mrs. Tomlinson with deadly accuracy. "Now girls," she would say, wagging her finger at me, "the most precious flowers are those unbruised by masculine hands," and then give one of Mrs. Tomlinson's sniffs, and my sides would ache with laughing.

She wasn't quite as drab as she first appeared, either. When I managed to coax her out shopping, I'd catch her dragging her hand through a rack of colorful ribbons, or fingering a bolt of silk. She loved beautiful things quite as much as I did. She could afford them, too. But whenever I urged her to buy a new hat or commission a new gown, she dug her heels in.

I had never met such a strange, closed-off girl in all my life. How my sisters would have stared if they knew that in the gay pleasure-palace that was Brighton, I was spending all my time with a girl who was more prim even than Mary.

She really was sickly, too. She would no sooner recover from one bout of sniffles or sore throat than the next would begin. I suggested that perhaps she would feel better if she stopped jumping in cold seawater every day, but she refused, saying it was the only thing that helped.

"It's not the seawater that's making me sick," she said. "I don't belong here, that's all. I never get sick like this at home."

"England is your home," I pointed out. "At least it will be if you marry an English fellow. And isn't that why you're here?"

She gave me a sharp look. "And why are you here?" she said.

"The same reason as anyone," I said. "For fun."

"Fun, is it?" she said. "And that's why the sea is trying to entice you with images of a sister you never speak of, who is apparently a cat?"

I was quite content to let her change the subject after that.

And still, I could not make out her connection to the Jewel of Propriety.

It was extremely vexing. Even if she never did any spells herself, she clearly had a gift for spotting other people's, so I dared not throw divining spells about. I did my best to look about her apartments, but I never saw anything that could be a Jewel of Propriety—or any kind of jewel at all, really, since she continued to dress like a nun. I knew from some careless words by Mrs. Tomlinson that Miss Maria Lambe owned some of the most exquisite jewels in the country, and even allowing for Mrs. Tomlinson's usual exaggeration that still implied a very well-stocked jewelry box. But she never brought it out.

I felt guilty, as well, that I had been neglecting Harriet so. Her husband was rarely at home, and now I had deserted her, too. I tried bringing her with me a few times, but Maria never warmed to her, so we agreed that it was better if she stayed at home.

"After all," Harriet said, "the jewel is the real reason you're in Brighton. You mustn't neglect the search on my account."

"I hope you are not too bored without me," I said.

She laughed. "You sweet thing. No, I've quite enough to occupy me."

This was true, I soon learned. I came home early one afternoon because Miss Lambe had a headache and found that Harriet had gone out. I heard a noise in her room and, thinking it was Sally, the maid, I went in to ask her to mend my apron. But it wasn't Sally. It was Captain Carteret, standing at the mirror and tying his cravat.

He waggled his eyebrows when he saw me. "Oh dear," he said. "Caught. Hope I haven't shocked you too much, country mouse?"

"No," I squeaked, sounding like the mouse he called me. "Excuse me," and I backed out and shut the door, his mocking, fond laughter following me.

Well, that was Brighton for you. It was a town where the Prince Regent was rumored to have had a tunnel dug from his pleasure-palace to the house of his mistress; and everyone seemed to take their cues from him and loosen their morals a step or two. It was quite common to see couples, red-faced with drink, disappear together behind curtains at balls, and the local gossips discussed the rumored love affairs with more relish than judgment. I tried not to be shocked. Harriet took me aside and told me I mustn't tell anyone, especially her husband; but once I had promised I would not, she seemed quite as unconcerned as Carteret had been.

"Don't look at me like that," she laughed. "Good heavens, your scandalized little face! Your eyes are the size of dinner plates. Really, Lydia, it's no great thing."

"No great thing?" I echoed.

"Not at all." She turned to the mirror and began arranging her hair. "I doubt if even Forster would mind so very much if he knew."

"I don't know about *that*. He dotes on you."

Her eyes were merry and amused. "Yes. That he does. As much as he dotes on his prize mare. And that is high praise, for Midnight is the best hunter in the county." She piled her hair up and held up a pink comb to consider the effect. "And I adore him, too, of course. He is such a darling. But if a man of five-and-forty marries a girl of nineteen, of course he must expect her to find *some* amusement with those of her own age. Everyone knows *that*."

I had not known that, but not wanting to be thought foolish, I stayed silent. I adored Harriet and I did not want to believe that anything she did could be wrong. After that, however, I was careful never to arrive home before the time I had promised.

I had high hopes that Miss Lambe would finally avail herself of her jewelry box for Lady Herrington's ball, which was to be the event of the season. However, the day of the ball, she had a worsening cold, and finally announced her intention to stay in.

I threw aside my embroidery in exasperation. "Again?" I cried. "How can you stand to miss a night like this? Come on, get dressed. You'll feel better once you get there and see how pretty everything is."

"No I won't. Parties make me feel worse, not better. Talking to be heard above the music hurts my throat."

"Then don't talk!" I cried. "Don't talk! *Dance*, for heaven's sake!"

"You know I don't," she said.

I was extremely close to calling her some choice words I'd overheard from my regiment friends, but I remembered just in time why I had to be sweet to her. "Then let me try to mend your throat," I said. "I used to fix my sore throats all the time. I daresay you didn't need it in the tropics but it's quite a simple spell, actually."

"You can't," she snapped.

"Certainly I can," I said. "It'll just take a bit of lemon and honey, which I know you have, and a very small sacrifice." I waved the handkerchief I was embroidering. "This will do. It's not very beautiful, but it's the first time I've ever got that loop stitch right, so I shall certainly cry when I burn it."

I got up to go to the fire and do just that, but she leapt from her seat and snatched it out of my hand. "Don't you dare," she said. "Not for me."

I threw my hands up. "Why do you hate magic so much?"

She sank back into her chair, frowning down at my handkerchief. "I don't hate it," she said. "I respect it."

I blinked. I had never thought of magic as something that cared one way or the other about our respect. "What on earth do you mean?"

She turned the handkerchief over, pulling it through her fingers, tracing over the stitches. "All magic requires a sacrifice," she murmured. "But have you ever wondered what the sacrifice is *for?*"

"Well, it's for—" I paused. "Actually, I don't know."

"Nor do I. And why don't we?" Her eyes were piercing. "Isn't that strange? Shouldn't that have been the first thing they taught us?"

"The first thing my aunt taught me was how to cast a confusion spell on Cook so I could sneak an extra biscuit," I said. "That's a spell I find useful to this day."

She shook her head. "Don't pretend to be stupid. I know you're not. You must see it's strange. Every time we do magic we pay a price, but who are we paying?"

This made me decidedly uncomfortable. It had always seemed logical to me that magic carried a price. Everything else did, after all, from my shoe-roses for balls (sixpence) to a baron's eldest son (ten thousand pounds dowry, minimum). But now she was forcing me to envision who was collecting that price, and I did not like it. Who was that shadowy merchant who dealt in pain?

But that was absurd. We weren't paying a *person*. We were just *paying*, because...well, just *because*.

"That's why I prefer not to do magic," she said. "I don't like to pay someone I can't see. Or some *thing*."

"Judging by your wardrobe, you don't like to pay anyone at all."

"I only wear free produce cotton," she said. "It's the same thing. I like to know who I'm paying."

It is very trying to be friends with someone who's right all the time. "All right," I said. "You dress like a nun and you won't do magic, because you don't want to traffic in suffering. But I can think of something you could enjoy that's guaranteed to hurt no one."

"What's that?"

"Dancing!" I said. "Who are you helping by staying in the corner? And you're certainly hurting yourself."

"I don't care to dance."

"Nonsense. I've seen you swaying to the fiddle. You *long* to dance." A pathetic possibility struck me. She had grown up on a remote island, after all. "Or did you never learn how?" I softened my voice with pity. "I could teach you, you know. Nobody need know."

"Miss Bennet, I am *perfectly* able to dance."

"If you say so, Miss Lambe, of course I believe you."

"Good." She took her embroidery up again and I did the same. The waves rumbled in the distance.

"But if you should like me to *remind* you—"

She glared at me. Really, she looked much better when she lost her temper. She forgot to be prim and her eyes looked very pretty when they burned with rage. "Very well," she said. "I'll prove it. Come to Lady Herrington's ball tonight and you'll see."

I went home to Harriet's to get ready, feeling rather guilty. I had rather enjoyed our scrap in the moment—it reminded me of all the little fights Kitty and I used to have, and it was a relief to talk to someone that way. But Miss Lambe was not Kitty and I shouldn't have needled her that way, and I certainly shouldn't have embarrassed her about her dancing. If the poor thing could not dance, I could hardly blame her for acting lofty about it—I probably would have done the same.

My guilt only increased when the Forsters and I arrived at Lady Herrington's ballroom. She was a rich woman of more money than sense—Brighton's favorite kind of person. She'd had to withdraw her daughter from London in the middle of last Season, after a small matter of a married viscount and a monogrammed snuff-box, and she was determined to conquer Brighton society instead. If she would continue to throw parties like this, Brighton would be happy to be conquered. The ballroom, so newly built that you could still smell the paint, was immense; candles and colored lanterns glittered at every corner, and the tables groaned with every kind of delicacy. The finest musicians in town were playing, and—most unusually—a whole row of windows at the south end overlooked the moonlit sea. It seemed that all of Brighton was there to enjoy the spectacle, except Maria Lambe.

I pushed aside my guilt and did my best to have an enjoyable evening. I danced with all my honor guard, ambushed Fulton with the introduction of a pretty young lady just to see him stammer and blush, and tried as many kinds of cakes as I could. They were all superb, but were surpassed by the punch, which was simply scrumptious. It made me feel light and sparkling and golden, like I was made of champagne bubbles.

When the clock struck half past nine, the time when Miss Lambe usually succumbed to her yawns and fled, I knew she wasn't coming. At the time I was dancing a thoroughly enjoyable reel with Denny. A young woman with seven thousand pounds and a feathered fascinator had cornered him a few minutes before and begun tapping his chest with her fan, so I'd marched over and induced him to ask me to dance. Denny might not be Kitty's anymore, but I was not about to let some other girl have him. I owed Kit that much.

As soon as I'd taken him away, Carteret and Wickham slid in to flirt with the delighted young heiress, and Denny groused good-naturedly at me, "What did you have to drag me away for, Bennet? I was doing so well!"

"Don't talk that way," I said sternly. "You're not a fortune-hunter. Leave that sort of thing to Carteret and Wickham."

"As if I don't need money just as much as those fellows," he grumbled.

"We all need money," I said. "Get it some other way."

He heaved a great sigh. "Why I let you scold me this way, Miss Bennet, I really do not know. Anyone would think you were my sister."

*I almost was*, I wanted to say.

I took his hand to go down the dance one final time and he winced. "Careful there, Hercules," he said. "Ease your iron grip. My poor hand is rather sore. I hurt it awfully badly."

"Oh, sorry. What happened?"

"Cut it on a gate," he said. "Carteret and Fulton did, too. Good heavens, is that your friend?"

I had opened my mouth to ask him about these matching cuts when I followed his gaze and trailed off into silence.

Miss Maria Lambe stood in the doorway, surveying the company. But this was a Miss Maria Lambe none of us had ever seen before. Her hair was dressed in a becoming riff on the latest fashion, piled high on her head with tiny ringlets tumbling down, but instead of being bunched by her ears they fell gently here and there, as though styled only by a gentle breeze. Her gown—oh, I'd sell my own mother for a gown like that. Just thinking of it makes me ache with envy. She'd cast off her usual gray cocoon in favor of a dress of brilliant teal blue. Even for Brighton it was a bold color to choose, but it suited her sun-kissed looks admirably. It was cut in the Grecian style, almost as simply as her normal fashion, but infinitely more becoming. She carried a lace fan of teal and gold, and a gold necklace sparkled at her neck.

She was a beauty. She'd been a rotten, stinking *beauty* this whole time, and she'd deceived us all.

Now, what you must understand about what I did that night and the next day is that I ~~had to could not did not know~~

No. I'll make no excuses this time. I did what I did, and some of it was awful, and all I can do is try to explain.

Miss Lambe looked about at the slack-jawed company for a moment. She locked eyes with Carteret, and she smiled. He was already moving toward her and when she smiled he stumbled—actually *stumbled*—and then bowed low. He said something to her, and she nodded and laid her hand on his arm, and they swept out onto the floor for the next set.

She hadn't been lying: The woman could dance. She knew the steps, and glided through them with the ease of long practice. Half the eyes in the ballroom seemed to be glued to her graceful form. She danced like she'd invented it. Carteret's gaze scarcely left her face. I thought he was laying it on rather thick. When the set was over he bowed over her hand and kissed it and then led the applause, which seemed to be as much for her as for the musicians. As she graciously curtsied to him, I could see her scanning the room through her lashes, until she found me. She flashed me a look of triumph.

Carteret conveyed her over to the punch table and to me. After he'd reluctantly taken his leave to find his next partner, she turned to me and said, "You see? I *can* dance."

"You certainly can!" I punched her in the arm. "Why on earth have you been hiding that all this time? Think of all the fun you've missed!"

She looked startled, and I realized she'd expected me to be upset. I wondered what her life had been, to think that. Maybe I would have been, a little—but I was having too good a time to spoil it with resentment. I still felt full of giddy golden bubbles, and whatever annoyance

I might have felt was lost in a wave of affection for this beautiful night and this wonderful city.

"You're not angry?"

"Of course I am, stupid. Every girl in this room is furious with you. Mostly, though, I'm relieved that I can now pass the time with you doing other things than reading essays." I handed her a glass of punch and threaded my arm through hers. "Now drink up, I see at least three young men getting their nerve up to come over here and ask you for a dance. I would be obliged if you'd say yes to Sir Graham first, as that will oblige Captain Andrews to ask me, since I am right here."

"Oh, I—Lydia, I don't know." Her arm flinched in mine and she took a nervous gulp of punch. "I oughtn't to have done this tonight—only you goaded me so, you see—"

"All this is to spite me? Good. At least you have *one* vice. That makes you a much more agreeable friend."

"I ought to go home," she said.

"No, you ought to dance, for this is a ball. Come *on*, Maria. You can put your hair shirt back on tomorrow."

Her eyes darted to mine. I could feel her sway with longing toward the dance floor.

"Well," she said. "Perhaps one more. This *is* a ball, after all."

She danced every dance after that. At first, there was a hard, bright edge to her joy—she was relishing how she'd shocked us. But as the evening wore on, and she danced and ate and drank and flirted, she seemed to simply give herself over to enjoyment. She smiled more that evening than I'd seen her do in all the weeks I'd known her. I swear I even heard her giggle.

I, too, was having a delightful evening. I'd been to many beautiful parties in Brighton, but none so lovely as this. The golden-bubble feeling was everywhere. Harriet and I made a turn about the room, arm in arm, complimenting people's gowns and laughing at jokes we could not have explained.

"Dear, dear Lydia. How lucky I am to have you with me," she said, and I was filled with such a rush of love for her it nearly choked me. A dance finished up and Miss Lambe came to join us, eyes bright and cheeks flushed. She and Harriet usually kept a wary distance, but now they greeted each other with cries of delight and we walked the balcony arm in arm.

My two dearest friends, now friends with each other. It brought a glad lump to my throat. We found a bench and looked up at the stars, which seemed to shiver in time to the music. Honor guard members and Miss Lambe's admirers drifted by, bringing us punch and cake and compliments, but we did not make room for them to sit. We three were enough, sitting there entwined in perfect friendship. For the first time since Kitty was torn from me, I felt complete.

Dimly, very dimly, I began to realize that something was wrong.

I did not even think the word *wrong*. I was too suffused with well-being and love for all humanity. All I managed was "Something has happened."

"Many things," Miss Lambe said solemnly. "The fall of Troy. The invention of the cotton gin." Harriet giggled.

"Yes," I said, half laughing, too, "I mean—no—I mean—we're too happy."

"Too happy!" Miss Lambe slapped my arm. "Don't be a wet dishrag. You sound like—" She snorted. "—like me."

This struck us all as so hilarious that we laughed until we could not breathe.

We remained there awhile longer, admiring the scarlet and bronze notes of the music—"Have we always been able to see the music?" Harriet asked, without much interest—and then during the musicians' break Maria's partner for the waltz came to collect her, and Harriet drifted off to find Carteret for the same.

I was content to wait for Wickham to find me, as he always did. I was longing to waltz, and though usually by this point in the evening my feet had begun to hurt, right now I was certain that nothing would ever hurt again.

He did not come, however, and I was beginning to be cold without my friends, so I stood and walked to the end of the balcony. From the French doors in the ballroom it appeared that the balcony ended before the house did, but as I drew nearer, I could see it actually wrapped around a ways. Past some tall, potted topiaries, one came to a small secluded area that couldn't be seen from the ballroom. And there was Wickham.

He was leaning against the wall with his head thrown back and his eyes closed. His normal carefully constructed look had rather fallen apart. His coat was flung over a chair, and his cravat was untied, exposing the skin of his throat. His painstaking pomade had shaken apart into a mass of waves, cresting over his forehead. He looked undone.

"Hello there, Lydia," he said, without opening his eyes.

A chill went over my skin at the sound of my first name on his lips. Every little sensation seemed magnified tonight.

"There you are," I said, striving to paddle back to shore from the deep waters I felt I'd somehow wandered into. "Aren't you going to waltz me? Listen, they're starting."

His eyes opened at that. "I know," he said. "I can hear. God, I can hear it. How do you humans bear it?"

The waltz had started slowly, and he thumped his hand against his chest in time. One-two-three, one-two-three.

"Bear what?" I said softly.

"The music," he said. "A man in Austria wrote this—just a man, just a stinking, selfish, distractible human—scratched it out on tree pulp, and then it traveled across countries and through wars and arrived here, and though none of us speak his language and most don't know his name, he speaks to us exactly as he intended to. He tells our bodies how to move to it almost without learning the steps. One-two-three, one-two-three." A smile flitted across his lips. I was astonished to see that he had tears in his eyes. "God! How beautiful it is! And you all talk over it about what Lady So-and-So said to the Honorable Whosit yesterday on the Steyne."

I had never seen him like this. I had no idea what to say. My own hand had risen to my chest, and my fingers fluttered out the rhythm, too.

"I'm made of fire, you know," he said. "Fire and stone. If he regained his full strength, my father could kill everyone in this ballroom before they could choke out a scream. But I'd rather have the tinder-flare of a human lifetime than go back to him. It's not just the waltz. The taste of a glass of punch, the curve of a barmaid's breast, the frost of a winter morning—it all pierces me to the heart. God, why am I telling you all this?"

I tried to fall back on teasing. The waltz was slowly picking up tempo, and my heart seemed to be matching it pulse for pulse. "No need for tears for a simple waltz," I mock-scolded in a whisper. "And you a great boy of eight-and-twenty."

He opened his eyes at that and surged away from the wall. "I am not eight-and-twenty. I am ten months old, or nine thousand years. Nothing in between." Before I could squeak, he'd seized me in a waltz hold, far closer than propriety allowed. "Yes," he said. "In answer to your question."

"What question," I said.

"Am I going to waltz you." He began, slowly, to move. "The answer is yes, at every opportunity."

Stuffy people say the waltz is immoral, indecent. Men and women, together for the whole length of a dance. In most cases the stuffy people are wrong. The waltz is as mannered and chaste as almost any other dance. Usually. In a crowded ballroom. When one's partner is not a demon.

The dark and the stars and the moonlit sea whirled around me. I could feel his breath on my hair, my ear, my throat. His fingers trailed lightly up and down my side, leaving dark shivers in their wake. The space was too small for a swooping, elegant waltz, so our turns were small, but his grace made it feel as easy as anything.

Around and around. His gaze on mine. I was waiting for him to goad me or scold me or threaten to eat me, but he just stared and stared, his eyes glinting in the deep shadows.

One wild spin brought me against the wall. A *hic* sound was jarred from my throat but his hand cupped the back of my head, keeping its landing soft. Our feet weren't turning anymore but somehow it felt as though the waltz went on, the rhythm burning through my veins. One-two-three—he undid three buttons on my left glove. One-two-three—his lips trailed up the skin he found there. My breath hitched—and again. *One-two-three.*

Dimly I was aware that I should push him away, but how could I? How could anyone expect that? How could anyone else exist, outside of our own little corner? They tell girls like me to avoid a rake, and they tell us why—but nobody tells us *how.*

He'd reached the end of the buttons and he tore off the glove, letting it fall. He was kneeling now, his mouth hot against my palm. *One-two-three.* "God, what you do to me," he groaned. "I was made for you." He growled a laugh. "Literally."

I hissed and raked my fingers through his hair, yanking his head back. He looked up at me, lips swollen, hair in disarray, eyes wild and dark and utterly out of control.

For a long moment we regarded each other. I tried to think what to say. I wondered what he saw. Then he surged to his feet, capturing my hand and pinning it against the wall, and then his lips were on mine.

The rhythm went on, but I could no longer hear the music—just my own heart pounding in my ears. His mouth slanted over mine like a man who had kissed a hundred girls, and I, who had never kissed anyone, gave it all back to him. My other hand came up to his back to grip his shirt as though for dear life. One of his hands threaded my fingers with his against the wall, the other roamed my gown with abandon, and then took hold of my skirt and began to ruck it up. I gasped at that, but all I could think was *yes, more, yes—*

"Lady Herrington, you have absolutely outdone yourself. It's simply the event of the season."

We froze. The voice was less than ten feet away, and coming closer.

"Thank you, Mrs. Tomlinson." Lady Herrington's drawling attempt at an upper-class accent drew nearer. "And that charge of yours! If this is the event of the season—and *I* do not say it is, you understand, I merely repeat what you said—if it *is*, then she is the absolute belle of the ball."

"Well, thank you." Mrs. Tomlinson sounded smug. "She was dreadfully shy at first of course, but it seems my little lessons are beginning to take hold. A girl like that—her mother was... well, you know, no matter how you dress it up, from that barbarous island—of course she'd feel overwhelmed at first until a respectable Englishwoman took her in hand." There was a creak and twin sighs and I realized with horror that they had settled themselves on the wicker love seat just beyond the topiaries. I could have reached out and touched them. "I daresay she'll make a good match, even with—" She lowered her voice. "—the mother."

"Yes, I daresay."

"And, of course, it helped to have a really *superior* hostess to draw her out," Mrs. Tomlinson said. "Everything so charming and gay! And the punch! She simply adores it. What is it that gives it that... unusual... flavor?"

"Thank you," said Lady Herrington. "Yes, I'm rather proud of that. It's the usual recipe, but with a dash of Brighton seawater."

There was a strained pause. "Seawater?" repeated Mrs. Tomlinson.

"Yes! Isn't it brilliant? We all drink it the morning after overindulging anyway, so I thought why not add it to the punch and we'll all wake up fresh as daisies."

"How charming," Mrs. Tomlinson said dubiously. They moved on to other bits of gossip, but Wickham and I stood rigid in horror. Even though just a couple of scrawny trees stood between us and social ruin, we were still touching each other: my fingers moving on his back, his lips ghosting against my throat. Now I knew why we couldn't control ourselves. That golden-bubble feeling, that love for all mankind—those weren't my feelings. They were *hers*. The sea.

I must have made some sound, because he pressed his hand over my mouth. "Make them go away," he whispered in my ear. "Do it now."

I had nothing to sacrifice, but this one would have to be on credit. I raised trembling hands and put a few quick spell-knots into the only knottable thing handy—his cravat—and whispered the spell into his palm. *Go away, go away*, I thought desperately, and hoped the price would not be too much. Or maybe I had already lost enough tonight to pay the tithe.

It worked. Lady Herrington grew eager for the praise of more guests than one poor widow, and they rose, shook out their skirts, and went back inside. We sagged in relief.

For a long moment we looked at each other. Then Wickham looked over his shoulder toward the waves below. "You old *bitch*," he whispered.

I took a few steps away and tried to smooth out my dress. "So sea-water works on demons, too?"

"Apparently." He scrubbed his hands over his face.

"You know, if you were a gentleman, you'd be apologizing right now."

"If you were a lady, I'd have nothing to apologize for." I started toward the row of trees but he grabbed my arm. "You can't go out there like that."

I was suddenly mortifyingly aware of the state his hands had left me in. My coiffure was slipping down my head, my petticoat peeked unevenly from beneath my hem, and there was a great brick-colored smudge on the back of my dress. He was little better off. "Dash it," I said.

"You'll have to do another spell," he said. "A glamour. Make it a good one. There are witches in the ballroom."

I shook my head dizzily. Even now that the euphoria had faded, my mind still wouldn't clear. "I already did one spell without a tithe," I whispered. "If I do another—"

"Here." He pulled out his pocketknife and cut a slash across his palm. He hissed and said, "Will that do?"

"I think so." I swallowed and tried again to gather my thoughts. "If it hurts you, that is. Like it would a man."

"Like the dickens."

"All right then. Give it here." I took his hand in mine and squeezed the blood onto my handkerchief. Meticulously I built a glamour to put us to rights, smoothing his hair, cleaning my gown, putting my hair back up. Hard without a mirror, but when I was done he looked me over and nodded in approval.

"You'll do. Now get out of here, quick as you can. Don't give any of the witches here time to look closely at you."

"Hopefully they won't notice. If they tried the punch they'll be drunk as lords, too." I stilled, a fresh wave of horror washing over me. "Oh God. *Miss Lambe.*"

Good heavens, I can't believe I wrote all that. Perhaps I'd better burn those last few pages and give you a briefer summary. "The sea got me and Wickham drunk and we almost ravished each other" gives you all the essentials really.

I just got carried away remembering, I suppose. It's a very compelling memory, don't you think? In fact, though the story of the evening is far from over, I think I'd better stop writing for tonight. Even now, when the sea's intoxication is entirely absent from my body, I still feel...

Well. I'm just going to sit here for a few minutes and think very, very hard about how Wickham is so awful that I regularly threaten to empty a chamber pot over his head.

# CHAPTER TWENTY-FOUR

I found out later that the normal folk didn't even like the punch. To them, the seawater tasted foul. It became a running joke among the men of the regiment: Move heaven and earth to go to one of Lady Herrington's parties, but bring your own flask. Funny, isn't it: One silly woman tries to set a new fashion in refreshments, and unwittingly rocks the magical community to its foundations.

After I'd laid the best glamours I could on Wickham and myself, and tied them on so hard it hurt, I dived back into the ballroom. Immediately I was waylaid by Colonel Forster. "There you are, my dear!" he said. "Haven't seen you in an age. Care for a reel? You know I love a reel, child, and the wife's tied up with that cub Carteret again."

Indeed, Harriet was dancing with Carteret for at least the third time that evening. Her smile was as brilliant as ever.

"My own fault," said Forster good-naturedly. "Told the men, you know, that if they could not get a partner they were to apply to her. Doesn't do to look like men of my regiment can't get partners! But that fluff-brained Carteret always fails to get his name down with any girl till it's too late, so poor Harriet's got to stand up with him again and again."

This was a truly startling read on the characters of both Harriet and Carteret, but there was nothing I could say, so I merely said, "I would love to, sir, but I don't think I shall dance anymore tonight. My feet hurt awfully."

His look shifted immediately to one of bluff concern. "Poor child! Of course, of course. Just you talk to Harriet after this dance and we'll see about getting you home."

"Thank you, sir, but I must make sure Miss Lambe is all right first."

He shook his head. "You really needn't! Girl's got her own chaperone. But go on, little chick, play mother hen."

Colonel Forster was a dear man, but the way he treated me like a child could be rather trying. I was only a few years younger than his wife, after all. But then, he sometimes treated her rather like a child, too.

I left his side and went to stand by the dance floor, staring until I managed to catch Harriet's eye as she whirled past. She saw instantly that something was wrong, and murmured in Carteret's ear. He obligingly pulled them out of the dance and led her over to my side. Her cheeks were flushed and her eyes starry. The effect of the punch was still on her. However, it didn't seem to be as strong as it was for me, for her gaze sharpened when I explained the effects of the drink (though not what it had led me and Wickham to do) and she understood immediately.

"We've got to get out of here," she said. "Go on, tell the footmen to call for our carriage. I'll collect Forster and meet you by the door."

I shook my head. "I can't. Not yet. I've got to see to Miss Lambe. She's drunk more of the stuff than any of us."

"Oh, right. Her." She sighed through her nose and looked to the corner of the ballroom.

I followed her gaze and found Miss Lambe. There she sat, like a songbird surrounded by ravens. Half a dozen young men flocked around her. Though she directed most of her conversation quite properly to the drowsing Mrs. Tomlinson, the frank friendliness of her smile and the relaxed lines of her shoulders seemed to invite them all in.

She was not doing anything wrong. The picture was quite as proper as it was beautiful. I could hear murmurs of admiration even on this side of the room. I'd begun to move toward her but my steps slowed. For a moment I wondered if I ought to leave her alone. Perhaps for one with morals stronger than mine, the drink was not so dangerous.

"Miss Bennet," said a voice in my ear. "You've got to get Miss Lambe to go home."

I turned, and was surprised to find Ensign Fulton. I'd never heard the shy young man speak with such a firm, resolute voice before.

"What are you talking of, Fulton?" I said. "This night is a triumph for her. The air is full of her praise."

"Yes," he said. "For now. The wind will soon shift. If she values her reputation she must go now."

"Don't be ridiculous. Why should her reputation be in danger? She's not doing anything wrong."

"No," he said grimly, and took my elbow to bring me over to her. "But one doesn't have to do anything wrong to lose face."

I shook my head. "Nonsense. This is *Brighton*."

"Is that what you think?" His hand tightened at my elbow. "Miss Bennet, it may appear that this town does not enforce such strict morals, but I have lived here all my life and I assure you, it can be every bit as judgmental as London, and ten times as harsh." He jerked his head to a little knot of party guests we were passing. "Ah. Listen."

A snatch of conversation came to me.

"Such a beauty, isn't she?"

"Yes. And so exotic. Quite the talk of Brighton."

"That chaperone of hers will have a deal of trouble keeping the men away."

"A hot-blooded tropical creature like that—she draws the fellows in before they even know what hits them."

"I, for one, am enchanted. I dearly hope she'll come to my card party next week."

"Do they play cards on that island of hers?"

"Oh, surely she must. Her father was English, you know. And he was *married* to her mother."

"Why do you think she's been so dowdy up till now?"

"No doubt the chaperone's idea. Quite wise, when you think about it. *I* do not think she's done anything wrong, but *some* might say it's rude to monopolize all the young men in the room. And some of them are even attached, like my Margery's betrothed. Though I am sure *he* is merely trying to make a poor foreign girl feel welcome."

"Yes, surely. And she has done nothing but what a young lady ought."

"Oh yes, surely. Still."

"Yes, still."

I looked at Fulton and swallowed. A hot-blooded tropical creature? Miss Lambe?

Fulton's jaw was set grimly. "Now do you see?" he said. "If she leaves now she's safe. If not, her reputation may be gone by dawn."

"Right," I said. "Go and ask for her carriage, would you? We'll meet you there shortly." He nodded and I turned to go.

"Say, Miss Bennet—" he said.

I looked over my shoulder. "Yes?"

He frowned. "Nothing. For a moment I thought your gown was— but it was just a trick of the candlelight."

Right. Time to leave, immediately. A quick word to Harriet to explain the situation and then Fulton helped me, Miss Lambe, and Mrs. Tomlinson into the carriage and we were safely away.

When we arrived back at Miss Lambe's lodgings, she tumbled onto the divan. Mrs. Tomlinson was no witch, but luckily, she'd drunk enough punch to render her nearly insensate anyway. She was too sleepy to notice anything amiss with her charges. After the maid had seen Mrs. T into her nightclothes, I sent both of them off to sleep with a flick of lavender—Lord, I was doing a lot of unplanned magic tonight!—and breathed a sigh of relief. No more witnesses. I loosened my corset-strings and let the shreds of my glamour drop away. Somewhere out in the night Wickham's glamour fell off, too, and I thought I felt an amused twitch. *Warn a fellow before you do that*, I seemed to hear him saying. He had left before we did so I was not sure why it mattered, since he must be home in bed by now. I had a dim impression of warmth and darkness and softness.

*Ah, but not in bed alone.*

I cut off the last strings of glamour and left him to his debauchery.

When I returned to the parlor, I did not see Miss Lambe. I thought for a moment she'd taken herself off to sleep, but then I heard a sigh from the floor.

There was a very large, very fine carpet in the middle of the parlor. Cream, with deep-blue flowers. Miss Lambe lay in the middle of it, staring up at the ceiling with a dreamy smile. She'd let her hair down and it flowed around her head in a pool of curls. "I'm here," she said.

"Come on," I said. "Get up. We've got to go sleep it off. Do you know what was in the punch? Seawater."

She pushed up on her elbows to look at me in surprise. "Seawater? Oh, that's terrible." She began to laugh so hard she had to lie down again.

I sighed. My head had cleared somewhat, but clearly she'd had much more than me. I got down on the floor to help her with her shoes. "How much of the stuff did you drink?"

"I don't know," she said. "A lot. There didn't seem to be much alcohol in it, so I let them bring me glass after glass after glass after..."

"I see."

She raised an arm to point at the ceiling. "That's pretty, isn't it?"

I followed her gaze. In the center of the ceiling was an ornate bit of molding—an oval, wound with vines and flowers. I had scarcely noticed it before. In the flickering candlelight, it looked almost like the vines were real. "Yes," I said. "Very pretty."

"So little is pretty here," she said. "I don't know how you stand it. I suppose you know no better."

"We have pretty things here," I said, rather affronted.

But she shook her head vigorously, rolling it from side to side. "Not like home," she said. "So much was pretty there we quite took it for granted. You're just like me, Lydia. You need beauty like you need to breathe. When I go back to Sainte-Josephine I'll bring you with me and you'll see."

"What do you mean?"

She fluttered her eyes open to glance at me, then let them fall shut again. There was a flicker of movement by my hand where it rested on the rug. I glanced downward. The flowers on the rug were no longer flat abstractions. They were growing up out of the carpet, deepening in color, a purplish blue I'd never seen before. The color was so deep and vivid it made my breath catch.

"Sainte-Josephine is an island of six thousand souls," she said. "Small though it is, it is an important jewel in the colonial crown. We grow a kind of indigo there that produces a depth of blue that takes your breath away. We cannot compete in volume or price with India, but for truly fine, deep colors, the indigo of St. J cannot be touched. The finest coutu-riers will pay whatever is demanded for it."

The vines curling around the molding on the ceiling were no longer dead plaster. They'd begun to move and grow and deepen in color. There were vines curling up the legs of the couch, too. The sharp, young green of early spring. I could hear the crash of the waves—not so unusual here, but the soft rhythm was subtly different than the crash on Brighton's rocky shores.

"My mother was a free woman of color. Herself the daughter of an enslaved woman and a plantation owner, her father had freed her and gave her enough to purchase a small boardinghouse in town. She worked as a landlady and a doctress, and, privately, as an obeah woman. She had learned the craft from her own mother, I suppose. I wish I had known her better. My memories of childhood in her house are all tinged with gold, and no doubt oversentimental. I can remember little, except learn-ing the basics of obeah at her knee. The blue candle though, not the black."

The teal of her dress seemed to be spreading. Gently undulating waves pulsed it farther and farther across the floor and it turned into the sea, a bluer, more sparkling sea than I had ever seen. A warm, humid breeze fluttered my hair. I looked down and found that the cream of the carpet was now pale, sun-warmed sand.

I wanted to ask about unfamiliar words like *obeah* and *doctress*, but I feared to break the spell. It was extraordinary. I'd never seen a glamour like it. The darkened, impersonal parlor had all but disappeared, and we were on a warm sunny beach, gazing out at the blue water. I had to squint against the sun. I heard a chirp and looked down to see a little frog hop onto the back of my hand. I could see and feel and smell it all—and she scarcely seemed to be trying.

"It's beautiful," I said.

"Yes."

"I thought you didn't like doing magic."

She was silent for a long moment, letting sand run through her fingers. Then she said, "I've already paid the price for this one."

"Why did you leave this place?" I asked.

"Ah." She twitched a hand and the beach was gone, replaced by a large, sun-faded house with a wraparound porch—her mother's boardinghouse, I realized. "My father was a white man, hardly unusual in those parts—but what was rather unusual was that he married my mother. That caused something of a stir. I am told that when they returned from their honeymoon, they found that the white merchants in town had painted their door half white and half yellow, because—well, you understand. That is what passed for wit among the white planters in those parts."

Peering closer, I could see three figures on the porch: a dark-skinned woman with a broom, and a man with Maria's eyes and mouth bent over a little girl with a book. Little Maria, clearly.

"Father was a clerk for a shipping company and in his spare time, he led church services for the slaves on the island. It must have been difficult for him to reconcile his godliness with Mother's obeah. Maybe she kept it a secret from him. Or maybe they simply loved each other enough to overlook their differences."

The man tickled the girl, making her squeal with laughter. *Someday, Maria,* he said, *I will bring you to England, and you will show them that your race is capable of all that their sons and daughters are. You will set your people free.*

*Do not put such pressure on the child,* her glamour-mother said. *She's only a little girl.*

*Miriam was a little girl when she led Pharaoh's daughter to Moses,* he said. *Sometimes He calls on children do to His work.*

Miss Lambe shifted, rolling her head away from the happy scene. "It was not until I was much older that I understood why his interference on other people's plantations was tolerated. My family was happy but poor, living on the top floor of Mamma's lodging house. We had nothing to do with the great plantation families, or so I thought; especially not with the Big Man."

She twitched a hand and the domestic scene was gone. For an eye-blink, I thought I saw another girl: a dark-skinned girl, laughing in the sun. I blinked, and the image was gone.

Now we were looking at the island itself, as though someone had built a model of it, large and intricately detailed. I stood and walked around it. It jutted out of the sea like a jewel, ringed with white coasts. Inland there were patches of dark-green jungle interspersed with the more regular squares of farmland. It was surmounted by a tall mountain, which came to just above my waist.

"The Big Man owned more than half the plantations on the island, and controlled the harbor, too. Even the smaller growers had to go through him. He set the indigo prices, arranged all the shipping—essentially, he owned Sainte-Josephine. He lived back in England, and I never thought him more concrete than the man in the moon—until I heard someone refer to him as 'Mr. Lambe.'"

The scene was drifting closer to the island, one of the farms enlarging in my view. The square of green divided into rows, then into plants, and the specks around them became the hats and headscarves of the field-workers. I had never seen so many Black people in one place.

"That is how I learned that my shabby, careworn father was the son of the richest slaver on the island," said Miss Lambe.

Our view swept past the fields, up to an immense manor house overlooking them. It was as cheerfully painted as the Lambes' boarding-house, and was far more elegant; but somehow, I had no wish to step inside.

"I suspect I will never know the full tale of what passed between Papa and his father," said Miss Lambe. She still was not looking at the scene she showed me; there was an illusory vine of purple-blue flowers growing around her wrist, and she was blowing on it gently, training it to encircle her finger like a ring. "The version I was told was sanitized for a child's ears. Suffice to say, old Mr. Lambe sent his troublesome son to the island to manage his estates; when my softhearted father arrived, he fell in love with the place and became horrified by the treatment of the people. He and his father quarreled; he was cut off; and hence the Big Man's son, who could have lived like a prince, instead ended up in three cramped rooms over a lodging house. I suppose we would have gone on like that, and I would now be running my mother's boardinghouse, but for an accident of fate. The Big Man came to tour his estates, and a sudden ill-ness obliged him to stay far longer than he had intended."

We were back on the comfortable porch of the boardinghouse, with that same little family of three, but now there was another figure. A dis-tinguished old gentleman with a trim white beard and an elegant black suit, so pale that he looked almost ghostly. The little Maria Lambe clung to her mother's skirts, but her mother pushed her gently toward the man.

"My mother urged a reconciliation," said Miss Lambe. "Life for Sainte-Josephineans of color was becoming more and more difficult, and she foresaw that our existence, caught between enslaved Black folk and white enslavers, belonging to neither, would become unsustainable. My mother and father agreed about slavery, but my mother prized bread and coin and a soft place to sleep. My father, who had grown up rich and could be rich again if he chose, could wear his poverty as a badge of honor, but being poor was all my mother had ever known, and she knew she must always be vigilant to keep the wolf from the door.

"And so the Big Man began to come round."

Now it was old Mr. Lambe who sat next to little Maria as she went about her studies. He looked at her with mixed incredulity and delight.

"At first I did not like him; he seemed unduly astounded to hear me sing 'Amazing Grace' and recite my times tables."

*She sounds for all the world like an English schoolroom miss!* said the image of her grandfather. *And she is not so dark as I expected; why, I have known Spanish ladies who were more brown.*

"I thought his astonishment was very stupid and dull, but to a certain degree he won me over. It is hard not to like someone who likes you so much. He made a pet of me, bringing me all the sweets and gifts he could get ahold of. Remember, I was very small.

"He was lonely, I think. He had married very young, to a lady who did not suit him; she was dead by the time we met, and most of their children had died, too, leaving him with only one hectoring daughter and a troublesome son. In me he found a relation who seemed to have little connection to his troubles, and he delighted in my company. It is thanks to him that I can dance, for when he found out that the lady who taught the planters' daughters would not teach me, he paid to bring a teacher from France. 'That will teach them to snub *my* granddaughter,' he said. He brought me dresses, too; but here my father put his foot down, for he would not have anything made by his father's slaves in the house.

"His three-week visit to St. J turned into six months, then a year; he was talking of staying on for good when a fever came and took my mother. The old gentleman brought me with him then to live in his house."

The scene dissolved again. Now Maria, a little older and dressed in an elaborate gown, was sitting for a portrait in the gloom of the plantation house parlor. Her gaze strayed to the window; a nursemaid came and forced her head back into position, none too gently.

"It was confusing for me. I thought my father must be angry with me, to send me away so. Only much later did I understand the arrangement they had made—the Big Man promised to leave all his slaves to my father, so he could free them upon his death. I suspect the Big Man meant it as a trick. He planned to look down from heaven with glee to see my father, softhearted but soft in every other way, too, realize that he could never turn a profit without his slaves, and to keep them. The Big Man would have been disappointed in the end, I think. Perhaps as the years rolled on, he realized that, and that is why he made the change that he did."

The little girl was still sitting for the portrait. She sat perfectly still, even as she grew older, and her child's dress became a fashionable young lady's gown.

"I lived with my grandfather from age nine to seventeen. He was still kind, in his way, but now that I was his responsibility that kindness became warped. He became obsessed with making me ready to take my place in society. I was scarcely allowed outside, for fear of growing darker in the sun, and all my hours were occupied with lady-like pursuits. He had a preoccupation with making me more English than the English; not only was I obliged to obtain every accomplishment, but I also learned the names of the ladies at Almack's, memorized every bit of society gossip, and so on. When he was pleased, he told me, 'It's as though I was in a drawing room on Grosvenor Street.' When he was not pleased...let us not speak of that.

"He thought he could train the Blackness out of me. Perhaps I would have let him, if not for Mistress Henny and Carmen."

The scene shifted again. Maria Lambe, now dressed in the height of fashion, was walking in town with her grandfather. It was dusk, but she still clutched a parasol.

"My mother's illness had taken her quickly, but somehow, she had found the time to reach out to a sister of the craft and beg her to continue my training. Obeah women usually work alone. I do not know what my mother offered Mistress Henny to take me on as an apprentice, but it must have been significant."

As they promenaded, an old woman with a dark, wrinkled face knelt about ten feet behind them. She scooped a bit of dirt out of Miss Lambe's footprint into a small bag. When Miss Lambe turned and saw her, the woman winked and turned away.

The scene shifted again. Under a starlit sky, Maria, her eyes closed, arrived at a fire on a hillside. Her nightgown was streaked with mud and grass stains, and her feet were bare. The old woman from before was there, along with several other young girls. Young Maria's eyes opened. She blinked as though just waking.

*There's the child*, said the old woman. *Took you long enough. Let us begin, girls.*

"So began my true lessons in obeah. My mother had taught me only the gentle stuff: a blue candle to summon love, a red candle for prosperity, that sort of thing. But apparently when she lay dying, she had a vision that I must be trained in all of it.

"So I learned it all. Even the black-candle sort, which was spoken of in terrified whispers throughout the island. I did not care for it. I have never wanted to smother a man by burying a live cockerel, or make his limbs swell by driving a nail through his footprint. Mistress Henny knew your English magic, too, which I preferred for a time, for it seemed prettier, full of rhymes and flowers. Eventually I realized it was just as brutal underneath. But I learned it, for my mother's sake, and so I could see Carmen."

Again, the girl laughing in the sun appeared. This time, the real Miss Lambe turned to look. One of her hands reached out to the illusory girl, then she drew it back.

"People in this country, when they wish to compliment me, tell me how fair my skin is," she said. "One young man once wrote a sonnet comparing my complexion favorably to a glass of milk, which was quite stupid. No one has skin like milk. If they did it would mean they were near death. If they could see Carmen, perhaps they would realize that pallor and beauty do not go hand in hand. To see her was to feel that any other shade was unnatural and sickly. If God made us in His image, He must be close to *that*."

Any clergyman would have been shocked to hear her; but I could see what she meant. The girl was strength and life personified; she was so beautiful that she simply looked *right*.

Miss Lambe passed a hand over her eyes. "How my head aches."

The scene shifted back to the fire on the hill. I realized that the laughing girl was one of Mistress Henny's other students. "Carmen was one of my grandfather's field hands. After the lessons we would walk home together, sheltered under a glamour that Carmen knit into my parasol so that we would not be seen."

The two girls were now walking on a starlit road, huddled together under a parasol as though the moon would burn them. Their fingers tangled together on its handle.

"I had never in my life had such a friend. I lived for those ten minutes a week when we walked together.

"And so I grew. After a few more years my grandfather grew ill, and stayed mostly in bed. My father's health, too, began to fail. I believe he hung on only for the hope of his inheritance.

"My grandfather slowly lost ground. Lawyers came and went from his bedroom. Letters from England came in a torrent. Carmen and I walked together in the night and whispered of what we would do when my father set her free."

The two girls were older now. Miss Lambe's fingers stroked Carmen's cheek; Carmen's lips brushed her ear.

"We were fools," said Miss Lambe.

"It was only a few months ago that my grandfather died. A week later, I got the shock of my life. His children had received sizable bequests, but he had left the great bulk of his estate—the land, the people, the fortune—to me."

I expected to see some of these events in her illusions; but still, she showed me only the two girls walking the starlit road.

"For poor Papa, this was one shock too many. He followed his father to the grave, leaving me to deal with the aftermath.

"On a Monday, the will was read. On Thursday, a letter arrived from my father's sister Augusta in England contesting it. There are laws, you see, allowing white heirs to push out upstarts like me. If my father had only lived—but that is not fair, is it?

"My grandfather, though he had been rather out of touch in the last few years, was no fool. He did what he could to ensure that my inheritance really would come to me. But it was his wish that I come to England, so when his daughter's lawyer produced an injunction ordering that his assets be sold, his own solicitors made no objection. His 'assets,' of course, including hundreds of souls, including the girl I loved.

"It was only then that I truly understood the horror of what we were a part of. Not a week went by before the first batch of slaves were ordered onto a ship to Jamaica to be sold. Carmen was among them."

Now Miss Lambe's illusion did shift, becoming so jagged and frantic that I could scarcely follow it. The girl called Carmen was being led onto a ship; Miss Lambe, weeping, was trying to reach her, but two white men—her grandfather's lawyers, perhaps—held her back. She screamed, but I could not hear a sound.

"I was frantic. Desperate. Life in our indigo fields was hard, but life on a sugar plantation was lethal. Most who were brought there lived no longer than five years."

We were looking at the island again. Down by our feet in the tiny harbor, the ship that had taken Carmen skimmed out to sea. The real Maria knelt and then lay down on her side, her face close to the tiny ship. She cupped her hand under it, like she could lift it like a child's bath toy. But it sailed on, and the sky grew grayer.

"All I meant to do," she said, "was to turn it back to the harbor. To bring her back to me. I was a talented witch. I was powerful. I thought I knew what I was doing."

Atop the mountain, I could see a tiny Maria, weaving an intricate spell, surrounded by black candles. When it was ready, she cupped her hands and blew it out toward the ship sailing away far below. But the stiff breeze the spell was supposed to carry tangled with the storm clouds, which roiled and grew and became a hurricane. The tiny ship was tossed on the waves.

"I was arrogant," she said.

Down on the ship, the crew struggled with the waves. They were good sailors, I could see, and Carmen was weaving strong charms around them, too, casting spell after desperate spell on credit. But then a monster of a wave loomed over it. Carmen, her hair and dress plastered to her skin, closed her eyes, and the rain and the wave slowed. Back on the mountain Maria was on her knees screaming, reaching out with both hands, trying to claw her wind spell back. For a moment both girls were dappled in the pearly moonlight they had so often shared. Then the wave crashed down and embraced the ship, and it was no more.

The scene shifted, yet again, back to Carmen, alive and whole, smiling in the sun.

"You know," said Miss Lambe conversationally, "I am not sure I ever saw her like this. I was rarely allowed out when the sun was high, for fear of getting brown. And even if I had been, she had not much leisure, nor cause to smile."

The illusion faded at last. I blinked to find myself in England once more, on the floor of expensive Brighton lodgings.

"So, I am here. My grandfather's dream of my arriving in England as a fine lady has come true. My grandfather's assets are frozen still. My lawyers and my aunt's battle in court. Old Mr. Lambe and his phalanx of bankers have ensured that I am still thoroughly rich—I have a fortune in jewels alone—but what do I care for that? The only 'property' I care for is Carmen's brothers and sisters and friends. I believe the only way I can prevail is to marry a white man with sufficient status and influence to sway the court. I will free them if it is the last thing I do. And when I have done that, I shall go and find Carmen again."

"Find her?" I asked softly. No one could survive a wreck like that, surely.

But Maria glared at me. "She's not dead," she said. "The sea would have told me if she was dead."

I was not at all sure that the sea understood that those she embraced to her bosom got drowned dead, but I said nothing.

With that, she turned and went into her bedroom without another word. I followed and helped her off with her ball gown and into her nightclothes. She did the same for me, though she scarcely seemed to know I was there. Then I left for her spare room and went to sleep.

# CHAPTER TWENTY-FIVE

That night Kitty came to me in a dream. I don't mean I dreamed of her; I mean I spoke to her, the real Kit, in my dreamscape. I suppose after the night I'd had I simply couldn't bear to be without her any longer. I fell asleep clutching a pillow, pretending it was Kit, and when I opened my eyes in the dream she was there instead of the pillow, purring under my arm.

She turned the purr to a growl when she saw me, and slunk from beneath my elbow. But when I put up a tentative hand she deigned to be stroked, and even arched her skull into my palm.

"How are you, Kit?" I said.

"Oh, fine," she answered in her girl-voice. "Meryton is the same as ever. Why are you bothering me? I'm still angry at you, you know."

"I know. I'm sorry," I said. "It's just, Kit, the night I've had—"

"Don't tell me. I don't want to hear about balls and dancing when I'm waiting here. I can feel it you know—all the fun you're having."

"I'm sorry," I said. "I am trying."

She reared up on her hind legs to bat at a green vine, and I realized that my bed was standing in the middle of the jungle. "Where are we?" she demanded.

"The island of Sainte-Josephine," I said.

"Pretty." She jumped down and began stalking a bright blue butterfly.

"Yes. Nastier than it looks, though. Kit, come back here and be cuddled, won't you? I've just listened to someone tell me about losing the love of her life."

"My sympathies to her. Was it your fault again?" she asked.

"No. It was hers, actually."

"Hmph. *Witches.*" But she hopped back up, leaving a series of muddy pawprints on the bedspread, and minced over to let me pet her. "Only because no one at Longbourn knows I'm a cat, so I never get stroked."

"Well, we'd better fix that."

She flopped down next to me and purred while I stroked her and told her the events of the evening. I knew she was still angry. When she did occasionally deign to reply it was sharp and cutting, and her tail swished and lashed. But I preferred to talk to an angry Kit than to anyone else at the moment.

"And how is Denny?" she asked, licking her paw with elaborate casualness.

"He's—the same." She rolled over and stretched out, displaying the soft warm fur of her belly. I knew a trap when I saw one, but I couldn't resist, and reached out a hand to stroke it. Quick as a flash, the trap closed, and I yelped as eighteen claws plus some needle-sharp teeth sank into my wrist.

"Tell me the truth," she growled around a mouthful of flesh.

"He's all right! Really!" But an image flashed in my head of Denny, red-faced, while the flirtatious heiress tapped him with her fan.

I knew Kitty saw. She made a sound like I'd stepped on her tail and jumped off the bed again. I reached for her, but she shied away.

"I'm sorry, Kit, I really am," I said.

"I don't care that you're sorry, don't you see? I—What's that?"

There was a strange trembling beneath our feet. The headboard muttered a nervous *b-d-d-d-d-d* as it rattled against the frame.

*You didn't really think I wasn't listening, did you?* drawled a familiar voice. *You two have no secrets from me anymore.*

The rumbling grew stronger. Birds rose in shrieking clouds from the foliage. Kitty crouched low to the ground, her tail switching.

"You've no call to interfere, Wormenheart," I said as stoutly as I could. "We've kept our agreement."

*So far,* he agreed. *But I grow impatient, little witchling. I grow hungry.* The air suddenly smelled strange, like smoke and burning tar.

Before I could respond, there was a great roar, and the air turned to fire.

The top of the mountain had exploded. Rivers of molten rock poured down the hillside toward us. I screamed for Kitty, but she climbed a tree instead. Before I knew it the bed was sinking in a glowing river. I gasped out a spell to protect it, but I knew it couldn't hold for long. Kitty clung to the top of the tree as long as she could. When the lava took it, she leapt to another, then another, until there was nowhere else to go. I watched helplessly as it dipped her toward the molten rock—

Then I woke.

The coverlet was covered in muddy pawprints and my wrist was ringed with puncture wounds, but I was all right. Frantically I groped for the connection to Kit, taking in the slack in great mental armfuls until I felt her at the other end. She was all right, too—her tail a bottle brush and a hiss in her throat, but not harmed. Now that we were awake I couldn't speak to her in words, but I did my best to send her the message: *I'm going to fix this.*

*You'd better,* the response came.

I threw back the covers and got up to open the window. It was still very early—I must have only slept for an hour or two—and dawn was just a sullen gray promise in an otherwise dark sky. I took in great lungfuls of cool night air, never so grateful to smell the mix of fish and refuse and salt that characterized Brighton's nighttime aroma.

"Just a dream," I murmured. "Just a dream."

And that was true enough—for now. But if I didn't stop wasting time, Kitty and I really would be consumed by fire.

The buoyant effects of last night's drinks had drained away and I felt absolutely vile. I don't care what all of Brighton's physicians say— drinking seawater is *not* good for you. My limbs ached, my stomach churned sourly, and I was raging with thirst.

The household was still asleep. I thought about waking the maid to ask for more tea, but decided to make it myself. My whole body was thrumming with worry, and I needed something to occupy my hands.

A runaway horse was thundering toward me, and I'd stood frozen in fear for weeks while it grew closer and closer. Perhaps I'd already wasted too much time. Well, I'd waste no more. Miss Lambe's story last night had made the possibility of losing Kitty feel much more real. From now on, every possible moment must be dedicated to finding the jewel.

I decided to bring Miss Lambe a cup of tea. If I had woken up feeling bad, she would probably want to die. I slipped into her room and left the steaming cup on her bedside table. She was so deeply asleep that I leaned close to see if she was breathing. She was, but her breath was terrible.

I was about to leave when I saw that a drawer on her vanity was open a crack. I went to close it and glimpsed something inside. A burgundy, velvet-covered box. Her jewel case.

*Wherever the Jewel of Propriety is, she has spent significant time in its proximity . . .*

It couldn't hurt to take a look, could it? This might be my only chance.

I glanced over my shoulder. She was still deeply asleep. Hadn't so much as stirred. Just to be sure, I whispered a quick sleep charm to keep her under. Then I slowly opened the drawer and removed the box.

It was locked of course, but I was able to sweet-talk it open with a charm Harriet had taught me and the promise to burn Mamma's latest letter. The latch opened with a soft *click* of luxury. I lifted the lid—

Treasures. Lord. It was like something out of a fairy tale. Most women I knew had little more than a strand of their grandmother's pearls or a thin gold chain—this trove made such finery look shabby. I stroked my hand over a diamond bracelet, lifted a great emerald ring so it caught the meager light. How beautiful to be rich and have such things.

However, none of them felt remotely magical. I poked through the trove gently, until I caught a glint of purple and my heart skipped a beat. I moved the fine silver chains and golden rings aside and found it: a brooch, delicately ringed with mother-of-pearl, with an enormous amethyst at the center. I lifted it from the case.

It was no more magical than the rest.

"What are you doing?"

I spun around to find Miss Lambe on her elbows, squinting at me. Her voice was a croak.

"I was just—I—I—"

"If you wanted me to stay asleep while you robbed me," she said, "you shouldn't have bothered with that sleep charm. You know I can always tell when I'm being spelled."

"Miss Lambe, please, let me explain—"

She rang the bell at her bedside as loud as she could. "The maid will be here in a moment," she said. "I'd put that away if I were you, unless you want it all over Brighton what a sneaking little thief you are."

Good Lord, I'd never live that down. I dropped the brooch back in the case and shoved it in the drawer. Just in time, for a sleepy maid poked her head in the door.

"You rang, miss?" she yawned.

"Yes," said Miss Lambe, still staring straight at me. "Please help Miss Bennet to dress and ask George to bring the carriage round. She will be going back to the Forsters' immediately."

# CHAPTER TWENTY-SIX

It's been a while since my writing hand has ached like this. I wrote the last three chapters in a little over two days, and when I was done I went to bed and didn't wake till noon. I had to get it all down before I had second thoughts, though, or tried to pretty it up. I am sure Darcy and Bingley think I'm nothing but a lazy sponge.

I am doing my best with Georgiana, but so far I've had no luck. All my scries return vague and contradictory results. The only consistent thing is the scent—a sort of burnt, sweet smell, like someone threw a bottle of cologne in a fire. And anytime I get impatient and try to just tear the dratted hex off her, she turns back into that *thing*. I can hardly analyze it then, for it always hisses and attacks me, no matter who else is about. I even had some steaks brought in one day, in the hope of distracting it, but clearly I'm the only meat it's hungry for.

There's something bothering me about this spell. I can't put my finger on it, but something about it is *wrong*. If I'm not careful, I know I shall make things worse.

I did my best to explain yesterday afternoon when Darcy came to see Georgiana. I've been spending my afternoons sitting with her, for, even half mad, she's better company than the gentlemen of the house. I brought her mathematics books and a blank notebook and pen, which nobody else bothered to do, and now she mostly writes in them instead of on the walls. Apparently her unsettling wall-writing habit wasn't part of the madness; they simply hadn't given her any paper. She still doesn't acknowledge my presence, but that's all right. We sit across from each other and each do our own work in silence. She even allows the nurse to braid her hair back now, so that she can see the page.

That's how Darcy found us yesterday. The nurse was drowsing by the fire as usual, and Georgiana had dozed off, too, curled up in her bed with her hand still resting on her latest equation. Darcy took it from her gently, his jaw tightening as he looked over her scribblings, then at me. "Well, Mrs. Wickham?" he whispered. "Have you made any progress?"

"Not yet."

"But—"

I shook my head. "I do not tell you how to manage an estate. Pray do not lecture me about witchcraft."

Darcy made a harrumphing sound. "God save me from Bennet women and their tongues."

I made a face at that. I had no wish to think of Lizzy's tongue as it related to my brother-in-law. Darcy looked amused.

"How's Lizzy?" I asked softly.

"She's well. I think."

"You think?"

"My mother was extremely well," he said. "Then one night she gave birth to my brother, and they both died before the sun was up."

"Don't talk that way. But here." I dug in the pocket of my apron and produced a handkerchief, heavily embroidered with bright tropical orchids and birds, and a tiny yellow bonnet with purplish-blue flowers. "For Lizzy and the baby."

He eyed my riotously colored creations. "Er...thank you."

"They're not for looking at," I said impatiently. "I thought I'd try my hand at some protection spells for them. There's not much a witch can do against the horrors of childbirth but I did my best."

He sucked in a breath and tucked them both into his breast pocket. Then he looked at me and said, more sincerely this time, "Thank you."

"It's nothing." I began gathering my writing and sewing things.

"Wait," he said. "I almost forgot. From Mrs. Dar—From Elizabeth." He produced a letter from Lizzy addressed to me.

I ran my hands over the familiar handwriting on the envelope. It was thick—no doubt stuffed with news and questions (and perhaps a bit of money, too). Lizzy might be highly irritating, but she is an excellent correspondent. She knows how I love clothes, so when she has nothing else to say (and is done scolding me), she'll send me accounts of the latest London fashions, and sometimes even cut out fashion plates to send me. What is more, I know Kitty has recently been to visit her. I longed to curl up and read it there and then.

Instead I put it in my pocket, and nodded to Darcy. "Good day."

"Don't you want to read it now?"

"Of course," I said, "but I'd better save it. I'm trying to bank plenty of sacrifices for my work on that one." I nodded to Miss Darcy. "When I finally find a way to lift the hex it'll carry a steep price, I'm sure."

He frowned. "Sacrifices? Price? I'm the one paying the price for all those herbs and thread."

"Not the price in money. Haven't I explained about spell-prices yet? Oh, I'd certainly better."

I did my best to walk him through it.

"You needn't make any sacrifice for us," he said. "I'll pay whatever's necessary out of my own coffers."

"Wrong on both counts. The spell will ask something from me at least—magic does not approve of disinterested bystanders. And you may certainly pay the bulk of the price, but it can't be paid in money."

"What, then?" he said. "Must I burn a letter, too?"

"Not unless that letter is very, very important to you. A spell-tithe has to be something that matters, something you'll miss. And the bigger the working, the dearer the sacrifice must be." I shrugged. "Think on it."

His lips tightened. He nodded. He looked as though he had more to say, but just then Georgiana stirred and said, "Fitz?"

"I'm here, Snubs."

"The level h of the binary tree contains 2 to the h nodes," she informed him, then went back to sleep.

Darcy balled his fists at his sides. "I just cannot stand another day of being *useless*."

"Well," I suggested, "you could try to talk to her about that." I pointed to the notebook he clutched.

His hand tightened on the book. "It's just ravings," he said.

"Is it?" I said. "Maybe. *I* certainly cannot make heads or tails of it. But then I never learned any more mathematics than what was necessary to make sure the housekeeper was not cheating me. Surely you have?"

"Well...yes." His frown deepened, if such a thing was possible. "I studied maths at Oxford. Never got as far with it as Snubs, though. She's a marvel." My respect for him went up a notch. Few men would admit that their younger sisters could best them at their studies, let alone boast of it. He flipped open the notebook.

"Why do you call her Snubs?" I asked.

"Hmm?" He was poring over the book. "Oh. She used to get shy of me when I came home from school for the holidays. There are twelve years between us, you know, and when I'd come home and try to play with her she'd hide in Mother's skirts. I'd have to coax her to be friends again. Father said she was snubbing me like a debutante does a penniless suitor. And the name stuck."

I could easily imagine how intimidating a half-grown Darcy must have been to the tiny girl. Indeed, many a grown woman would still be intimidated by such a lordly brother. But Miss Darcy showed no such fear now. He must have been patient indeed.

"You know," he said, running his finger down a page of equations, "you may be right. There is something here. This almost tracks." Then he flipped a page and sighed. "But then it just descends into nonsense again."

"Still," I said. "If it's a way to reach her..."

"Yes, quite. What did you say she was trying to prove? Goldbach's conjecture?" He chuckled. "Lord, she does have the Darcy pride, doesn't she? The wisest men in Europe have been tearing their hair out over that for a hundred years, and this schoolroom miss plans to solve it before she comes of age." He turned to me. "Would you mind staying with her for a few minutes longer? I'll just go down to Bingley's library and see if he has any books on the subject. We can go mad over it together." He looked almost happy for a moment, and I realized how much he must have missed being able to really talk to her.

"Certainly."

"Thank you." He made for the door, then paused at the threshold. "This matter of the price—I do not like the idea of being indebted to a young lady, especially one of my wife's relations. There's really no way to take it all on myself?"

*Blood pouring onto a snow-white handkerchief.* "There are ways," I admitted, "but I don't like where they lead."

"Mrs. Wickham," he said. "I've seen you do what seem to me to be some fairly large magics. Does that mean that the price was correspondingly large?"

I nodded. He seemed to be waiting for me to say more, but what business is it of his what price I've paid? I should think it was fairly obvious anyway.

"You know," he said, "I begin to see I've underestimated you." And he closed the door.

Well. *Of course* he underestimates me.


Now, where was I? Ah yes. The worst morning of my life. Up to that point, anyway.

I rode home in Miss Lambe's carriage as the sun was rising, gritting my teeth with all my might. Late-night revelers from Lady Herrington's ball were wandering the streets, and I was determined that they should not see me cry. I knew, though, that the tears could not be avoided, only delayed.

I had never been so ashamed in my entire life. To be caught (so it appeared) stealing from one I had begun to consider a friend! And just a few hours after I had nearly given up my virtue to Wickham! Drink or no drink, there was no excuse for it. And worst of all, it was all for nothing. I was farther that day from finding the jewel than I had been when I arrived. I wanted to die. And, thanks to my idiocy, I soon would, and I'd take Kitty with me.

I had hoped that the Forsters would still be asleep, so that I could sneak into my room without facing them. But Harriet had found it as hard as I had to sleep with a bellyful of seawater, and when the carriage came rattling up to the front door, I saw her poke her nightcapped head out an upper window.

She met me at the door, a crease of alarm between her eyes. "Lydia! Why are you home so early? Did Miss Lambe take ill?"

I shook my head, but couldn't get a word out. With a swift glance at the curious maid, she said, "No matter. Let's get you off to bed, you must still be exhausted." She and the maid got me back into my nightclothes, and then Harriet shooed her girl away, took my hand, and said, "Now tell me."

The dam broke. I put my head on her shoulder and sobbed out as much of the story as I could stand to tell. I was vague about what had gone on between me and Wickham, and omitted Miss Lambe's story altogether—but on the subject of the jewelry box I felt I must be shamefully accurate. It was very possible that, since the Forsters were my temporary guardians, Miss Lambe might write them a letter describing my conduct. Horrors. She'd best hear it from me.

Harriet hugged me and made shushing noises and stroked my braid. "Oh, my poor Lydia," she sighed. "Is that all?"

I drew back and endeavored to wipe my face. "All!" I cried. "Isn't it enough?"

"Don't be so hard on yourself," she said kindly. "There were a number of witches there last night and we all behaved rather unlike ourselves. I heard Mrs. Carr actually rode home on the roof of her carriage. Better than Miss Pollitt, who rode home on her groom. Poor Lady Herrington will probably find herself the recipient of a number of hexes and curses in the next week or so. After the night Brighton society has had, nobody is going to mind *your* little schoolgirl indiscretions, even if they learn of them."

"R-really?" I hiccuped.

"Well—not that you should tell anyone, mind you. Still, I should think you'll be all right." And she recounted some more scandalous witch behavior from the party. I began to feel a little better. There is no better balm for shame than hearing that others have debased themselves far worse.

"But," I said, a fresh lump rising in my throat, "I'm no closer to finding the jewel, and Miss Lambe hates me now."

"Piffle," she said firmly. "She was there last night, too. I am sure when she's had time to reflect, she'll forgive you. Just you have a sleep for a few hours, then go over there this afternoon and explain the whole thing."

But Miss Lambe was not at home to me that afternoon, nor the next day, nor the day after that. In a last-ditch attempt to justify myself, I wrote her a long letter explaining about Kitty and Wormenheart and the jewel—she never responded. When we passed each other on the street she cut me dead, and after a few days of increasingly desperate attempts to reach her I arrived at her house one day to find she had left town.

"She's gone to London to see her lawyers," the maid told me. "She don't know when she'll be back. She mayn't be at all, she said."

Well. That was it, then.

After that I stopped caring about balls and parties. I stayed in unless Harriet insisted otherwise. I scried endlessly, cast divination after divination, trying to find the Jewel of Propriety's location. Sometimes Harriet helped me, but even when she was busy I carried on by myself. None of it did any good. Sometimes I thought I caught a flicker of something, but it was never helpful—more often than not, it was just a feeling, a touch of loneliness or amusement or anger, as though the jewel had feelings as people did. And I often got an impression of great power. It was that power, I supposed, that shielded it from me.

I grew careless and desperate. I poured more and more into my spells. What did it matter? All that mattered was the jewel. One day Colonel Forster walked in on me holding a handkerchief to my bloody hand, weeping with the pain of it. He went brick red and backed out, muttering an apology, and called for Harriet. I heard him whisper something to her about "female troubles."

*Oh God*, I thought.

Harriet came in and helped me bandage my hand, then cleaned up the remains of my latest failure. Then she sat me down in front of the mirror and brushed out my hair.

"Look at yourself," she said. "You've gone all pale and mousy. What happened to the Lydia I know?"

It was true. My skin was pasty, my hair lank and uncurled. "She's trying not to die," I croaked.

"She won't," said Harriet firmly. "Really, Lydia, I won't let that happen to my dearest friend. I know what you need: a distraction. I've a garden party to go to tomorrow, and you, Miss Bennet, are coming with me."

"Oh, Harriet, I don't know—"

"Nonsense," she said. "I brought you here as my companion, you know, and you have not been offering much in the way of companionship lately."

"I'm sorry."

"It's all right. Just come with me tomorrow. I promise you'll enjoy yourself." She bent down behind me and put her arms round me, her cheek pressed against mine. "Two such pretty girls shouldn't languish inside," she said. "And who knows—perhaps you'll even find the answers you seek. Besides, she wants to meet you specifically. It's a great honor." She rose and handed me the invitation.

*Miss Ada Beaumont*
*Requests the honor of the presence of MRS. COLONEL JAMES FORSTER*
*And*

MISS LYDIA BENNET
*For a garden party at her home*
*To celebrate midsummer with the members of the Order of the Rose*
*RSVP.*

"The Order of the Rose?" I said. "What's that?"

"It's a sort of social club," she said. "Very exclusive."

Now that she mentioned it, I had heard the name murmured at parties—frustrated debutantes sighing with the impossibility of obtaining an invitation to join. Perhaps a few hours of fun would help me to clear my head.

"Very well," I said. "I'll come."

"Of course you will. Now let's go for a walk. Your complexion needs brightening up if we're to impress tomorrow."

I had a most peculiar dream that night. It seemed to be a message of some sort from Kitty—I could feel her trying to communicate with me, a sense of babbling urgency and questions, but she wasn't making herself at all clear. In the dream I *was* Kitty, standing in the parlor, but everything was confused. Someone was standing in the parlor speaking to the family, someone they did not know—I could hear Mamma's respectful confusion, though I couldn't make out the words. I tried to look at the newcomer, but my vision would not focus. I seemed to be both a tall girl of seventeen and a cat crouching on the carpet, my vision flicking back and forth dizzily between girl-height and cat-height. Someone was holding me pinned, forcing me to exist in both states at once.

With a great effort, I managed to focus on the visitor. It was Miss Lambe.

I woke with a start and a pounding headache. I tried to reach out to Kitty, but the effort to contact me seemed to have exhausted her, and all

I felt was a plaintive *mew* of confusion. Mrs. Forster poked her head in the door. "Come on, sleepyhead," she said. "It's time to get ready."

I did not expect to enjoy the garden party, but from the moment we arrived, it seemed designed to appeal just to me. Miss Beaumont lived in a house a little way out of town that did not look terribly grand from the street, but once the maid had shown us through to the gardens, I caught my breath. They were far more extensive than one would normally see for a house of that size, and beautifully cultivated. A healthy, sunny, green smell rose from the plants, a balm to my aching heart. If afternoons like this existed, surely my mistakes could not be so insurmountable.

We wandered the grounds for twenty minutes or so, then, according to some invisible signal, all the guests began drifting toward the rear of the garden. Here there was a pretty yellow-and-white-striped awning, its sides tied up to admit the fresh air. Lady Octavia De Vere, whom we'd met at parties but whom I would have assumed was too grand to take much notice of Harriet or me, gave a cry of delight when she spotted us and crossed the tent to where we were standing.

"So you've brought the dear girl at last!" she exclaimed to Harriet. "We've been wondering when you would introduce this sweet thing to the Order. A seventh of a seventh! And a familiar, too, I believe? How do you do, Miss Bennet? Here, child, this is for you." And she held out a piece of chocolate.

"Thank you, my lady." I was surprised, but I'm powerfully fond of chocolate, so I took it and popped it in my mouth. I felt my eyes widen. The chocolate was stuffed with magic. (And caramel.) After all my attempts to find the jewel, my magical reservoir was rather raw and empty, and this little morsel of magic was like a sip of ginger beer on a hot day.

"*Thank you*, my lady," I said more fervently. "That's extremely kind of you."

And it really was. True, she had not given me much—but it was more than I would have given to a near stranger. Magic is not cheap. I expected she would ask something in return, but she merely crinkled up her eyes in a smile and patted my hand. "Nonsense, nonsense. It's my pleasure. How lucky you are, Harriet, to have such an apt young witch as an apprentice! If you ever tire of her, child, you come to me, eh?"

"Not trying to steal my apprentice, are you, my lady?" Harriet said with a laugh. It sounded like a joke, but there was a hint of steel beneath.

Lady De Vere looked startled. "No, no, of course not. I beg your pardon. Only funning. Won't you excuse me." She gave me another kindly smile. "Welcome, Miss Bennet. And good luck."

"So this is your coven then?" I whispered to Harriet after she'd moved away.

"You could call it that," she said, "but we usually call it the Order of the Rose."

"Oh dear," I said.

"What? Don't you like it?"

"It's lovely. I just wish you'd told me. I shall have a great deal of trouble getting this dress off without a maid."

"What? Oh, *Lydia*." She laughed so hard she had to hang on my arm to stand up. "We're not among your country coven anymore. No one is getting naked here, pet."

"Oh." I felt my cheeks flame.

"I'm sorry." She wiped tears of laughter from her eyes. "I absolutely should have prepared you. I just wanted to give you a nice surprise."

Across the room, another woman—another witch—gave a glad cry at the sight of us and began to make her way over. I could not remember her name, but she certainly seemed to know me. "It is a nice surprise," I said to Harriet. "The nicest."

"Good. And it's only just begun."

For the next hour or so we mingled and chatted. I hadn't lied—it really was nice. The warmth and approval of the members of the Order of the Rose was a balm to my soul after the last few days. Many of them pressed magic-stuffed sweets upon me, as Lady Octavia had. I welcomed them eagerly, especially at first. It felt delightful to replenish myself, and the selfless kindness shown by these women made me want to cry. After a dozen or so both my stomach and my magical reserves began to feel over-full, but Harriet dug her nails into my arm warningly and I knew it would be rude to refuse. And I wanted badly not to offend. This, I felt, was the coven I had been waiting for all my life.

There was only one sour note: One of the witches who approached us was Mary King.

"How do you do, Mrs. Forster, Miss Bennet," she said in a drawling voice.

"Miss King," said Harriet coolly. "Haven't seen you in Brighton this summer."

"Yes, well, it's so crowded this year, isn't it? I hate when a place becomes faddish, don't you? It becomes overrun with the dullest people." She looked at me with the faintest curl of her lip.

"Then what brings you to town now?" I asked. "Surely you can afford to travel elsewhere. What was the point of murdering your grandfather otherwise?"

Mary ignored that last bit. "I am in town to keep an eye on you, of course," she said. "My master grows impatient. He's not sure you're up to the task." She laughed lightly. "Wouldn't it be a lark if I were to find the gem instead of you! He could have the jewel *and* his snack. Oh my, he'd be pleased with me then."

"She'll find it, all right," said Harriet. "Especially once she's got the Order behind her."

"That's if the Order accepts her," Mary said. "In friendship I must warn you, Lydia, I do not like your chances. Your little country coven may take all comers, but the Order has standards. Your association with that so-called Miss Lambe, for instance, will not stand you in good stead here." She sniffed. "How it galls me to see that creature come to *my* town using *my* family's name."

My eyes narrowed at that. Surely it could not be...? But the deaths of wealthy grandfathers certainly lined up. "You're her *cousin!*" I blurted. "The spell that we—that was old Mr. Lambe."

Mary's jaw clenched. "She's no cousin of mine. Once our lawyers are through with her, she'll never see the inside of a ballroom again. She'll be lucky if we allow her to live in our house as a servant."

"Go away, Mary," Harriet said pleasantly, "or I shall make you smell like a tannery for the next fortnight. You know I can."

Mary smirked and moved off.

I was beginning to feel a little sick when, luckily, the meeting was called to order. Servants entered with round tables and chairs and we all found seats. I noticed that all the women at our table nodded to Harriet with great respect.

A fluttering woman came to the front of the room and read off some rather dull business—apparently the Order had raised twenty pounds for the widows and orphans of Brighton, which they all politely applauded—then cleared her throat.

"And now, sisters, without further ado," she said, "I shall turn matters over to Miss Ada Beaumont, our dear Regent!"

The applause was much more enthusiastic this time. A woman with a determined, energetic air made her way to the dais. It was difficult to tell her age. Her hair was all white, but her face was smooth and red-cheeked with health, and her eyes were sparkling and alert.

"Why is she called the Regent?" I whispered to Harriet. Unfortunately, just as I did so the applause died down, and my voice sounded clearly in the silence. Miss Beaumont turned her gaze upon me.

"It seems our new prospects are rather inquisitive," she said gravely to the crowd, who rippled with warm laughter. "It's all right, dear. Stand up. What's your name?"

"Miss Lydia Bennet, ma'am."

"And what did you ask our Harriet, Miss Lydia Bennet?"

"I was just curious," I said, "why you are called the Regent. Is it after the Prince Regent?"

The laughter was louder this time, but still seemed affectionate. "Certainly not," she said. "Brighton's witches have been ruled by a Regent far longer than the nation has. The Regent stands in for the Witch-Queen of Brighton, who was lost generations ago. Until her heir returns, Brighton's witches are under the care of Regents. I had the honor of being chosen by my sisters for the task." She inclined her head humbly, accepting another smattering of applause. "Of course," she said confidingly, "there are those who say that the Witch-Queen is never coming back, or that there never was such a person. I, for one, hope that they're wrong! I should dearly love to hand off the responsibility. These parties are rather hard on my lawns."

Another ripple of fond laughter from the crowd. She may not have been born to her post, but she was clearly popular with those who had placed her there. "Does that answer your question, dear?" she said.

"Yes, quite," I said, and sat down again.

"Good." She clapped briskly. "Now. Who is our Great Working for tonight?"

"Me! Me!" A gawky young woman in the back with a prominent overbite rose and hurried forward. "It's my turn tonight!"

"Certainly." She smiled. "Sit here." Two witches carried out a large wicker chair, overgrown with climbing roses, and the young woman sat down, looking thrilled.

"Young Celia Ward here," said Miss Beaumont to the crowd, "has been an exemplary member of the Order of the Rose. Since joining Mrs. Hayes's branch, she has attended every meeting, volunteers her time to organize our soirees, and is a dedicated help to both her sisters and her mistress. Isn't that right, Mrs. Hayes?" A woman who was sitting at Miss Ward's former table nodded proudly.

"Most important," Miss Beaumont continued, "Miss Ward has contributed no fewer than forty pints of power to the Order."

A murmur of admiration went around the room. Miss Ward looked proud. I had never heard of magical power being measured in pints, but apparently forty of them were quite a lot.

"She has richly rewarded us with her time and efforts," Miss Beaumont said. "And so, the time has come to reward her. What is it to be, Miss Ward?"

"My face," said Miss Ward. "My face, my *face.*"

"Very well," said Miss Beaumont. "Sisters, to work."

As Miss Ward settled herself expectantly back against the rose chair and closed her eyes, a rustle broke out among the witches seated around the tables. They took hands with one another—the two witches on either side of me reached over my lap, omitting me from the circle—and I could feel power begin to flow through them. To my surprise, it went into the vase of flowers at the center of the table. Each table had a different arrangement—ours was a collection of snow-white roses and yellow tulips. As I watched, the power flowed into the bouquet. Their blooms opened a little wider, their leaves and stems turning a deeper green. A hint of blush appeared at the center of the white roses, and the tulips became shot through with crimson.

Our table was shaking slightly—not from magic, I realized, but from the sheer physical effort of the women sitting around it. One was jiggling her leg against the leg of the table, shaking the whole structure. Another was whispering her power spell through clenched teeth. She caught me looking and made an obvious effort to relax and look as though she were enjoying herself, but I could see the sweat standing out on her brow.

Harriet, however, looked quite undisturbed. Her color was high, and there was a faint smile on her lips. She seemed as if she were in the midst of a vigorous dance with a favorite partner. She must be the best of them, I thought with a swell of pride.

In the center of the arrangement, two new blossoms arose. One rose and one tulip, both such a deep crimson that I could hardly tear my eyes from them. As I watched, they transformed from buds to tight knots of petals before bursting into glorious bloom, all in less than a minute. The sweet scent of a summer garden wafted through the tent.

Harriet pulled the vase toward her. She cupped it in her hands for a moment, as though warming them, then drew the two crimson blossoms out. She tucked the rose behind her ear and then stood and made her way to the front of the room carrying the tulip. She was not alone. One woman from each table, I saw, was making her way toward the dais, wearing one blossom and carrying another. They were different flowers, but all the same crimson hue. Mary King was among them. She looked much like Harriet—thrilled and energized, more than exhausted.

"Thank you, mistresses," Miss Beaumont said. "Give them to me." One by one, they curtsied before her, and laid the flower they carried in her arms. She held each blossom to her nose and sniffed appreciatively. She had a particularly warm smile for Harriet's. When they were through, Miss Beaumont took her armful of scarlet and turned to Miss Ward's chair. One by one, she took the flowers and threaded them through the weave of the wicker chair. Harriet's tulip she tucked into Miss Ward's hand. Then, finally, almost shimmering with the power handed over by dozens of women, she began her spell. At first it seemed a simple glamour, but then I listened closer, and I almost fell out of my chair when I realized what she was trying to do.

No, not a glamour. They were *changing her face.*

I daresay that to a non-magical person, this would seem like a meaningless distinction. (Once they had stopped gibbering with terror upon learning that magic was real, I mean.) Since beauty is only in the eye of the beholder, what's the difference between someone who *seems* beautiful and someone who *is*? The answer, of course, is power. It is by far the easiest kind of magic to alter the way a thing is perceived. Doing anything physical and permanent is harder, especially if one wants to be precise. And altering the body of a living being, permanently, without disfiguring them or killing them stone-dead, is just about the hardest task of all. The cyclone I'd raised on the standing stones, wild as it was, had been far simpler than this.

There was one more important difference, I realized as I watched Miss

Ward's eyes grow wider and wider and her fingers clutch the arms of her chair. A glamour, at worst, tickles a little. As Miss Ward's lower jaw began to lengthen, her chin to sharpen, her buck teeth to shrink, I could actually hear the creaking of her bones changing shape.

Soon she was shaking so hard that Miss Beaumont actually paused her working. She knelt down and took the trembling girl's hand, loosening her grasp on the blossom she held. "Gently, my dear Miss Ward, gently," she said. "Do not crush your totem. Are you well? Are you in pain?"

Miss Ward shook her head. "I took the tincture you gave me. It doesn't hurt," she said. "But I can *hear it*."

I shuddered. If I could hear the creaking from where I sat, I could only imagine how distressing it must be to have it within one's own head.

Miss Beaumont was carefully blotting Miss Ward's forehead with a handkerchief. "It's not too late to stop, you know," she said. "The tithes I've gathered can simply be added to your account."

But Miss Ward, breathing hard through clenched teeth, shook her head. "This is why I joined," she said. "This is everything."

Miss Beaumont patted her shoulder. "Very well," she said. "I think you very brave. Don't you, sisters?" The women at the tables applauded warmly. She rose and lifted her hands to continue the spell, then paused in dismay.

"Oh dear," she said. "I'm afraid we don't have quite enough to continue."

A mutter of consternation rose from the tables. Various women grumbled under their breaths.

"More, she says? After I'm already milked drier than when I had the twins."

"It's those girls at Camellia Table. Never pulling their weight. Such weaklings ought never to have been let in."

"Just you wait till I'm a table-mistress. Then at least I'll be draining as well as being drained."

Miss Beaumont raised her hands for silence. "I know, ladies, that I am asking a great deal of you. But you must remember, we only get out of the Order what we put in. Look." She stood aside to show them the chair, and I saw now that the table-blossoms had reverted to their previous colors with just a bit of crimson shot through. "The entire point of the Order is to support one another. Surely when it is your turn for a Great Working, you won't wish your sisters to skimp?"

The grumbling subsided into a sullen silence.

"Excellent," said Miss Beaumont. "Come on now, dig deep. I know you can."

Harriet took a rose from the vase and passed it to the woman on her left. The woman looked at her pleadingly—she was the one who had shaken the table before—but Harriet merely held her gaze, and at last the woman took the rose and pulled the vase over to her. Setting her chin, she pressed her thumb into a thorn, letting three drops of blood fall to the water, then she shoved the rose and the vase to the next woman to her left.

As the vases made their way around the tables, the flowers wound through Miss Ward's chair began to turn red again. The collective effort seemed much harder this time. I realized that the women had come prepared with a surplus of power for this event, but now many of them were cutting into their own strength.

The woman to Harriet's left had turned quite pale. I was afraid she was going to faint. I began to reach for my own well of magic, but Harriet warned me off with a glance. "You'll need it later," she said.

It wasn't enough, though. The red was still fading from Miss Ward's blossoms. The spell wasn't going to hold.

Then Mary King stood.

"Good heavens, the quality of magic in the Order has fallen off dreadfully," she drawled. "I see I'd better lend an extra hand. Beaton, Smith, to me." Two blank-faced young women dressed as lady's maids came to stand at her side.

Mary wore a small smile. Producing a knife and a small bronze bowl, she rolled up the sleeves of the two uncomplaining women—"It's easier to make the cut at the elbow than the palm, so they can still dress me and tend my things," she explained, as though giving a lesson—and then cut each one at the bend of the arm. Blood splashed into the bowl, first a trickle from one girl, then a gush from the other.

Once she had what she wanted from them, Mary bent their arms to put pressure on the wounds with the ease of long practice and moved them off to the side. She mixed a few more items in her bloody bowl—some herbs, and a vial of clear liquid—while chanting softly, then, with a sudden cry, she tossed its contents high into the air.

The women in the front row flinched, but the bloody mixture never came down. The flowers around Miss Ward grew fully crimson again—Miss Beaumont raised her arms—Miss Ward said "Oh *my*," very thickly—the creaks crescendoed into a final *pop*—and it was done.

Miss Ward lifted her head up, trembling a little. Her overbite was gone, replaced by an extremely normal jaw and a rather adorable pointed chin. She glanced in the hand mirror that Miss Beaumont held up for her and burst into tears. "Thank you," she said. "Oh, sisters, *thank you*. You're all so wonderful."

A burst of warm applause filled the room. The woman at Harriet's left had indeed fainted, but at this she woke. "Oh, we did it," she said, "how marvelous," and she too began, vaguely, to clap.

Mary King sketched a curtsy in response to the cheers directed her way. "It was nothing, sisters," she simpered. "Just mind you remember it when it's my turn for a Great Working." Behind her, the two young women stood, staring at nothing.

The ladies surged up from their tables, gathering around Miss Ward to shower her with compliments, basking in the glory of their own accomplishment. Miss Ward, though still trembling slightly, was glowing with pride and hope. She laughed and joked and thanked everyone prettily, her fingers stroking her new face with absent wonder.

The next time I saw her after that was at a public ball a few days later.

She was dancing with a fine-looking young man who was said to have recently taken possession of an unusually valuable living near Norwich. They were married before the month was out. They say *be careful what you wish for*—Miss Ward was careful, and wished for exactly the right thing.

# CHAPTER TWENTY-SEVEN

After watching Miss Ward's transformation at the hands of the Order of the Rose, I would have liked to go home and think over what I had seen that day; but the Order did not allow time for rumination. After just a few minutes of triumphant chitchat, Miss Beaumont clapped her hands and gathered everyone's attention. "Would Miss Bennet please come forward?" she asked. "The time has come to make your application for membership."

"Application?" I whispered to Harriet.

"You'll do a spell," she said. "If it is sufficiently impressive, you'll be admitted."

I felt an uneasiness in the pit of my stomach. "Must I? I haven't prepared a sacrifice."

"You've been gorging yourself on spell-sweets all day," she whispered through a fixed smile. "Really, Lydia, it would be awfully rude to walk away with all the gifts these ladies gave you and not give them anything in return."

I felt ashamed then, and made no further objections. Besides, I could clearly see why Harriet had brought me here: If the power of the Order could give a girl a new face, surely they could help me find the jewel.

"But what spell am I to do?"

"Anything you like." Harriet twisted her mouth. "So long as it's better than that nasty butchery Miss King performed on her servants."

I shuddered. "I couldn't do that even if I wanted." I considered. Despite the spell-sweets, I was awfully tired. "Perhaps a nice glamour? I could change the color of your dress."

Harriet grimaced. "I don't think that will be enough. Can't you do something bigger? Oh, I suppose you are right—you will need more than those drops of candied magic. But don't fret." She rose to her feet. "Table-mistress for Yellow Tulip requests a short recess," she said.

Miss Mary King scoffed loudly at that, but Miss Beaumont ignored her. "Agreed, Yellow Tulip," she said. "But make it quick."

The women got up from their tables and the tent was soon filled with the dull, cheery roar of mingling. Harriet stayed seated, her hand mirror propped against the vase; I started to inquire, but she held up her hand for silence. "Drat, they're all on maneuvers," she said. "All of them except—Ah!"

She muttered a quick summoning charm. Five minutes later, the honor guard walked in.

They were looking somewhat disheveled, out of uniform, cravats undone, and Wickham and Carteret still held playing cards. From that and the look of shame on Fulton's face, I gathered they had been playing hooky from the regiment's drills. A certain amount of that was tolerated, though from the colonel's grumbling at the dinner table I had a feeling that Carteret and Wickham were pushing their luck.

Carteret stepped forward and sketched Harriet a bow. "Well, here we are," he said. "We came as soon as we got your note." He frowned. "Or no, not a note, but rather—"

"You're here now," Harriet said swiftly. "That's what matters. Miss Bennet has need of you."

"I do?" I said.

"Yes," she said firmly. "If Mary King can use blood-letters, so can you. Indeed, so *must* you."

A sick feeling crawled in my stomach. "I had rather not. I did eat all those spell-sweets, after all. I'm sure I've enough for quite a jolly illusion—"

Harriet grabbed me by the forearms and looked into my eyes. "Listen to me, Lydia," she said. "A jolly illusion won't suffice. You've got to show the Order what a remarkable witch you really are. Do you know how long Miss Ward waited for her Great Working? Five years."

I sucked in a breath. I didn't have even one year.

"If you want the Order to make an exception for you, you've got to prove you'll be an exceptional member." She nodded to the four officers. "Use our friends here. They're your only chance."

My queasy feeling increased. Except for that night at Lady Herrington's, I'd never done any blood-magic—not with blood other than my own. But what choice did I have? Besides, none of them had shown any lasting effects from Harriet's use of them. Surely taking a little more would do them no harm.

"Use us for what?" drawled Carteret.

I looked at Harriet in alarm. The men of the honor guard bore none of the look of empty-headed goodwill that Harriet's vessels the night on the hill had worn. They were their normal selves, if a little confused. She whispered in my ear, "I've no dram of biddability for them. I can make them forget afterward, but we'll have to persuade them in the normal way."

Harriet stepped forward and raised her hands in placation, a charming smile on her face. "Listen, fellows," she said. "I know this is strange, but can Lydia cut your hands just a bit? It's a silly women's game, you see, but silly as it is, Lydia *must* win it."

They stared at me. Except for Wickham, they all looked utterly poleaxed. Denny was blinking in confusion. Fulton looked uncertainly at the others to see how to react. Carteret looked like he wasn't sure whether to laugh or beat a retreat. How little they really knew me.

"You want our *blood*?" said Carteret slowly. "For a...silly women's game? I thought women's games were things like lottery tickets, not... whatever this is."

"I've been cutting my hand rather a lot lately," said Fulton.

I was losing them. I opened my mouth to beg, but before I could, Wickham stepped forward. "Well," he said firmly, "I'm game. These ladies have never steered us wrong, have they, fellows?"

With an uncertain murmur, the others agreed. I started to shoot him a grateful glance, but he continued, "Of course, she's got to make it worth our while. What will you have of Miss Bennet, in exchange for a few drops of blood?"

Drat him. "Really, Wickham?"

"Debts must be paid, Miss Bennet." His eyes sparkled with lazy amusement.

"Very well." I looked to Denny first. "What can I do for you, Denny?"

He looked apologetic. "Awfully sorry, Bennet, but the fact is that the sight of me own blood makes me go all swoony. Silly thing for a grown man and a soldier, but there it is. I think I'd better sit this one out."

"It's for Kitty," I blurted.

"I'm in," he said immediately.

Lucky Kit. The man loved her even when he didn't love her anymore. I turned to Carteret. He was smiling quizzically. "Really, Miss Bennet, this is the strangest thing anyone has ever asked of me. I know you ladies have your whims and fancies, but this is damned odd."

"I know," I said.

He held up a hand. "Odd as it is, I am always delighted to get someone honorable in my debt. This seems like a small price to pay for a favor from you. Hmm." He wrinkled his brow. "What shall it be?" His gaze flicked to Harriet for a moment. She smiled and trailed her fingers down her neck. But he looked back to me and said, "Here's what I want. You're to help me to ingratiate myself with Miss Maria Lambe."

"What?" said Harriet. "Her?"

"I don't know if I can," I said. "Miss Lambe and I have had a falling-out."

Carteret's face was unyielding. "That's what I want, Miss Bennet."

"Oh, very well, I'll do my best." My best would certainly not get him anywhere, but that was his problem.

Harriet had gone very white, but she nodded when Carteret stepped forward to join Denny and Wickham.

I thought I would have the least trouble with Fulton. Where Wickham and Carteret led, he followed. But when I turned to him, I found he was wearing the same grim expression he'd had the night of the ball, when he'd warned me to take Miss Lambe home. "The Order of the Rose," he said. "I've heard strange whispers about these ladies."

I tried to smile. "It's just—it's a social club."

But he was shaking his head. "You oughtn't to be involved in such things, Miss Bennet. You're too good a woman for this."

"Where on earth did you get the idea that I was good?" I said irritably.

To my surprise, he took my hands. "If there's ever anything I can do to extricate you from all this, I want you to ask it of me," he said. "Make me a promise of that. That's all I want."

"You don't even know what 'all this' is."

"No, but you do." His eyes bored into mine. "Promise me."

"Very well," I said, and tried to pull my hands away. He would not let me.

"Say it," he said. "Say *I promise.*"

I strongly suspect that Fulton's mother or sister or something is a witch. The boy has an instinctual understanding of the way the witching world works that is quite inconvenient at times. "I promise," I said.

He nodded and let me go.

At least they'd all fallen in line. I drew a deep breath and turned to go to the dais when a hand shot out and gripped my wrist, detaining me. It was Wickham.

"Not so fast," he said. "What about my favor?"

I yanked my hand free. "If I succeed here, it benefits you as much as me," I pointed out.

"True. But an opportunity to extract a favor from you is too good to pass up."

I sighed. The women were beginning to take their seats. "What's it to be then? Be quick about it."

"Manners, manners. I'm doing you a good turn, remember." He

smiled. "If you're so rushed, you can promise me a boon to be specified later."

"Oh no. What kind of fool do you take me for? I know better than to give an open-ended promise to one of your family."

"All right," he said. "I'll take a kiss."

My face flamed. I had a sudden memory of his hand at my waist, his mouth over mine, so vivid it felt like everyone else must be able to see it on me. "You must be joking."

"I am not. And it's rather a small price to pay. My blood is quite powerful."

In that light, it was rather a small price. "Not a magical kiss?" I demanded. "Not some sort of dragon kiss that will turn me into a toad or something?"

"Just the normal kind," he said. "Lips and lips. Not here, of course. I'll take it in a more private setting to preserve your honor."

"You're a vile rake."

"Yes. And you're out of time." He nodded to the dais, where Miss Beaumont was gesturing for quiet.

One kiss. In exchange, quite possibly, for Kitty's life, and mine. One kiss for a man whom, after all, I'd already quite thoroughly kissed.

"Very well," I snapped. "Get up there with the others."

He bowed slightly over my hand, and joined his brother officers near the dais. When books talk of the "primrose path to damnation" they ought to have an illustration of me in them.

Miss Beaumont gave me a warm smile when I joined her on the dais. I had a feeling she was hoping to see me show up Miss King. But when the four officers filed up behind me, there were some shocked cries from the crowd. "Men!" someone yelled. "She brought men here!"

Miss Beaumont held up her hands once more. "I know, ladies, this is turning into quite an unorthodox day," she said. "But if Miss King was allowed to siphon off those servant girls, I think it only fair to let Miss Bennet bend the rules a bit as well." Her eyes turned to bore into mine. "After all, Mrs. Forster tells us she's quite a prodigy. I am sure that whatever she's about to show us will *certainly* be worth it. Isn't that right, Miss Bennet?"

I swallowed. "I'll do my best, ma'am. Thank you, ma'am." I bobbed a little curtsy.

"Sweet child," she said. "You may begin."

And I did.

Even as I began gathering my power, I was not sure what I would do. I'd been so focused on securing the men's cooperation, I'd had no time to think of what spell I would actually use. What would impress this formidable coven?

I glanced over at Mary King's table. She was staring at me sourly. Behind her, pale, blank-faced, stood her maids. One of them was swaying slightly. And then I knew what to do.

Denny looked away and whistled "Rule Britannia" while I cut him. His face was the color of cottage cheese. Carteret gave an exaggerated hiss of pain, then shot me a wink when I looked at him in alarm. Fulton stared straight at me and did not flinch. As for Wickham, I did my best not to look at him at all, and only noticed how very, very hot his hand was.

When I was done, I turned to the crowd, holding the little basin of my friends' blood. Funny, I thought, looking into the bowl—once it was mixed up, you could no longer tell dragon's blood from human, or noble from common. It was all just a mass of red.

"If you please," I said, "could Miss King's maids join me here?"

"Absolutely not," snapped Mary King. "You've your own blood-letters, you've no business using ours."

"They're not my spell's fuel, they're its object."

Mary frowned, but the two women, obedient as ever, came slowly forward when I beckoned.

"These gentlemen," I said to the crowd, indicating my honor guard, "are cut quite shallowly. Oh, it stings, I'm sure, but it will heal up without leaving even a scar." I set the bowl on the podium and put my hands at the backs of the two girls. I could feel them trembling a little. "I wish I could say the same for these two girls. I fear Miss King's blade was not sharp enough."

Gently, I bent their left arms forward just a hair, and the crowd gasped.

The girl on my left was wearing a black dress. Still, when she unbent her arm you could see that her whole arm was covered in a spreading wet stain. She bit her lip. The other girl was even worse off. As soon as I took the pressure off her elbow, blood spurted into the air. I hastily reapplied the pressure.

Miss Beaumont frowned. "Really, Mary, you ought to have been more careful with these poor girls. Have a little respect for your blood-letters. Suppose one of them should die? The most awkward questions would be asked."

"They're *my* maids," said Mary King sullenly.

"Don't be alarmed," I said. "I intend to fix the problem."

And I began my spell.

Anything to do with altering the human body, as I've mentioned, is quite difficult. Healing is not as bad as what had been done to Miss Ward's face—the body *wants* to heal, so one needn't work too hard to persuade it to seal up any unusual holes in it. It is more a question of giving it the power to do so. Still, it was quite the most complex spell I'd ever done. If not for my weeks of study with Harriet I'd never have attempted it.

The first few lines of my spell were a basic *how now*—a what-have-we-here chant to get the lay of the land. It was as I'd thought: They were quite badly hurt, especially the girl on the right. She'd quietly bled half to death in the corner while Mary King chatted and ate scones.

I glanced at Harriet. *Durire*, she mouthed.

Right. A few more lines of a hardening spell, slapped over their arms, made their wounds clot rapidly, and the bleeding stopped. Even just that much required all the magic I'd got from the spell-sweets.

A few people offered confused applause when I unbent the girls' arms to examine my work and they saw the grisly scabs, but I held up a hand for silence. I could feel fresh blood pulsing underneath, and knew that it would soon burst forth again. And they could not afford to lose one more drop.

The next step was to feed them strength. Their bodies were nearly depleted, so I simply put my hands in theirs and gave them all I could spare. It wouldn't have been enough, but for the otherworldly strength in Wickham's blood. *Much obliged, Wormenheart,* I thought, as the girls stopped trembling and began to stand up straighter.

For the girl on the left, that was nearly enough. She still had some of her own strength. Feeding her just a little more power and laying a speed charm over her wound was sufficient for her body to begin to heal the gash. I could feel it closing up as I let go of her.

The other girl was further gone. Her wound was too deep to heal on its own. Miss King had inadvertently tapped a large vein. If left to her own devices, she would soon bleed to death.

I was shaking now. My own strength was nearly gone, even with what my friends and Wickham had lent me. The smell of blood mixed with the other scents in the air—flowers, canvas, well-bred lady sweat—to form a sickly perfume.

I wiped the sweat from my forehead with a trembling hand. I had nothing left to give.

Somewhere, far away, I heard a disgruntled, contrary *mrow.*

I don't know how Kit knew I needed her. She was far too distant to talk to me. But somehow, she did know. And she had what I needed. I had never realized how strong Kit really was until she shoved that lump of power along the bond stretched from Hertfordshire to this garden near the sea. It was grudgingly given, and it felt unpleasantly like a dead mouse—Kitty had left enough of those on my bed when we were younger. But it was enough.

I heard excited murmurs of the word *familiar* darting through the crowd. So this was why witches were always so fascinated to hear about Kit. "If you knew what trouble she was, you wouldn't envy me," I muttered. Then I turned, slapped a rapid-healing charm over the second girl's arm, and finished the job.

The Order of the Rose surged to their feet in a standing ovation. I could barely hear it over the blood pounding in my ears. The last thing I felt was the hands of the honor guard, catching me as I collapsed in a faint.

I woke several minutes later, surrounded by well-wishers. It seemed my spell had greatly impressed the Order, and I was offered membership.

I suppose you are quite disgusted with me for not refusing their invitation. I assure you, I am quite disgusted with myself. Yes, I was a naive country mouse; yes, I was afraid for my life, and Kitty's; but to join a group that let two servant girls nearly bleed to death in the corner while they chattered and ate lemon cakes is beyond excuse. I suppose I chose to frame it as an excess of Miss King's, and to ignore the way the other women tolerated it as though it were a mere faux pas.

All I knew, really, was that I could not see any other choice. I told myself that I was exaggerating what I had seen—that someone else would have saved the two girls if I had not. Join, I told myself, just join, and survive, and sort out everything else later.

Besides, Harriet was there: Harriet with her arm around my shoulders, Harriet pressing a damp handkerchief to my forehead, Harriet ordering the others back so I could get a breath of fresh air. If Harriet said it was all right, it must be.

So I said the words they told me to say, and opened my mouth for Harriet's thumb to drop three drops of liquid from the yellow tulip vase onto my tongue. It was only at the end, when Miss Beaumont ordered me to prick my thumb and drop blood into the vase, that something in me went stock-still and refused to move. It was not a moral stand; not consciously, at least—I only knew that, surrounded by the scent of blood and flowers and lemon cakes, if I had to transact one more drop of anyone's blood I would be sick.

There was a little of that fuzzy, country-smelling power left from Kitty's delivery. Just a tuft, but it was enough. I held the rose thorn to my thumb, but the blood that welled up and dropped into the vase was merely an illusion.

It was a very good illusion, though, for none of the witches standing around watching caught it. Instead they all cheered and applauded and welcomed me as their newest member.

I curtsied and smiled through their well-wishes after. Miss Beaumont invited me and Harriet to stay for dinner, but Harriet, who could no doubt feel my hand trembling on her arm, declined on our behalf.

Most people had gone by then. Miss King had taken her servants and departed. I was still shaking so Harriet gave me Wickham's arm to lean on and walked ahead with Miss Beaumont and the rest of the honor guard to give them their Dram of Lethe and make them forget the day's events.

Leaving the tent made me blink: The sun had sunk low in the sky. Deep green-black shadows lengthened from the hedgerows, and I could see Miss Beaumont's servants lighting lamps inside. It was later than I realized.

"Are they all right?" I asked Wickham. "Carteret and Denny and Fulton?"

"They'll be fine." He patted my hand. "Call someone other than Denny next time, though. I thought the poor fellow was going to swoon. Heaven help him if we're ever in battle."

I swallowed hard. Next time? But I knew he was right. Pints of power, drops in vases, cuts on hands and elbows—blood, blood, blood. This was not the last time the Order would expect me to contribute. The table-mistresses' power flowed to Miss Beaumont, everyone's power to the table-mistresses—and all the witches around those tables, where did their reserves of power come from? Were all of them enchanting their friends and servants, doing their best not to commit the faux pas of taking too much?

That reminded me of the promises the honor guard had extracted from me—Wickham in particular. "You won't really make me kiss you, will you?"

His hand tightened on mine. "Not backing out, are you? I don't believe magic looks kindly on broken promises."

"It's not broken if you let me out of it."

"Ah, but I'm not going to let you out of it."

"You, sir, are taking shameless advantage—"

"You took my *blood*," he said sharply. "Do you really think I am the one taking advantage?"

I looked away, a sick wave of shame swamping me.

To my surprise, he looked chagrined. "No, don't look like that," he said. "I know you are only doing what you must."

"Then you will let me out of it?"

"No."

"I could give you something else. Copy you out some of Cowper's poems, perhaps—"

"No."

"Why not? I know you love them. I saw your face when Harriet and I read them aloud when it rained last week, and you all piled into her drawing room."

"Yes," he said, "they're lovely."

"Then why—"

His boot scuffed a bit of dirt from the rose beds onto the impeccable stone path. "If you must know," he said, "I can't."

"Can't what?"

"Read."

"Oh, come now."

"It's true," he muttered. "I had to choose which bits of Wickham's knowledge to maintain. I couldn't keep it all—there isn't room in one head for two people. Foolishly, I chose to drop the alphabet and keep his knowledge of how to cheat at cards."

"But I've seen you read letters."

"I can read people, and the imprints they leave," he said. "But a witch does not leave such imprints, and nor do printing presses, and there it is."

I could not help it. I gave a snort of laughter. "You can't read."

"Shut up," he said.

But the giggles would not stop bubbling up. "You're a demon who loves poetry and cries at waltzes and can't *read*," I gasped.

"Enough," he said. "Or I'll take my kiss in the middle of a public ballroom."

That threat was enough to douse my laughter. My cheeks flamed. "You wouldn't."

"Probably not, but I shall enjoy holding it over your head. In fact, I rather think I won't take it right away. I quite fancy being able to make you blush like that whenever I choose."

That thought was quelling indeed. I looked down the path. Harriet and Miss Beaumont were quite a way ahead of us. I grabbed Wickham's elbow and yanked him behind a tall hedgerow. He gave a slight yelp of surprise. Before he could say anything more, I grabbed his face in my hands and kissed him.

Magic makes no allowance for those who follow the letter of the law but not the spirit. I knew I had to make the kiss a good one, and I did. I shoved my body against his, threw my arms around his neck, and did my utmost to make him the best-kissed man in England at that moment. He stood frozen in shock for an instant, then wound his arms around my waist.

Somehow, when he began to kiss me back, I started to forget that I was merely settling a debt. Indeed, I stopped thinking of anything at all, except his mouth and his hands and the press of his body against mine.

It ended when the backs of my knees ran into a stone bench. I fell back with an *oof* and Wickham tumbled down on top of me. For a moment we lay frozen, staring at each other.

Then I crowed, "Hah!" and smacked him in the chest. "Kiss delivered. Promise discharged."

"So it most certainly was." He did not look angry. He was staring at me with the oddest expression on his face. One of his arms was trapped underneath me. I realized that, just as he had the night of Lady Herrington's ball, he'd cupped the back of my head to keep it from striking the stone.

I swallowed hard. The moment stretched and slowed. I leaned up toward him again.

I truly am the most wanton creature, for it was he who stopped things from going any further. He placed three fingers on my lips, keeping them from his. "Don't," he said, his voice gravelly. "You may need to buy my blood again. Keep your coffers full."

And he stood, dusted himself off, and offered me his hand to help me to my feet. He walked me to the front of the house, where Harriet was waiting in the carriage, and bowed us away without another word. I must be the only girl in the world who has threatened the virtue of a demon, rather than the other way round.

When Harriet and I arrived home, I wanted to go straight to my room and collapse into bed. But it was not to be. "You've a visitor, Miss Bennet," said Sally when she opened the door to us. "It's that Miss Lambe."

I'll leave it there for now. I went into the village today, and spent most of the afternoon scribbling on a bench in the town square. I've a crick in my neck and I suspect I've sunburnt my nose, but that's all right. It was lovely to be out of doors.

I wrote so long that I quite lost track of time and Wickham came to collect me in Bingley's carriage. I saw more than one admiring eye turned to him as he rolled into the square in the smart little phaeton. He's an excellent driver and does cut a fine figure if you don't know what a rat he is.

"You are stiff from sitting so long," he said, when he saw me rubbing my neck. "Shall we take a walk about the square before we go back?"

"To give the village girls more time to admire you, you mean?"

He merely offered his arm and waited. And I *was* stiff, so I took it.

The late-afternoon sun was turning everything all golden. There was still a springlike warmth in the air, but it was colder in the shadows in a way that promised harsher weather to come. I tucked my arm in his and we walked slowly around, examining the shop windows.

"How goes the writing?" he asked.

"Wouldn't you like to know."

He huffed but let that pass. "Which bit are you writing about?"

"Brighton. The Order."

"Ah."

We walked a bit more. The muscles of my neck were unknotting themselves. "Do you ever miss it?" I asked. "Brighton, I mean?"

"Of course. Do you?"

"I don't know."

"Oh, come now. You were like a child in a sweet shop there."

"True," I admitted. "But that was then. I don't think it would be the same if I were to go back."

"No, I suppose not."

We paused in front of a haberdashery window so I could examine the new bonnets on display. Instead of the bonnets, though, I found myself looking at our reflection in the glass. He is really a very fine-looking man.

I was so tired from writing, and I knew that I would face more pressure from Darcy at supper. For a moment I had an almost overpowering urge to lean my head on his shoulder.

It may not be much, but his is the only shoulder in the world I've any right to lean on.

I pulled back from the abyss. It wouldn't do to start thinking of him in those terms. I mustn't go soft toward him. It's only because I'm writing about that strange time, those days in Brighton when it really seemed that perhaps, he and I—

*Stop it, Lydia. Enough.*

I shan't be able to write outdoors anymore. Though the weather has been briefly so fine, there's a nasty storm coming.

That sounds like a metaphor, but I just mean it's going to rain tomorrow.

# CHAPTER TWENTY-EIGHT

Miss Lambe was waiting in the Forsters' sitting room, as gray and buttoned-up as she had been the day I met her. All traces of the exuberant belle from Lady Herrington's ball were gone. The only dash of color about her person was a little bunch of purple and blue flowers, pinned to her dress in place of a brooch. I briefly wondered how she'd managed to grow the tropical blooms without using magic, but chose not to think too hard about it. Right now the very idea of flowers made me want to be sick.

"Good evening, Miss Lambe," Harriet said. "I am glad to see you back in Brighton. No one was sure if you would return."

"I was not sure myself."

"Your family in London is well?"

"What? Oh yes, certainly. Mrs. Forster, may I speak to Miss Bennet alone for a few minutes?"

Harriet glanced at me and I nodded. She withdrew, shutting the parlor door behind her.

I sat down on the couch opposite Miss Lambe's high-backed chair. It was the most uncomfortable chair in the room, but from the rigid perfection of her posture I doubt she noticed. She was regarding me intensely. "You've a spot of blood on your petticoat," she said.

"Have I?" I pulled my skirts around until I saw she was right. "Dash it. Lord knows how I am to explain that to Sally."

"You've been doing blood-magic."

"Just a bit with Harriet's coven."

"I see."

She lapsed into silence again. I was intensely aware of the sound of Cook banging pots in the kitchen. I smoothed my skirts, trying not to let my hands bunch nervously into the folds.

"I'm sorry," I blurted. "I really am."

"I know," she said. "I read your letter."

"You did?"

"Yes. I did not believe it at first. But after visiting your family in Hertfordshire—"

*"What?"*

"Didn't they tell you?"

I thought of my strange dream where I was Kitty, and someone was forcing me to hold both my shapes at once. "Kitty tried, I think. I thought it was just a dream."

"Well, it was not. She and I had a long talk. Why didn't you simply tell me that you needed the Jewel of Propriety to save her?"

I sighed. "It was hard enough going as it was, getting you not to despise me. How was I to tell you I needed to take one of your jewels?"

She frowned. "I did not despise you."

"Oh," I said miserably. *Did not*, not *do not*.

"None of my jewels are magical, anyway."

"I know that now."

"I want to help you find the Jewel of Propriety," she said.

I was dumbfounded. "You do?"

"Yes."

"Glory be. Why?"

Her keen eyes flashed to mine. "We're not friends," she said.

"I know."

"We're not friends, but I understand why you did what you did. You were desperate. I've been where you are. But believe me, that kind of panic only makes things worse."

I thought of that girl screaming on the mountaintop, trying to claw back a hurricane as it slipped through her fingers, and shivered.

"And I heard what you did for Nellie and Fay," she said.

"Nellie and Fay?"

"Miss Mary King's maids."

"Ah." I had never asked their names.

"You're a gifted girl, Lydia. It's no wonder the Order wants you. But if you continue with them, you'll need your own Nellies and Fays soon enough."

The memory of my friends' blood closed my throat. She was right.

"Suppose I help you instead," she said. "I should not like to see your power fall into the hands of that—of the Order. We can find your jewel together, you and I."

Right then, I knew, was the moment to admit I had already joined the Order. But I was too embarrassed. Besides, if I did, Miss Lambe might not help me, and if a small lie of omission could save Kit, surely the scales more than balanced. "Very well," I said. "Thank you. So where is it?"

"Where is what?"

"The Jewel of Propriety."

She looked quite startled. "I have no idea. What makes you think I have it?"

I told her about what Wickham had shown me.

"*I* do not have it," she said. "I've never seen the thing, nor the traces of it you claim you saw on me. And I'm quite good at seeing magic, you know."

"I know," I said ruefully.

She shook her head decisively. "No, I think you've been going about this all wrong. Throwing more and more magic away on aimless spells isn't getting you anywhere. Why, you don't even know what this jewel is."

I was rather startled to realize she was right. For all I'd been desperately seeking it, I had no idea of its true nature. "Then where do you suggest we start?"

"With rigorous research of course," she said, and laughed when she saw my face. "Come to my lodgings tomorrow morning. It will not be so bad, I assure you."

Did you know that in Roman times Sussex was ruled over by a fellow with the excellent name of Cogidubnus? It is quite true, I assure you. This and many other exceedingly dull facts Miss Lambe had learned in her research, and imparted to me the next morning.

"If you are looking for an object of power that is tied to the region," she said as I yawned, "it stands to reason to research the region. You have been floundering about, casting general scries, rather than learning more."

"So you know something about the jewel then?"

"Not much," she admitted. "Magical scholarship is decidedly lacking in these parts. Still, I've discovered a thing or two."

She produced several dusty volumes with titles like *A Brighthelmstone Grimoire* and *Witchery of the Sussex Parts*. It seemed the Jewel of Propriety was so called because it was a tool of Brighton's Witch-Queen—"Shee doth use the jewelles power to garde against chaoss and wickednesse," said *A Brighthelmstone Grimoire*. *Witchery of the Sussex Parts* had a diagram of the Witch-Queen holding the Jewel of Propriety, which appeared to be growing out of her hand, and using it to burn away some thorny brambles that probably symbolized gluttony or something.

It was all disappointingly pious.

"This is a great deal more than I knew before," I admitted. "But people hereabouts say this Witch-Queen vanished ages ago. How does this help us?"

"We may not be able to consult the Witch-Queen, but there are other great powers hereabouts," pointed out Miss Lambe, and flipped to a spell titled *To Call the Long Man*.

What was it Fulton had said? *It's said he'll strengthen your hand against your enemies, or bring you knowledge you seek.* Worth a try, certainly. Miss Lambe and I cast it. It was a peculiar spell—it sounded a bit like a summoning, such as one might use on a lost lamb or calf, but somehow more respectful. Less a command than an invitation. Strangest of all, it required no spell-price. I had never encountered such a working before; even the most trifling usually require one to pluck out a few hairs or the like. Miss Lambe and I were both of the opinion that it probably would not work, cast midafternoon in a hired parlor—probably we'd have to climb the hill at midnight and dance naked or something.

After we'd finished, we thought at first we'd been right. Nothing seemed to change, except the wind. Normally the breeze came in through the front windows overlooking the sea, carrying the scent of salt and faraway places. Now, though, the wind blew in from the French windows at the rear of the parlor, the ones that opened directly onto a rolling green hill. There were sheep grazing higher up the hill, and I could hear their placid, faraway baas. The air smelled of grass—green and summery, with a hint of sweet hay and clover. I felt a squeeze in my chest. I would not have said up to that moment that I was homesick, but those scents reminded me that I had been away for months now from the farmland where I'd grown up.

I was about to suggest that we try the spell again when I heard "Halloo!" from outside. A man came tramping in through the French windows. He was a gangly fellow, so tall he had to duck his head to come inside the doorway. He was wearing an old-fashioned green shepherd's tunic and a green hat, and he carried two staffs. He had the tan, craggy face of a man who spent his life out of doors, deeply creased with smile lines. "Evening, ladies," he said, tugging his forelock to us. "Ah, I'd best stay by the door, for this is as handsome a dwelling as any I've seen, and my shoes are all over mud and the Lord knows what else. I'll just leave these here." He leaned his two staffs against a decorative bust by the doors. "Now then. Let's to business, you fine folks, afore my flock's had a chance to run off to mischief." And he smiled upon us.

"Good day, sir," I said.

"Good day to you, mistress."

"Who are you?" asked Miss Lambe.

"A humble shepherd, mistress, at your service."

"We wish to contact the Long Man," I said. "We were told he knew something of how to find the Jewel of Propriety."

The man gave a low whistle. "A jewel, is it? I'm sure I don't know owt about it. No one speaks to shepherds of such things. If the Long Man could have brung home the jewel, he'd've done so many a year ago. But you're in luck, mistresses. 'Tis almost Lammas Day, a great strong time for the Long Man. Aye, in a few weeks, go you to an echoing place and call him, and mayhap he'll have some answers for you. Aye, I'm sure he will."

"An echoing place?" I repeated. "What's that?"

"A place that loudens the voice of the supplicant, the better to reach the ear of the power you call," he said. "The closest one be a day's journey away. The Shell Grotto, they call it. Go you there three nights afore Lammas and the Long Man will have enough power to reveal to you the jewel you seek." A distant, plaintive bleat drifted through the window. "Well, I think I hear one of my lambs, so I'm best off." He bowed to us once more, donned his cap, seized his staffs, and set off back out the French windows and up the hill. I watched him go for a time, the green-gold light of the summer evening blending with the green of his tunic and the grass and the soft sound of his sheep's bells.

"Lydia? *Lydia!*"

I blinked and found myself being violently shaken. I opened my eyes and found Wickham standing over me, his hands tight on my shoulders, shaking me so hard my teeth rattled. Before I could regain my wits he had seized a jug of water from the side table and held it over my head, as though to dash its contents in my face.

"Stop!" I cried. "What are you doing?"

Wickham froze. Slowly, he lowered the jug. "Are you all right?"

"If I say yes, will you promise not to drench me with water?"

He put the jug down. "You were dumb," he said. "Both of you. I could not make you answer me."

Next to me, Miss Lambe was also blinking and looking around in confusion. "Nonsense," I said. "We were just talking to the—" I made to gesture in the direction the shepherd had left, but my hand stilled in midair. The rear wall of the parlor had no windows at all. If it had, they would have looked out onto a crowded Brighton street.

"Well," said Miss Lambe. "That was odd."

"What happened?" Wickham demanded.

"I believe we met the Long Man," she said. "He strongly suggested that in two weeks we take a journey to someplace called the Shell Grotto."

# CHAPTER TWENTY-NINE

The Shell Grotto was known to the local witches. "It was quite fashionable a few years ago," said Harriet when I told her about the Long Man's advice. "The Order used to go there sometimes for special spells. Common folk don't know it's there, and no one knows who made it, which makes the whole thing quite thrilling. But it's so dreary to get there and back, and it never seemed to strengthen our spells, so we gave it up."

So we made plans to travel to the grotto a few days before Lammas Day. There were weeks until then, though, and in the interim we had little to do. So we carried on—I will not say "as normal," for what does that mean in such circumstances?—but as expected of us. We walked, we danced, we flirted (some of us), we practiced our spells.

My two social sets now merged, more or less, into one. Wickham took to stopping by Miss Lambe's lodgings most afternoons; his presence in her drawing room drew a possessive Carteret, who drew a jealous Harriet, and all of us drew a lonely Fulton. Before long the lot of us were sitting around Miss Lambe's parlor nearly every day.

Carteret was not one to waste an opportunity presented. He had recently acquired a fine curricle and a beautiful pair of horses through dubious means; he lured me out in it on the pretense of a ride and, once he had me trapped, grilled me about Miss Lambe. Who were her family? Did she like him at all? What did she seek in a husband?

Remembering my promise, and mindful of the still-healing cut across his palm, I did my best to answer him. Her family were dead, and, yes, had left her in possession of quite as enormous a fortune as any could wish. As for what she looked for in a husband—

"Influence," I said. "She has all the money she could ever need—more, for she hardly spends a penny. What she wants is a man with enough influence to fight the relations who would rob her of it. Sorry, Carteret, that counts you out, doesn't it?"

He leaned back in the driver's seat, a faraway look in his eye. "Influence," he mused. "I could have influence."

"Could you?" I asked, startled.

He slanted an amused glance at me. "Do you doubt me, country mouse?"

"I have never known you to have any influence, is all," I said. "I've never known you to have much of anything really. My guess is that by next week you will no longer have this carriage."

"Ah, my creditors will have to catch me first," he said, and clucked the horses faster. "I am from a prominent family. For the right woman, I could be anything at all, except rich."

"And Miss Lambe is the right woman?"

"If she agrees to marry me, she is."

"She is my friend, you know. I shall have to warn her about you."

"Warn her what? That I am a fortune-hunter? She is a clever girl and knows that already, I assure you. I shall do my best to convince her that I am worth letting herself be hunted."

Some devil made me ask, "What about Harriet?"

"For heaven's sake, girl, keep your voice down. We're nearly back on the high street. Harriet and I understand each other. We've passed a lovely summer together but she would never expect me to ruin my own prospects over her for no reason."

I rather doubted that Harriet would consider her devotion to be *no reason*, but I knew if I asked her about it she would just laugh at me and say he was quite right, so I said no more.

I did warn Miss Lambe as best I could. As Carteret had predicted, she was unsurprised.

"So he believes he has influence enough to woo me, does he?" she said. "I have seen little evidence, but let him try."

So try he did.

At first, she just laughed at him. His florid attempts at seduction were quite, quite wrong for a woman such as she. When he showed her the locket he had had made with a little portrait of her inside, she said it looked like a picture of a bear and teased him mercilessly. But Carteret was no ordinary rake. When he realized that he was getting nowhere, he merely joined her laughter and said, "Very well, Miss Lambe, I shall try less conventional roads to your heart. One of them somewhere must be open."

"I doubt it," she said.

What she had not reckoned on, I think, was pride. Her own. She knew that Carteret could not win her heart; it was not free to be won, by him or by any man. So she thought there was no harm in letting him flatter and pursue her. However, human beings are soft creatures. We like warm touches and admiring glances. No matter how we try to constrict those impulses in a cage of morality, they will return, stronger than when we tried to force them away. Miss Lambe had been punishing herself for a long time. She thought she could relax her strictures, just a little. But one cannot open a dam *just a little*.

It became quite commonplace to see Miss Lambe about town on Carteret's arm.

Nor was Carteret's charm the only weapon in his arsenal. In the days after I told him about Miss Lambe's desire for a partner with influence, he went about with an intent, abstracted look on his face. I soon heard that he had begun borrowing large sums of money from his brother officers. The men of the regiment were always getting into terrible debts to one another, not to mention to merchants and moneylenders; but even for them, this was striking behavior.

I thought he had some investment scheme in mind—dubious property in the colonies, or a share in a factory—and I fretted that he would ruin himself. But what he had in mind was actually far riskier.

Carteret, it seemed, had no plan for the money at all, except to lose it at gambling.

Brighton was a very gambling town. We all played cards a great deal; we could not dance and have assignations *all* the time, and we had to fill the hours that better folk passed with reading improving literature and honing their accomplishments. I had too little money and was too distracted by my own troubles to get into much debt, luckily. The men of the regiment, I knew, played even more than the rest of us. When we innocent ladies had gone home to our beds, they stayed up in inns and back rooms and gambled away the little money they had.

Carteret suddenly became a much more extravagant player than he had been. He had large sums of money to bet and did not appear to mind much when he lost them. It is my understanding that in serious gambling circles such a man is called a "fish," and is as highly prized as a pretty, stupid girl with ten thousand pounds is in the marriage market. Thus, Carteret soon found himself invited to much loftier tables than those he had frequented before.

And why? Well. For some time, Miss Lambe had been rather upset about a bit of news of her home. There was talk of stationing a garrison of English soldiers on Sainte-Josephine permanently. She was determined that this must be prevented.

"Sainte-Josephine is not like your other colonies," she told us, pacing in her living room. "It has its own way of doing things. It must retain at least some of its independence. It *must*."

Carteret looked at her for a long moment. "So, Miss Lambe, the garrison must not come to your Sainte-Josephine." And he gave a sharp nod. The next day was when he began to borrow.

His new spendthrift ways, coupled with his charming, well-bred manners, soon brought him into company with men who moved in the first circles. Not only his own colonel, but other higher-ranked officers, even a general or two. It was rumored that the Prince Regent himself had appeared at Carteret's table once or twice—true or not, this of course made him even more in demand.

And still, he lost money, more and more and more. Money he had never had in the first place.

I fretted about it to Harriet. She, as usual, laughed at me. "Can you really not see?" she said. "Oh, he is a clever fellow. I think it's brilliant, myself."

Indeed, if Harriet had ever been jealous of Miss Lambe, she now seemed determined to be aloof and amused, even encouraging. She constantly talked of Carteret's virtues to Miss Lambe, and talked to Carteret as though they were co-conspirators in attempting to achieve the match. She laughed about it a great deal, and whenever Miss Lambe was not about Harriet loudly offered him advice on how to steal time with her and which gambling tables he ought to frequent. Carteret accepted her help with equanimity, but did not admit her into his confidence any more than the rest of us.

I finally learned what he was about when he paid a call on Miss Lambe one morning. It was fairly early, around ten o'clock, and the heat of the day had not yet become unbearable. We sat out on the balcony, enjoying the sea breeze, and were surprised to see Carteret coming up the street. He looked disheveled, still in his evening clothes, and I assumed he had not yet been to bed. Stumbling along beside him was a man whom at first I thought I did not know. He was even more disheveled than Carteret—cravat untied, his gait wavering, his wig turned sideways on his head to reveal a thatch of gray hair. He looked a thoroughly unsavory character.

Carteret brought his companion to a shaky halt in front of Miss Lambe's lodgings and, propping his companion up with one arm, waved up at us with the other. "Good morning, Miss Lambe, Miss Bennet," he called up. "I believe you are acquainted with Admiral Whitcombe?"

"La!" I said, and craned my neck over the railing. "Why, it is him." I had only exchanged a few words with the tall, dignified admiral, one of the most respected and awe-inspiring figures in Brighton society. Well, he inspired neither respect nor awe at the moment.

He looked around blearily, then said, "Eh, Porter—Carter—Carteret—tha's not my lodgings."

"I know," Carteret said. "But you owe me a debt of honor, sir. Remember?"

The admiral grumbled, attempting to straighten his wig. He overshot and it ended up sideways in the other direction. "Remember—yes," he muttered. "Yes, very well. Last time I sit down at the gaming table with you, young cove." He peered up at us. "Which one is it? The Creole or the baby?"

"Miss Lambe is the one on the right."

"Evening, Miss Lambe," the admiral called up. "I am to tell you that none of the ships under my command will carry troops to—where was it?"

"Sainte-Josephine."

"To Sainte-Josephine. Lord knows why a lady should care." He turned back to Carteret. "There, I have done it. You'll give me back my marker." Carteret handed him a crumpled bit of paper from his pocket, gave us a lazy salute, and conveyed the admiral away down the street. We stared after him in shock. Miss Lambe's mouth hung open. Carteret glanced back and, apparently liking what he saw, winked.

"Good heavens," I said.

Miss Lambe made a visible effort to collect herself. "It will come to nothing. Drunken promises mean nothing in the light of day."

However, Admiral Whitcombe kept his promise. To some men, gambling debts are like marriage vows. He made it quite clear that none of his ships would be troop transports for Sainte-Josephine. Miss Lambe looked upon Carteret with a great deal more respect after that.

I demanded to know how Carteret planned to recoup all he had lost in this scheme. He shrugged. "Once she agrees to marry me, she will discharge my debts," he said. "It was a worthwhile investment."

"That's rather mercenary of you."

"Marriage is mercenary, country mouse. How many times must I tell you?"

Despite this triumph—or perhaps because of it—Harriet's enthusiasm for his marriage plot began to wane. She no longer egged Carteret on, and tended to go white and leave the room when she saw him and Miss Lambe together. Once I saw Harriet and Carteret in a whispered argument; she gripped his sleeve till he shook her off. I wanted to comfort Harriet, but was not sure how. When I asked her about it, she still insisted that "Carteret's scheme was famous."

Miss Lambe steadfastly refused our invitations to attend meetings of the Order; she believed that I went only to oblige Harriet, and I am afraid I did not disabuse her. However, she was now a little more willing than she had been to perform magic. We were doing our best to prepare for Lammas Day, which required a certain amount of scrying and defensive spells, and to my surprise she shouldered the burden of performing them without a word.

I asked her about it, and she said, "I've agreed to help you. I may be cautious of the price that magic extracts, but it would be selfish to force you to pay all of it."

I certainly made no objection. It was a pleasure to watch her work. She was an extraordinary witch. Her workings were as neat and precise as the rest of her, and she never extracted the price from anyone but herself. Some of her spells were familiar to me, chants in old English or Latin, while others were more foreign concoctions of French and Spanish and various Creole languages. The prices she exacted on herself were usually abstract—she did not favor bodily pain or cuts—and frequently took the form of self-improvement. She would forgo something she enjoyed, like walking by the sea, and spend an hour declining Latin verbs or practicing on the harp. It had never occurred to me as a child, when I gave up the pursuit of accomplishments, that I could have saved time in this way. I wish I did not know it now. It removes my excuse for not practicing my drawing, which I am certainly not going to do.

I was grateful to her for taking her share of the spell-work—more than her share, really—for I was finding magic increasingly difficult for some reason. A simple don't-notice-me that Miss Lambe could fuel with a few scales on the harp took a much steeper price from me, and left me shaky and gasping. It was only by reaching out to Kitty for help that I managed any spells at all. Kitty, naturally, did not care for this, and the magic she sent me felt sour and thin.

She did send it, though, and I was glad. Every time she sent me magic, it was like clasping hands with her for a moment. I assumed that my increased weakness was due to Wormenheart, and it occurred to me for the first time that if we failed at the Shell Grotto, I would probably never see Kitty again. We would perish hundreds of miles apart. This bothered me more than the idea of dying itself. Kitty and I belonged together. That was the natural state of things. I had been able to ignore it in the first frenzy of the summer, but now I longed to have her with me so much it was like a physical ache.

Miss Lambe noted my frequent exhaustion, though she attributed it to the cloying heat wave that had settled over Brighton. She shouldered even more of the spell burden and, whenever she saw my hands shaking, ordered Wickham to take me down to the seaside. I resisted this at first, for I no longer trusted the sea and had never trusted Wickham, but was usually too tired to win out.

And Wickham? What of him during this strange time?

On our walks by the sea, he astonished me by being something approaching a gentleman. He was careful of my stamina, found me places to sit and brought me cool things to drink, and changed the subject when a topic upset me. I was reminded of how charmed all of Meryton had been when he first arrived. He certainly knew how to please when he chose to. I supposed that he was keeping me amused so as not to let me think too hard about what his father was doing to me; but as I did not wish to think about it, either, I was glad of the distraction. He mostly did so by telling me things a young lady ought not to know—how to conceal an ace up one's sleeve, how to pick a winner in a cockfight, the best way to win a drinking contest. How to unlace a corset one-handed, which he offered, with a sweet smile, to demonstrate. I said no thank you, and turned to the sea to let the breeze cool my heated cheeks. (Something *approaching* a gentleman, I said.)

I was tired, and frightened, and he was there. I wanted so much to lean on somebody, and for all his faults, his arm was strong and steady. And, for reasons I could not understand, he seemed to want to be leaned on.

Occasionally Fulton would join us on these walks. He was not precisely invited, and his presence limited what we could talk about—all magical topics were off the table, and we had no wish to shock him by talking of bodices or cheating at cards—so we mostly spent those walks in silence, all three of us staring out to sea. Fulton looked older than he had at the beginning of the summer. He acted older, too. He was still a quiet fellow, especially around Wickham, but his reticence now seemed less awed than speculative. I often saw him looking between me and his friend with a question in his eyes.

Brighton society began to talk of me and Wickham as a pair, just as they spoke of Miss Lambe and Carteret. If I had been listening properly, I would have seen that we were not *quite* the same. Wickham was a well-known fortune-hunter, and unlike Miss Lambe, I had no fortune to hunt. For me to be so much in the company of a man who could not possibly mean to marry me was not at all the thing, even in freewheeling Brighton. I see all this in retrospect, but at the time, I paid it scarcely any attention. I had no intention of marrying Wickham; I always behaved with perfect propriety in public (well, close enough to perfect propriety, anyway); so what did it matter if Wickham was there?

If Miss Lambe's cardinal sin at that time was pride, then mine was certainly naïveté.

As the days wound on, our tangled knots grew tighter. Miss Lambe no longer flinched when anyone hinted that she and Carteret were soon to be engaged. Wickham was nearly always at my elbow. He waltzed with me as usual, but those were practically the only dances I did dance. I was too tired for the others, and usually sat down with a lemonade or a punch (unseawatered). Fulton always asked me to stand up with him, but since I was so tired and he did not waltz, I rarely accepted. I think he believed it was Wickham's influence, and often scowled at him.

Now it was I, not Miss Lambe, begging to go home early from even the liveliest ball or entertainment. What had once invigorated me now wore me down, and the close, pressing heat of the ballroom made me feel like I was suffocating. Harriet had little patience for what she called "my airs." She wanted to stay out and dance all night, and when I asked to go home she upbraided me for my dullness.

"When I asked you here, I wanted a young companion who could enjoy the pleasures of Brighton," she said. "*You* are not five-and-forty, like my husband, so do not behave so."

Tears sprang to my eyes when she said things like that. I wanted above all things to be the companion Harriet wanted. I despised the dullness that had sprung up in me as much as she did, but I could not seem to overcome it. At first I did my best, and when she assured me that all it would take to refresh my spirits was one more country dance and a strong glass of punch, I followed her advice. But I always ended up with my muscles aching and heart pounding, longing for a quiet cool place to rest. Most nights I left with Miss Lambe and Mrs. Tomlinson, since they kept hours more like I now preferred. I practically lived in their spare room.

I was not the only one who was out of sorts just then. I supposed everyone was becoming weary of the endless pleasure parade of Brighton. Denny stopped doing magic tricks, Carteret no longer flirted reflexively with everyone who walked by, and Fulton was quieter than ever. Miss Lambe seemed unaffected, but then she had never been very lively to begin with. Nor did Wickham seem to have lost his spirits, but he had the opposite problem. If anything, after he'd waved good night to us, he began a whole other life. I began to hear tales of his wild exploits:

gambling, fighting, horse racing. He'd always been a rogue of course, but people used to speak of him admiringly. Now they lowered their voices and wondered where it would end.

One morning he showed up at Miss Lambe's house, clearly in the clothes he'd worn the night before. "Is everything well with you, Wickham?" I said.

"Quite well, Miss Bennet, whyever should you ask?" He had a pair of dice that he was rolling over and over and did not look up from his task. He smelled faintly of beer and tobacco.

"Because half the town is fretting on your behalf over your gambling debts, and the other half is threatening to beat your head in if you don't pay them."

He gave a tired grin. "I admit I have had something of a bad run of it these last weeks. But a man must do something to keep himself amused. However do you humans sleep this time of year when the sun's always up?"

"We manage. Is it true you've gambled away all you had?"

"What do you care?" He tossed the dice again.

"I don't. But I need your help with Wormenheart, remember? You won't be able to help me if you're thrown in debtors' prison."

"Ah yes, my father. Never fear, Miss Bennet, I shall be here to fulfill your requirements of me. Remember, my attributes include luck and charm. No one will want to throw such a delightful fellow as I in jail, and regardless, I shall soon begin to win again. I daresay this next toss will be double sixes." But he threw snake eyes.

Harriet seemed full of a wild energy. She flirted outrageously with Carteret, sometimes right in front of her husband. When she could not get Carteret to herself, she flirted with other men, and looked to see if Carteret was jealous. Carteret visited her less often, but when she was able to get him to come, she no longer seemed to care about getting caught. Once Carteret slipped out the back door while the colonel was entering at the front. It was only Carteret's sense of self-preservation that saved them—Harriet had hung round his neck and tried to get him, against all reason, to stay.

Even the colonel's easy temper had its limits. I was glad to spend most of my nights at Miss Lambe's, because Harriet's breakfast table had become rather uncomfortable. Colonel Forster would growl about her behavior the night before, she would insist she had no idea what he was talking about, and all would subside into icy silence.

"You know," he said on one of those awful mornings, "there were those who said I oughtn't to marry you. Your mother, the natural daughter of somebody-or-other—bad blood will out, they said."

"There were many who said I oughtn't to marry an old man like you," she said coolly. "But my mother did not give me the option of refusing."

Neither of them seemed to notice I was there. I watched in horror as they tore each other to shreds, before muttering my excuses and escaping to Miss Lambe's. Lord, I had thought my parents' marriage was bad.

Somehow we made it through that horrible July, and a few days before the end of the month, Miss Lambe, Harriet, the honor guard, and I prepared to set out for the Shell Grotto.

# CHAPTER THIRTY

When we had first planned the journey to the Shell Grotto, I looked forward to it, not only because it might save my life, but because I thought it would be fun. Me, Miss Lambe, Harriet, the honor guard: It seemed to me the perfect party. I was sure that all of young Brighton would be eaten up with envy if they did not obtain an invitation.

Who knows, perhaps they were—but if so, it was probably out of curiosity to see such a potent mix of personalities explode. What a difference a few weeks make.

The night before we set off, we were all at another ball at Lady Herrington's. I was in my typical seat, catching my breath and waiting until it was polite to leave. I saw Colonel Forster and Carteret having words in a corner. Carteret used to be one of the colonel's favorites—though he was never what you'd call a model soldier, he made himself very agreeable, and the colonel enjoyed his company—but lately, there had grown up a certain stiffness between them. The colonel still had some willful blindness where his wife and Carteret were concerned, but not even he could believe that they were behaving quite as they ought. The colonel had a tight grip on Carteret's shoulder and was speaking some low words in his ear. Carteret at first tried to laugh it away, but then went quite pale. It occurred to me for the first time that the kindly, bumbling colonel was a man of some importance who could make or break livelihoods and reputations whenever he chose.

Carteret seemed to be explaining something rather desperately to the unmoved colonel. After a moment Carteret broke off and went over to Miss Lambe and spoke briefly. She looked surprised, but nodded. A dance had just ended, and Carteret approached the musicians. Then he turned to the assembled crowd and raised his hands for our attention.

"Ladies and gentlemen," he cried. "A moment, please. I will not long delay your enjoyment of this lovely evening, but my beloved has given me permission to share our joyous news: Miss Maria Lambe has agreed to be my wife."

The expected coos and applause met his announcement. A flock of women pressed around Maria to offer congratulations. She smiled and looked as composed as ever. Fulton and Denny slapped Carteret on the back. The musicians struck up a waltz, one of Carteret's favorites, and he and Miss Lambe swept onto the floor. The colonel watched, grimly satisfied.

None of them, however, were the faces I sought. My eyes continued to scan the crowd anxiously until I saw her: Harriet, by the French doors, her face rigid with shock.

Harriet had been looking very well lately, and tonight was no exception. Her cheeks bloomed, her eyes were dark and starry, and her brown curls bobbed and shone with every movement. She drew admiring eyes wherever we went. Now, though, I suspected she would not welcome the attention. She managed a ghastly smile for a moment, but it quickly wavered and dropped away. She stared resolutely off into the distance, avoiding the stares of the curious or pitying that turned her way. Slowly, as though without thought, she took a bit of ribbon from her purse and began to knot it.

I hurried over to her. I had no idea what spell she intended, or if she even knew; but I was certain she would realize once her wits had returned that it was a bad idea to perform it in public. Before she could continue, I took her by the elbow and led her back outside. Luckily there was no one else out there at the moment. I led her to the wicker bench where I had once heard Lady Herrington disclose her punch's secret ingredient.

"Yes, Lydia?" she said. "What is it? I suppose you are tired again, you silly thing. Have a little more to eat and you'll be ready to dance again."

Her voice, except for being a little louder than usual, sounded completely normal. But I could feel her arm shaking against mine.

"I *am* tired, Harriet," I said softly. "Very tired. Can't we leave this place? This party is awfully dull. Let's go back to your lodgings, put on our nightgowns, and have Sally make us some hot chocolate."

She gave a despairing little sound. I think she meant it to be a scornful laugh but it sounded more like a sob. "Leave now?" she said. "Let everyone *see me* leaving now? That would be worse than anything."

"But Harriet dear—"

"*No.*"

It struck me, as though for the first time, that Harriet was only a few years older than I was. I had always considered her completely an adult, but she was very young really.

I wanted to offer some words of sympathy, but the clenching in her jaw was familiar to me. She had the look of someone who would burst into tears if their defenses were breached by one kind word.

"Very well," I said. "What can I do, then?"

"Do?" she said. "Aside from telling that Miss Lambe to—to let him loose from her clutches?"

"But Harriet, what good would it do if she did? You're married."

That was a mistake. She muttered a curse, buried her face in her hands, and sobbed.

I put an arm around her and shushed her and rubbed her back, trying to be for her what she had been for me after the affair of Miss Lambe's necklace. I felt woefully inadequate. I had come to rely on Harriet's strength and maturity like the North Star. It made me queasy to be the one comforting her instead.

I do not think she much liked it, either. It was not long before she was wiping her face and catching her breath. "There, that's enough," she said. "I'm all right."

We stared up at the stars, swirling in and out of view above the clouds.

"I never wanted to marry Forster, you know," she said presently.

"Really?"

"Yes. Oh, I thought he was good fun, for an old man. But when I first heard that he'd made me an offer I thought it was a joke. He was so old." She gave a shaky sigh. "But Mamma said it was the best offer I would get. She said if I did not say yes she would stop bringing me out to parties and leave me at home until I had no choice but to be a governess or something equally horrid. She'd sacrificed a great deal of magic to bring about the match and she nearly tore my head off when I told her I intended to refuse."

I shivered. Before Brighton, the Forsters had seemed such a happy couple—my model of what a marriage ought to be. Harriet had never told me she'd been forced into it.

"So I agreed. It wouldn't be so bad, Mamma promised. Forster was a tolerant man, and she taught me some charms to help him turn a blind eye. *He won't mind if you indulge in a few summer flirtations, or discreet entanglements*, she said. *He's a sensible man.*"

I wanted to look at her, but I suspected that would break the spell. So I stayed still and kept my gaze on the stars.

"I tried to do what she said," Harriet continued. "I tried. Summer flirtations..." She sighed. "Well, maybe I'll learn to leave them behind with practice."

"Oh, Harriet," I said. "You love Carteret, don't you?"

She was silent for a moment. Then she gave me a light smack on the arm, the way she did to scold me when I tried to leave a ball too early. "Of course not, you goose," she said. "If Carteret wants to throw himself away on that tiresome creature, I am well rid of him. There are plenty of handsome young men who will dance with me in his stead."

She jumped to her feet and I followed. "What can I do?" I asked. "Harriet, how can I help?"

Her eyes flashed. The moment had passed, I realized, when she would accept any help from me. She wanted me to be her admiring young friend again. "Help?" she said. "You can help yourself by straightening your shoe-roses and coming back to dance." She seized my hands. "Come on, Lydia. *Dance.*"

And I did. I would have forced my tired feet to move, for her sake, if I had to—but in fact, it seemed that evening that my old strength returned. Harriet and I danced long into the night; and though we knew we had to leave early the next day for the grotto, the sun was already up when we finally went home to sleep.

# CHAPTER THIRTY-ONE

It was a worn-out, headachy, decidedly sullen group of young people who set out the next morning. Miss Lambe, of course, arrived promptly on time at our lodgings, but I had had trouble dragging myself from sleep and was twenty minutes late to meet her. Harriet took half an hour more, finally emerging without a word of apology or explanation. The men had yet to arrive. Still sensible of what had happened to her the night before, I tried to make Harriet's excuses to Miss Lambe, which only led Harriet to snap at me to mind my own affairs. Lord, travel is a curse. So are friends, and love, and mornings.

"Do you know," Harriet said, with a strange, bright smile for Miss Lambe, "in her little village Lydia here is considered quite the troublemaker? I cannot fathom it, for as far as I can see she goes all to pieces when anyone says a cross word to anyone else. The country must be a dull place indeed, if our Lydia is considered a dangerous woman."

I looked down to hide my hurt under my bonnet. Miss Lambe regarded us both coldly, then checked her pocket watch again. Harriet gazed up at the sky with a sigh of apparent contentment. Considering what she had been through the night before, she looked well. Blooming, really. There was a sort of gleam of exhilaration in her eyes that I could not explain. At one point while we waited I saw her staring at an upper window; I looked up and saw Colonel Forster there, staring back at her. He seemed solemn. When he saw me watching he let the curtains fall shut.

The men arrived one by one, walking or riding, all of them squinting against the bright sun and complaining about the early start. We could not tell them the true reason for our journey, but nor did we wish to travel the open road without male protection, so we had simply said that we ladies were wild to sketch some particularly picturesque cliffs. They'd been happy enough to acquiesce in theory, but now that the prospect of a hot, dusty journey to a place that promised none of Brighton's amusements was upon them, they were full of complaints. Even Wickham, who knew the truth, grumbled.

We set off at last, the sun already hot above. We stopped after a stuffy, drowsy hour for a picnic luncheon, arranged as a surprise by Miss Lambe. "For," she whispered in my ear, "we must keep up the pretense that this is just a pleasure trip." Her servants met us on the grounds of a local estate with meat pies, fresh fruit, and lemonade, all laid out on beautiful linens.

It was a beautiful spot, and we all admired it as we ate. Harriet said sweetly, "Isn't it a bit rude, though, for us to stop on someone's property without thanking them?"

"I suppose it would be," said Miss Lambe. "As it happens, I am the owner."

"It must be lovely to be rich," said Harriet to no one in particular. "You can arrange everyone's affairs so perfectly to your liking."

Carteret, who had been drowsing in the grass, opened one eye to look at her. "Curb your tongue, Harriet."

"That's Mrs. Forster to you."

We subsided into silence. The bees buzzed. Denny tried to liven us up with one of his tricks, but not one of us would pick a card.

I felt a tickle at my arm and jumped. I turned to find Wickham's fingers brushing my skin. "Ant," he said, and held it up.

"Oh. Thank you."

Fulton jumped to his feet. "I've something to say to you all," he said. "I am leaving the regiment."

That at least woke us up a bit. "Leaving!" I said. "Why?"

"You were always too virtuous to be a soldier," said Wickham.

The look Fulton shot him was surprisingly venomous, but he made no direct reply. "My great-aunt died a few weeks ago," he said. "I was always a great favorite with her, and my mother hoped she'd leave me a small legacy, to help me climb the ranks as an officer. Instead, she—she left me nearly her entire estate, which was more sizable than anyone knew." He looked awkward. "I am—well—I am now a man of independent fortune."

We all gaped. Then Wickham laughed. "Well done!" he cried. "Carteret and I work ourselves to the bone fortune-hunting, and young Fulton stumbles into one without even trying. Well, that's two of us sorted. Has anyone got an heiress or a great-aunt for me?"

"It would take more than one fortune to dig you out of the hole you're in, Wickham," drawled Carteret.

"What hole?" I asked.

Wickham gave me a lazy smile. "Do not worry about it." He plucked a buttercup and passed it under my chin. "Look, everyone, she likes butter."

To my surprise, Fulton stuck his hand between us. "Miss Bennet, will you go for a walk with me to see the view?"

I put my hand in his and let him help me to my feet. When I looked back, Wickham was staring after us.

Fulton led me a little way up the hill. The view was not much different than what we'd had before, but I dutifully admired it. Fulton found a stump for me to sit on, then made me get up again so he could wipe it off with his handkerchief.

"What is it, Fulton?" I said with a laugh. "You've not been this nervous since the spring. Go on, out with it."

Fulton knelt next to me, then stood, then knelt again. "Miss Bennet," he said. "Lydia—will you do me the—will you make me the—" He blinked, squared his shoulders, and to my astonishment, took my hand. "Lydia," he said simply, "marry me."

I am afraid I gaped in a most un-lady-like fashion. Fulton! Fulton, whom I teased mercilessly, and shoved into the path of heiresses, and danced with when I wanted a break from more intimidating men. Fulton, whom I treated like a younger brother, despite his being several years my senior.

Fulton, who now gazed at me quite gravely, and not like a younger brother at all.

"You cannot be serious," I said faintly.

He twitched but did not appear to take offense. "I assure you, I am in earnest."

"But you—" I shook my head. "Fulton, it's *me*."

"I am too late? Your affections are engaged?"

"What? No."

"Then please, Lydia. Consider what I can offer. I have money now. An estate of my own. You are a good woman and you deserve a respectable, elegant life. Let me take you away, before he has a chance to ruin you."

I pulled my hand away. "This is—this is so sudden. Fulton, you're excited about your inheritance, that's all. When you calm down you'll see you can have anybody now. You could marry the queen of Sheba."

"I don't want the queen of Sheba, and this is not sudden," he said softly. "I have loved you for many weeks. You're better than any of them, Lydia. Don't let them drag you down with them. Don't let *him*."

"Him?" I whispered. But I found I knew.

"Wickham will never marry you," he said. "And if he does, what life can he give you? He has ruined his own finances. He will have to flee soon, or face debtors' prison. I do not know what he's told you, promised you, but all he can bring you is ruin and pain."

For a wild moment I considered it. A quiet, comfortable life. A kind, sensible husband. A life like Mamma's, only better, without entailments, with a husband for whom I felt—if not love—at least genuine friendship. After watching Harriet and Kitty's torments, I was beginning to think that was better anyway.

And the thing that pulled and tugged and burned between me and Wickham—when had it brought me anything but fear and shame?

He took my hand again. Across his palm, I felt the faint, raised line of a scar. If I asked, I knew he would say he'd cut it on a gate.

"I cannot," I choked. "I am sorry. Truly. I am not the good woman you think I am." I pressed my hands to my cheeks. When one does finally manage to blush, it is at the most inconvenient times.

His mouth became a grim line. "You love him, then."

"No!" I said. "Stop saying that!"

"Then please, reconsider. I promise you, whatever he—" He paused. "Whatever mistakes you've made, I promise you, they are in my power to forgive."

I was not sure whether to be angry at his presumption or guilty that what I had actually done was much worse than he could imagine. Before I could respond, he held a gentle hand to my lips. "No, please. Do not refuse me again. I could not bear it. I chose my moment ill, I see now. Will you at least allow me to ask again at a later date?"

Helplessly, I nodded. It seemed the least I could do.

Do you know what I wish? I wish I could tell Lizzy about that day. I wish I could tell her how close I was to accepting a proposal from a kind, wealthy man for a life much like hers. She believes I have never had a sensible thought in my head. I wish I could tell her how clearly I saw the value of such a life. That such a man saw value in me.

But that would entail telling her everything else as well. And that, of course, I cannot do, can I?

# CHAPTER THIRTY-TWO

There had been some talk of spending the night in an inn before continuing in the morning, but after that horrid afternoon none of us cared to prolong the journey. Without a word, we piled back into the carriages and pressed straight on.

The sun had set when we arrived. We dined at an inn, during which Harriet slipped a dram of biddability into our honor guard's wine. I watched the now-familiar look of amiable stupidity slide over their faces with a twist in my stomach. Of the men, only Wickham remained as alert as ever.

Though there was a full moon, it was shrouded behind heavy clouds, and the night was dark and unseasonably cool. Harriet, clutching a lantern, found a nearly invisible track and led us down the steep, rocky path toward the shore.

I kept my eyes on Miss Lambe's back, trying my best not to stumble over the loose stones in the dark. Harriet had never been to the grotto on her own and had some trouble finding the entrance. Eventually Wickham made us all stand still, then raised his face and sniffed the air. I thought I saw a glint of red in his eyes.

"That way," he said, and pointed to a spear of rock jutting up toward the sky. It appeared solid, but when we approached we found it actually hid a narrow crevasse, just wide enough for someone to slip through. Beyond it there lay a dark pathway, sloping down under the ground.

"How did you know it was here?" I whispered.

"It smelled like my father," he said.

We left Carteret, Fulton, and Denny standing outside—an honor guard indeed, now, though I doubted they would do anything to protect us other than smile foolishly. It had been Harriet's idea to bring them along—"They will keep anyone from disturbing us," she had said. It occurred to me now, looking at their blank faces, that this was rather a flimsy excuse. There was, I realized, another reason she thought we might need them. I had seen her pack her little knife. I shook off the thought as we raised our lamps, Wickham hoisted our bag of supplies, and we went inside.

The steep path downward ended in an even steeper set of winding spiral steps that creaked as we walked. When I reached the bottom, I raised my lamp and gasped. It is an astonishing place. I wish people other than witches could go and see it. I did find a hair ribbon on the floor and a boiled sweet, so some girls had probably stumbled onto it.

Every inch of the walls and ceiling were covered in seashells. Thousands upon thousands of them, all sorts, from those smaller than a fingernail to others larger than my hand, carefully arranged in an elaborate mosaic of whorls, sunbursts, symbols I did not recognize and a few I did.

The pattern could have been five years old or a thousand. It smelled of the earth but of the sea, too. And something else—a sort of ancient power, sunk into the very walls. After all, when I thought of all the months and years someone had spent, carefully sticking on shell after shell in this cramped, musty hole, I realized that they had sacrificed a great deal indeed to make this place.

The four of us exchanged an uneasy glance. Harriet raised her chin and started forward first.

"Come," she commanded. "Let's go and find this so-called jewel."

We come now to the bit you particularly wanted to know about—the bit I have successfully avoided telling you about for over two hundred pages now. I can certainly understand why you'd have questions, but oh—are you sure you want the answers? They do none of us much credit. Perhaps you'd rather hear more about my childhood? I could tell you about the time I made Mary invisible, and no one noticed for a week. Or

the time Kitty was frightened by a dog and ran up a tree to the Lucases'
roof and Sir Lucas had to carry her down again. He never did understand how a girl of ten managed to run across that skinny branch.

But no. I can practically hear you telling me to get on with it. Very
well. At least I have a great deal of practice now at telling uncomfortable
truths. The secret is for me to plunge straight ahead, like jumping into
cold water, and not think about your face when you read it. Oh drat.
Now I am thinking about it.

The Shell Grotto was not large. The winding stairs opened out into a
circular room with vaulted ceilings and a large pillar in the middle. The
feeling of power grew, making my skin itch and my ears buzz. I could
see the others felt it, too. The shapes in the walls seemed to flicker and
twist in the light of our lamps as we made our way through the rotunda
and down the passage that followed. My stomach fluttered. Had we been
wise to so blindly follow the advice of a strange local demigod? Why
should we come to a place like this to talk to the Long Man? He was a
lord of grass and sunshine and growing things. This place smelled of cold
rock and old seawater. Had we been so distracted by our own entanglements that we'd failed to consider if this was wise?

I was about to call out to the others to come back, that this was a
mistake, when the narrow passage opened out into a larger room. At one
end the designs seemed to come to a crescendo over a little platform that
protruded from the wall. Around it swirled complicated circular patterns, each surrounding a large shell. Unlike most of the others, which
were bleached white, these glowed a soft pink, and their bumpy exteriors
curved open to hint at unseen whorls within themselves. I knew if I
stuck my fingers in them, they would be smooth as glass. These came
from no English beach.

"Conchs," Miss Lambe said. "We have those at home."

"Well," Wickham said, "that's a good omen, isn't it?"

"An omen at least." Miss Lambe set her lantern on the altar. "Come,
let's set to work. It's almost midnight."

The spell was another odd one. It was a bit like what we'd used before to speak to the Long Man, but bigger, more complicated, and more formal somehow—if the first spell was like a casual note to a friend, this one was like an invitation to court.

It was hard to see to the bottom of that deep, murky spell, so we were as careful as we could be. We had prepared sage bundles and the pungent smoke now filled the cavern as we laid out multiple circles of protection in salt and ash. Whatever personal complications divided us, we were uniformly focused now. However, the more precautions we took, the more anxious I became. In this place of power, our little salt-circle felt like a parasol in a hurricane.

However, there was nothing to do but press on. Standing in a semicircle around the altar, we took turns placing the required ingredients in a bowl—a few drops of salt water, a sprig of fresh grass, a sprinkle of cinnamon, some bones charred black—and chanted the words of the spell. As we spoke the final words, Wickham pricked his finger and dropped a few drops of blood in the bowl, whose contents burst into flames.

Miss Lambe, Harriet, and I spoke the words to seal the spell together. Miss Lambe had gone very still, as she does when she's uneasy. Harriet's eyes glittered in the firelight. Wickham had a hand half raised toward me, as if he was about to pull me away from the altar.

Then the fire went out.

Not just the fire in the bowl, either. Our lamps extinguished without so much as a flicker, leaving us in total darkness. Someone gasped—I was not sure who. Maybe me—

And then a voice drawled, "Well, cousins, ain't this prettily done on my part?"

My eyes were beginning to adjust to the darkness. I could dimly make out the shapes of the others. Or, no—it was not that my eyes were adjusting. There was a very weak, greenish light. Faint, but growing stronger. I could now make out the others' faces, turned toward me with fear.

The voice continued in its Sussex drawl, "I druv these mortals here, to neutral ground, that belongs to none of us. Weren't that courteous of me? This matter concerns us all, I says to myself, when the little witches calls upon me, and I'd best speak to t'others in a place of no advantage to none."

The green light was growing brighter. With it came the scent of grass. The green light and the voice, I realized, were coming from me.

I gave a half-choked gasp and tried to look down at myself. I was glowing green, my form superimposed with that of a tall man in rough clothes. The Long Man.

"Easy, child," he said, and made soft chucking noises like he might to soothe a lamb. "I'll not harm ye, if ye trouble me not. Well, cousins?"

"What is it that concerns us, peasant man?" hissed a voice. "Why disturb you a Great Lord?"

"No, no, no," sighed another voice, its sound a rhythmic rush and retreat. The green glow was joined now by other light: a smoky redness glowing around Wickham, and a rippling gray-blue that poured off Harriet. Her curls waved lazily about her face, as if submerged in water. "This place, this place—dry and dead. Let me go, let me go, let me go."

My own throat gave a low man's chuckle. "I promise, Sister Sea, you'll want to hear 'n. For these little mortals have been striving to bring back the Witch-Queen o' Brighton."

Miss Lambe gave a gasp. I tried to do the same but my throat was not my own. The Long Man made the chucking noise at me again. "This one would have me tell you," he said, "that they've no interest in the Queen, just her jewel." He chuckled. "Sweet little fools don't even realize they're one and the same."

With that, Miss Lambe, too, began to glow. A soft purple light grew stronger and stronger as her eyes slipped shut.

"The Queen," sighed the sea. "The Queen, the Queen."

"My jewel," snarled Wormenheart.

My mind was a whirl. If I could have screamed, I would have. So this was why I'd never been able to find the jewel, no matter how close

I got to Miss Lambe. I thought the traces of magic I saw on her meant she'd been close to the jewel. But no. She *was* the Jewel of Propriety. The Queen was the jewel was the girl, and I'd dropped her in the clutches of not one but *three* other Great Powers.

"So what are we to do with her?" asked the Long Man. "We've all three made claims. For myself, I druther let her come home to her domain. She's an orderly creature, like me. Stands for straight hedgerows and clean streets. The Long Man and the Witch-Queen o' Brighton have always been friends." I felt a fierce grin stretch my face. "Mostly."

I could *feel*, suddenly, how ancient he was. Yes, the Long Man could be kindly, the cuddler of newborn lambs and guide of wayward witches. But to carve sheep-meadows from ancient woods—that takes a kind of ruthlessness, too. He took the wild lands and let the wolves starve.

"You do not know this Queen," sighed the sea. "I do, I do. Give her to me. She longs for me."

"No doubt," said the Long Man drily. "Since you took her lover."

"Lover, lover," the sea agreed. "I love her, love her, love her." She stretched out one glowing hand toward Miss Lambe's—the Witch-Queen's—cheek.

But a brilliant purple spark leapt from it, and the sea hissed and drew back. "I'm afear'd she may not be quite ready to walk down into your embrace," said the Long Man. "She belongs at your shore, not in your depths."

"Come now, Long Man," drawled Wormenheart's aristocratic voice. "Don't play the voice of reason. You want her merely to enrich your own domain."

"Maybe," said Long Man. "Partly. What's your claim then?"

A curl of smoke drifted from Wickham's finger to spiral around Miss Lambe. "My claim is the oldest. I was the first to spot the jewel's return. First to dispatch my servants after it."

"Perhaps," said the Long Man cheerfully, "but your domain do be far from here. Me, I doubt you could enforce t' claim." He drew a deep breath, puffed out his cheeks—my cheeks—and blew the smoke away. "I dunno, cousins. No claim seems strong enough to me. What are we to do?"

"If you will not give me what is mine," snarled Wormenheart, "then none shall have it. Collapse this place before the jewel comes into its full power. Kill it and its companions. I will take it the next time it is reborn."

"Seems a waste," the Long Man said. "I've missed the Queen, I have. Still, perhaps it's best." And I felt all three of them gathering their power.

I gave an inner moan of despair. All our maneuvering and researching, all our petty intrigues and entanglements—all for nothing. We had always been pawns of Great Powers that we could not even see. Like vassals to a faraway lord we'd never met.

But then, the power of feudal lords wasn't what it once had been, now was it?

A desperate notion began to form in my head.

*Wait*, I begged silently. *Please, wait!*

"Yes?" my own lips asked in the Long Man's amused voice.

I did my best to gather my foggy ideas into words. How I wished Miss Lambe was awake. *You all have your own domains*, I said. *Is that right?*

"'Tis true," agreed the Long Man. "I'm a creature of fields and farmland, my sister there rules aspects of the sea, and yon dragon over there—well, I don't rightly know what he cares for. Evilness, p'r'aps. What of it?"

*The Witch-Queen—her domain is people, isn't it?*

"True enough," he agreed. "Witches and magical folk in these parts. 'Tis why she's a line of reborn human vessels, 'stead of immortal like us, I warrant."

*So don't we—her subjects—have a right to decide which of you is to have her?*

The Long Man gave a low whistle. "An audacious notion, missy. 'Ere, cousins, you hear yon little witchling?"

"I hear, I hear," said the sea cautiously.

"Nonsense," spat Wormenheart. "These mortals have already failed to deliver on one bargain. Why should I agree to another?"

*Surely it is better to leave her power in play than to destroy her altogether?*

I did not know what I meant, precisely, but what I showed them was the excitement that had pervaded Brighton society when Miss Lambe had arrived. A rich, young, beautiful heiress—even though only one person could win her hand, *everyone* had had a chance at it. The potential was a thrill in itself.

"She thinks us fortune-hunters," Wormenheart growled, sounding a little amused in spite of himself. I knew him well enough now to be sure that he thought himself capable of winning such a hunt.

"Let them choose their path to joy," said the sea hopefully.

The Long Man ducked his head. "Clever creature you are," he muttered, just for me to hear. Then he raised his voice. "We're agreed then?"

"Let them go, go, let them go," said the sea.

"They'll make the wise choice," said Wormenheart smugly. "Remember, witchling, I have your cat-creature."

"Right," said the Long Man. "Yon Witch-Queen will be in a state of transformation for some hours yet. When she finishes, one of us will come for her, and you'd best decide by then which it's to be. Go now, afore we change our minds."

With that, they released us from our bonds. We all gasped and looked around, except for Miss Lambe, still purple and frozen.

"Come," said Harriet, "let's get out of here," and Wickham nodded.

We quickly found that Miss Lambe, though still and hard as though she were carved from a massive chunk of amethyst, was not difficult to move. Her feet hovered several inches off the ground, but a slight push would set her moving as easily as a pat of butter on a hot stove. If a pat of butter was five and a half feet tall, glowing, and purple, that is. We slid her to the entrance and Wickham managed to nudge her up the stairs. I gave a sigh of relief once we left that place of power. We'd made it.

*Careful, missy,* the Long Man whispered to me. *We pledged not to use our power against the jewel. To leave her fate in the hands of you mortals.*

*We never promised not to make offers to those mortals...*

Luckily, the coachmen were asleep. We quickly maneuvered Miss Lambe into her carriage and drew down the blinds.

"Let's get back to Brighton," said Harriet. "We can figure out what to do from there."

I agreed fervently. Harriet piled the honor guard into her carriage and Wickham and I joined Miss Lambe and followed them back onto the road.

The road back to Brighton had never seemed longer. Normally we never would have attempted it in the middle of the night, but I hardly saw what choice we had. We could not check a glowing, purple girl into an inn, now could we? No, the best thing was to get her to her own lodgings.

And then what?

I stared at her softly glowing form in the dark. All summer I had sought the Jewel of Propriety. Some magical object that I could borrow or buy or steal and bring back to a dragon to save my life, and Kitty's. But no. The jewel was a person.

She was not completely frozen, I realized. She was moving, just very, very slowly. One of her hands was drifting, an inch an hour, up toward her face—probably to put her palm over her forehead, a gesture of irritation I'd seen her do a thousand times.

What was it like in there? Could she hear us? See us? Did the woman I knew still exist?

The weakness I'd been feeling for weeks suddenly returned. My heart fluttered in my chest and I leaned back against the seat. Wickham quickly moved over next to me and took my hand. "Are you all right, Miss Bennet?"

I gave him a tired smile. "I hardly know."

A crease of alarm appeared between his brows. "Can you reach out to Kitty? Or I can cut my hand, I can—"

"No, no, I am quite well, I assure you. I only meant—la, I meant I hardly know what to do now."

His gaze followed mine to Miss Lambe. "It is remarkable," he said softly. "To think that all this time, all those weeks we sought the jewel so desperately, there she was."

"Yes," I said. "There she was."

There she was, ruining my fun, raising questions I would rather not consider, missing her home, and loathing it. I could feel, now, the monumental waves of power rolling off her—and yet she seemed to me diminished. "I hope she is finished with this 'transformation' soon," I said. "Then she can decide for herself what ought to be done."

"I suppose," Wickham said.

The carriage wheels rolled on. I leaned my head against the window. Through a crack in the shade, I saw that the sun was rising. The scent of roses drifted in the morning air. I supposed we were passing some great person's garden. Strange after a night like this to remember that something as simple as roses existed.

"Lydia," Wickham said presently.

I rolled my head to look at him. "You know," I said, "I never gave you permission to call me by my Christian name."

"Do you want me to stop?" he asked softly.

Slowly I shook my head.

"Lydia," he said again, as though tasting it. I wanted to close my eyes and hear it again. I kept them open.

"We made a promise to my father, you know," he said.

"To bring him a jewel," I pointed out. "Not a person."

"She *is* the jewel. What do you think will become of us if we fail? What will become of your sister?"

I shook my head. "I did not know what I was promising. He *cannot* hold us to it. It wouldn't be fair."

"That is not how promises work, particularly not magical ones."

Before I could answer, the other inhabitant of the carriage spoke.

"Mnnn," said Miss Lambe. She sounded like someone talking in her sleep. Her glow had muted somewhat. She looked a bit more like a person. "Miss Lambe? Can you hear me?"

"M'ss Benn'?" she muttered. Her movements, still sluggish, were growing a little more deliberate. "Whr—wha—"

"It's all right. We're in your carriage. Are you all right? Do you remember?"

"Mnnn." She moved restlessly. "Llll...lllooo..."

"What? What is it?"

Her eyes flew open. "*Look out.*"

At that moment I realized that the clatter and jolt of our carriage racing along the highway had given way to the slower, softer crunch of wheels over gravel. The scent of roses returned, tenfold stronger.

The carriage drew to a halt. Wickham frowned. "What is this? We are not in Brighton town yet."

I threw the door open. I already knew what I would find. No, we were not in Brighton proper. We were in Miss Beaumont's garden. Arrayed in a circle around the coaches were a number of members of the Order of the Rose. And standing directly in front of my door, her smile even more superior than usual, was Miss Mary King.

# CHAPTER THIRTY-THREE

I had the oddest conversation with Miss Darcy today. She can have conversations now, after a fashion. I haven't lifted the spell yet, but I managed to work up a simple draught that keeps her mind fairly grounded. It also makes her as sluggish as she was when I first met her, but Darcy is still pleased with the result. Anyhow, I was sitting with her, and suddenly she said—

No. I haven't got time to go into it. I'm near the end of my tale, and I've nearly got the shape of the spell on Miss Darcy. Oh, I wish I could talk to someone about it, though. I wish I could talk to *you*. I miss being able to ask your advice. I'm not just saying that to turn you up sweet, either. (Notice I say nothing about *taking* your advice.) I'm alone here. I want someone to tell me whether I'm doing the right thing.

Now where did I leave off? Ah yes, Mary King.

I stepped out of the carriage on feet shaking with fatigue, but inside I felt strangely calm. A glance to the left told me that, indeed, Harriet's carriage had been lured here as well. She quickly got out and stood beside me.

"What is this, Miss King?" I demanded. "Where is Miss Beaumont?"

"She's gone away," Mary drawled. "Seems the heat did not agree with her. Not to worry, though. The Order of the Rose is in good hands. The last thing she did before she—left—was to make me her successor as Regent."

With great casualness, she leaned down to sniff a blossom on a rosebush. It was still just a tightly closed bud, but when she blew on it, it burst into full bloom. Not an illusory bloom, either. A real one. It certainly appeared that she had the power of the Order behind her.

"Congratulations," I said. "Let us go."

"I'm afraid not," she said. Her gaze shifted over my shoulder. "Ah. Ladies, if you please."

I glanced back and saw that Miss Lambe had followed me out of the carriage. She still had a faint purple haze drifting about her form, but she was looking considerably more like a person. She started to lift her hand—

All the ladies of the Order joined hands and shouted in unison. With a discordant hiss, sparks raced from Mary King's hands to strike Miss Lambe. She reared back, hand still half raised, and froze, suddenly looking more like a large block of milky-purple gemstone than ever. Her features were now rough-hewn and indistinct. If I had not seen it happen, I would never have known that the immense stone had once been a person.

"Apologies," said Miss King. "We cannot allow this transformation to continue. The witches of Brighton are quite content with a Regent. We've no need for a Queen." She stepped forward, gazing at Miss Lambe in fascination. "Besides, if we keep her caught partway through like this, we can use the gem's power on behalf of the Order."

"She's not a gem, she's a Miss Lambe, and you've no right."

Miss King gave a scornful laugh. "You needn't get on your high horse with me. I was with you in Meryton, remember? I know quite well that you intend to feed it to a dragon." She walked a slow, appreciative circle around Miss Lambe, like a connoisseur enjoying a fine sculpture. "So did I, of course—initially. That was before I understood what a delicious thing the jewel really was. Why bow and scrape to some old dragon when I can simply use its power directly? Far more modern, I think."

"You just want her out of the way so your family can steal her fortune."

"It should save us a great deal on legal costs, I own. Now, let us see—" She lifted her hand, and I felt her begin to tug at the power that made up Miss Lambe.

"No!" I threw myself in front of her and knocked Miss King's arm aside. "I won't let you!"

"Oh yes you will," said Miss King. "You really think you can stand alone against all of us? Impertinent girl."

"Maybe not," I said as stoutly as I could. "But I shall try."

"And," drawled Wickham at his most insolent, as he stepped forward and took my right hand, "she's hardly alone."

Miss King looked furious at that, but quickly masked it with an insouciance as elaborate as his own. "Ah yes, Papa's good boy," she sneered.

"If you like," Wickham said, and squeezed my hand. I reached out my other for Harriet.

I have dreams about that moment, you know. At least once a week. Nearly as often as my dreams where I am called upon to recite Shakespeare onstage at Drury Lane despite never having learned a word of it. In my dream I stretch out my hand and Harriet takes it, and flashes that warm smile she always gave me when I was being a goose but she was still going to make everything all right, and together we face the forces arrayed against us. Sometimes we triumph, but usually I wake up before the battle begins. The important thing is that my friends stand with me.

Instead, in the waking world, the real Harriet stepped past my hand, turned, and stood with Mary King.

Oddly, what I was most conscious of in that moment was thinking, *You must not cry. Lydia, you must not cry.* But oh, I wanted to. I felt like a stupid child. Harriet, her face frozen in a hard version of her kind smile, took Miss King's hand.

"Come now, Lydia," she said sweetly. "This is quite the most practical solution, you know. If we keep the jewel here among the Order, we can *all* get what we want. Why, its power could fuel our spells for decades, I daresay."

"She's not an *it*," I said, and despite my best efforts my voice was thick with tears.

"Besides," said Wickham, "if you keep the jewel here, my father will destroy me and Miss Bennet."

Miss King gave a shrug. "He cannot reach you here. Simply stay out of his domain, and you will be safe enough under our protection."

"What about Kitty?" I said. "She is still in his domain."

Miss King shrugged again. "Some sacrifices must be made."

I turned to Harriet, aghast. She gave me a rueful grimace. "I am sorry, Lydia. But you have been managing quite well this summer without your familiar, you know."

"I am not without her," I whispered. "I am never without her. Harriet, how could you do this? You called me your dearest friend."

"And so you are," she said. "But Lydia, can't you see? I have to. I *have to.*"

"But why?"

Her eyes blazed. "To escape," she said.

Good Lord, she was beautiful in that moment. All the bloom that had blessed her that summer seemed to glow in her face. Passion made her cheeks bright and her eyes starry. She looked like someone whom I would be proud to follow anywhere.

"I have to," Harriet continued. "I must escape my marriage, Lydia, or I will die, I swear it. Marrying Forster was a horrible, horrible mistake. How can I be a wife to that ancient fellow?" She wrung her hands, and tears glittered on her cheeks. "Can you not see? All the years of my life, stretching ahead of me, decades and decades, with nothing but boredom and loneliness? *I am nineteen years old.* I must get away from him. *I must.*"

"What will you do?" I asked. "Kill him, like Miss Lambe did her grandfather?"

She shook her head. "No, no, I'll not kill anyone. At first I thought I'd simply glamour myself a new name and face, and start over somewhere new. But that wouldn't be enough, would it? I would still need fortune, and family. No, there is only one way. I am going to make it so my marriage never existed."

"What the devil do you mean, 'never existed'?" demanded Wickham. "Magic cannot change the past."

"Can it not?" she said. "It can change memories, which amounts to the same thing. Lydia here has done it before—when she was just a child she made the whole world forget that her sister was really a barn cat. Why should I not make the world forget the fact of my marriage? Forster will be at liberty to find a wife who suits him better, and I will be Miss Weber again." She flicked a glance at her carriage. "And then, perhaps— we shall see."

"You don't want to be Miss Weber," Wickham said. "You want to be Mrs. Carteret."

She flinched at that.

"Harriet," I said, "even if no one knows you are married to Forster, you still will be. Marriage is not just a pretense everyone agrees upon."

She laughed rather hysterically. "That is *exactly* what it is."

"How can you force Miss Lambe to fuel this glamour?"

"Because that is exactly what *she* is. Fuel. She was made for this, Lydia, can't you see? She's been nothing but unhappy as an English lady—because she's not one. She will be much happier fulfilling her purpose."

I was not sure anyone could enjoy being a slab of rock. "If you're so sure of that, why not wake her up and ask her?"

"People don't always know what's good for them," said Harriet.

"But you do?"

"Enough of this," said Mary, more bored than ever. "I loathe being up this early. Are we going to do battle, or will you lot come quietly? You're badly outnumbered, you know."

"Not quite so outnumbered as you think," said Fulton from behind me.

I turned to find him, and Denny, and Carteret behind me.

"Fellows," I babbled, "you don't know, I can explain—"

"I find I do not need you to," said Fulton.

"I have been having the most peculiar dreams all summer," Carteret added. "Dreams where some lady—usually Mrs. Forster—cuts me up to fuel her dark designs. Quite medieval."

"You neglected to give us the forgetting-drink tonight, ma'am," said Denny to Harriet, almost apologetically. "We remember all we've seen this night, and the other nights as well."

Harriet had gone quite white. "Carteret," she said. "Carteret, you must understand—"

"Oh, I do." He stepped forward, took her hand, and kissed it. "You are going to take Miss Lambe here and use her as your personal bank, but I am quite set on having her as mine, you see."

"I can give you everything she has and more."

"I doubt that. If you could, all you witches would be rich as Croesus." His voice went hard. "Let her go, Harriet."

"Carteret," she whispered. "You said things—made me promises—"

"I never dreamed you would take them seriously."

Without another word, Harriet sent him tumbling backward with a blow of pure power.

If the people of Brighton knew about the battle that followed, it would explain a number of things that puzzled them excessively. Why their drinking water turned a peculiar shade of purple for days, for example. Or why a number of ladies in the town—specifically, those who belonged to the social club known as the Order of the Rose—all became prostrate with nervous exhaustion at once. Why the Steyne— normally such a carefully maintained expanse of smooth green lawn— was suddenly broken by rosebushes, violets, tulips, peonies, and climbing purple flowers.

At first, I thought we would defeat the Order easily. I had not only my own power at my disposal, but Miss Lambe's, too—I found that when I put my hand on her cool stone flank, her power flowed quite as easily to me as my own. I wanted to believe that meant she was aware on some level of our situation, and chose to join the fight; but whether she was or not, I knew the only hope for us both was to use her stores of power, so

I did. Somehow, though, it was not enough. Given the immense depth of her magical coffers, we ought to have been able to hold our own, but the Order swatted aside everything I tried. Before long, my throat was hoarse from reciting my strongest spells, and my fingers ached with the effort of channeling all that power into the correct arcane gestures. It was more magic than I'd ever done in a month, and ought to have been enough to flatten a dozen Mary Kings. But she and the Order showed no worse effects than slightly limp coiffures and the odd nosebleed. I felt that heart-trembling weakness that had plagued me these last few weeks creep over me, and I knew my strength would soon fail. Why? Yes, there were dozens of them tied into the Order's web of power, but they should not have been a match for the combined strength of Miss Lambe and me, not to mention the honor guard. I could feel their strength flowing through me, without them even needing to cut their hands—

And then I understood.

*You must not cry, Lydia.*

No doubt you think me extremely stupid for not understanding it before; well, I must remind you that at the time, *you* did not suspect anything of the sort either. All my sickly weakness—the honor guard's sulks and headaches—the sudden loss of Wickham's luck and charm—none of it was simple late-summer malaise. We were *being drained*. And it was my fault.

I was fighting on both sides of this battle. For weeks now, my strength, and that of the men I had cut to please the Order, had been flowing to my table-mistress. To Harriet.

This was why she had looked so blooming and starry-eyed—why she had the energy to dance and dance while I felt like I was fading away. Harriet. My dearest friend.

*You must not cry.*

I stopped fighting. What else could I do? I was only making things worse, as I always do. Instantly the scent of roses overwhelmed me. I dropped hard to my knees, as two rose vines slithered out from the flower bed and wrapped themselves around my wrists. The thorns bit into me, but I did not care. Stupid, stupid country mouse. I had worshiped Harriet, idolized her—loved her—and she had used me. Well, no more.

She felt it, the moment I tried to take my own magic back. "Now, Lydia, stop that," she said in her sweetest voice. "Have you forgotten that it was I who saved you from the dragon last spring? I who took you from that dull little village and made you part of my world? Surely you're not so ungrateful as to begrudge me a little help?"

"If you'd asked," I said, "I'd have given you anything. If you'd only *asked*."

"Enough." Her voice was hard now. "Let go. Your table-mistress commands you." And with a sharp yank, she tore my own magic away from me once more.

There was nothing I could do. I gasped, trying to tug it back to me, but it was like trying to wrap my hands around a river. I'd said the words, swallowed the bloody drops from the vase. I'd given my permission for her to take her fill of me. And, by extension, of our friends.

I remembered, then, that the honor guard were beside me. I turned and found that they were on their knees, too. Carteret, Denny, and Fulton were gray in the face and fighting for breath. Wickham was flickering between his human form and something else—something with a dark stone face, riven with dull red cracks, and glowing yellow eyes.

It was Denny who drew my gaze. Denny, my first friend in the regiment. Denny, who had loved Kitty. In the spring I'd taken his love; now, it seemed, he would lose his life. Good old Denny—even as he collapsed onto his hands, he felt my gaze on him and tried to give me his old reassuring smile. His mouth worked to speak.

"What?" I whispered.

"Sleight of hand," he croaked. "Palmed the card. Saw you. At that ruddy party."

"What?"

"The blood, Bennet," he whispered, and collapsed.

Sleight of hand? What on earth did he—?

*Oh.*

The day I had joined the Order, I had said the words, yes, and I drank the bloody water—but the blood I had offered to seal the pact had been just an illusion. Denny, with his love of conjuring tricks, had seen and remembered. The Order was using my magic via a contract that had never actually been sealed.

Could I get it back, though? Already they had taken so much. Where even to begin? I whispered a quick how-now divining, fed with a bit of Miss Lambe's strength. The whole structure of the Order's magic spread out before me like a complex embroidery—my contract with the Order, their contracts with one another, the whole beautiful, interwoven mess of it. There! A dropped stitch—a loose thread! Where my contract was meant to be, there was a tiny fault in the design. I ought to be able to—I reached out, making my nails as sharp as a seam-picker, and tugged loose one stitch, then the one before, and back and back, faster than I could ever do it in real life, the thread of my magic eagerly undoing one stitch after another in its haste to return to me.

Mary King screamed in outrage and tried to make a grab for it, but now it was she who was on the defensive. At last my magic was free, and not only did I belong to myself again, but there was now a massive flaw running through the whole of the Order's organization where my thread should have been. Their ability to do spells as one was lost; they were thrown into confusion. Behind me the honor guard gulped in great breaths, raised their heads, and got to their feet.

My strength slammed back into me. I felt better than I had in weeks, and angrier than I ever had in my life. "I was your *friend*, Harriet," I said, my voice breaking. My face was wet. So much for *you must not cry*.

"You were a *sponge*," she said, in a voice quite as shaky as mine. She was the one on her hands and knees now. "Dreary little nobody. No connections or conversation. Following me about. I should never have taken you on." Her cheeks were wet, too.

"I hate you!" I screamed.

"Well, I hate you!"

I wanted to seize the whole embroidery of the Order and set it on fire. What would become of its members? Would they lose their magic permanently? Perhaps they'd even die? I did not care. As long as Harriet and Mary King suffered, they could all go to blazes as far as I was concerned. I made ready to burn the whole damned thing to the ground.

It was not the horror of the honor guard that stopped me. Not Miss Lambe's cool disapproval, either. No, ultimately it was Harriet herself. I found myself speaking a fire spell that Harriet had taught me. A simple but effective one—it could light green wood in a downpour. A neat little spell, and one she'd practiced with me a great deal.

There is a certain point in the middle of it where one has to perform a particular gesture, a sort of twist and upward thrust of the hand, fingers opening—"like a flame igniting," Harriet explained—and I can never get it right. My twist is too twisty, my fingers not open enough. As I reached the moment now, I saw Harriet's hand twitch toward mine in a familiar gesture. How many times, in our practice sessions, had she patiently taken my hand in hers to correct that little mistake? How many times had she laughed off my frustration, soothed my declarations that I would never get it? She never lost her patience, just took my hand again and again and showed me how to do it right.

Now her hand reached out of its own accord—not to attack, but to correct her pupil's little mistake.

I dropped my own hand, let the spell unravel. Harriet glared up at me. "Do it, if you're going to," she said.

"Of course I'm not, stupid," I said.

Oh, I did not merely leave them to their own devices, of course. I seized the Order's embroidery once more and examined it. The way I'd yanked my own thread free had left it in some disarray—stitches loose, threads hanging off, snags and gaps—but they would soon be able to put it right if I left it as it was. However, I had no intention of doing so. If there is one gift I have in spades, it is ruining embroidery. I sent the loose threads chasing back through the wrong stitches, tangling with one another, here too loose and here so tight they bunched the fabric. When I was done, what had once been a neat embroidery was now a snarled, wrinkled mess.

That was the moment, I believe, that Order members all over Brighton fell into hysterics. It is a good thing this all happened in modern times, for if it had been a few hundred years ago we might have actually been arrested for witchcraft. Instead, it was blamed on miasmas.

When I was done, and I stood panting on the gravel drive, my knees shaking under me, I realized my skin was burning and hot. More magic? No, not exactly—the sky in the west was tinged with pink and orange. It was late afternoon, almost evening. We'd been dueling all day. I was sunburnt.

The Order of the Rose and its Regent lay crumpled on the ground, unconscious. "Good heavens," said Wickham. "You killed them."

"They've only fainted," I said wearily. "They'll be all right. Come, we'd better get out of here before they sort themselves out."

He and the other officers were groaning and stiff, as they slowly pulled themselves to their feet. They looked at me with new caution. "*Cor*, Bennet," said Denny with feeling.

"Sorry," I said. I held out a hand to help Fulton up; he, ever the gentleman, ignored it, and made his own way to standing. He found a handkerchief I'd dropped and handed it to me with a little bow.

"Thank you," I said. "Still want to marry me, Fulton?"

"I—Of course!" he said. I turned away. There'd been the slightest hesitation before his answer.

No time to think of that. I held my breath as I turned to Miss Lambe. Would my blow to the Order restore her on the path back to humanity? For a moment I was sure I would find her perfectly well and glaring at me. But my heart crashed into my boots when I saw that the stone was unchanged. Whatever the Order had done, it had knocked her well off the path the Great Powers had expected.

We piled back into the two coaches, leaving the Order where they lay. Not sure where else to go, I took them back to Miss Lambe's lodgings. Mrs. Tomlinson, not expecting us back until the next day, had taken herself off somewhere, and we had the place to ourselves. I mixed up some Dram of Lethe and brought it to the men.

"I will not force you to drink this," I told them. "I've done quite enough forcing and tricking my friends for one lifetime. But if you wish to go back to your lives before today, you may drink, and forget."

I went to Carteret first. He gave me a pale imitation of his usual ironical look. "Was all of this my fault?" he asked me.

"Certainly a great deal of it was."

"I don't suppose I deserve to forget, do I."

"I don't suppose you do."

He gave a great sigh, rubbing a hand over his face. "And yet," he said, "I am a selfish bastard," and he seized the dram and drank deep. Last I heard of Carteret, he was engaged to a pretty young heiress, and had rented a fine house in Kent. People who tell you how selfish they are usually are not joking.

Next I went to Fulton. He avoided my gaze.

"Well, Fulton?" I said as briskly as I could. "What will it be?"

He took my hand in his. Looked up into my face. I really thought, then, that he was going to say, *No dram. You're still the best of them. Say you'll marry me.*

Instead, he dropped his eyes, muttered, "I'm sorry, Miss Bennet," and drank it down. Fulton, too, is engaged now, to a virtuous young vicar's daughter who has never once set foot in the wicked city of Brighton.

Well. That was that.

I took a few deep breaths to collect myself, then turned to my last victim. Denny. He was absently twirling a coin between his fingers, staring off into the distance.

"Denny?" I prompted.

"Oh," he said. "Right. You know, Bennet, I'm remembering more and more. Forgive me if this sounds absurd, but—was I in love with a cat?"

"Yes," I said. "Kitty. All this was to save her, Denny, I swear, or I never would have—"

He held up his hand to cut me off. "It's all right, Bennet, I remember." His face changed. Softened. "Kitty."

I swallowed a lump in my throat.

"I don't suppose," he said, "even if you manage to sort out all this dragon business, that there's any way for me to marry a cat?"

"I don't think so," I said. "She's my familiar really."

"But she loved me, too?"

"More than anything."

He nodded slowly. "It's an awfully jolly summer I've had, not being in love," he said. "The jolliest of my life. And I can't see that it will be very amusing in the future, loving and loving a cat-girl I can never wed."

I nodded. Held out the drink.

"No," he said. "No thank you, Miss Bennet. I think I'd rather have the memory, all the same." And he pushed the dram away.

Carteret and Fulton had already gone glassy-eyed. Wickham, blessedly, took charge, and shepherded all three men toward the door. He gave Denny some whispered instructions and then sent them off.

Then it was just us. Me and Wickham, and Miss Lambe's unseeing, glowing gaze.

Wickham and I stared at each other. I had collapsed in an armchair and he sprawled on a chaise. His cravat was undone, his clothes covered in dust from travel and battle.

"We cannot stay here," he said. "The Order will sort themselves out. They'll come for her."

"I know," I said.

"We must get off their territory."

I gave a slight, hysterical laugh. "And go *where*?"

"Let us get away first. We can consider that question from the road."

There seemed no alternative, so I agreed. I spun a fierce don't-notice-me and threw it over Miss Lambe's glowing form, then we piled into her carriage and were off. Within an hour, without so much as returning to the Forsters' for my trunk, I had left Brighton for the last time. And that is how I came, quite accidentally, and entirely chastely, to run off with George Wickham.

# CHAPTER THIRTY-FOUR

Darcy is ever so pleased with me. I am almost like one of the family now. I can understand a bit more how Lizzy stands him—he can be quite charming when he chooses. Darcy is rather like a cat—he is horribly cold and aloof to one for ages and ages, and just when one has despaired of ever earning a kind look, he goes all warm and friendly.

The reason he is now purring for me is that I have done a superb job of understanding what is amiss with Miss Darcy. I was quite right to proceed so slowly.

Here is what I believe happened: Someone attempted to cast a rather nasty hex on Miss Darcy. This took some doing, for I had of course adorned her with excellent protection spells; but with a burst of raw power, they were able to blast them away. And here is where it gets interesting.

I do not know what that hex was intended to do, but I doubt it had anything to do with madness or owls. However, when our mystery witch went to cast said hex, she found that Miss Darcy was *already* under a powerful enchantment.

It must have been a thing of beauty, that enchantment. I wish I could have had a look at it before Miss Darcy's tormentor got her hands on it. So delicate it must have been that I never realized it was there during our weeks of acquaintance, yet so strong that it never faded or weakened during all the years of her life.

I explained all this to Darcy the other night, who was quite astounded. "Is there any history of madness or illness in your family?" I asked.

His face took on that shuttered-window look it gets. "You presume greatly, Mrs. Wickham."

"Yes, I generally do," I agreed. "Is there?"

His face reddened. He muttered something about a great-grandmother, and a sister of his mother's, and a whole branch of cousins whom no one spoke of but whom he maintained at a house deep in the country with a litany of discreet caretakers.

"Mmm," I said. "Yes, I thought so. Papa always said that the best families all carry some strain of eccentricity."

"Snubs *never* showed any sign of mental weakness," he protested.

"Well, she wouldn't, would she," I said, "for your parents had her thoroughly spelled against it when she was born."

Darcy was so astonished at that that he collapsed in a chair. "My parents?"

"I assume so," I said. "An elaborate spell like this would have taken weeks. If it was not your parents, they were certainly not very attentive."

"After Snubs was born," Darcy said slowly, "they sent me to stay with Lady Catherine for the entire summer. They told me the baby was sickly and they couldn't have me underfoot."

"Yes, I imagine that's when they did it. Probably they enlisted some old nurse or village woman who was a witch. A jolly good one, too."

He frowned. "So that's what this stranger did to her? Took off the spell that's been preserving Georgiana's sanity?"

"Not on purpose, I think. I believe they got partway through their nasty working and found that there was already this other spell in their way. They probably tried to lay the hex on top of it, but it would not stick. I've seen your sister repel a hex before. I attributed it to my own protections, but perhaps it was this original spell that shielded her." I shrugged. "Anyhow, they tried to peel off this original protection spell, but it had been on her for too long—it's been with her since she was born, and it had sunk into her very bones. When they tried to pry it off it wouldn't come away cleanly, but only warped and got tangled with the new spell they were trying to shove beneath. At that point I believe they gave up the whole business, probably deciding that bungling the spell that badly would cause quite as much trouble as the hex they originally intended."

"So they did not intend to make her run mad?"

"No, I do not believe so."

"And you can fix it?"

"Well," I said. "Yes and no. You see, the lump of magic on her now is an utter mess. There are two choices for where we go from here. One is to do my best to repair the sanity charm that's kept her in her right mind all her life. It's not so badly damaged, really—only twisted out of alignment, but the pieces are mostly still there. I believe I could patch it up, get it functioning again as it did before." I drew a deep breath. "However, after so long being subject to so many spells, Miss Darcy's aura has become rather tangled. The half-done hex has melted partway into the protection spell. I could no more separate them than I could pick out the butter from a scone already baked." (Actually I think I could do that, with the right spell, but it was a useful analogy.)

Darcy frowned. "What does this mean?"

"It means that if I repair the charm and give her back her sanity, Miss Darcy will transform into an owl every night for the rest of her life."

"Unacceptable. You said there were two choices?"

"Well, yes, but—"

"Tell me."

"The other choice," I said, "is to take the whole mess off altogether. Protection spell, hex, all of it. She will essentially be bare of magic, as she would have been had your parents never granted her the charm. She will no longer transform, but her sanity will not be her own. Mentally, she will be as you know her now."

"You are quite sure that these are my only options?" he said.

"Quite sure. You could ask another witch, I suppose, but I'm as certain of this as any working I've ever done."

I expected him to be torn, to rant and storm, but he merely said, "The second option. That's what we'll do."

I blinked. "Just like that?"

"Those draughts you've been giving her to bring her some lucidity—they will continue to function if you remove the spells?"

I nodded. "Certainly. But as you've seen, those draughts are hardly a perfect solution."

His jaw clenched. "Perhaps not, but better for her to be a bit foggy at times than to be a wild beast every night."

"Is it?" I said. "I think being an owl looks rather fun."

The look he gave me was that mixture of exasperation and pity that I seem to so often bring out in respectable people. "I am sure you do," he said. "But pray, how is she to live like that? How is she to find a husband? I cannot keep her secreted away here forever, and I dare not subject my wife to this disgrace." (Note that he had no trouble subjecting *me*, however.) "Georgiana is handsome, accomplished, respectable, and kind. Moreover, she has a sizable fortune. There are many fine men who would be proud to wed such a creature, even if she was a bit...foggy."

"Do you really think she could be happy with a man who did not care about her brain?" I cried.

"In her current state? Yes, I do," he said simply. "In fact, she might well be happier than she was when she was torturing herself with proofs she will never solve. Besides, what is the alternative? No man would ever wed an owl."

"But she—"

"Enough!" he shouted.

I am ashamed to admit I flinched.

He softened his tone immediately. "I do not care to do this, either," he said. "But you leave me no choice. I must do what I can to preserve my sister's future safety and happiness, Mrs. Wickham. This is the only path forward."

And, I had to admit, he was probably right. I had given him two bad choices; he had picked the less bad one. I had no business bothering him about it. I cleared my throat. "Very well," I said. "I will make my preparations to remove the spells."

He smiled then. "Thank you. I know I have asked a great deal of you, Mrs. Wickham, and I must tell you—you have impressed me."

"How nice."

"I am quite serious," he said. "This has been one of the hardest times of my life. I know I have been brusque, impatient, even rude at times—and you have borne it with patience. Thank you."

"Yes, well," I said. "I like Miss Darcy, you know."

"I know," he said. "And I am glad. I am going to take steps to ensure that your life becomes easier, I promise you. Perhaps I could even find Wickham a living somewhere."

A loud laugh burst from me. "I believe if Wickham set foot in a church wearing clergyman's robes the place would combust."

He gave me a rueful grin. "Yes, perhaps that's a bridge too far. But there must be something." He hesitated. "You could be a companion to Mrs. Darcy."

I could not believe my ears. "Me, live at Pemberley?"

"Indeed—you *only*, that is. Your husband would need to make other arrangements." He abruptly turned away to gaze out the window, his hands clasped behind his back. "We have wronged you," he said. "All of us. I see that now. No matter what you did, we should never have cast you out into the world with only that—creature for company. Make your home with us, my dear. We should be glad—proud—to have you."

Just when you think Darcy is an intolerable stuffed shirt, he goes and says something like that! I blinked back the sudden sting in my eyes. "You might find my presence rather hard to explain to Elizabeth," I pointed out.

"Then I shall simply have to tell her the truth," he said. "It's past time she knew who you really are."

I wanted to answer, but I found my throat had gone rather tight.

Darcy, looking massively uncomfortable himself, gave me a brisk nod and made his escape.

Imagine, me at Pemberley! I must say it is a tempting prospect. I never dreamed of making my way as one of my sisters' poor relations, but it certainly would be an improvement on the cold and hunger and uneasy détente of living with Wickham. And, of course, from what I hear, Kit practically lives at Pemberley.

I am going to do what Darcy asked. I am going to put that strange conversation with Miss Darcy quite out of my head, and do what is best for all of us, and then I am going to go and live at Pemberley and finally, after this horrible year, I won't be alone.

I must simply put my misgivings aside.

Even the fact that the hex stinks of roses.

We left the coachman at home—the poor fellow had been through quite enough—and Wickham took his place. Young men of fashion often took the reins themselves. It was late and the roads were clear, and Wickham drove like the demon he was. Still, it seemed to take an eternity to get clear of Brighton and its environs, and at least five eternities to get out of Sussex. I had left the Order of the Rose in turmoil, but their power was strong and deep-rooted in this county, and now that I had yanked myself free of their organization I could no longer sense whether they were still in disarray or were in pursuit of us.

I had nothing to do as we jostled along but to stare at Miss Lambe's purple form and brood about our situation. Her lilac light blended with the oranges and yellows of the setting sun. The array of colors would have made a very pretty brooch.

While the carriage and I bounced along, she floated serenely, except when we went over an exceptionally large stone or pothole. Then the floor rose up to meet her, and she bounced back and forth between floor and roof before finding equilibrium once more. I hoped we would not have to go too far, or she'd tear a hole in the roof. To steady her, I laid my hand on hers—or rather, on the spike of stone that her hand had once been. "Excuse me, Miss Lambe," I murmured. I had no reason to believe that she could hear me, but best to be polite just in case. She was not one to suffer indignity lightly.

Her power thrummed through me when I touched her. I was aching and weary and I had not slept in almost two days, and it felt like a warm bath. I thought seriously of throwing my arms around her and letting her goodness flow all over my poor tired limbs. No wonder the Order had wanted her: This was *delicious*. But if she could see, I knew that the liberty would mortify her. Besides, once I had groaned in delight at how her power soothed my sore muscles and my sunburn, I could feel that there was a slight wrongness to it. She was full of power, certainly, but it was power that was meant to be *doing* something, surging forward to its goal. Instead, it was trapped in a loop. I could feel its—her?—frustration beginning to build.

*Your Witch-Queen will be in a state of transformation for some hours*, the Long Man had said. But the Order had arrested that process midway through. Was there a way to start it up again? To let her continue to become what she was meant to be? Was that even the right thing to do?

After some hours the carriage drew to a stop, interrupting my musings. Wickham hopped down and opened the door. "We're over the border into Surrey," he told me. "There's an inn up ahead. Shall we stop there?"

"I suppose." I had, at least, thought to bring all the money I had on hand, but it was not a great deal. Still, it was dark, and we would have to stop somewhere.

I tied the don't-notice-me even tighter about Miss Lambe, using a bit of her own power. "Sorry," I whispered. "I'll pay you back." I was not at all sure I would be able to, but better to be in debt to her than to magic at large. Wickham dealt with the inn's stable boy and then helped me down, Miss Lambe trailing invisibly behind me.

Wickham managed to secure two rooms for himself and his "sister" and we hastily retired. The innkeeper leered at me, and I suspected he did not believe us to be brother and sister for a moment. But he sent up a bit of supper for us, and after swiftly eating, I collapsed into bed and was asleep instantly.

The clatter of a coach arriving in haste in the courtyard woke me in the middle of the night. Urgent voices called out, heedless of the late hour. I stiffened, recognizing one of them: Peter, Colonel Forster's manservant.

I lay frozen, my heart pounding. Was the colonel here, too? Was Harriet? She mustn't find us. Miss Lambe was floating beside me, her glow dimmed by the blanket I'd thrown over her so I could sleep, and I reached for her power.

As soon as I touched her, the world seemed to tilt in two different directions at once. There was more power in her than ever, but it was *wrong*—more wrong with every passing second. It wasn't flowing the way it should, and instead it churned and frothed angrily inside her. A wave of it raced into me when I touched her, overfilling me, roiling within me till it was all I could do not to be sick.

"Good for you, Miss Lambe," I gasped through clenched teeth. "At least if they catch us you won't make it easy for them." After that I had to squeeze my eyes and mouth shut.

Distantly, I could hear the innkeeper and Peter conversing downstairs. I wanted to listen in, but since I currently felt like I was on a boat in stormy seas, I had little attention to spare. Presently I heard the innkeeper come upstairs and knock on Wickham's door. He and Wickham spoke in low voices for a few moments, then the innkeeper departed.

After he'd gone back down, I heard my own door creak open. "Are you awake?" Wickham asked in a low voice.

"Mm," I said. I had no wish to open my mouth.

Wickham crept into the room and stood by my bed. "Colonel Forster's men are looking for us," he said. "They believe we've eloped together."

"Mm?" I said.

"Yes. Harriet forged rather a convincing little note from you, apparently." He laughed bitterly. "By God, I underestimated that woman. It seems she's playing the distraught, betrayed chaperone to the hilt." He frowned and knelt down beside me. "I say, are you all right?"

"Miss Lambe's power," I managed to grit out. "'Swrong."

"Yes, I can see that." He laid a hand on my forehead, then quickly withdrew it and fell to his hands and knees, retching. "Lord, how unpleasant. It's like bad gin. You'd better get rid of it."

"Need to spell them away."

"No need. Listen." He jerked his head toward the window. The crunch of gravel indicated the carriage was departing.

*Oh, thank God*, I thought. I blew out a tight breath. Sweat broke out across my face—I tried to focus on that sensation rather than the roiling in my stomach. "How?" I demanded. "A charm?"

He laughed. "Not in the way you mean. No, I charmed the innkeeper quite unmagically with half a crown to keep his mouth shut." He sighed. "My last half crown, as it happens."

I was barely listening. Now that I knew I would not need it anytime soon, my only aim was to rid myself of the noxious magic I'd unwisely borrowed. Never in my life had I had that particular problem before— too much magic to spend, and nothing to spend it on—so I did the first spell that came to mind, an illusion.

I haven't Miss Lambe's artistic eye, nor her attention to detail. My illusion was not as pretty as her portrait of Sainte-Josephine. Still, I think I did it rather well. It was more a series of impressions than a detailed re-creation, but those impressions, taken together, were home. Without consciously choosing, I began to paint the sitting room at Longbourn on a bright spring morning. I let the sickly magic pour out of me to paint in details—the rasp of a page turning in the book Lizzie was reading, the smell of Papa's tobacco and Mamma's perfume, the wind rattling the drafty door to the hall. I placed myself on the love seat over in the corner, and I could feel the press of Kitty's warm arm against mine as we whispered together in our usual nook.

Wickham looked about the room, in my illusion but not of it. He drew in a sharp breath when he saw me with Kit. However, all he said was, "Good heavens, you have learned a great deal this summer, haven't you?"

I used the last wriggling worm of power to add the off-key sound of Mary singing at the piano, then blew out a sigh of relief and let the illusion fade. The sickness faded away, too, and I felt quite well again, if rather tired.

"All right now?" Wickham asked.

"I think so." I stared up at the moonlit ceiling, which was no longer swaying on an invisible ocean.

"Here." He rustled in his pockets and then pressed something small and squashy into my hand. "It's a ginger sweet," he said. "It will help settle your stomach."

Doubtfully, I popped it into my mouth. The sweet taste of ginger did, indeed, quiet the last of my stomach's complaints. When he saw me relax he grinned. "Marvelous, aren't they? We use them to get on our feet for roll call when we're a little the worse for wear."

I sat up on my elbow to look at him. His smile faded. I realized suddenly that our faces were only a few inches apart. I was, to all intents and purposes, alone with a man in an inn. In my short career, this was the most scandalous thing I had ever done.

Except it wasn't, was it? Not in the eyes of the world. Now that I was no longer sick, the things he'd said came rushing to the fore. "Did you say—" I had to force the words past a lump in my throat. "—did you say they think we eloped?"

He nodded.

"Oh God," I said, "I'm ruined," and I burst into tears.

"Oh no. Oh Lydia, please don't cry. I'm no good when females cry. Oh love, please don't." His distress would have been rather comical, were I not sobbing my heart out.

It all came crashing in on me at once. Every step I'd taken this summer, every bit of borrowed magic, every ill-advised flirtation, had been a jolly step toward utter ruin. If the colonel's servants were now openly seeking me on the king's roads, then that meant my flight with Wickham was generally known—no doubt Harriet had made sure of it. Even if I somehow survived these next few days, I had no life to go back to.

Wickham put his arms around me and I sobbed into his shoulder. I knew I should push him away, try to preserve what little decency I had left—but he was the last friend I had in the world, and I clung to him helplessly.

"There, there," he said, when at last my sobs began to quiet. "It will be all right."

I pulled back to glare at him. "How on earth can it be all right?" I demanded.

He handed me his handkerchief and I wiped my face. He said, "My father is not ungenerous to those who please him. Once we deliver the jewel to him, I daresay he will lend you enough power to glamour and charm your way out of this mess."

I looked him in the eye. "Deliver Miss Lambe to your father?"

His arms stiffened about me. "Yes. Of course. If we ride hard tomorrow we can be back on his land by nightfall."

"But we can't!" I blurted.

"We must. We promised."

"That was when I thought I was bringing him a *thing*. She's a person. I cannot simply hand her off to do with as he chooses. It's too horrible."

"People do that to other people all the time," he said. "It's practically all you mortals do. Think of Mrs. Forster's marriage. Listen, Lydia, if you shirk this promise my father will come after us. We will *all* die—first your familiar, then you and me, no matter where we try to run. And for what? A hunk of glowing rock?" He gestured to Miss Lambe. "Would you even know how to restore her to human form?"

"No," I admitted, "but—"

"But nothing. For all you know, she is gone forever." He gripped my shoulders. "Lydia. If you defy my father this way, *you will die.* You have barely seen what he is capable of, even in his weakened state. Will you not save yourself?"

"I should certainly prefer to," I said. *Stop there*, I willed myself. But I could not. "But she's a person."

"Damn it," he said. "Do you expect me to throw my life away for you, selfish girl? Do you think you are the only one who wants to live?"

"We have made it this far," I said. "We will find a way."

I could see from the set of his jaw that he wanted to argue further. Instead he sighed, then smiled and cupped my face in his hands. "Let us not fight," he murmured. "Isn't it nicer when we're friends? Come, let us be friends again."

The kindness and affection in his voice made my eyes fill with tears again. He wiped them away with his thumbs, and then, leaning closer, kissed them away. His lips found mine.

This kiss was different from those we had shared before. There was no frenzied seawater powering it, nor was it the payoff of a complicated transaction. It was just sweet comfort, the sweetest thing I thought I had ever felt. The gentle, tender touch of his lips, the soothing strokes of his hands, the press of his body on mine, all of it rushed into the parts of me that had been filled with queasy despair. It felt inevitable. As though nothing could be more right than Wickham and me, intertwined, his lips whispering endearments in my ear and then finding mine once again.

So there you have it. I really am as wicked as everyone says. Wickeder, for I lay with a rake, and never actually married him after as everyone thought. If that is enough to make you utterly disgusted with me and read no further, I can certainly understand. I am quite disappointed with myself. For heaven's sake, I *knew* what he was—a demon, in the body of a rake, gifted with charm and skilled at seduction—and yet I let myself be seduced. The worst part is I cannot entirely regret it. When I am falling asleep at night, and feeling too lonely to live, I take my mind back to the small hours of that morning, when Wickham lay with his arm round my waist and his chest against my back, murmuring sweet lies to me until I fell asleep. Even now, the memory warms me. That is how I know how irredeemably wicked I really am.

I woke to a pounding at the door. Bright sunlight streamed through the window and I squinted against it. "It's nearly eleven o'clock, miss," the innkeeper's wife said through the door. "Time to check out."

"All right," I croaked. "We'll be down directly."

A pause. "'We'? Miss, your brother left hours ago."

I looked around the room. Sure enough, Wickham was gone. And so was Miss Lambe.

# CHAPTER THIRTY-FIVE

There is a kind of terrible calm that comes over a person when the worst possible thing has happened. As though from a distance, I heard myself tell the innkeeper's wife that I would be down directly, thank you.

I found myself sitting on the floor in the middle of the room, staring at nothing. Last night, when I found that all the world thought I had run off with a rake, I did not think my situation could possibly get worse; but now I had lost the rake as well. I truly was alone and friendless, and I had no notion what to do. The world is not made for friendless ladies. If I could even call myself a lady anymore.

Presently I made inquiries and found that Wickham—and, I was sure, Miss Lambe, still with my helpful don't-notice-me tied about her—had departed in Miss Lambe's coach for London. He had not said why he was leaving his young "sister" behind and unchaperoned, and it seemed no one had thought to ask—now that I'd severed the Order's hold on him, he was on his way back to full strength, and his charm was, too. No doubt he would quickly continue on to Meryton to give her to his father and save his miserable hide.

And what was I to do? Where was I to go? If I went home, alone, after all the county knew I'd run off with a man, my father might well turn me from his door. Perhaps there was a way to invert Kitty's glamour, and turn us both into cats? I'd had quite enough of being a human woman. Every paltry moment of joy it brought was followed by misery times a hundredfold. For example, last night, with Wickham. I'd let my guard down with him, and now, thanks to me, Miss Lambe was as good as Wormenheart's.

There was something pushing up from within me, disturbing the surface of my eerie calm. What would Wickham do after delivering Miss Lambe to his father's predation? Whatever he pleased, I supposed. I could see now that he had only seduced me last night to pacify me so he could sneak away with her. He was a man. His reputation might suffer, but few doors would be closed to him as they were now to me.

Ah yes. That was the feeling surging up within me. Rage. Pure fury.

Say what you will about going from respectable Miss Lydia Bennet of Longbourn to a fallen woman in a single night, the horrific cost of it was certainly enough to power a few spells. I threw on a don't-notice-me and climbed aboard the next mail coach. It was rather comical to see the driver try to make sense of why he had too few seats for all the ticketed passengers—he counted again and again, skipping right over me each time—and in the end he left a sour-faced clergyman huffing in indignation in the yard while I relaxed in his seat.

It had been the impulse of a moment, sneaking onto the coach to follow Wickham, but as I stared out the window I felt sure it was the right decision. I still did not care to hand Miss Lambe over to a dragon. Magic does not like unpaid debts, and I certainly owed her a great many. More important at the moment, I wanted Wickham to pay. Every time flashes of last night came back to me, I shivered in shame and huddled back into my spell. I was sure that were it not for that, everyone in the coach would see my disgrace written all over me. I had visions of delivering Wickham to his father to devour, or completing Miss Lambe's transformation and letting her blast him to cinders with a bolt of purple lightning, and many other jolly fantasies of the sort.

A quick scry-spell gave me a hazy picture of where they were—in London already, changing horses and then probably heading on. I could hardly allow that. I whispered a hex, not at all sure it would work at that distance, but my rage and betrayal came to my rescue. I had only meant to bend the axle or make a horse throw a shoe, but the spell came out surprisingly powerful, and from the sense of confusion that echoed back

at me I was fairly certain that both horses had escaped and the carriage
had more or less exploded.

Wickham was out of money, too. He would be unable to hire a coach
to take him the rest of the way. For the moment, he was stuck in London.

I felt him snarl as he saw what I'd done. A flash of red-hot power
burned away my scrying; after I hissed at the sting, I reached out again,
and realized I could no longer find a trace of them. I had no real idea of
the nature or extent of Wickham's abilities. I was fairly certain he could
not recite spells as I did, but there was a kind of raw power in him, a bit
like Kitty's, that could apparently shield him from detection. Bother.

Well. To London then.

When we arrived in Clapham I alighted from the coach, only to realize that I had no idea where to go. My knees were trembling from doing
two strong spells already that day. The street was crowded with people,
shoving and jostling and taking no notice of me (yes, I know I'd spelled
them not to. I was still hurt) and I had very little money and was all
alone. However, my don't-notice-me felt as strong as ever, so I hopped
in behind another passenger into a hackney chaise that was headed for
the city.

I changed hansoms several times—it may be more economical, but it
is very tiresome to sneak onto cabs using magic, for you cannot tell the
driver where you wish to go—until I made it close enough to walk the
rest of the way to my destination: Gracechurch Street.

I had not really thought my plan through. My aunt and uncle Gardiner lived there, and they were the last people I wanted to see, but they
were also the only people in London that I knew. I was *fairly* certain that
they would at least let me in. I knocked at their door, gritting my teeth
for the tongue-lashing I was sure to get, but when the butler opened it,
he merely frowned at me, looking puzzled, and let me walk past him.
My don't-notice-me, which I had expected to fade away by this time, was
still going strong.

It really was an excellent don't-notice-me. I kept it on for days and it never frayed. I moved smoothly through Uncle's house like a ghost, eating their food, sleeping in one of their guest rooms, and no one ever quite realized I was there. The servants set a place for me at table, and brought me fresh linens; I even borrowed one of my aunt's nightdresses, but they had no idea I was in the room with them. At first it was just the servants there, and I recollected that my aunt and uncle had gone away on holiday with Lizzy; but after a few days my uncle returned in great haste, and he did not see me, either.

In some ways, I suppose, the spell lasted so long because it was not taxed very hard in my uncle's house. He and my aunt had never taken much notice of me. The vague way my uncle looked over my head now was not so different from how he and my aunt had always reacted when they thought I was talking too much or laughing too loud. They are good people, I must emphasize; but they had never liked me, and like most well-bred people who do not like someone, they had coped by ignoring me. I was merely helping my uncle's natural inclination along with a little magic.

If, on some level, my uncle was aware of my presence, he probably felt deep down that ignoring me was the right thing to do. He had come back, I soon found, because they had heard about me and Wickham, and he was wild to track us down and make us marry; but from how he talked of me to his valet, I knew that as soon as that disagreeable task was done, he and his wife would quite happily never mention my name again. Some part of them was probably glad to ignore me, the way one does one's best to ignore a spider crawling across the ceiling. I had already fallen out of their world.

Presently my father came to stay with my uncle, too, and that did give me a pang of conscience. He looked twenty years older, and appeared to feel some genuine remorse for how he'd neglected me. *Yes, Papa, maybe if you had not treated all of us but Lizzy like so many millstones round your neck, I might have come to you with my troubles.*

Once I found him alone in the parlor, his shaking hands covering his face, and I realized he was either weeping or trying not to. He had always been fairly useless to me but I defy any girl to see her father in such a state and not feel it; I felt close to tears myself.

"Lydia," he muttered to himself. "My poor little Lydia. Oh, my littlest one."

"It's all right, Papa," I said, though I knew he could not hear. "I'm here. I'm all right."

"Little one," he whispered. "I have failed you. Where can you be?"

"Oh, Papa." I could not stand it, and almost lifted the glamour and let him see I was there, but then he continued.

"I failed to keep you from wickedness," he said. "And now you are sunk beneath reproach...what is to become of your sisters after what you've done?"

And so I kept the glamour in place, and watched my father weep for how utterly despicable I was.

I had a morbid fascination for the way they spoke of the need to find me, sometimes over my very head. Sometimes it was *poor Lydia* and sometimes *foolish Lydia* and occasionally *wicked, wicked Lydia*; but Wickham was always *that horrid Wickham*, so at least they had one thing right. Colonel Forster came and conferred with my uncle in low voices, pulling at his mustache, the picture of concerned fatherliness; I wanted to scream that if he was old enough to be my father, he was old enough to be his wife's, too.

I wanted to scream a great deal in that house. These men knew nothing, understood even less. They spoke of me with a mix of pity and disgust usually reserved for those with communicable diseases. They would cure me if they could, but their main goal was to keep my disgrace from infecting others. I had fantasies of dropping my concealment spell in the middle of one of their grave, officious conferences and showing them how much of what they thought they knew was wrong.

Luckily for them, I had a higher goal: Make Wickham pay. I knew he and Miss Lambe must still be in London after what I'd done to the carriage, and after his summer of being drained by the Order, his luck and power must still be at low ebb. He'd have to wait until they refilled to make the rest of the journey. I was determined to find them.

It was the search for the jewel all over again. I knew that I could not scry for Miss Lambe directly, because of her magic-jewel-queenliness; and now Wickham, too, had managed to hide himself from my magical gaze.

I did not know London at all well, and its witching world, not at all. I considered seeking out sisters of the craft to ask for their assistance, but after all that had passed with the Order, I decided I'd best take my chances alone. After a few days of scrying and wandering, however, I was footsore and at my wits' end. Perhaps I would have to let Wickham take her to Wormenheart after all.

That night I had a dream. I found myself in Miss Lambe's Brighton parlor, sitting across from her in my usual spot on the loveseat. She sat very upright and correct, with a bit of embroidery.

The room, however, was a disaster. The rug became a beach of Sainte-Josephine halfway down. The back wall opened onto an imaginary hill. Ripples of purple light spread out from Miss Lambe herself, ebbing and flowing, and red-gold cinders floated in the air. It was all too much—too much magic, too much power, concentrated queasily in too small a space with nowhere to go.

"Apologies for the mess," she said. Her voice had a queer echo, as if bouncing off stone walls. "It's the maid's day off."

"I'm trying to find you," I said. "I really am. Wickham tricked me, he—"

She shook her head. "Always excuses with you, Miss Bennet."

"Well—he did though."

"I am only in this situation because I tried to help you," she said.

"Can you tell me where you are?"

She shook her head. "I'm stuck inside myself. I can't see anything beyond."

"I've tried every spell I know to find you," I said.

"In the end, we did not discover the jewel's location with spells," she said. "We did the reading."

I frowned. "Wickham is only a year old. There can't be any books about him."

"Perhaps not, but the knowledge he possesses is mostly left over from the mortal Wickham, is it not? There must be those who knew him."

I shook my head doubtfully. "I do not know any of his acquaintances. I suppose I could scry for them, but—"

She sighed. "You are too dependent on magic, Miss Bennet. *Use your brain.* You would have a fine one, if you ever exercised it."

I found that so insulting that I woke myself up. When my eyes sprang open, I heard a well-bred male voice downstairs. One of Uncle's friends? No, he was at home to no one. Besides, this voice was faintly familiar.

*Mr. Darcy.*

I hurried into my day dress (I may have been nearly invisible, but I still liked to dress smartly) and ran downstairs. There he was: Mr. Darcy, Netherfield's brief visitor of last year. It had taken me a moment to place him. We had barely spoken ten words to each other, and because he was so widely agreed to be unpleasant and proud, the young ladies of the town had paid him little attention, preferring to sigh over his more amiable friend Bingley. Particularly in our household, because Mr. Bingley had so distinguished Jane, he had quite eclipsed this silent, scowling fellow.

Mr. Darcy was now as silent and scowling as ever, turning and turning his hat brim in his hands until the butler almost took it from him by force. I followed him to the parlor, where Mr. Darcy paced up and down like a caged animal until he finally sank into a chair, only to leap up again when my uncle came in.

"It is my fault," he blurted.

My uncle gave a great sigh. "Sit down, Darcy. What can I do for you?"

"What happened to Miss Lydia—" He clenched his jaw. "I could have stopped it."

"What on earth do you mean? You were in Derbyshire when those two idiots ran off."

"Wickham and I grew up together," he said. "His father was my father's steward. He—became angry with me after a dispute about my father's will. I will not bore you with the details but suffice to say I did my best to provide for him according to my father's wishes and Wickham chose to believe I cheated him. Eighteen months ago he attempted to take his revenge." His jaw clenched, somehow, even harder. "With my fifteen-year-old sister."

*The last thing he did before losing his soul to me was to try to seduce a fifteen-year-old heiress.*

"Oh, Darcy." My uncle placed a hand on his arm.

"Luckily, Georgiana chose to confide in me. Would that Miss Lydia had had such a confidant—but no, it should not have been necessary. I should have made at least a part of his infamous conduct more generally known." He drew a deep breath and stood. "I alone am responsible for another young girl being imperiled by him. I alone must repair the damage. Only tell me how I can help."

I was leaning forward on the sofa with my chin in my hands, staring at him with narrowed eyes. I appreciated that he, at least, saw that none of this was my fault. I did not entirely understand why he was choosing to involve himself in this matter, or even how he knew about it, however.

As though he heard me, my uncle said, "I suppose Lizzy told you of all this?"

"Yes. On your last day in Derbyshire, sir, I happened to be present when a letter arrived from Miss Jane Bennet—Miss Elizabeth was—" He cleared his throat. "She was quite overcome. The thought that, through my actions, such grief should befall such a dear, sweet creature as—as all the Bennet sisters, I cannot bear."

Oh. *Oh.*

It is much easier, I think, to judge what is passing through other people's heads when they cannot see you doing it. It was written all over his face that he loved Lizzy. How peculiar! She, above all of us, had always loathed him. Had her feelings changed? How had they even stayed in contact all this time? To this day I do not know all the answers. Isn't it strange to see that, even as one's own story unfolds, others are traveling through their own, which may be just as interesting? (Except for Mary. Nothing interesting will ever happen to Mary.)

A stab of something like envy ripped through me. Of course Lizzy had managed to ensnare this elegant, rich man, and even, it seemed, taught him to behave. Why must she always be right? Probably they would marry, and she would have everything I had felt on my one night with Wickham, with none of the pain that followed.

I shoved the thought away. I did not wish to think of that night, except in the context of the bloody revenge I would wreak on Wickham for it. My uncle and Darcy were in the process of agreeing that Darcy would try to find out where Wickham had gone to ground.

*There must be those who knew him.*

When Darcy left, I followed him into his carriage. I did the same each day that came after. His voyage through what he knew of Wickham's past associates was quite an education for me. Disreputable as some members of the honor guard had been, they had never allowed me to come along with them in the pursuit of manly vices. Now I saw all the debauchery that London had to offer a weak-moraled young man, whether flush with cash or empty of pocket. Gambling dens, clubs, boxing, what Darcy called "nunneries," which were filled with extravagantly made-up young women who were, I was quite certain, not nuns—we visited them all.

Perhaps you think I was unkind, not to tell Darcy or any of the people who were so desperately seeking me that I was there and quite safe. But keep in mind, they would not have much cared. As far as they were concerned, I was about as safe as a lit grenade unless they found Wickham as well and made us marry. I, too, needed to find Wickham, so I felt it best to avoid tiresome conversations until then. Besides, so long as I remained invisible, I found Darcy to be surprisingly good company. He placed all the blame on Wickham, not me—which is quite true!—and never described me as wicked, only misled. I decided I rather liked him.

And of course, I had other reasons for remaining invisible. There had been something growing inside of me—I do not call it love, for *that* would be ridiculous, but *something*—for many weeks. Perhaps since the night of the seawater in the punch. Perhaps even longer. Waking to find that Wickham had deserted me had ripped out this tender shoot by the roots, leaving an empty, dry hollow behind that threatened to crumble me from the inside out. For the first time in my life, the thought of being looked at was unbearable.

Occasionally, though, someone would see me. Small children, I found, were not always susceptible to my spell, and I had to come to an arrangement with Uncle's boot boy so he would not yap to the whole household about the strange girl staying in the house. (I became quite proficient at polishing boots.) One woman at a nunnery stared right at me and laughed and said "Hail, sister," but the others said she was drunk and not to mind her. Mostly, though, the glamour held. It felt different—less like a cloak and more like a hard, shiny shell keeping the world away. It drained me awfully, but I did not care. I had misery enough to pay for it.

Darcy, too, became gradually half aware of my presence. He never fully saw me, and certainly never recognized that the girl whom he desperately sought was at his side eating a pasty he had paid for, but after I had accompanied him for some days, he seemed absently aware of my company. If I dawdled on the way into his coach he would growl "Come *on*," and hold the door for me, and sometimes he would mutter, as much to himself as to me, about where we would search next. I believe what happened is that he became gradually immune to my spell and began to see through it; but he was by that time so used to my presence that he simply accepted me there without thinking about it.

This had distinct advantages. I began, cautiously, to respond when he spoke to me, and then to ask him questions, and I found that he would sometimes absently answer them. He did not speak to me as a lady, but more like a groom or a steward—someone who required no special formality, but who was close enough to confide in.

He told me how he had come to love Lizzy, and how pained he was that he had treated her so badly at first. Apparently he had persuaded Bingley not to offer for Jane, an act that threatened to drive a permanent wedge between Darcy and Lizzy. He was quite wretched over it, dwelling over and over upon his longing to go back and fix past mistakes—it made me think of Harriet, and her desperate desire to erase her marriage from the face of the earth. It is a good thing magic cannot really turn back time, or we would all be going ceaselessly backward and forward trying to fix everyone's love affairs.

He told me, too, about growing up with Wickham—the old, human Wickham—and I felt even more sympathy for him. No wonder Darcy had become so withdrawn and stern. He had been told throughout childhood that he must be kind to Wickham—but Wickham, so charming and obliging when adults could see, was in private an utter terror to Darcy. He was a year older than Darcy and, for most of their childhoods, several inches taller, and so he relieved his feelings about the unfairness of Darcy being the heir by beating his so-called friend nearly senseless. Darcy still has scars on his back from when Wickham had deliberately frightened Darcy's horse into rearing and Darcy fell on a rocky riverbank. And so Darcy distrusts charm, in himself more than in anyone else, and I do not blame him a bit. Not for *that* anyway.

Some of what he described to me sounded a little familiar from the early days of my Wickham. I remembered how he had gleefully terrified me with the news that he was causing Kitty's illness. Mostly, though, it sounded like he was speaking of a complete stranger. My Wickham was selfish, vain, and unreliable, but after those first few weeks I had never seen him be deliberately cruel. How much of the original Wickham really remained? Was that fellow's nature still a part of him, or was my Wickham now his own man? And did it really matter, since he was a demon anyway?

And, of course, when I thought about it, I realized that there might not be such a difference between the old Wickham and the new one after all. The man had made love to me and then abandoned me. What was that, if not gleeful cruelty?

Aside from giving me a fascinating education in debauchery, my travels with Darcy at first accomplished little. Many of those he approached knew Wickham, but most had not seen him in some time, and none in the last few days. Darcy grew increasingly tense and frustrated, until finally he ordered his coach to stop at the side of the road.

He stared straight ahead. "I do not know where else to go," he said finally. "I have failed."

"Oh come now. Have we really visited *all* the dens of vice in London that a young man might enjoy?"

"All that I know of."

"Hmm."

We sat in silence for some time, Darcy in dejection, me trying to rack my brains for any charm, any spell I hadn't tried.

*You are too dependent on magic. Use your brain.*

"Is there no other acquaintance of Wickham's you know?" I said. "Forget the debauched ones—he must have some connections in polite society. He does so love to play at being a gentleman."

Darcy moved restlessly. "There's *her*, of course," he murmured to himself. "But to seek out her company—it is too much."

Excitement stirred in my breast. "Her who?"

Darcy gave a great sigh. "Yes—I suppose I have no choice. She will know, if anyone does."

And so we went to see Mrs. Younge.

Mrs. Younge lived in a respectable house in a respectable street and a respectable maid opened the door to us and ushered us into a respectable parlor. I gaped unashamedly. In a way, this was more fascinating than any of the dens of vice I had been to before; they were places quite outside the sphere of polite society. What I knew of Mrs. Younge made it all the more interesting that she was able to live with such apparent propriety.

"Mr. Darcy," a cool voice said presently. "I did not expect the honor of your company."

Darcy jumped to his feet. "Mrs. Younge. My visit finds you well, I... trust?"

*I trust.* Not, I noticed, *I hope.*

Mrs. Younge looked as though she'd noticed as well, and her mouth quirked in cool amusement. She was a woman in her mid-thirties, I estimated, impeccably dressed and coiffed in the latest fashion, without looking overdone—I found myself noting the subtle yellow trim that raised her day dress beyond the ordinary, wondering if I could reproduce it. She had a kind of calm, amused poise that made me feel like a gawky child.

"Oh, well enough, I suppose. I've a number of boarders at the moment—young ladies in need of a respectable chaperone." She raised an eyebrow. "My time as a governess in the Darcy household has made me quite in demand."

Darcy growled. "Any decent family ought not to let their daughters within fifty miles of you."

"I daresay you're right." She smiled. "Who's to tell them? You?"

Darcy growled again.

"And how is dear Georgiana?" she asked. "Keeping up with her Italian, I hope?"

"Do not speak of her," he said. "I am here for another reason. Seeking a friend of yours. Wickham."

"Ah yes. Quite the talk of the town, this adventure of his with the little country girl."

"Do you know where he is?"

"Perhaps. But why not simply ask the girl herself?" and she gestured to me.

Darcy, following her movement, turned to me. As his eyes focused directly at me for the first time since he'd come to London, they widened in astonishment. *"Miss Lydia Bennet?"*

"Hail, sister," I said to Mrs. Younge weakly.

# CHAPTER THIRTY-SIX

Mrs. Younge waved off my greeting. "I am no witch, child, though I am acquainted with several. No, I am merely a lady who makes her way in the world by seeing what others choose not to." That cool amusement crinkled her nose. "In this case, a runaway."

"Miss Bennet," Mr. Darcy said. "How on earth did you get here? Are you staying with this...this woman?"

"No," I said. "I came with you, remember?"

Darcy opened his mouth to speak, then closed it, then shook his head as though to clear it. "No, I...that is..."

"Oh dear," said Mrs. Younge with interest. "You've fractured his wits. I think I like you."

Darcy blew out a breath. "It does not signify where you came from. Miss Bennet, where is Wickham? Are you married?"

"No, we are not."

"Tell me where he is at once."

"I wish I knew."

At this they both looked at me in astonishment. "You don't know?" she said.

"No."

Darcy advanced on me with such fury in his eyes that I actually took a step back. "I know not what game you are playing, Miss Bennet," he said. "Sneaking around, following me, somehow concealing yourself...but it ends now. Have you any idea what you have put your family through? Your father?" He drew in a sharp breath. "Your sisters? Tell me where Wickham is, this instant. You are going to marry him without delay, if I have to march you two down the aisle at the end of my pistol!"

I felt naked without my concealment spell. Darcy's eyes burned like a brand on my skin. I bit the inside of my cheek, hard. I would *not* cry before him like a naughty child. "I don't *know*," I repeated. "We stayed at an inn. When I woke, he was gone."

Darcy's eyes widened. "He abandoned you on the road?"

I crossed my arms. "Yes."

"Even for him, that is truly..."

"Yes, well." I had no wish to dwell on that night. "The point is, I want to find him as badly as you do." I turned to Mrs. Younge. "*Do* you know where he is? Someone must."

"First things first." Darcy grabbed my upper arm. "I am taking you back to your uncle's. You've done enough damage."

"Ow! That you are not. You know perfectly well that having me under their roof will do more damage to their own reputation, unless we find Wickham." I wrenched my arm away. "Besides, is it really me who's done the damage? You told me yourself that this is all your fault."

His eyes widened. I could see him searching his memory—not quite able to remember, but not quite able to refute it, either. "It does not signify," he said again. "Come along."

Mrs. Younge intervened. "I believe I can help," she said. "Darcy, are you willing to make a donation to my little school? The same sum you paid me to hush up the Georgiana affair will do nicely."

"Very well," Darcy growled. "If you tell me where he is."

"I don't believe I will," she said. "But I will tell Miss Bennet."

"What!"

"Yes, that is the most amusing way, I think," she mused. "Darcy, step out of my parlor. Go on now. Go and bring your carriage round."

Darcy, still grumbling, made his way out the door, and Mrs. Younge turned to me. "What an interesting day this is turning out to be," she said. "Come, let's sit and have a cozy chat." She saw the strain on my face.

"No? Very well, I suppose you are in a hurry." She went to a desk and took out a scrap of paper. As she wrote on it, she continued, "It is really for your sake that I do this, I tell you. I don't care for Darcy—he spoilt all my lovely plans. Do you have any idea how hard it was to persuade that tiresome brat Georgiana to take her nose out of her mathematics books and fall in love with Wickham?" She sighed. "I was promised ten percent of her fortune, you know, once Wickham had her...but Darcy ruined it all."

The warm, confiding tone in which she said all this made me feel uneasy. *She thinks I'm like her*, I realized.

Her sharp eyes scanned my face. "You still have illusions," she deduced. "You are judging me harshly."

"For a non-witch, you see things very clearly, ma'am."

"Yes, well, you make it easy. For the life you're going to lead, you'd best learn to hide your feelings better than that." She ripped off the page with a flourish and handed it to me. "Wickham's address. Take him and welcome. I don't like him anymore. He's more complicated than the man I knew."

I took it. "Thank you."

Her sharp eyes raked over me once more. "You need not look down on me so, you know. You have already started down a path you can't turn back from. You will soon find what it takes for women like us to survive."

"I am not a woman like you."

"That's what we all think," she said. "At the beginning."

Darcy tried again to take me back to my uncle's, but I refused to give him the address I'd got from Mrs. Younge until he agreed to take me along. When we arrived at our destination, the door was opened a crack by a woman with suspicious eyes and no teeth. "I 'eard there was a new witch about," she said. "You'd best leg it, witch, for this 'ere's Ellie Snuff's patch and she don't take kindly to competition."

"I'm not here to trouble any fellow witch," I said. "Is Wickham here?"

A crafty look stole over her face. "Ah. Maybe he is, maybe he ain't."

"Darcy, give this woman a large sum of money, if you please."

Darcy did so, and we were allowed inside. Up a winding, creaking staircase we went, past four floors of crying children, dull-eyed women, and men who looked greedily over Darcy's fine coat and boots and my quality gown. The house smelled of cooking and smoke and worse things. So this was where one landed when one fell.

When we arrived at the landing on the fifth floor, our hostess jerked her head at the door, said "There's your man," and went back downstairs. Darcy, seeming to recollect his place, stepped in front of me and knocked on the door. "Wickham!" he called. "Open up, I know you're in there."

To my great surprise, he did so.

That was the last thing I remembered for quite some time.

# CHAPTER THIRTY-SEVEN

"...not to mention what you have done to the prospects of your poor sisters with your scandalous conduct. Lydia? Lydia, are you listening to me?"

I blinked, and blinked again, trying to clear my vision. It was a most disorienting sensation. As far as I knew, a moment before, I had been in the rookery of St. Giles, watching Wickham throw open the door; now I was standing on a footstool in my aunt's sitting room, one arm held stiffly out to the side, while her maid pinned a sleeve in place. It had been late afternoon in St. Giles, but now the morning sun streamed through the windows.

"Honestly, girl, I believe you haven't heard a word I've said in days. It's as though you're a thousand miles away." My aunt jerked my other arm up and began moving the pins, none too gently. "All I can say is, you had better behave impeccably after you are Mrs. Wickham, or no one will know you. Hold *still*."

"When I am Mrs.—" I drew in a sharp breath. Some of it began to come back. "Wickham! Look out! He's—"

"Yes," drawled a voice from the doorway. "Wickham *is* here."

Wickham sauntered in, forcing the maid Ellis to move aside, and leaned in to kiss my cheek. I froze, like a mouse hypnotized by a snake. "Hello, dear Lydia."

*"Hello, dear Lydia."*

*Those had been his words when the door opened. A whiff of sulfur blew out with the open door; I thought for an instant too long that it might be simply one of the St. Giles slum's many stinks. I soon realized my mistake.*

*I had generously wreathed both myself and Darcy in protective spells, but I had not really expected much trouble; I had never seen any sign that Wickham could do magic the way I could. But now, as I felt the familiar sensation of coils tightening about me, I realized this was not my Wickham.*

I blinked away the shard of memory. I was in my aunt's sitting room, not on a rickety staircase in St. Giles. But the danger was no less.

"Mr. Wickham." My aunt's lips thinned. "It's not proper for you to be here. Go down to the parlor, and Lydia will receive you there—*briefly.*"

"Ah, but surely we need not stand on ceremony. We are to be married tomorrow." His smug gaze raked over me. "And it is such a delight to see my darling preparing herself for me."

My aunt hissed out a breath between her teeth. "And *when* you are married, you may be as disrespectful as you like to her; but while she is under *my* roof, the proprieties will be observed."

"Of course, madam." He made her a slight bow and withdrew.

After I had dressed, my aunt accompanied me down to the parlor. "Do not ask to see him alone, Lydia," she whispered to me on the stairs. "It may be the accepted thing for an engaged couple, but *you* are no ordinary engaged couple. I shall chaperone you every moment."

"Very well, Aunt," I said meekly. I had no desire to spend any time alone with Wormenheart.

He stood and bowed to us when we entered the parlor. He was in splendid form. Over the last few weeks, as Wickham's luck failed him and then we took flight, he had grown shabbier; his boots less shiny, his hair undone, his cravat rather dirty and mussed. But now his hair was impeccably pomaded, his boots were expertly polished, and his cravat was a brilliant white.

"Let's have some privacy," he said, and flicked his fingers at my aunt.

Normally, when I wanted privacy, I would use a don't-notice-me or a sleep spell. This was considerably less subtle. My aunt froze mid-step, one foot off the floor, her mouth open to greet him. A halo of shimmering red heat surrounded her. He turned to me.

"Wormenheart," I said.

"What have I told you?" he said. "I am a Great Lord and you are to address me as such." He cocked his head. "Since we are to be married, 'my lord and master' would be appropriate."

"You cannot really mean to marry me."

"You think not?" he said. "I do, though. I shall marry you to this body at least. A Great Lord cannot be bound by your earthly marriage ceremony." He sauntered toward me. "I am quite enchanted by your little marriage vows, though. They are almost as good as a spell, with no magic at all. I make you say the words, and then all that you have, all that you are, is mine."

"I will never be yours," I choked out.

He chuckled warmly. "Still fighting as hard as ever. You have been wriggling in my coils since you were seven years old, child. Surely you see now that you cannot escape?"

"What are you going to do?" I managed.

"Exactly as I please." He took my hand. His skin was hot, but I could not pull away. "You should have delivered the jewel to me when you had the chance. Instead you broke our agreement, and now everything—the jewel, the cat, you—will be mine." His expression grew dreamy. "What will I do with all that power? Oh, I don't know. Your little friend was right, the days of flying about roasting sheep are over—but there are so many more delicious things to eat nowadays, aren't there? I am quite taken with some of the goings-on in your South Seas. Thousands of souls eaten up every year, and no one bats an eye. How would you like being the wife of a plantation owner?"

"I should hate it."

"Well, it does not matter." He kissed my hand. "I am glad you are awake. That haze I threw over you was quite a bit more powerful than I expected. I have been interested to see when it might finally wear off. It would have been quite amusing if you had come to your senses at the altar." He gave a happy sigh. "This is better, though. I like that you have time now to dwell on what is coming."

"You cannot do this," I said. "We are out of your territory."

"Ah, but I have a vessel now." He gestured grandly to Wickham's body. "It is your fault, you know, Miss Bennet. When you blew up Wickham's carriage you left him with no choice. He reached out to me in desperation. I do not think he expected me to take over so wholly, but he always was a foolish boy. So you see, I can do what I like." He gave me a polite bow. "Go on, though. Try to escape me."

I did not like his obliging tone, but nevertheless I reached for my power. I could at least blast that smug look off his face—

It was gone.

Frantically, I scrabbled for my magic. It was as though a well in me had been drained, leaving only dry, crumbling walls within. I did not have the smallest shred of magic.

"No," I muttered. "It's not possible."

He laughed in delight. "But it is! My dear Miss Bennet, it is! Go on, try again."

Even if my store of magic was entirely gone, I ought to be able to get more. I was in a state of utter misery and despair; that ought to buy a spell or two. I whispered a spell, trying to call on my store of sacrifice, and for a moment hope swelled as magic began to well within me—

Then it drained away.

Wormenheart was licking his lips, like he'd had a gulp of beer on a hot day. "Ahh," he said. "Delicious. How glad I am that I did not eat you up when you were a child! How much better it will be to let you feed me slowly. Your familiar will keep you alive, though I don't know if it will keep its shape—I hope you've said your farewells." He kissed my hand again, then flicked his fingers at my aunt, who began to move. "Until tomorrow, ladies," he said, and took his leave.

The rest of the day passed in a blur of lectures from my aunt, fittings for my hastily got-up wedding clothes, and awkward meals. I paid it all as little attention as I had when I was under Wormenheart's daze. I was too busy trying everything I could to reach my power. It was no good. It was gone.

That night, I lay awake for a long time, staring at the ceiling. I suppose after a time I fell asleep, for I began to fancy that I could see past it, up beyond the roof and the smoke of London's chimneys, to the stars above. Idly I picked out stars for myself and for Kitty—a large twinkly one for me, and another nearby, smaller but very bright, for Kit.

I continued the game. The North Star was Miss Lambe, of course, steady and strong—or she had been, before I had come along. A bright star with a flight of smaller stars behind it, angling down toward mine as though attacking it—that would do for Harriet. Thank God that she, at least, had not come after me, though I was sure she would hear of my downfall. Orion's belt was the honor guard, my sisters were the Pleiades.

And what about Wickham?

At first, I thought to give him a large, pale star near my own, a little above it. I could almost imagine it as a face, shining down on my star.

*"What are you staring at?" I had asked him, in the dim moonlight as he trailed his fingers over my collarbone.*

*"Nothing." He wrapped a curious finger with a lock of my hair. "You."*

*"Well... stop it. It's keeping me awake."*

*"I cannot help it. You're too beautiful." He lifted the lock into the moonlight. "Why on earth do you ladies keep your hair bound up? It's so lovely like this."*

*"Why do you gentlemen keep it pomaded within an inch of its life?" I rolled over to look at him. His face, sleepy and content and affectionate, was so beautiful it made me ache. Shyly, despite what we'd just done, I reached out a hand to push his hair back from his face. He caught my hand in his and kissed the palm. I shivered. I hadn't known I could feel like this.*

*"Tomorrow," I began.*

*But he silenced me with a kiss. "Sleep now, Lydia. Trust me. I'll take care of everything in the morning."*

My star, and Kitty's, and Miss Lambe's, were disappearing. A cloud must be passing across the sky. That would do—the cloud. For Wickham and Wormenheart both. I was no longer under the illusion that there was any meaningful distinction between the two.

Wormenheart had won. Carefully, he'd clouded each of us over, swallowed up our light. Collected us all as prizes.

But people aren't prizes. Prizes are inert things. When they're won they don't care. But people—even when they've lost everything, people can do things out of *spite*.

The dream, or whatever it was, was drifting away. True sleep was swallowing me up. The last thing I felt was a tickle on my nose, as though someone had laid her furry tail across my face.

# CHAPTER THIRTY-EIGHT

I was not terribly surprised to wake to Kitty's claws kneading my chest rhythmically. She was purring, her eyes half closed in pleasure. I'd have purred, too, if I could, despite the dire circumstances. She was here. Kitty was *here*. I was whole again.

"Hello, Kit," I said in a voice creaky with sleep. "How did you get here so fast? We haven't any magic anymore."

*How does any cat get in where it's not expected?* she said, butting her forehead under my chin. *I've told you, Lydia, we cats have ways unknown to mortals.*

I buried my face in her fur. She smelled of home. "It is good to see you."

*Yes, well. I thought it was right we should be together today.*

"Does that mean you're not angry with me anymore?"

*There doesn't seem any point anymore, does there?*

"You know then. What I mean to do."

*Yes. I don't see that there is much choice.*

Tears sprang to my eyes. "I am sorry, Kit. I tried. Really I did."

Her rough tongue bathed a tear from my cheek. *There now. Do not apologize. When we cats make a mistake, we merely show the world that it was what we meant to do all along.*

I gave a watery laugh. "You don't fool us, you know."

*Yes we do. Shut up.*

An hour or so later when my aunt came in, she stared when she saw Kitty in my arms. "Good heavens. Is that a cat? How on earth did it get here? Ellis, come and shut it up in the sitting room."

"Please let me have her with me today, Aunt," I said.

My aunt's expression softened when she saw my tear-streaked face. "Very well, if it will keep you calm. Now come, it's time to make ready."

I was even less attentive to my aunt's homilies that day. I am sure she thought me horrid ungrateful, but I hardly think anyone on their way to the noose is a jolly conversationalist. I merely let her and her maids dress me and ready me, only interfering when they would have left my front hair flat instead of curled. Even on the day of my doom, I could not stand to look *too* dowdy.

There was another little argument when I insisted on bringing Kitty in the carriage. I quickly prevailed, though. They were so relieved to be almost rid of their scandalous niece, they would have let me bring a whole menagerie.

The church was nearly empty when we arrived. The parson, Darcy, and Wormenheart waited at the altar. Hovering next to them, looking less person-like than ever, was the jewel. Of course. Probably Wormenheart meant to use her magic to seal my fate. He smirked a little when he saw Kitty trotting along next to me, and made her a small bow.

I reached the altar. My stomach was in knots.

The ceremony began. The priest droned on about honor and fidelity, about chastity and love. Lots of things that did not apply in this case.

"...and do you, Lydia Charlotte Augusta, take this man George David James, to honor and obey, for as long as you both shall—"

I threw up at the altar. Darcy jumped back in disgust lest my sick splash on his shoes. Wormenheart rolled his eyes.

"Tried to use the jewel, did you?" he said. "It's no good, remember. Any power that passes through you or your kitty-cat drains straight to me." He turned to the priest. "Get on with it."

The priest, looking rather taken aback, turned to me. "Do you take this man, my dear?"

"Not much choice, have I?" I muttered. "Yes, I take this man."

"And do you, George David James, take this woman Lydia Charlotte

Augusta, to honor and obey, to belong to and to follow, for as long as you exist on this mortal plane?"

"I do," Wormenheart said with a smirk, then frowned. "Wait, those aren't the words—"

"Then by the power vested in me by sacrifice," said the rather confused-looking priest, "I now pronounce you witch and familiar."

Wormenheart's eyes widened. "Familiar?"

"Yes," I said. "Familiar. I'm sure you'll enjoy helping me in my spells."

"That's not possible. That flea-ridden creature is her familiar—"

*Not anymore*, yowled Kitty.

Wormenheart's face twisted into a mask of rage. He lifted a hand. But it was too late. We'd done it.

*Kitty's tail had swished with curiosity that morning as she'd watched me laying out my spell.*

Are you sure this will work? *she'd asked.*

*I bit my lip in concentration, trying to keep the lines of the complicated shape I was drawing in salt neat and precise. I was modeling my spell on the one Harriet had done on the hillside all those months ago, but despite her tutelage I was by no means sure I'd got it right.* "Quiet," *I said.* "No, I'm not sure, so keep still, would you?"

You've smudged a bit. *She gently patted a stray herb back into place with her paw.* There.

"Thank you." *I sat back with a sigh.* "That's the best I can do, I think. We'll just have to hope it works."

How can it, *she asked,* if we've no magic anymore?

"If I make a very great sacrifice, I shall have enough magic to power it," *I said.* "Just for an instant. I think. I hope."

That will have to do, I suppose. *She regarded me carefully.* A very great sacrifice. Yes, I think you're capable of that now. You've changed a great deal this summer, you know.

"And yet, the sacrifice is still partly yours. Kit, I'm sorry."

Pooh. Such pride! As if it's a sacrifice to no longer be *your* familiar,

Miss Lydia. *She turned up her nose.* I daresay I shall do quite well on my own.

"I daresay you will." *I gave a watery laugh.* "But oh, Kit, I shall miss you so much."

Lydia. *She jumped into my arms and let me cry into her fur until our aunt came.*

In the church, Wormenheart had twisted Wickham's handsome face into such a mask of hate it was almost unrecognizable. He raised a hand, but I was too quick for him. His eyes widened as the power he was gathering flowed away to me.

"Not a nice feeling, is it?" I panted. His power was hot and unpleasant to hold. "Turnabout is fair play."

"Don't be a fool, girl. Do you honestly think you've the strength to hold me as your familiar? *Me?*" He grabbed me by the hair. The mortals were staring at us in confusion. Darcy stepped forward as though to take my arm. I held up a hand to stop him. Wormenheart continued, "My power will burn you to a crisp from the inside out. Let me go or I'll make you sorry for it."

"I daresay—you're right—about not being able to hold you," I gritted out. "But—I don't—intend to." And I reached out and grabbed the jewel.

And then the church fell away.

I found myself in a familiar place. A clifftop, overlooking a tropical isle. The grass would have been a brilliant jewel green in sunlight, but the sky was roiling with dark clouds. Wind and rain beat the hilltop, the raindrops nearly horizontal.

A figure in a gray dress was at the cliff's edge. I went to join her.

"Miss Lambe," I said.

"Miss Bennet."

"I've come to ask a favor," I said.

She huffed a laugh, not looking at me. "You always want a favor."

"This is the last one. I need you to come out now. Take your crown."

She shook her head. "I can't. They've left me stuck. All my power is turned inward."

"Ah, but I've a gift for you." I held out the roiling, red-black mass of power I'd taken from Wormenheart.

She wrinkled her nose. "That's a nasty thing."

"Yes, but it's enough." I held it out. "Take it."

But she did not move. Just sat there staring at it. "If I come out," she said slowly, "if I take my throne, I shall be bound to that horrid little town forever. Surrounded by quarreling witches and people with complexions like uncooked dough."

"Yes," I said. "I suppose that's true." I frowned. "Do you really think my skin is like uncooked dough?"

"I'd rather stay here," she said. "At least this way I'm home."

"This is not your home," I said firmly.

"I beg your pardon? Sainte-Josephine is most certainly my home."

"Perhaps. But you did not just bring yourself to Sainte-Josephine. You brought yourself to this moment. Don't you see?" And I pointed out past the harbor. Far below, a valiant little ship was fighting a losing battle against the enormous waves.

Miss Lambe sucked in a breath and raised her hands. "Get out of my way. I can still save her. I can still—"

"No. You cannot. She's not here."

Slowly, Miss Lambe let her hands drop.

"This moment is not your home," I said. "You have lived here far too long. It is time to walk on."

She did not reply. Just kept staring out at the waves.

"You know," I said, "my sister told me this morning that I had changed this summer. If I've learned anything, it's because of you." I took her hand. "Come on."

She stared out to sea, and pressed her fingers to her lips. Then she turned and started down the hill. "Very well," she said. "I see I shall have to clean up one more of your messes."

Sainte-Josephine faded away, and I was standing at the altar once again.

"—boil your insides! I'll burn your toenails off one by one! I'll—" Wormenheart stopped mid-rant when a great purple light suddenly flared in the chamber.

Miss Lambe was no longer a rock. She was a pretty young lady again—neatly dressed, with her feet on the floor once more—who just happened to have a blinding violet halo.

"Enough now," she said. "This nonsense has gone on far too long. Begone, Wormenheart."

Wormenheart recovered from his shock and turned to her. "Will you really try your strength against mine?" he snarled. "You are a newborn. I am as ancient as the Hertfordshire hills."

"Ah," said Miss Lambe. "But we are not in Hertfordshire. And I am not the only one who has objections to that."

Suddenly the chamber was full of people—well, some of them looked like people. I spotted the Long Man among the crowd, and thought I could hear the sea's rhythmic sighs, but there were so many more. A knight in armor. A lady in a Roman toga. Sprites and giants and animals and trees. I wonder if anyone's wedding has ever had so many Great Lords of Britain in attendance as mine did.

"Lord Wormenheart," said the knight, "you stand accused of crimes against your fellow Great Lords, of stealing magic from them, and of trespassing upon their turf." He sighed. "At the moment, *my* turf. How do you plead? Never mind, I don't care. Go home and sleep, wyrm."

Wormenheart opened his mouth to scream—

And then his body collapsed.

After a moment, he stirred and groaned. Wickham opened his eyes. The red glow was gone. He was my Wickham again. I crossed my arms.

"What—" He moaned. "Father, please don't—" His eyes lit on me and he surged to his feet. "Lydia!"

"Hail," I said. "Familiar."

His hand had been reaching toward me. He let it drop. "So that's how it is," he said, and sank back onto the altar, put his head in his hands, and laughed.

The cleanup took some time, both magical and real. I do think that all those Great Lords could have stuck around a *little* longer to help.

You know the rest, of course, Miss Lambe. How I glamoured my uncle and aunt and the priest to believe they'd seen a normal marriage. I tried to do Darcy, too, but it did not work so well, for he knew more, and I was still unaccustomed to my power being bound up with Wickham's.

Then you opened a sort of gate—gracious, magic is easy for you now!—and told Kitty it was time to go home. We were both rather surprised that she'd ended up in girl-shape when the bond was severed, but I was glad, for it meant I could catch her in a quick, hard hug. Her hair smelled of Meryton sunshine and her human heart beat steady and strong. I may have made a mess of things, but at least Kit was still in the world.

Then you cleared your throat and my sister stepped back through the portal and was gone. When all was restored, you turned to me.

"Well," you said. "Is this mess of yours finally tidied away?"

"I think so," I said. "As much as it can be. I really am sorry, but you see—"

You raised a hand. "If you make me any excuses, I shall box your ears."

"Very well." With difficulty, I resisted the urge to explain. "What will you do now?"

You sighed. "What I must. Thanks to you, I've had to accept the crown. It's Brighton for me."

"Well... that's not so bad. I can come visit you. We can practice our glamours—"

"No. Miss Bennet, your selfish, shortsighted use of magic has caused immeasurable distress in at least three different counties. You are not to do magic anymore unless absolutely necessary. Is that understood?"

I looked at you. You seemed tired, but stood tall. Your mouth was set in a grim line. The witches of Brighton wouldn't know what had hit them.

I was not even sure I could do much magic, to be honest. Kitty was gone. The spot where she had been was numb but also somehow ached. In her place, my new familiar was tugging at his bonds, testing if he could get away, and it took considerable amounts of my power to keep him in check—and it has been that way ever since.

"All right," I said. "I promise. On one condition."

You raised your eyebrows. "You demand conditions of me?"

"Just one," I said. "Stop wearing gray."

I fancied, just for a moment, that I saw your hard eyes soften. You looked down at yourself. Your dress became a soft coral pink. It suited you admirably.

"Very well," you said. "Goodbye, Lydia."

Wickham and I went to visit my family for two weeks, and it was the hardest fortnight of my life. I had to pretend to be as empty-headed and foolish as everyone thought me, playing the happy newlywed and trying to ignore the pitying looks from Jane and the angry ones from Lizzy. My father barely looked at me at all. Now that I was married, he'd forgotten his self-reproach and seemed perfectly ready to wash his hands of me altogether. My mother was sweet at least.

Hardest of all was Kitty. We'd gone through life hand in hand, and now it was as though there was a pane of glass between us.

Wickham tried to persuade me that he'd done it all for my own good. He'd taken Miss Lambe from the inn, he claimed, to deliver her to his father in order to save my life. Of course I knew better, and soon enough he gave up his protestations and professions of affection and subsided into the sullen silence that has defined our domestic life ever since.

Then, of course, we went north. I tried, at first, to endure the life of solitude to which I'd sentenced myself. I wrote endless letters to Kit, and lived for her letters back. Then, a few days before I first wrote you, I got the following from her.

> *Dear Lydia,*
>
> *I shan't write to you again after this. It hurts too much. Everything I was—a familiar, a fine mouser, a magical creature—is all gone, except for being a young lady, which is the dullest part. Your letters make me miss you and miss you, and I don't care for the sensation. I am rather lost without you, and if I am to find a way forward I must do so on my own. If we cannot be witch and familiar anymore I think it is best if we do not correspond so often, and allow our intimacy to subside. Grown-up sisters usually do, you know, when one gets married and moves away.*
>
> *Love,*
>
> *Kitty Bennet*

I tried to do as she asked. I really did. But oh, I missed her so. That is why I wrote to you. Why I've done as you asked and written this leviathan. (Be careful what you wish for! It'll take you ages to read, I daresay, and cost a fortune in postage.)

As you asked, I have tried to be as honest as possible. Is it enough to earn one last favor in return?

Please say it is. I know I am a wicked creature—I know I do not deserve it—but please give Kitty back to me. Somehow. I think I could stand all of it, the poverty, the isolation, the handsome, hateful husband, if only my sister and I were together.

I have to go now. I'll send this off with the afternoon mail. I may not be at the Bingleys' much longer but I shall send you my new address as soon as I can. I remain, still, though you are practically the only one who knows it—

LYDIA BENNET.

# CHAPTER THIRTY-NINE

FROM THE DESK OF
Miss Maria Lambe, 13 —— Street, Brighton
To Mrs. Lydia Wickham, Baily Hall, Derbyshire

Dear Miss Bennet—

I was astounded to receive your—*letter* does not seem quite the right word. When I did not hear from you after writing you all those weeks ago, I assumed you had simply declined my request to elucidate the events of last year. I am afraid you quite misunderstood me. I merely wanted a few lines explaining some points that confused me. Not hundreds of pages about your childhood. You always did enjoy talking about yourself.

In fact, my dear, you have misunderstood me in every possible way. If I had had to read one more line where you castigated yourself for your wickedness, I would have hexed the whole thing into ashes. Was such self-flagellation meant to appeal to my character? It does not flatter me, I assure you, that you see me as a kind of stern confessor. Or—is it possible—do you really think yourself as wicked as all that? I suppose everyone tells you you are—and for all the wrong reasons. This smug nation of yours certainly enjoys grinding its daughters down to a powder.

You have been selfish, thoughtless, lazy, and vain, it is true. You have also been brave, and kind, and insisted on seeing me as a person when everyone else saw only a resource to be exploited. Do not think I am ignorant of that.

I think, in order to avoid future misunderstandings, we had better meet in person. The spell you requested may be possible. Can you come to Brighton?

I have one more thing to thank you for. I do not miss the gray gowns.

Cordially,

MISS MARIA LAMBE.

P.S. For heaven's sake, call me Maria. We have been through enough.

~⌒◡

FROM THE DESK OF

Fitzwilliam Darcy, Pemberley, Derbyshire

To: Miss Maria Lambe

Miss Lambe—

Forbid my impertinence in writing to you when we have never met. Indeed, you have more impertinence to forgive than you know, for I opened a letter from you to my sister-in-law Mrs. Lydia Wickham that arrived yesterday at my friend Bingley's house. My only excuse is that it was a dire emergency.

I gather from the tone of your letter that you are familiar with certain extraordinary facts about my sister. I shall hold nothing back. Mrs. Wickham, who had promised to aid me in lifting a terrible enchantment from my own sister Miss Darcy, has instead disappeared, and taken my sister with her. Her husband is quite frantic, as am I. I pray, if you know anything at all about her whereabouts, write at once. I am desperate.

In haste,

FITZWILLIAM DARCY.

~⌒◡

## END OF PART TWO.

# PART THREE

# CHAPTER FORTY

From: Miss Georgiana Darcy, ▮▮▮▮▮▮▮▮▮▮▮▮▮▮▮▮▮▮▮▮▮
▮▮▮▮▮▮▮▮▮▮

To: Mr. Fitzwilliam Darcy, Pemberley, Derbyshire

Dearest Fitz,

I am so, so, so sorry for making you worry. I ought certainly to have left you a note, but at the time that Lydia and I left I was quite incapable of it. (Owl.) My wits as you know have been very sluggish of late, and it was not until this morning that I realized that you must be tearing your hair out with fear. It seems I continue to bring you nothing but trouble. You have no idea how that pains me. After last year's business with—well, you know who—I solemnly promised myself that I would be a model sister and never cause you a moment's pain and what do I do instead? Get myself somehow drenched with magic. You must be thoroughly sick of me.

Really, though, you mustn't worry. I am perfectly all right—better, in fact, than I have been in some time. Lydia has done a partial repair on my mind spell (though she says it is only temporary and will not hold) and my head is clearer than it has been in weeks. I am *myself* again, and oh, it is glorious. We have taken lodgings ▮▮▮▮▮▮▮▮▮▮▮▮
▮▮▮▮▮▮▮▮▮▮▮▮▮▮▮▮▮▮▮▮▮▮▮▮▮▮▮▮▮▮▮▮
▮▮▮▮▮▮▮▮▮▮▮▮▮▮▮▮▮▮▮▮▮▮▮▮▮▮▮▮▮▮
▮▮▮▮▮▮▮▮▮▮▮▮▮▮▮▮▮▮▮▮▮▮▮▮▮▮▮▮
▮▮▮▮▮▮▮▮▮▮▮▮▮▮▮▮▮▮▮▮▮▮▮▮

Lydia walked by just then and exclaimed when she saw what I was writing. She pointed out that if I described our lodgings you would quite easily be able to track us down, and she made me black it all out. Isn't she wonderful? So *practical*. I feel quite stupid beside her. I am sure you can have no fear for me, knowing that she is here to watch over me.

She read that last bit and now is laughing so hard she is crying. *I* do not see what is so funny. I know she has had moments in her past that were—well, not exactly respectable—but then, so have I. It is only luck that she is Mrs. Wickham and not I. And she knows about so many things—not only magic, but also how to catch the mail coach, and how to get a good cut of meat at the butcher's, and all sorts of useful things. And she can talk to people! La, she makes it look so easy! (Do you mind if I say "la"? I know it is Slang, but I like it.)

You know, I do not think I ever loved Wickham—I only wanted to be the kind of girl who *would* love him. A girl like Lydia, a smiling, dancing kind of girl who knows how to converse and be amusing and does not cry when her corset is laced up. Even when I am a girl, I often feel like an owl.

Lydia says that as long as we are on the subject of how wonderful she is, could I please tell you that I came away with her of my own free will and to please not send the Runners after her for kidnapping. It is quite true, you know—in fact, leaving was my idea. I am *truly* sorry, Fitz, for going against your wishes, but I am afraid I begged her to do it. I remember little of the last few weeks, but I do remember, whenever I had Lydia alone and my head was halfway clear, imploring her to help me get my mind back. At any cost. I told her—and I remember this, for it took all my concentration to get the words out—that I would rather be an owl twenty-three hours a day if it meant I could get my mind back for just one.

I had to, Fitz. Truly I did. I know you had only my best interests at heart when you asked her to remove the owl spell and let my mind stay sluggish—perhaps you are right, and I could have learned to be happy like that—but I do not think so. I certainly do not wish for a husband, except to please you. I should be quite happy for the rest of my life doing mathematics all day and flying about the countryside all night. I know it is selfish of me, but there it is.

Now I have my mind back and oh, the glory of it. Lydia says it is only a temporary patch and that she will have to work much harder to make the repair to the spell permanent (and so will I—something about a spell-price?), but for now I am simply enjoying it. My decision is not purely selfish, either—my brain is necessary for the world. Which brings me to my reason for writing.

I have some most exciting news: I have almost solved Goldbach's conjecture! My long period of madness seems to have worked on my brain like a good sleep. When Lydia spelled me back to myself I found that almost all the pieces were there in my mind. Is that not wonderful? It requires only a little more tinkering. Could you please send me some of my mathematics books when you have a moment? The Newton of course, and the Leibniz, and whatever else you think might be fun. You may send them to this address:

Goodbye for now, Fitz. Pray do not be *too* angry. I shall be home as soon as I can. After this I will strive to be the best sister and the least troublesome ward who ever lived. All my love to Mrs. Darcy.

Your loving sister,

GEORGIANA DARCY

P.S. Lydia has pointed out that it would be quite inadvisable to give you our address. Ah well. I have most of Newton memorized, anyway.

P.P.S. Pray do not be too worried. I really am quite safe with Lydia.

⟳

FROM THE DESK OF
Fitzwilliam Darcy, Pemberley, Derbyshire
To: Miss Maria Lambe

MISS LAMBE:
I enclose a copy of a letter I have received from my missing sister. As you can see, the situation is dire. I pray you will assist me in tracking them down.
All the best,
FITZWILLIAM DARCY

⟳

From Miss Lydia Bennet, Rookery of St. Giles, London
To Miss Maria Lambe, 13 —— Street, Brighton

Dear Miss Lambe,
By now you will have received my account of the last year. Unfortunately, I was obliged to leave Baily Hall before you could send a response (if, indeed, you sent one at all). If you read my account—and if you have not, I do strongly urge you to do so, for though it is dauntingly long I daresay it is charmingly written—you will know that at the end I begged a favor, and promised it would be the last I would ever ask of you. Well, I am afraid I am now going to break that promise.

It is not for me that I beg this favor, though. It is for the young lady you met in the pages of my account—Miss Georgiana Darcy. Oh, what a muddle she and I are in! If you do not help us, I am sure I do not know what will become of us.

I had no intention of rescuing her at first, I assure you. I do not have a noble bone in my body. But she begged me and begged me to help her get her mind back, and every time she looked at me I was reminded of that kid goat Aunt Philips wanted to sacrifice, the one I finally stole away and gave to a tenant farmer, and so I gave in.

At first I thought it would be all right. I took her to London, and got us some cheap lodgings in St. Giles. I was sure no one would think to look for us here. We pawned some of her jewelry to pay for room and board, and our lodgings, while not elegant, are clean and spacious enough for us, and most important there is a skylight so Miss Darcy can come and go at night. I am sure her presence is greatly improving the health of the neighborhood by decimating the rat population.

My plan was simply this: take her away for a few days, repair her mind-shield spell as best I could, and return her to Darcy with her mind clear and her owlish habits intact as a *fait accompli*. I was sure he would be furious, but that he would accept her in time, for he loves his sister dearly; and perhaps Miss Darcy could even persuade him to let me stay on as her companion. Having one person in his household who knows about the owl business would surely be useful.

However, I am afraid my original plan is not possible. My attempts to repair the spell have been for naught. Every time I try to patch up the parts of her mind-shield that were damaged by the hex, it merely reactivates the hex itself.

As I mentioned, the spell smells of roses, which suggests the caster is among your domain. Will you help me? I hope you will, for as I write this we are already packing up to go to Brighton. We have been evicted from our lodgings. A St. Giles landlady will put up with almost anything, but not, it seems, acid dripping down the stairs. This is *really* the last favor I will ask.

Your friend (I hope),
LYDIA BENNET.

~◯

FROM THE DESK OF
Miss Maria Lambe, 13 —— Street, Brighton
To: Mr. Fitzwilliam Darcy, Pemberley, Derbyshire

SIR:

I understand your disquiet on your sister's behalf, but be assured that I expect to see her and Lydia shortly and will do my best to ensure Miss Darcy's safety. I pray you, remain at home and wait for word from me. This is the best thing you can do for your sister and yourself.

Sincerely,
MISS MARIA LAMBE.

~◯

FROM: Miss Kitty Bennet
To: Mrs. Lydia Wickham, care of Miss Maria Lambe

Lydia—

What do you think? I am on my way to Brighton with Darcy! I must confess I am quite curious to see the town that ruined you so utterly. It must be a frightfully fascinating place. I am writing from his carriage, which is thundering down the road as we speak, so please forgive me if my handwriting is harder to read than usual.

Wickham is here, too. He is the one who bade me come with them. Darcy was all against it—you know Darcy, he is usually against things— but Wickham said that this was witch business and I knew more about that than either of them, and Darcy said what was that supposed to mean, and Wickham said I was really a cat, and Darcy went and leaned against the windowsill for a while. So, here I am.

Am I to see you there? Darcy seems to think we will find you at the address I am writing to. I hope not. I do not feel at all ready to see you again now that our bond is gone. But I thought I'd better write and prepare you for the possibility.

Do you want to know something strange? Both gentlemen are extremely anxious and cross, but of the two of them the more distraught one is Wickham! He is quite tense and keeps muttering about what manner of hex you may be facing, and cursing himself for not anticipating your flight, and asking Darcy if those d—ed nags of his can go any faster.

He asks me to send his love (!), and to implore you not to do anything foolish, but to wait for him for any sacrifice that may be needed. What on earth have you done to him? Is he just putting on a show for me and Darcy? Or have you actually made him attached to you?

Your loving sister,

KITTY BENNET.


P.S. Ah, we have stopped for supper and Wickham is flirting with the barmaid. That is the brother-in-law I know.

# CHAPTER FORTY-ONE

FROM THE DESK OF
Miss Maria Lambe, 13 —— Street, Brighton
To: Mr. Fitzwilliam Darcy, Royal Hotel, Brighton

SIR:

It has been three days now since your sister-in-law Miss Bennet fell unconscious and was ensconced in my spare room. Since then I have, at your request, allowed all the physicians you selected to come and see her and endeavor to bring her back to her wits. As I predicted, none have succeeded. She remains insensate, suspended between life and death. This is to notify you—in writing, since you do not seem to hear it when I say it aloud—that I will admit them no longer.

Her condition is simply not something a normal physician can understand. I have endeavored to explain that to you, but you will not hear it. I shall now set down a complete account of the last few days here. If you cannot see me to interrupt, perhaps you will be more willing to attend to me.

Four days ago, your sister and sister-in-law arrived at my home in Brighton. I cannot exactly accuse them of coming unannounced, for Lydia did write a letter informing me of their intention, but as it arrived a mere six hours before they did, I was not entirely prepared.

"I know, I know," she told me the instant she tumbled out of their hired carriage. "Frightfully rude of me to drop in this way. But really, I had no choice. How are you? I like your hair like that." She dropped distracted kisses on my cheeks. A rather shy-looking young lady dismounted behind her, whom she introduced as your sister.

I settled them in my guest rooms, and then we retired to my parlor, where Lydia asked me again to help her repair the spell on your sister.

"I am sorry, Miss Darcy," I said. "I do not believe I can remove your hex."

Lydia frowned. "But you're ever so powerful now. Couldn't you just—?" She waved a vague hand.

I shook my head. "As a Great Lord, my power is bound to my land and the witches who live on it. In many ways, I am more restricted than ever."

"Oh pooh." Lydia pouted. "You were my last hope."

Miss Darcy put up a timid hand. "Does this mean I shall lose my mind again?"

"Yes," Lydia said. "Sorry."

"Perhaps there's another way I can help," I said. "You said the spell smelled of roses. That means at least some of its power was probably reaped here. I cannot remove the spell, but I can summon its caster."

Lydia frowned. "Is that all? If the Order did it, summon them all here and turn them into toads or something."

I shook my head. "Some of the magic was gathered on my land, but it was cast elsewhere. I can summon the caster for you, but no more. The rest is up to you."

"Well, that's something, at least."

"Yes," I said. "But are you sure you want that, knowing who the spell's target was?"

"You mean Miss Darcy?"

"No, Lydia," I said. "You said that every time the spell activated, the creature came straight for you. This spell was intended to make Miss Darcy kill *you*."

Her eyes widened. "My God, I think you're right. How did I not see it before? Someday you'll have to teach me how you do that."

"Do what? Observe things and think them through?"

"Yes, that thing." She frowned. "Well. Let us go ahead with it then."

"You are quite sure?"

"Yes. I want to know who's trying to kill me." She made a face. "It is probably that odious Miss King."

I tended to agree—the Miss King in question is a relation of mine, and has ensnared me in some rather tiresome legal proceedings I shall not bore you with—but for once we were both wrong. The next morning, after we'd laid our spells and I'd made the summons, it was not Miss King who came stumbling up the beach to us.

We'd chosen a spot on the seaside, sheltered by some rocks, because the sand marked the border between my land and Mother Sea's. Borders are powerful places. We were there at dawn, both because the border between night and day is powerful as well, and because we were less likely to encounter holiday-makers. The summoning was not a showy spell—there was no shower of sparks or puff of colored smoke, to Lydia's disappointment. Instead, our target simply appeared on the sand half a mile down, and marched toward us. Lydia exclaimed softly as her features became clear.

"Harriet," she said.

Harriet Forster was not the woman I remembered from the previous summer. She wore a gown I had seen her wear on the hottest days last year, but now the weather was nowhere near warm enough for it; moreover the dress looked shabby and worn. In a darkened room it might pass for elegant, or at least attractive, but in the glare of the morning sun its poor state could not be hidden.

Her face, however, was the greatest change. She was still a very pretty woman, but the flush of youthful energy that had made her so admired was gone. Her features were hard and pale. Harriet Forster, it appeared, had fallen on hard times since we'd seen her last.

Lydia took a step toward her when she reached us, but her former friend did not even look at her. "You called, my Queen?" she drawled, managing to make my title sound like an insult.

Lydia stepped closer. "No," she said. "I did."

Still, Harriet would not look at her. "You may have the power to call me," she said to me, "but I live and practice my craft in London. You have no further power over me, I think."

"Harriet," Lydia said. "Harriet, you must take the spell off Miss Darcy. It's gone terribly wrong, you see, and—"

At last, Harriet turned to her, a wild look in her eye. "Wrong?" she said. "Wrong? Yes, I can see that, for you are still standing here."

"Then—" Lydia faltered. "Then—you really did mean to..."

"Kill you? Of course, you stupid girl."

"But why?" Lydia whispered.

"Because thanks to you, *I lost everything.*" Harriet's lips curled into a snarl. "The Order cast me out. So did Forster. I have spent the last few months under the protection of men I previously would not have allowed to speak to me." She made a sound halfway between a growl and a sob. "I'm *ruined.*"

"But so am I!" Lydia said. "I am ruined, too! Why, we could be ruined together at least."

I looked at her in astonishment. "She tried to kill you," I pointed out.

Lydia waved a vague hand. "Yes, but if she stopped, we could have such fun."

It is one of the nicer things about Miss Lydia Bennet, I think, that she is incapable of holding a grudge. Probably it is because she lacks the attention span that God gave a gnat, but still. The hopeful look she directed at her former friend was entirely in earnest.

However, Mrs. Forster was not moved. "You're not ruined," she said. "A little marred, perhaps, that is all. My own mother will not speak to me."

She took a few ribbons out of her purse and began slowly to braid them together.

I nudged Lydia in the ribs. "Remember," I said, "all I could do was the summons. You must see to your own defense."

But Lydia ignored the strands of magic slowly gathering in Mrs. Forster's hand. Her eyes were glued to her former friend's face.

"I still had a bit of magic saved," Mrs. Forster was saying dreamily to Lydia. "Being a table-mistress was profitable. And of course my downfall afforded me still more. I had to use a great deal of it to keep body and soul together after Forster cast me out, but there was enough left for one great spell." She smiled. "At first I thought to attack you through one of your sisters, but they're well warded—your little country coven is good for some things, it seems. And then I learned, quite by chance, that you and Miss Darcy both lived in Newcastle."

"That was stupid," Lydia said briskly. "She had wards as well, as you know now." Despite her firm tone, there were now tears on her cheeks.

"Yes," said Harriet. "It was. I should have come for you directly." And she attacked. A wild burst of power careened into Lydia, knocking her off her feet and throwing sand in her eyes. Lydia stood, bit her hand till blood came, and responded in kind.

It was not much of a duel, really. Nothing compared with their previous one, which had spilled out all over Brighton. Back then, Harriet had the Order behind her, and Lydia had my power and that of her familiar. Now Harriet was all alone, and Lydia was, too.

They sweated and gritted their teeth and bled, hurling sickly heaves of magic back and forth, blocking them clumsily. It was not long before they had both used up their stores of magic, but they did not stop—Mrs. Forster gouged into her own life force to hurl another spell, and Lydia followed suit.

"Stop!" I cried. "Both of you, stop!" But they ignored me. Or maybe they could not hear me.

Mrs. Forster dug deep and flung one more curse, and Lydia failed to block it. She clutched her throat, gasping for breath.

Do not think I stood idly by. But the restrictions upon me are strong, and the power I tried to feed Lydia merely flowed back to me. I watched in despair as she fell to her knees. She was suffocating before my eyes.

Tears glittered in Mrs. Forster's eyes. She was shaking her head, as though part of her wanted to stop, but still she held her hands up, and still Lydia gasped vainly.

Then, just as she began to turn blue, Lydia lifted her head up. She drew in a deep breath, then another, and rose to her feet. "At last," she murmured to herself, "he's good for something," and she broke Harriet's spell into a thousand pieces.

Harriet collapsed. It was over.

"Are you all right?" I demanded. "What happened?"

"Hmm?" she said. She tried to wobble toward me and sank down again. "Wickham. Fin'lly behaved like a familiar." She blinked slowly. "Oh. Harriet."

I turned.

Harriet Forster did not have a drop of magic left to her name. She lay crumpled in a heap on the shore, sobbing. Her gown was torn and streaked with sand.

As I approached, she tried to fling a spell at me, and then another; it was like a child playing make-believe. She had dug too deep. She was powerless, and would be ever more.

"Stop that," I said. "You'll kill yourself."

She glared at me through tangles of hair. "Good!" she said. "Better than to stay here! Go on, strike at me!" and she screamed in frustration and tried again and again.

I do not know what would have happened, had it been just the three of us on the beach. Perhaps I would have had to kill her after all. But of course there was someone else there. As Harriet collapsed, one cheek to the sand, the tide rolled in.

A wavelet flowed just up to her, barely reaching her cheek, a curious, tickling touch.

*Come away?* asked the sea. *Come, come away?*

Slowly, Harriet sat up. She put a hand in the damp sand, let the next wave flow up to cover it.

*Come away*, the sea said more firmly. *Love, love, come away.*

Harriet looked at me defiantly, as though she expected me to stop her. I said nothing.

With trembling fingers, Harriet reached for the buttons of her gown. She was shaking too hard to manage them, but another pair of hands joined hers to help. Lydia had dragged herself over to her former friend. I joined them. Together, we helped her to undress.

Harriet Forster walked out into the sea, her head up and back straight, without a backward glance. As she went deeper, her trembles ceased, and the bloom of health and youth returned to her face. The waves reached her knees, her waist, her shoulders, then she ducked her head under. We caught a glimpse of a sleek, brown-furred back, the flip of a trim tail, and then she was gone.

I turned to see how Lydia had taken Mrs. Forster's departure, and was just in time to catch her as she sank into a faint.

A voice shouted her name, and the next thing I knew Wickham was there. He snatched her from my arms into his own, patting her face, stroking back her hair. "Is she all right?" he demanded. "Is she dying?"

"I do not know," I said. And indeed, I still do not.

That is the scene that you and Miss Kitty Bennet joined shortly thereafter. The rest you know: We took her back to my house. With Mrs. Forster no longer there to anchor the hex, I was able to work her curse on your sister loose enough to repair her mind-shield, and you have since divided your time between haranguing me to remove the owl hex altogether (I cannot. Lydia was quite correct about that. Let me be) and surrounding Miss Bennet with useless physicians.

Believe me, Mr. Darcy, I want to see Lydia come back to us quite as much as you do. More, perhaps, for she is, in spite of everything, my friend.

I confess, however, that I am as much at a loss as your many physicians. All we can do now is hope.

Sincerely,

MARIA LAMBE.

⁓

[The following is written in a very large, awkward hand, with many blots of ink and smudges, as though written by a child.]

Deer Lidya.

Now you see I am not such a fool as you tack me for. Nore such a wastrul eether. Sumtimes when you thoght I was out drinking or gambleing I was acktually lurning my lettrs.

It is 3 days now girl that you have been lieing in Miss Lambs gest room and we begin to dispare that you will ever wake from your ~~unkonksh~~ ~~unconsc~~ oh HEL

[The letter is now continued by a much more accomplished and legible hand.]

Your Miss Lambe has agreed to act as my scribe for the remainder. She heard some of the noises I was making and decided writing it for me was preferable to my smashing the inkwell against her wall. This writing is a frustrating business. I do not like to do a thing unless I can do it well.

She has hardly left your bedside, you know, trying everything she can to bring you back. So have I. Still you lie there, white and silent, inching closer to death.

Miss Kitty has just poked her head in. She thinks that, instead of wasting time on correspondence, I ought to try to call out to you yet again as your familiar. She can be very persistent, your sister. In this case she is wrong. I have called and called and got no reply. Even if I could somehow reach you, is hearing from me not more likely to induce you to retreat even farther from us? I know how much you have longed to escape me this past year.

Anyhow, girl, there are things you ought to know, and as we've always been hopeless at conversation, I thought I'd try this way.

First is the writing. I confess I began it so I could better read your correspondence, but so far it has not been much good for that—I find reading and writing far more difficult than I anticipated, and your handwriting is atrocious. I can hardly make out a word. So why have I kept on? I suppose I wanted to surprise you. Picturing how your eyes would go wide, the way they do when something has shocked you, kept me from giving it up. I have lived every day of these past eight months under your open contempt. It would be nice to show you that you do not know *everything* about me.

The second is something Miss Lambe says I must tell you. She was horrified when she read your missive and found you did not know. I am sure she is quite wrong to think you would care, but she says if I do not tell you she will, so I suppose I must.

It concerns those frantic days in London last year, after I took my leave of you in that inn. I intended, as you know, to bring the jewel straight to my father, and save your life—our lives—but you took care of that. Charlotte Street will talk for many years of the abrupt implosion of my carriage.

You left me no choice but to remain in town, and I took the cheapest lodgings that I could. Luckily I was near St. Giles when it happened, and no one there asks questions. I set about trying to raise the funds for a new carriage. I had thought, now that those rose-reeking she-devils were no longer sucking me dry, I could gamble for the money, but I overestimated how much of my luck had returned and soon found myself poorer than when I started. I had no alternative. I simply had to hide away until my luck grew back. And that is where the trouble began.

Stuck in those squalid little lodgings, with no company besides the jewel, I had nothing to do but think. Oh, I tried not to. But the trouble was I kept hearing your voice, Lydia. I did my best to think of my violet companion only as *the jewel*, not *Miss Lambe*, but I found that every time I looked at her I heard your voice, saying, *But she's a person.*

I told myself it did not matter. So what if she was? You, I, and Kitty were *three* people, and we would all die if I did not deliver her. Anyhow, she wasn't. She was very clearly a rock now. I was right to make use of her.

Still, as the days crept by, your voice only grew louder. *She's a person.*

It can be deucedly uncomfortable when a fellow has too much time to think. Yes, she was a stone, but what was I, if not fire and stone poured into man-shape? I, who had been created solely to be of use to another, had done all I could to escape that fate—and now I was delivering another into it.

Miss Lambe, must I really go on? It is mortifying, and she will not care. No, don't write that down, dash it. Very well.

When I found she was now Miss Lambe to me, and not the jewel, I grew desperate. I could not make use of her power the way you had. The thought of bringing her to my father had grown difficult to bear, but the thought of letting him destroy you was unthinkable. In my panic, I made the stupidest mistake of my short life. I still held a tenuous connection to my father's power; I thought perhaps I could siphon off just enough of it to shield us—you, me, Miss Lambe, Miss Kitty—from him, so that we could all survive long enough to escape his reach.

As I said, it was stupid. The moment I tried to drain a drop from him, he rushed through the opening I had created and took me over. The rest you know.

Miss Lambe would like to ask why I never told you this. But how could I admit such an error? I would rather have you think me irredeemably wicked than such a weak, softhearted fool.

Besides, I knew you would not believe me.

I can feel you still. A little. You are in a dark place, and very far off. If I traced the thread of our bond I think perhaps I could follow you down there, but then we'd both be stuck there, and I know that spending an eternity alone with me is the last thing you would want.

Cannot you please climb out on your own? Come, do not be lazy. Hitch up your skirts and come back to us. It is almost summer and we are in Brighton again. There is a whole new crop of young officers for you to beguile. You should be dancing and laughing and teasing your friends, not lying there as quiet and pale as the grave. I cannot bear to see you like that. I cannot bear it. Lydia,

Enough of that. Your Miss Lambe is looking at me with something like pity and that will not do. I shall close this letter with the only title I can honestly claim. I remain,

Your familiar,

GEORGE WICKHAM.

# CHAPTER FORTY-TWO

From: Miss Lydia Bennet

To: Mrs. Darcy, Pemberley, Derbyshire

Dear Lizzy,

I know—you must be most awfully confused to see me write my name as *Miss Bennet*. There is a reason for that, I promise. I am enclosing with this letter a rather lengthy manuscript. You will find I addressed it to a Miss Lambe, but as it turned out she never wanted it in the first place—and the more I think of it, the more I believe the person I really wanted to explain myself to was you.

You and I were never close, exactly. I had my Kitty and you had your Jane, and for all that we grew up side by side, we lived remarkably different lives. (How different, you will see once you have read the attached.) Our interactions consisted mainly of you scolding me and me mocking you.

But for all that, Lizzy, you are the one person in our family whom I most wish could see me as I really am—could understand why I did the things that I did. Oh, dash it—I respect you, Lizzy. You are clever, the cleverest of all of us, and you care in a way our parents never really did. If you accepted me, that would mean I really deserved it.

So go off and read my manuscript, now, please. I will wait.

Did you read it? I suppose it took you a few weeks at least. I know I ought to have cut it down, but all my writing is so good I really could not decide what to remove. Apologies for the racier bits, but I was trying to do the thing thoroughly. I included a few letters from others, including your husband and sister-in-law, which will hopefully help you to believe the more unbelievable parts, which I suppose is all of them.

So now you know all. Almost, anyway.

I am writing this at the desk in Miss Lambe's spare room. It is my first day sitting up on my own since I woke. Yes, I woke up. There is a cup of tea at my elbow, heavily sugared to keep my strength up, and the sea breeze is ruffling my curls. I feel almost my old self again. Almost.

After I collapsed on the beach that day, I knew nothing of Wickham's arrival, or being carried to Miss Lambe's lodgings, or the fuss Darcy apparently made. I seemed to be somewhere else, and getting farther away by the second. I was on a raft, bobbing gently on the waves, the stars above me and reflected all around.

It was calm. Peaceful.

That was how I knew I was dying. When have I ever liked peace?

I did, though. I lay there and waited for death and was perfectly content.

Then my raft rocked violently. I sat up, throwing my weight to the side to prevent it from capsizing, and then Wickham, dripping and glaring, pulled himself aboard.

"Not like this," he said.

"Wickham?" I scrambled away from the slosh of water he'd brought onto my little vessel. "How on earth are you here?"

His scowl deepened. His hair was stuck to his face, which made him look like an angry cat, but the way his white shirt was plastered to his chest was really rather flattering. "I'm your familiar, remember?" he said. "I can go where you go."

"Well, where I'm going is death, so I do not think you want to follow. Have you come to be released from our bond? You'll have to petition Miss Lambe, I haven't the strength to light a candle."

A strange look passed over his face—one I had never seen. He looked—sad. "After all this," he said, "is that what you really think of me?"

I swallowed. "You did seduce me, abandon me, and try to feed my friend to your father," I pointed out.

"Lydia," he said quietly, "I did that for you."

I scoffed. "Oh, certainly."

"Really. My father would have killed you. I did it to save your life."

I opened my mouth to contradict him again, but no sound came out. Because I wanted it to be true.

"You will never believe it, I know," he said, "if I tell you how much I want you to be safe and happy." His throat bobbed. "How much it killed me, these last few months, to know that I was bringing you misery instead. Oh, I tried to stop loving you. I indulged in every vice and pleasure the mortal plane offered, but it was no good. The damned parasite's got its hooks in deep."

*You love me?* I thought. But still the words would not come out.

Oh, Lizzy, did you feel like this, when the proud Darcy fellow you despised told you that he was laid low with love for you? Did a hundred little strangenesses suddenly make sense? Did you tell yourself nevertheless that, no, it could not possibly be true—even as a part of you hoped desperately that it was?

"You do not believe me," Wickham said. "That is no matter. You will." And he cupped my cheek in his hand, and kissed me.

His touch worked on me as it always did, and I sank into him. I wound my arms round his waist, and he laid me back gently. His lips on mine, his arms around me, one hand cupping the back of my head—heavens, why hadn't we been doing this all year? I felt stronger than I had in days.

No—I did not just *feel* stronger. I *was* stronger.

I broke the kiss on a gasp and pushed him away, but it did not matter. Wickham's strength was still flowing into me. "Stop it," I breathed. "Stop it! Don't you dare!"

Wickham gave me a weak smile. He took the hand that was pushing him away and kissed it. "Believe me now?" he whispered. His eyes drifted closed and he collapsed.

"No. No! Wake up!" I shook him, pounded on his chest, even slapped

him. It was no good. Even as I swiped the tears from my cheeks, I could still feel the last of his strength flowing into me. In a moment, he would be gone.

Then the sky exploded above us.

Fireworks of a hundred colors and shapes exploded and whistled and boomed. The night flared bright as day, again and again. I stared up in wonder, raised an arm to shield my eyes from the brightness—

And when I lowered it, I was in Miss Lambe's spare room, and the unbearable brightness was the morning sun streaming through the window.

Kitty was holding one of my hands, coughing and choking. I could see why: The air in the room was full of smoke and a peculiar smell. I craned my neck to look at the fireplace. There stood Georgiana Darcy, her face nearly black with soot, looking triumphant. "Oh good," she said. "It worked."

"What did you do?" I croaked.

"Burned my proof of Goldbach's conjecture," she said. "She"—she nodded to Kitty—"said that a very great sacrifice would be needed to save you, and your husband got a funny look on his face and said he would take care of it, and I realized he meant to kill himself, and then I thought, well, I have something better than that."

"My husband—"

And yes. He was there. He was sprawled out across me, one arm across my waist, perfectly still.

"Oh," said Miss Darcy in a small voice. "Was I too late?"

Carefully, I pushed his hair back from his forehead. Unruly, unpomaded, as though he'd just rolled out of bed—just the way I liked it.

A wave of unfairness swamped me. All those hard, cold, lonely months we'd been angry at each other—we'd been so *stupid*! If only he'd told me, we could have had a gay time despite our poverty and poor characters. And now it was too late.

Then his fingers twitched.

I caught my breath. "Wickham?" I whispered.

He drew a breath, then another—then coughed. With a groan, he sat up. "Really, Miss Darcy?" he groaned. "Fireworks?"

"I threw some phosphorus in the fire with the proof," she said. "I thought the sparks would make it seem, well, witchier."

I laughed. "You cannot just burn things and call it witchcraft! You have to do spells! You have to—to be a witch!" My laughter sounded hysterical even to myself. I did not care. Wickham was grinning at me, as confident and rakish and alive as ever.

"Apparently you do not," Miss Darcy said. "For you're both alive, and I've quite forgotten the proof." She shrugged. "No matter. It was figuring it out that was fun. Perhaps I'll turn to chemistry now. That phosphorus was delightful."

The next few days were an utter joy. To actually have friends about me again—to have a man who loved me—to have Kitty! It was as though the world was making up for all the misery I have dwelled in this year. Even Darcy got into the spirit of things, and actually waved to the Prince of Wales's mistress on the Steyne. Of course, it cannot last, not entirely. The Darcys will depart tomorrow. Miss Lambe must return to her duties as Queen.

And then there is Kitty.

Once I was strong enough, Kit and I went for a long walk through Brighton. I showed her all my favorite spots—the balcony where Wickham and I kissed, the best ballrooms, the spot on the seaside where I used to go and sit with the honor guard—and she was suitably appreciative. Too appreciative, I ought to have realized.

"I wish you could have been here with me, Kit," I said. We were sitting on my favorite rock, staring out at the sea. "I never thought when I left that we would be apart for so long."

She nodded and said carefully, "Miss Lambe says she could put us back together again."

I nodded. "We'd have to come up with some sort of fairly enormous sacrifice, of course, but it could be done."

"Is that what you want?" she asked.

I considered it. For nearly a year now, it had been all I wanted. I'd missed her every minute of every day. I missed her still.

I had a new familiar now, and I was only just beginning to realize the potential we had together. But did that potential really stand up to the years and years of Kit and me? "Perhaps I could have two familiars," I said hopefully.

She nudged me. "You know you cannot."

"No."

We watched the sea for a moment. Then Kitty said, "I have something to tell you, Lydia." She drew a deep breath. "I am engaged."

I blinked. "You are? But—" But what? Kit was a mortal woman now. There was no reason why not. "Oh, Kit! You're going to be married?"

She nodded, her eyes brimming with tears, and I hugged her. I was crying, too. I wish I could say they were tears of joy, but I am far more selfish than that. Kit, who used to be as much a part of me as my right arm, was getting married, and this was the first I was hearing of it. My insides ached.

"Best, best, best wishes, Kit," I whispered, and squeezed her tight. "Who is he?"

She drew back a little and wiped her face. With a deep breath, she said, "A clergyman. He has a very fine living not far from here."

"Do you love him?"

"Very much," she said. "Actually, I told him to meet us here. Ah, here he is now."

I turned. Denny was striding up the beach toward us.

He was not Denny as I had known him. He had abandoned the rakish fashions of the regiment and was dressed soberly. He looked five years older. But his grin was the same.

"Hello, Bennet," he greeted me. "I see you're acquainted with my bride-to-be."

I put a hand to my mouth. "But I—your love—I sacrificed it! How did you break the spell?"

Denny's smile faded. "Ah. We didn't, I'm afraid."

He reached out a hand toward Kit, as though to stroke her cheek. She leaned into him, but the moment they touched, Kitty flickered and was replaced by a mottled gray cat.

"That happens every time we try to touch, you see," Denny said. "Damned inconvenient, I must say." He drew his hand back and girl-Kit returned. She turned to me with pleading eyes.

"I see" was all I could say.

Denny stayed with us for a few minutes, updating me on the changes to his situation. Apparently after the events of last year, he'd soured on regimental life. Fulton, now the owner of a great estate, offered him a living, and he'd jumped at the chance. He also showed us a number of new magic tricks, each more terrible than the last.

Eventually, though, he said he could see that I was tiring, and left to fetch us a carriage. The sun was getting lower. I put my head on Kit's shoulder.

"Well?" she said, patting my bonnet.

"It would take a great sacrifice indeed," I said. "Are you sure it's what you want? I could rid myself of Wickham and we could go off and have adventures together, you and me."

"It is what I want," she said.

"I know."

"I could name my firstborn child after you," she offered. "Perhaps that would do for a sacrifice."

I raised my head to look at her. "How is that a sacrifice?"

"I have never cared overmuch for the name Lydia."

I made a face at her.

"I am sorry to ask it," she said. "I was awful to you last year. I know you were only trying to help me."

"It's all right," I said. "You were in love. I understand."

"Do you?"

"I think so."

We watched the waves for a few more moments, just Kit and me. One last time like it used to be. But I was beginning to grow cold, and besides, I knew what my sacrifice would have to be.

I wish I could send you this letter, Lizzy. I wish you could sit down and learn who your silly, selfish little sister really is. Instead, it, along with my manuscript, will go straight into the fire like Miss Darcy's proof. Undoing a spell is a tricky business. If I am to convince the universe to let Kit and Denny love each other, I have to give it something in return that I will never take back.

It's not so bad, really. The Darcys have their part in the sacrifice, too. Darcy, who loves you to distraction, will always have a secret from you, and Miss Darcy, who so admires you, will appear very odd indeed in your eyes and will never be able to explain why her room is full of mouse bones.

As for me, I am used to your disapproval at least. I have had years to learn to ignore it. Besides, things are really going quite well for me. I shall soon have a third respectably married sister to visit. My worst enemy is now a seal, and my other worst enemy is asleep for two hundred years. And best of all, I am going to have productive employment. Miss Lambe has decided that she needs a sort of second-in-command—a witch who can leave her lands when necessary. Good thing she is so rich—she has settled her lawsuit with the Kings (apparently they thought it unwise to try to bankrupt the most powerful witch in southern England) and she intends to send us to the Indies to release her friends. Wickham and I will be quite comfortable in her service—financially, anyway. I do not know if things between us will ever be *comfortable*. For one thing, he is still a demon. For another, what are you to do when someone falls violently in love with you, and it's your husband, but you're not actually married?

He offered to marry me properly, but I found, when I thought about it, that I do not want to. I am too young to get married. So for now we'll go on as we have been, with perhaps a bit less threatening to overturn chamber pots and a bit more kissing. And perhaps, someday . . . but then again, perhaps not.

Goodbye, Lizzy. I will see you again, of course—but you will not see me. Not really. You never have. It is too bad. This is the part, I suppose, where the novel would wrap up with a tidy boring moral, so I will say this: Love your best friends. Forgive your worst friends. Remember, always, not to judge people too hastily, for everyone is living out a story of their own, and you only get to read the pages you appear on. And no matter what your physician may say, do not drink seawater. It is bad for you.

Love (really),

Your sister,

LYDIA BENNET.


P.S. I forgot to mention—when I visited Longbourn after my wedding, and I "accidentally" let slip that Darcy had been there, and you realized that he must have paid Wickham off to marry me and ergo must still adore you? That was on purpose of course. Ha! You owe your whole marriage to me.

P.P.S. Congratulations on the upcoming birth of your daughter. She's going to be a witch.

~∾

THE END.

# ACKNOWLEDGMENTS

Guys, I did so much damn research for this book. I could write a ten-page bibliography. But I am told it's already too long, so I will try to just pick out the sources I relied on the most: Pemberley.com, whose *Pride and Prejudice* timeline (based on the work of R. W. Chapman and Frank MacKinnon) is so painstaking that they actually caught *Jane Austen* in a mistake; Moira Ferguson, whose *Nine Black Women* introduced me to the Hart sisters, who inspired much of Miss Lambe's biography, including the yellow and white door, presumably painted by ancestors of today's Twitter trolls; and Clifford Musgrave, whose *Life in Brighton* allowed me to visit a city I'd never seen at the height of a pandemic without ever leaving the Upper West Side.

I'm deeply indebted to my early readers and advisers, including Sophie Gee, Charlie Baily, Hannah Taub, Razan Ghalayini, Kristen Bartlett, and Ashley Nicole Black. This book would not exist without Amanda Taub, who kept me writing by saying, "When can I read more Lydia?" when I would have preferred to play video games. My agent Jenn Joel is a powerhouse like no other. My incredible editors, Elizabeth Kulhanek and Jo Fletcher, made the book what it is (especially vis-à-vis the word *gotten*).

Hmm, who am I forgetting? Oh right. Thank you to Jane Austen. Even if I'd never written this book, I would owe her so much.

Finally, a thank-you to Austen fans everywhere. I know we're all very protective of Jane and her legacy. I hope you feel that the liberties I've taken are worth it. Lydia may have mixed feelings, but my love for Lizzy Bennet and Mr. Darcy knows no bounds.

# AUTHOR'S NOTE
## What's Real, What's Mine, and What's Jane's

This book is an amalgam of history, folklore, one and a half Jane Austen novels, and a bunch of stuff I made up from whole cloth. For those who are curious, I've tried to sort out where some of the various pieces came from.

### Real (well, sort of ):

Wormenheart the dragon is an actual Hertfordshire myth. His cave is said to be under St. Albans Cathedral in Hertfordshire. His nasty personality and his appetite for witches are my invention.

The Long Man really is carved into a hillside in East Sussex. No one knows for sure who made him or why. The current prevailing theory is that he's only a couple centuries old, but where's the fun in that?

The Shell Grotto is real, though actually located in the Kentish town of Margate. It is just as mysterious and beautiful as I tried to paint it in the book. If you ever get the chance to go, I highly recommend it. As far as I know, it does not actually amplify magic spells, but if anywhere could, it would be the Grotto.

The portrayal of magic in this book is mostly my invention, but it draws on real traditions and folklore from England, Scotland, and the Caribbean.

### Made up (by Jane Austen):

Miss Lambe is not my creation—she's Miss Austen's. She is referenced in Austen's final novel fragment, *Sanditon*. Sadly, Austen died before she could bring her Miss Lambe onstage. I hope she doesn't mind me borrowing her here. I guess that's the least of my sins.

Sadly, the fact that her own aunt and cousin almost stole her fortune is very much based in fact. At this time, mixed-race heirs were often disinherited by English courts in favor of their white relatives. If you'd like to hear from some actual mixed-race women of the nineteenth century, I'd suggest you check out the writing of Anne Hart Gilbert and Elizabeth Hart Thwaites, two Antiguan sisters and abolitionists. You might also be interested in *The Woman of Colour*, an anonymous 1807 novel about a biracial heiress, which some scholars think might have been written by an actual woman of color. (It's at least as likely that it was written by a white person with abolitionist leanings. There were a large number of those at the time. Next time someone tries to defend a slave-owning historical figure as "a product of their time," feel free to point that out.)

Unlike Denny and the Forsters, who are mentioned in *Pride and Prejudice*, Fulton and Carteret are entirely mine. (There's a "Captain Carter" in *P and P*, so maybe Carteret is in there and Lydia just got his name wrong.) However, the name "Willoughby Carteret" suggests he's related to some of the more unsavory people in the Austen cinematic universe—the shady Willoughby from *Sense and Sensibility* and the snobby Carterets from *Persuasion*.

## Made up (by me):

The island of Sainte-Josephine is not real. It's heavily influenced by my reading on Barbados, Jamaica, and other Caribbean islands at the time, but this book tells only a fraction of Miss Lambe's much larger story, and I felt like she needed a brand-new canvas to live it upon. I named Sainte-Josephine after Saint Josephine Bakhita, a formerly enslaved Sudanese woman who was canonized in 2000. She is the patron saint of human trafficking survivors.

The Order of the Rose is completely invented, thank goodness.

Magic also isn't real. Probably. You know what? No comment.

# ABOUT THE AUTHOR

**Melinda Taub** is an Emmy- and Writers Guild Award–winning writer. The former head writer and executive producer of *Full Frontal with Samantha Bee*, she is also the author of *Still Star-Crossed*, a young adult novel that was adapted for television by Shondaland. (She also wrote that thing about the Baroness in *The Sound of Music* that your aunt likes.) She lives in Brooklyn.